Liberty Girls

Fiona Ford is the author of the Liberty Girls series, which is set in London during the Second World War.

Fiona spent many years as a journalist writing for women's weekly and monthly magazines. She has written two novels under the pseudonym, Fiona Harrison, as well as two sagas in her own name in the Spark Girls series.

Fiona lives in Berkshire with her husband.

The Liberty Girls

Fiona Ford

arrow books

3 5 7 9 10 8 6 4 2

Arrow Books
20 Vauxhall Bridge Road
London SW1V 2SA

Arrow Books is part of the Penguin Random House group
of companies whose addresses can be found at global.
penguinrandomhouse.com

Penguin
Random House
UK

First published in Great Britain by Arrow Books in 2019

www.penguin.co.uk

A CIP catalogue record for this book is available from the British Library

ISBN 9781787461383

Typeset in 10.75/13.5 pt Palatino
by Integra Software Services Pvt. Ltd, Pondicherry

Printed and bound in Great Britain by Clays Ltd, Elcograf S.p.A.

For the McLaughlins –
true friends indeed

Acknowledgements

I always say that writing a book is a team effort, and I would be completely lost without the superstars in my life who make all of this possible. First of all, I'd like to say a very heartfelt thank you to my wonderful agent Kate Burke of Blake Friedmann. Generous with her time, patient to the nth degree and fabulously blunt yet kind with it, I'm so grateful for all you do Kate. The same can also be said for the ever lovely Emily Griffin and Cassandra Di Bello. Thank you, Emily, for your kindness, wisdom and exceptional talent for pointing out things that always make the story better and, Cass, your tolerance when I send stupid questions and changes your way is always appreciated.

To everyone at Arrow: huge, huge thanks for all the hard work that goes on behind the scenes. I know just how much effort you put into everything and I'm truly grateful to everyone from Sales, Marketing, and Design, who create such wonderful covers, not to mention the always ingenious PR guru, Rachel Kennedy.

My brilliant writer friends – Jean Fullerton, Kate Thompson, Dani Atkins, Elaine Everest, Rosie Hendry, Di Redmond and Amanda Revell Walton – it's a great honour to have you all in my life. Nothing gives me greater pleasure than swapping stories and sharing the highs, lows and general perplexities that go hand in hand with being a writer – thank you all.

To the incredibly patient staff at City of Westminster Archives Centre and Central Bath Library, you're all absolute treasures. Thank you for answering my daft questions and putting up with me loitering for far too long. The terrific people involved in the Bath Blitz Memorial Project who have set up bathblitz.org to record the memories of those involved in the blitz and provide a historic record of the bombing in Bath – what a wealth of information. Special mention must also be given to the wonderful staff at Liberty's, who yet again have allowed me to take the store's name in vain and create my own fictional wonderland. As always, I should stress that this book is a pure fabrication and in no way bears any resemblance to what really happened at Liberty's during the Second World War. Thanks must also go to the Facebook groups 'I'm From SE London' and 'Memories of London'. Your posts are such a great source of information and I'm indebted to you all for your help.

Finally, thanks must be given to my rather brilliant husband Chris Lobina, who never tires of helping me thrash out plot points, and to my fabulous parents, Barry and Maureen Ford, who were born during the war. Consequently they are forced to answer my ridiculously detailed questions on everything from social attitudes to old money with patience. Your help and support has not and never will be taken for granted – thank you.

No minute gone comes back again,
Take heed and see ye do nothing in vain

Father Time quotation, inscribed into the Kingly Street
arch of Liberty's

Prologue

June 1930

It was the thudding Alice Harris heard first. Then finally a large bang of what she suspected was a door being slammed in anger. Pausing on the stairs of the modest two-up, two-down she lived in with her father and sister, the fourteen-year-old listened again as the sound of angry voices being exchanged in her father's bedroom floated down towards her.

'How many times do I have to tell you to do what's right by those girls, Jack Harris?' fired a voice Alice knew to be a friend of her mother's, Dorothy Hanson, better known as Dot.

'And how many times have I gotta tell you, mind your bleedin' business. What goes on in this house ain't none of your concern,' she heard her father shout in reply. 'Alice is old enough and ugly enough to stand on her own two feet, and take care of Joy.'

'They're a pair of kids,' Dot thundered. 'Their mother's been dead ten years; it's a father they need, even if that father happens to be you.'

At the mention of her mother Alice winced. Even though as Dot rightly said her mum had been gone longer than she had known her, Alice still missed her.

'Christ, when I was her age I'd been working for years already,' came her father's voice again. 'That kid's had it easy. I wouldn't mind but she's shown no interest in the family business—'

1

The sound of Dot's raucous laughter cut her father off mid-flow. 'That's rich coming from you. You don't know the first thing about work; the only thing you know about is thieving, that and making money out of other people's misery. Round here, people might fear you, tip their caps to you out of so-called respect, Jimmy, but to me you're nothing more than a common criminal. It's a good job you're running off to America, because if it were down to me I'd see you land in jail for this latest stunt. Knocking off the wife of one of the Newcastle Mob? What are you, stupid?'

There was a pause then and Alice held her breath in disbelief, worries whirling around in her head as she tried to make sense of everything she had just heard. Her father had come home covered in blood two nights ago. He'd told Alice that he'd been involved in a bar fight, but the way he had shoved his clothes in a bin and demanded Alice drag the old tin bath out so he could scrub himself clean made her think differently. Was that what had happened? Alice needed answers.

Running up the stairs, she burst into her father's bedroom. The wardrobe was bare and on the bed lay two open suitcases, one stuffed with clothes, the other with bank notes. 'So you're finally leaving us then?' she snarled.

Jimmy lifted his chin and stared at her in anger, his blue eyes the match of her own. 'You had no right to eavesdrop, girl. What have I told you about that?'

Alice rolled her eyes at the predictability of it all. Her father, the great King of South London, had a lesson for everything. Never let anyone take advantage; make sure you're respected; never let anyone make a fool of you; and her favourite: an eye for an eye. Unlike her younger sister Joy, who had lapped up these lessons like a sponge, Alice knew it all meant nothing. They were just excuses for doing exactly as you pleased and, looking at the bulging suitcases on the bed, it looked as if her father was once again doing just that.

Panic enveloped her. She might not like her father, or approve of who he was, but he was the only parent they had and he always made sure there was food on the table, clothes on her back and coal in the scuttle. 'Dad,' she said cautiously, 'what's really going on?'

'Nothing to do with you,' her father said gruffly, slamming the lid of one of the cases shut.

'Please don't leave, Dad, I'm begging you,' she said, her voice full of fear.

Jimmy's lined face hardened; he had always hated weakness and Alice cursed herself for showing him her true feelings. Drawing himself up to his full height he took a step forward and towered over his daughter. 'Don't start whining, girl. Dot here's going to keep an eye on you. Besides, you're old enough now to fend for yourselves. You'll need to clear out the house by next month, the rent'll be due.'

Alice turned to Dot, whose face was so contorted with anger, Alice could tell she was having difficulty speaking. 'You're really going away to America and leaving us without a penny or even a house?' Alice said in disbelief. 'Joy's ten, she adores you, how do you think she's going to feel? Her mum's dead, you're buggering off to the other side of the world and now we're out on the streets?'

There was a pause then as Jimmy looked at his daughter and Alice could see him thinking it all through. Relief started to flood her. He was going to change his mind; it was going to be all right.

'Here you are,' Jimmy said at last, pulling out a fistful of notes and a handful of change from his trouser pockets. 'This ought to keep you going 'til you get a full-time job at least. Now, don't say your old man ain't generous. I know how to take care of me own.'

At the sight of the money in his hands Alice knew she was supposed to be grateful but all she really wanted to do was roar with laughter at the stupidity of it all. She also knew it wasn't the time. Not if she wanted to avoid a black eye anyway. Instead she took a step back and surveyed the man who was her father. He looked old, she thought. His cauliflower ears, scarred cheeks and broken nose made him seem more advanced in years than he actually was. Alice knew that he wasn't running away because he was worried about retribution, or even about the police turning up at his door. He was going because he was worried about losing his position as leader of the Elephant Boys. The only thing that mattered to him was his stupid pride.

'Shove your bleedin' money,' she said, her eyes blazing angrily. 'We'll be better off without you.'

'Alice, love,' Jimmy wheedled, reaching for her hand, palms still full of money, 'there's no need for that. I'll write, course I will, when I can.'

As Dot snorted in disgust once more, Alice rounded on her father. 'Don't bother. We don't need nothing off you, Jimmy Harris. You're an ageing two-bob crook who's always let me and Joy down. I hope I never see you again.'

At his daughter's outburst Jimmy opened and closed his mouth. Then with an angry shrug, he shoved the money he had offered her back in his pocket, slammed the last of his suitcases shut and pushed past her without a backward glance.

When Alice heard the front door slam, the tears started to flow. He really had gone. She might have hated him, but he was all she had. Her body heaving with sobs, Alice turned to Dot and whispered, 'What do I do now?'

Chapter One

April 1942

Twelve years later

It was no good, Alice Milwood thought glumly as she stared at her reflection in the mirror, she just wasn't ready to return to Liberty's, it was as simple as that. Her once bright skin was sallow and grey, her forehead had more lines than one of Dot's string shopping bags, her blonde curls looked weighted down by life and the sparkling blue eyes she had once been so proud of looked dull and lifeless.

Sweeping a finger under her eye, she pulled gently at the bags that hung like sacks of coal and shook her head in despair – how could she not have noticed how dreadful she looked? A cry pulled her from her self-loathing. Sneaking a sidelong glance into the large wooden cot that rested on the floor beside her bed, Alice smiled, knowing perfectly well why her appearance had been the last thing on her mind: her son Arthur. Since giving birth to him just four months ago, Alice's own wants and needs had ceased to exist as she concentrated solely on her new job of caring for her son.

Consequently she had thought nothing of long days scrubbing nappies by hand, and even longer nights where she would do nothing but sit in the always warm kitchen of the little terrace house she shared with Dorothy Hanson, nursing her son back to sleep. Enveloped by the lonely darkness Alice found her mind would wander between sheer happiness at her new role as a mother and extreme fear as she fretted over the kind of future her little boy would have. Born in the midst of war with his father missing in action, possibly dead, Alice had spent almost every waking hour wondering just how she would provide for him as well as herself.

Today was the day she was returning to her role as deputy fabric manager at Liberty's – a day she had been dreading and looking forward to in equal measure and one which she wasn't remotely ready for, if the snug fit of her once-loose-fitting, treasured teal-and-grey skirt was anything to by. Downhearted that she couldn't find one single dress from her pre-pregnancy days to fit, Alice gave the waistband a final tug to try and get it over her thighs, before admitting defeat.

Sliding the skirt off, she breathed a sigh of relief before turning her attention back to the rest of her clothes. Running her eye across the few outfits that hung in the cupboard of the room she rented in the Elephant and Castle terrace, she reached for a dress she had worn before giving birth. Slipping the loose-fitting navy tea dress over her head, Alice was comfortable but looking at her reflection again felt a stab of despair. She knew it was vain, but the dress swamped her and Alice had wanted nothing more than to make a good impression on her first day back at work.

Just then a wail from the cot beside her dragged her from all thoughts of Liberty's and instead brought her attention solely to the cause of all that noise.

'Come on then, darlin'!' Alice beamed, reaching down to pick her son up for a cuddle.

Arthur gave a whimper in reply as his mother rocked him gently in her arms.

The motion didn't just soothe her son, it helped Alice's nerves too as she held Arthur close to her chest enjoying the weight of him. Glancing down at the precious bundle, she tried to swallow the rising sense of guilt she felt at returning to work.

Before the war, mothers wouldn't have been at work earning a crust to feed their family; instead they would have stayed put, looking after a home and keeping their children safe. Now they had to leave their offspring with anyone who would take them while they went out to work.

It wasn't right, she thought as she stared down at the little face she loved more than anything in the world. Stroking the slope of his fat cheeks she planted a kiss on Arthur's forehead and placed him gently back in the cot. Her heart was breaking at the thought of leaving him for the day, especially when he was still so tiny, but what choice did she have?

A knock at the door dragged Alice from her train of thought. Turning around she saw Dot, beaming in the doorway, clutching a very welcome cup of tea.

'Thought you might need this.'

'Thanks.' Alice took the cup gratefully.

'I don't suppose I need to ask how you're feeling,' Dot said, elbowing her way into the room and taking a seat on Alice's bed. 'It's written all over your face.'

Alice sighed. 'That obvious?'

Dot chuckled knowingly, a lock of greying chestnut hair falling loose from the scarf wrapped tightly around her head. 'Let's just hope Beatrice Claremont has the good sense to put you below stairs today until you're feeling more yourself.'

'Not a good start, is it?' Alice smiled ruefully, perching beside Dot. 'Not only is it my first day back but my first day with a new boss who don't know me from Adam.'

'Oh, Beatrice'll be all right.' Dot shrugged, her grey eyes filled with kindness. 'She was widowed in the last war and raised her two kiddies single-handed. She'll appreciate how difficult it is to leave your baby with a stranger while you go off to provide.'

'I didn't know you were calling yourself a stranger, Dot.' Alice laughed, reaching down to stroke Arthur's sleeping face once more.

Dot gave her a playful nudge. 'You know what I mean. But now you bring it up, you could have it worse. You've landed on your feet really, darlin', what with you and me job-sharing now so I can help you out with Arthur.'

'You're right. And I owe Mary for agreeing to let me move back in here while she helps out with Rose and her dad.' Alice set her cup down on the wooden bedside table and got to her feet, her thoughts full of her friend. Mary Holmes-Fotherington had been the last person she had expected to find friendship with when the girl with the double-barrelled name had arrived on the doorstep of Dot's terrace last September. Homeless and jobless after being discharged from the Auxiliary Territorial Army under horrific circumstances, Mary had turned up with her fancy raven hair cut into a posh bob, an equally posh accent, and secretive past, the hurt of which her green eyes couldn't disguise. Alice had wondered if the two of them would ever get on, but, sensing the girl needed help, she had put that aside and helped Mary get a job in the fabric department of Liberty's, where she had become a firm favourite amongst staff and customers, as well as a very dear friend to Alice.

'Well, they're only round the corner,' Dot reminded her as she took a gulp of her own tea. 'But I agree, it was a sensible suggestion of Mary's for you to move back in here so we could share care for Arthur. I think she's having the time of her life there, though, always telling me how welcoming Rose's dad is. But then that's Malcolm all over.'

'Is Mary still working for the Red Cross?' Alice asked.

'Yes, every spare moment she can. Wants to do her bit to help, put those skills she learned in the army to good use.'

'I don't know how she finds the time,' Alice said admiringly. 'I haven't been able to carry out many of my ARP duties since Arthur came along.'

Dot roared with laughter. 'You've had a baby, Alice. You don't have to do everything, you know.'

'I know, but I actually want to do my bit.'

Dot patted her knee consolingly. 'You are and you will. Just give it time.'

Alice looked at her watch. 'I'd better get a move on. The last thing I want is to be late on my first day – even if I do look a fright.'

'Why don't you let me alter a couple of these things for you today? It won't take long.'

'Would you? I would have done it myself, but what with Arthur and moving out of Rose's just last week, I haven't had time. I also thought I'd be back in my old clothes by now.'

'Stop being so hard on yourself Alice,' Dot scolded. 'You've not got it easy. Now let me have a couple of those old dresses and I'll see what I can alter while his lordship's sleeping.'

Alice kissed Dot on her cheek, making her blush. 'Thank you. I mean that.'

'Get away with you,' Dot said, playfully shooing her out of the door. 'Any more affection from you, Alice Milwood, and people'll be wondering if you should be off down Bedlam Mental Hospital rather than back at Liberty's.'

Chapter Two

An hour later and Alice was nervously walking along Oxford Street. She hadn't been into central London since she'd given birth to Arthur just before Christmas, but the sight of the devastated buildings were a very real reminder the country was still at war. Alice could see in an instant how teams of volunteers had made excellent progress, sweeping and tidying the rubble and debris, but the sight of lives half-lived still shocked her to the core: partially destroyed walls bearing cracked mirrors or crooked pictures lined the streets. And although Hitler hadn't raided the city for almost a year, Londoners were still braced for attack, with barrage balloons lining the Thames, and of course the nightly blackout continued in full force.

It was a stark reminder for Alice of what was really important. Yes, she might feel terrible at leaving Arthur but she would feel even worse if he starved because he didn't even have one parent to care for him in this world. Her husband Luke had been missing in action for almost eight months and the RAF payout she received in his absence was barely enough to cover food for them both, never mind anything else.

As she turned into Argyll Street, the early morning sunshine giving the capital a glorious golden glow, Liberty's came into view. At the sight of the mock Tudor building Alice let out a gasp of delight – the store still had the power to take her breath away. She was reminded in an instant of her early days working at Liberty's. She had been just sixteen years old when, thanks to a friend of one of the rag-trade sellers down the Lane, she had been taken on in deliveries as a Saturday girl. It wasn't long before she became a full-time employee down in the stores, fetching, carrying and acting as general dogsbody to Mr Percy Wilmington, who was in charge of the department and had been a firm but very fair boss. Although Alice hadn't known at the time, Percy had heard through the grapevine how Alice's father, Jimmy Harris, had suddenly hightailed it to America, leaving Alice to look after herself and her little sister Joy. Nor did she know how Percy had vouched for her with the Liberty family, who were worried about her father's criminal background, but she repaid him with hard work – not only because she loved the store from the moment she set foot in it but also because Alice understood from a very early age that hard work, not crime, was the best way through life.

Reaching the shop floor now, Alice felt as if she had never been away. As she neared the counter, she saw a straight-backed unsmiling woman with thick brown hair piled neatly on the top of her head crossing things off a list with gusto and guessed this was the new fabric manager. Alice regarded her for a moment. She thought she must be about fifty-five, and noticed that despite the fact she was widowed she still wore a gold wedding ring on her finger. She looked miserable, Alice thought, before catching herself. She shouldn't find fault with the woman already, just because she wasn't her pal and old boss Flo.

Florence, now better known as Flo Canning following her Boxing Day wedding, had worked with Alice as a Saturday girl in the stores, also under Percy's guidance. The girls had quickly become friends, climbing the ranks together – Flo always that little bit further forward than Alice thanks to the fact she had started six months earlier.

They both found their natural home in fabrics where they had worked contentedly side by side with Flo eventually being promoted to department manager and Alice her deputy. Recently, however, things had shifted as Flo had been made deputy manager across the entire store. Alice was delighted for her, but watching this stiff-backed, unsmiling woman narrow her eyes as she glanced over the day's takings, Alice felt a pang of sadness as she realised how different the department would now be without Flo. Still, she thought sternly, that didn't mean she shouldn't give Beatrice Claremont a chance.

'Hello,' Alice said brightly, extending her hand towards the woman, determined to make a good impression. 'You must be Beatrice. I'm Alice.'

The woman's head snapped up as she regarded Alice for a second; then she wrapped her cool long fingers around Alice's to shake her hand. 'You're my second in command, I understand.'

'That's right.' Alice nodded. 'Any help you need with anything do let me know; I've been down here years.'

Beatrice stared at her appraisingly. 'Then you'll know that at Liberty's we call each other Miss or Mrs, never by our first names.'

Alice blushed at her mistake. 'Yes, of course, I am sorry, Mrs Claremont. I was just trying to be friendly; we never used the terms in this department.'

'Yes, well, I'll let you off this once,' Beatrice replied, lips pursed. 'Now I don't know what life was like when you worked under Mrs Canning, but I can tell you that she and I have rather different management styles and I'll expect you to follow my lead. There's a war on here, Mrs Milwood, and I don't have time for pleasantries, niceties or friendships; what I have time for is work. I won't stand for idle gossip on the shop floor and I won't stand for shirking.

There is always work to do and I expect the very best from my girls, is that understood?'

Alice nodded meekly. 'Of course, Mrs Claremont.'

'Good,' Beatrice replied, her tone a little softer now. 'Now, I have a meeting with Mr Button. Mrs Milwood, I don't mean to be unkind when I say this, but that outfit you're wearing is most unbecoming and until you are in more flattering attire I suggest you work downstairs in the stockroom familiarising yourself with our current stock levels and sales books.'

Without waiting for a reply, Beatrice swept past Alice, leaving her open-mouthed in surprise at the new fabric manager's bluntness.

By lunchtime Alice's back was aching and the dress she had dreaded wearing that morning was covered in grime. Beatrice had not only set her the task of going through the stock and guard books, but she had also instructed Alice to clean the room from top to bottom, insisting that it would be a good way for her to become reacquainted with the fabric department.

It was almost one when Mary tapped her on the shoulder and presented her with a cheeky slice of bread and butter, along with a scalding hot cup of tea.

'What are you doing?' Alice asked, aghast, as she saw Mary's hands full of treats.

Mary grinned, her emerald eyes alive with merriment as she set the cup and plate on the wooden floor and held a finger to her lips. 'I thought you might need some sustenance. Besides, Beatrice is out for lunch.'

'Don't you mean Mrs Claremont?' Alice replied sulkily.

'She's a funny one, isn't she?' Mary giggled, perching on one of the upturned boxes Alice had neatly stacked away.

'She's very direct!' Alice said diplomatically, taking a sip of the illicit tea and savouring it. 'Why on earth did old Buttons think she belonged here?'

'You know what Mr Button is like.' Mary shrugged, tucking a lock of raven hair behind her ear. 'He's a kindly store manager who likes to see the good in everyone. I think he thought that as she managed to boost profits over in gifts as number two last year she might be good in fabrics, which has been dwindling.'

Alice fell silent as she pondered Mary's remark. Edwin Button, store manager, who had recently rekindled his love affair with childhood sweetheart Dot, was famed across the store for being a good, decent and fair man – and he felt like a father to the Liberty girls. Together with Mary, he had even helped deliver Arthur on the shop floor when her baby arrived unexpectedly, so it seemed strange that he would saddle them with a woman who, on first impressions, did not appear to be a natural fit.

'I suppose he knows what he's doing,' said Alice, ripping off a chunk of bread with her fingers. 'I mean Buttons doesn't tend to get too much wrong too often.'

'Who doesn't?' a voice boomed, before Flo's smiling face appeared around the corner.

'Hello, stranger!' Alice exclaimed, getting to her feet so quickly she almost knocked herself out on one of the low hanging beams,

'Hello yourself.' Flo beamed, her green eyes crinkling with delight as she pulled Alice in for a hug. 'Thought I'd look in on you while I've got five minutes and see how you're getting on.'

Alice glanced around at the pristine stockroom and spread out her arms. 'As you can see, I haven't lost my ability to clean and tidy.'

'It's beautiful,' Flo breathed admiringly, 'I can't believe you had time to do all this. There's no flies on you, Alice Milwood.'

Alice revelled in the praise. 'Just trying to keep on the right side of Beatrice – sorry, Mrs Claremont.'

Flo raised a perfectly arched eyebrow, her chestnut bob dancing on her shoulders, 'I gather Mrs Claremont has given you the lecture on not using first names.'

As Alice rolled her eyes in acknowledgement, Mary chuckled. 'I had to admit it took me back to my army days when she instructed me never to use her first name. I rather thought she was going to start barking orders at me and get me on latrine duty.'

At that the girls fell about laughing. Despite her misgivings about returning to work Alice had missed these women more than she realised and she couldn't help grinning with pleasure at the sight of Flo.

Like Alice, Flo was passionate about all things Liberty, especially the fabric. She had proven herself to be a wonderful department manager, and so it was no wonder Mr Button had insisted to the Liberty board that Flo be promoted into the role of deputy store manager after her predecessor, Mabel Matravers, had been sent to prison earlier that year. It had been quite the scandal when it was discovered that Mrs Matravers had masterminded a hooch ring with her husband Alf, selling illegal alcohol across the city. She had insisted it had been because she needed the money – she was pregnant with her first child and Alf had no job. But Alice had no sympathy. With a father like Jimmy Harris, and a mother who'd thought the world of him no matter what trouble he brought to the door, she had faced her own set of difficulties in life, yet she had never turned to crime and she never would.

Just the thought of their former deputy store manager made Alice's blood boil. Mrs Matravers and her thirst for money had sent several people blind, including their friend and fellow Liberty girl, Rose Harper.

'How's Rose?' Alice asked, an image of the girl suddenly at the forefront of her mind.

'Rose is doing very well,' replied Mary. 'She's been learning braille, and we're hoping that will mean she can help out with some of the admin and the organisation in the office of things like staff rotas – and of course she's marvellous on the phone with all our customers.'

'She's returning to work this week too,' Flo said, her tone full of excitement. 'The Liberty family were determined to get her back in as soon as she was ready.'

'That's the best news I've had all day.' Alice beamed. 'She's such an asset to Liberty's—'

'In a way that cow Mabel Matravers wasn't,' Flo said hotly.

Alice pursed her lips. 'Yes, well, I suppose she's suffering in her own way. Not only did she have to give birth in prison but her month-old daughter is in the care of strangers now.'

'Best place for the child,' Mary muttered angrily.

'I can't say I disagree.' Alice sniffed. 'But we've got to move on.'

Flo leaned her head back against one of the stone pillars. 'I know, my aunt Aggie's always saying the same thing to me.'

'Your aunt's a very wise woman.' Mary agreed.

Flo gave a watery smile by way of reply and in that moment Alice saw just how tired her friend was. The fresh, dewy appearance she had been sporting following her wedding was long gone; instead she looked to be at the end of her tether.

'How are you doing, Flo?' Alice asked, her voice full of concern as she patted the space in between her and Mary.

'Oh, I'm fine,' Flo replied, taking the seat Alice offered her. 'I suppose I'm finding the new job a bit tough, if I'm honest. And I'm worried about Aggie.'

'What's wrong with her?' Mary frowned. 'I thought she seemed as strong as an ox when I visited you both last month.'

Flo shrugged. 'She's fine really. But her nerves have been on edge ever since Dad turned up at the wedding threatening revenge. She keeps getting up in the middle of the night thinking he's lying in wait for us.'

Alice paused for a moment. Flo had never had much to do with her father, Bill Wilson, but when she wed last Boxing Day he had suddenly turned up at the reception uninvited, shouting the odds. It was then that Flo, along with everyone else, had discovered that he was the third wheel in the hooch ring that had destroyed Rose's sight – and wanted by the police. Little wonder, Alice thought as she remembered the events, that Flo's aunt Aggie's nerves were frayed at the thought of him turning up again.

'But your old man's long gone now, isn't he?' Alice ventured. 'If he's anything like my father he'll be too terrified of the police to come sniffing back now.'

'I think so. Dad doesn't usually stick around when the police are after him but Aggie's still terrified and I don't know what else I can say to reassure her. Anyway,' Flo said, getting to her feet, 'I had better get back up to the office. I've got a mountain of paperwork to get through.'

Just as the girls got up to wave goodbye to Flo, they heard the sound of footsteps on the stairs.

'What's all this?' Mrs Claremont exclaimed, her expression taut. 'There's to be no drinking or eating on the premises. Why on earth is there a cup and plate on the floor?'

Alice and Mary reddened, equally ready to take the blame, but Flo stepped forward. 'Mrs Claremont, forgive me but those are mine. I simply haven't had a moment to escape for a lunch break and I wanted to speak with Mrs Milwood.'

'Oh, I see,' Mrs Claremont said flatly. 'I didn't realise. I'm so sorry, Mrs Canning.'

'Quite all right, Mrs Claremont,' Flo said evenly as she gathered the cup and plate from the floor and exchanged a knowing look with Mary and Alice.

With that Flo walked up the stairs, leaving Mrs Claremont opening and closing her mouth like a goldfish and Alice chuckling inwardly. Even though she and Mrs Claremont hadn't got off to the start she was hoping for, it was good to see that the Liberty girls still truly ruled the roost.

Chapter Three

The happy sounds of Arthur's gurgles were like a balm to Alice's tired soul as she walked through the front door of the Elephant and Castle terrace that evening. Without even bothering to take off her coat and shoes she ran straight into the kitchen to find Arthur and Dot.

'Oh, you two are a sight for sore eyes,' she said, hands outstretched to take her son. This was the longest they had ever been apart and she had missed him more than she had expected.

'Well, he's been as good as gold,' Dot revealed. 'Eaten all his food and settled down for his afternoon nap without complaint.'

'Thank you so much, Dot.'

Dot waved her gratitude away with a swipe of her hand. 'Don't be daft. We all look out for each other round this way, you know that.'

Alice sniffed the air appreciatively, suddenly aware of a delicious scent of onions filling the house. 'Is that what I think it is?' she begged, eyes widening in delight.

'Thought you deserved a treat after your first day back,' Dot said. 'Tripe and onions.'

As Dot lifted the lid to check the pan's contents, Alice gawped at the amount of food her landlady had cooked. 'Blimey, who are you expecting?'

'I've invited Rose and her dad around – oh, and Edwin, Mary, Flo and Aggie too. We met for a cup of tea earlier on down the Lane. Aggie seemed a bit down so I thought a nice tea would cheer her up,' Dot replied, wiping her hands on the tea towel conveniently placed next to the pot.

Since Flo and Neil's wedding, Aggie and Dot had become firm friends. The two had a lot in common: not only were they without children but they had devoted their lives to caring for others. Alice was glad the two older women were forming a bond but the news of a gathering had taken her by surprise.

'Nobody said anything to me at work.'

'I asked them to keep it a secret,' Dot said playfully. 'Thought it would be nice for you to have a bit of a do to celebrate going back to work. It'll be ready in an hour, so that gives you time to play with his lordship here. Oh, and while I think about it, I've taken in two of your old maternity dresses. They're hanging on the back of your door.'

There wasn't much that took Alice's breath away but that did. Over-awed by her landlady's kindness, she gave Dot a kiss on the cheek.

Dot shooed her away in mock annoyance. 'Go on, have a rest, you daft sod.'

Alice did just as she was told, but as she turned half-way up the staircase, Arthur balanced on one hip, she was delighted to find her landlady was wearing a smile a mile wide.

Even though she had only seen most of them less than a few hours ago, Alice found herself hugging Flo, Aggie, Mary and even Mr Button as if they were long-lost strangers as they arrived at the little Bell Street terrace.

'It's so nice to see you,' she whispered into Mr Button's ear.

'And you, my dear,' Mr Button replied warmly. 'I am so sorry I wasn't there to welcome you back today but I had a rather long meeting with the Liberty board.'

'That's all right. To be honest, I spent the day reacquainting myself with everything.'

'Come here, darlin'.' Aggie grinned, her green eyes the very spit of Flo's. 'It feels like it's been forever since I ran me eyes over you.'

Alice returned Flo's aunt's hug, unable to ignore the fact the older woman appeared to have lost a lot of weight since she had last seen her. Flo was right, the worry of Bill Wilson had been taking its toll. 'How've you been, Aggie?' she asked gently.

Aggie offered Alice a watery smile as she pulled away and patted Alice's hand. 'I'm all right, darlin', keeping busy. You know how it is.'

'Only too well.' Alice sighed as the sound of Arthur's cries filled the hallway.

Chuckling, Aggie jerked her head towards Flo. 'This one was the same as a nipper. Always bawling.'

'I was not!' Flo protested as she took her aunt's coat. 'I was a good baby, that's what you always used to say.'

'And you were.' Aggie laughed again, shaking her grey curls free from her hat. 'Just a flamin' noisy one!'

All too soon Dot bustled out into the hallway. 'Come on, you lot. I'm working me dogs off and you lot are in here gabbing like it's going on ration.'

'Sorry,' Alice said meekly.

'Never mind sorry, lady, you can get in here and help me plate up,' Dot said huffily. 'Anyone seen Rose and Malcolm? Not like them to be late.'

As everyone glanced at one another there was another rap at the door.

'Speak of the devil,' Mary said, swinging the front door open with as much ease as if she still lived in the terrace.

As Rose and Malcolm stepped inside, Alice paused for a moment to take in Rose's appearance. She was the youngest of the Liberty girls and with her luminous pale skin, flaming red hair and smattering of freckles across her nose, she always had an air of innocence about her. Yet it was the sight of the round glasses Rose continued to wear, despite the fact they were largely redundant, which framed her pretty blue eyes, that made Alice want to cry. It was a sign of hope, she thought, taking both coats and hanging them on the bannister, that Rose hadn't given up, which made Alice both delighted and sad in equal measure.

'Is that the latecomers?' Dot shouted, and, without waiting for a response: 'You'd all better come through and sit down if you don't want a cold tea.'

Not wanting to risk further rebuke, everyone trooped into the kitchen and sat down at Dot's large scrubbed wooden kitchen table, Alice settling Arthur in his basket next to her.

'Right then,' Dot said, setting the huge pot on the table between them all, 'you're all to help yourselves and I don't want any standing on ceremony.'

'No chance of that, my love.' Mr Button gave a half-smile as he started ladling the tripe and onions on to her plate before going on to serve everyone else.

Before long the only sound around the table was chews and murmurs of satisfaction as everyone tucked into Dot's plate of delights.

'I dunno how you do it, Dot,' Aggie said. 'It's a triumph.'

'Best not to ask,' Dot replied, tapping her nose.

'You should know, Agatha, I learned that very early on,' Mr Button said teasingly.

Glaring briefly at Mr Button, Dot turned back to Aggie. 'You still singing up the Lamb and Flag, love?'

Aggie nodded and Alice noticed her relax for the first time that evening. 'I am. Twice a week now. I really enjoy it.'

'She's ever so good,' Flo added proudly. 'The pub's full when she's on the bill.'

'I can't say I'm surprised, you have a lovely voice, Aggie,' Mary agreed.

'You're both very kind. I keep trying to get Flo to come and do a turn with me but she refuses.'

Alice's right eyebrow shot up. 'I didn't know you could sing, Flo.'

Flo blushed. 'Not as well as Aggie.'

'Nonsense,' Aggie replied firmly. 'She's a voice better than mine.'

'I haven't got time, Aggie,' Flo said. 'You know I've my new job to think about now.'

Sensing the signs of an argument brewing, Alice turned to Rose. 'Am I right in thinking I'm not the only one starting back at work this week?'

Rose's face flushed with pleasure at Alice's question. 'Yes! I start back on Thursday.'

'We can't wait to welcome you back,' Mr Button said warmly.

'That's right,' Flo replied, her eyes brimming with pleasure. 'You'll be working with me in the office, if that's all right?'

'Oh Flo!' Rose clamped her hands to her mouth in delight. 'That will be wonderful.'

'I hoped you wouldn't mind,' Flo said, a hint of relief in her voice. 'I just thought we might be able to help each other out that way, though of course we've got everything all ready for you on the shop floor so you can find your way around a bit more easily.'

'Are you giving me my own commissionaire to open all the doors for me?' Rose asked cheekily. 'You know, complete with top hat and tails?'

'Not likely.' Flo laughed. 'You don't get one of those before I do.'

'It'll be nice, though, to get back to the world you love, won't it?' Mary enquired.

'Of course.' Rose nodded enthusiastically. 'And what's more, I've started getting a little of my sight back.'

At the girl's welcome announcement everyone at the table started to clap and gasp in delight.

'When?' Alice cried, cutting through all the noise.

'Last week,' Rose said happily. 'It's not much, just shapes and a bit of colour.'

'But it's a start, love,' Malcolm said encouragingly, laying his hand on his daughter's arm.

'It's more than a start, it's wonderful,' Mary enthused. 'You'll be back to your old self before you know it.'

At that Rose's face darkened. 'I'll never be that.'

'Perhaps not, but it's good news,' Alice said consolingly. 'Just think how lovely it will be to be back and to work alongside Flo.'

At that Rose suddenly brightened. 'Yes, I have missed you girls.'

'And we've missed you,' Flo replied earnestly. 'I can't wait to have you back with us, Rose love. It's not been the same without you. I don't see anyone when I'm up in my little office all day.'

Mr Button raised an eyebrow in concern. 'You sound rather sad about that. Mrs Matravers used to say the best bit about her job was cherry-picking the best customers to hobnob with.'

'Well, Flo ain't no Mabel Matravers,' Dot said hotly.

'No I'm not,' Flo said cautiously. 'But I actually miss the customers. Especially some of the regulars.'

'How's your David, Mary?' Dot asked, changing the subject. 'I haven't heard you talk about him much.'

Mary nodded. 'He's fine. He wrote to me last week and said he thought he would be off to a new destination

24

but of course couldn't say where. If I'm, honest I'm a bit worried.'

'Well, I think that's good news,' Dot said brightly. 'It'll take his mind off his sister's incarceration if nothing else.'

Alice shook her head in disbelief. 'Dot! I don't think that being shipped off to some far-flung destination in the pursuit of war is going to help take his mind off the fact that Mrs Matravers is in prison.'

As Dot opened her mouth ready to fire off in protest, Mary intervened. 'No, it is good news. It's just that to me the war seems never-ending. How much worse does it have to get before it gets better?'

Alice nodded in agreement. 'It seems like we've got no chance. Did you read about that American ship the Japs destroyed last month near Christmas Island?'

'I keep thinking what if that happens to Neil. We've only just got married,' Flo put in, worry etched across her face as she rested her knife and fork on her plate. 'I've not seen him since the day after our wedding; I keep wondering when or if we'll ever see each other again.'

Dot banged her fist down on the table, making everyone jump. 'Listen to the lot of you,' she fumed. 'The way you're all carrying on you'd think we'd lost the war already. Our boys need your support not your worry.'

'I couldn't agree more,' Malcolm began, his face grave. 'When I was injured in the last war it was thoughts of family, friends and the freedoms we were fighting for that gave me the strength to battle on.'

There was a silence then as everyone reflected on what had been said. Alice glanced around the table, feeling humbled by his words.

'I would like to raise a toast,' she said loudly. 'To carrying on in troubled times.'

The assembled group lifted their glasses high and clinked them together. 'To carrying on in troubled times,' they echoed.

Glancing around once more, Alice felt a sturdy sense of resolve. Yes, times were hard, but they had food on the table, a roof over their heads and each other to lean on. Together, they would survive whatever life threw at them.

Chapter Four

Alice woke the next morning feeling hot and clammy. Rising from her bed, she reached for Arthur who was just waking up and kissed him on the forehead. As she held her son in her arms, she tried to make sense of her dreams. She and Luke had been reunited at Waterloo train station. As they looked at each other through the crowds they had waved and smiled, but every time Alice went to reach for him he slipped through her grasp.

As Alice blinked her eyes open in the pitch black, trying to adjust to her woken state, she felt a rush of grief flood through her the likes of which she hadn't felt since she had first received the news that Luke had gone missing. She physically ached for him. He was her soul mate, something she had known all those years ago when she had been a farthing short of a cinema seat at the Coronet and he had offered to pay the difference.

The force of the memory took her by surprise. Alice had never forgotten the feel of his palm against hers as he slipped her the coin, or the warmth of his body as he sat next to her in the cinema. Now she brought his handsome face to mind, closing her eyes, determined to remember every last detail of her husband as if the very act of doing so would bring him back into her life.

Alice had fallen for him as soon as she laid eyes on him. Luke hadn't been shy about his feelings either. The moment the film was over he had introduced himself, telling her he worked at the nearby docks. She had been impressed, and when he asked her out to the pictures the following night, Alice hadn't hesitated. They had talked all the way through the film, snuggling up together in the back row, comparing notes on their lives.

She had told Luke all about her father's criminal ways and the fact that she had been only four when her mother had died giving birth to her sister Joy. She had her pride and she wanted to be upfront. If Luke Milwood had a problem with her or her upbringing better to find out now.

But in fact Luke had no problem at all. Instead he merely remarked that it was sad Alice had been forced to endure so much when she was so very young. In turn he had told her how he had been raised in Aberdeen, his father a dock worker from Bermondsey and his mother a proud Scot. The two had met when his father had gone on a training course at the docks in Aberdeen where his mother was a cleaner in the offices. It had been love at first sight, Luke explained, and so heady that his father had given up his life in London and settled in Scotland immediately. It had been a love story Luke and his younger brother Chris had grown up with. His family never had very much, Luke told Alice, but the one thing they had always had was love, and Luke very much wanted to recreate for himself the love his parents shared. Moving down to London at eighteen to follow in his father's footsteps at the docks, Luke had been looking for the right girl but never found her until now. Six months later when Luke proposed, Alice had felt giddy at the thought of this very handsome man stepping into her life and had immediately said yes. That had been six years ago, when she was just twenty, and they had married the day she turned twenty-one.

As her son stirred in her arms, she immediately sprang to life. 'Good morning, sweetheart,' she crooned.

Arthur merely gurgled delightedly.

'This morning it's just you and me while Grandma Dot goes out to work,' she whispered softly. 'What do you think about that?'

Arthur of course said nothing, simply happy to enjoy a precious cuddle with his mother.

Setting her son down on her bed, Alice quickly changed him, and as she looked into his large round eyes she realised just how much her son looked like Luke. Of course she knew all babies looked like their father when they were so small but in that moment she could see the resemblance as she never had before. The sight of her husband, alive before her, took her breath away. She needed more than anything to feel Luke with her, to feel as though he was more than just a distant memory.

Her eyes never leaving her son, she opened the door of the little teak cupboard that stood next to her bed. Reaching inside for the large bundle of letters her husband had written to her since he had joined the war, she immediately found the one she wanted – her favourite was always on the top, carrying the very essence of the man she loved. Pulling it from the bundle, she began to read aloud to Arthur:

16th June 1941

My darling,
 It has been a quiet day for once, no sorties and no drills, just time to sit down with a cup of tea and catch our breath. It's been a welcome break for some of the lads here, they've all been working their fingers to the bone, they need the chance to let off a bit of steam. But not for me, my love, I hate the lulls. I know it sounds daft, I can hear you now telling me I should enjoy the chance to put my feet up when I can, but I just can't do it. I like to work because the harder I graft, the more exercises I'm a part of, and the closer I am to getting

home and getting back to you and our beautiful baby boy or girl. You've always told me to shoot for the stars, Alice. I would never have had the strength to face all the tests I have without you – I can't wait to do the same for our son or daughter. I want them to have the world.

I miss you so much, my love, my body aches to feel your arms wrapped around me. Your braveness, your strength and your devotion carry me through each day.

There are times when it seems that we will never get home, that we will never win this war and that all this suffering is in vain. There are times I feel as though it's pointless to carry on, but then an image of you will appear in my mind, and I know that despite everything, I am still the luckiest man on earth. The day I slipped you a farthing in the cinema queue was the best of my life. Who knew you could buy so much happiness with so very little?

Stay strong for me, my love. We will be reunited soon and I cannot wait for the day when that happens.

Your ever-loving husband,
Luke

The strength of love wrapped up in Luke's words was the tonic Alice needed. She could feel him with her in her every movement.

Wiping her tears, Alice put the letter back in her bedside cabinet and then picked up her son, who was still gurgling away, and carried him downstairs balanced on her hip. As she walked down the steps she realised how much heavier her son was getting and the thought that this little person she and her husband had created was beginning to grow and thrive, despite the hardships of war, helped give her a much needed lift. Setting her son back down in his makeshift cot of a kitchen drawer, she filled the kettle and reached for a pair of cups.

'Morning,' Dot called drowsily behind her. 'Thought I heard you rootling about down here. Didn't you sleep well?'

Alice shrugged. She had become used to nights fuelled with nothing but broken sleep as Arthur woke crying in the dead of night, demanding to be fed or changed.

'Sort of,' she managed in reply.

'We ought to offer him up to the War Office,' Dot chuckled. 'As an alternative to the all-clear siren.'

'He's got a pair of lungs on him, make no mistake,' Alice said wryly over the whistle of the kettle.

'Like his father!'

Alice regarded her landlady fondly. She had known the older woman since she was a child – since before her father had run off to America to work for the mob in Los Angeles. Dot had been a treasure then, showing her how to wash, cook and clean. 'You remember what life was like when my old man left, don't you?'

Dot frowned. ''Course. He tried leaving you a pile of ten-bob notes before buggering off leaving you and Joy high and dry.'

'When he left, I wanted things to change, I wanted to give Joy a proper start in life, a start I'd never had.'

'And look how she repaid you!' Dot exclaimed.

'Joy never took it quite that far. But you're right, I worked my fingers to the bone at that horrible tearoom on the Walworth Road for that girl and look how it turned out.'

'So what are you bringing it up now for?' Dot asked, getting to the point.

'When I was working all hours of the day in that café, I promised it would be different when I had children of me

31

own,' Alice said firmly. 'I wanted him or her to have the very best I could afford. Not just in clothes, shoes and food, but love as well. This might sound daft to you, Dot, but I want that for Arthur – I want him to have a better childhood than I did and he won't have it if his own father don't come home soon.'

As Alice finished speaking, Dot was up on her feet and pulling Alice into her arms. 'I don't think you're daft, 'course I don't,' she said soothingly as she rocked Alice gently. 'I think what you've just said makes a lot of sense, but, darlin', the thing about life is that it's not perfect, and if you're waiting for the day it will be before you start thinking you're giving Arthur a decent childhood then you'll be waiting a bloody long time.'

Alice snorted with laughter at the bluntness of Dot's statement as she untangled herself from her landlady's arms. 'I don't want everything to be perfect; I just want it to be right.'

'Things are right,' Dot said firmly, her grey eyes brimming with earnestness.

'But it's not enough.' Alice sniffed miserably. 'I mean I think of you and the girls as family, 'course I do, but he deserves the best and what's he got? A grandfather who thought a life of crime would pay, an auntie who's supplementing her waitressing wages at Claridge's by thieving her way around the West End, and a dad who's missing God knows where.'

'Look, Alice, in my experience there are certain things you can control in life and certain things you can't. Look how your Arthur arrived in this world, on the shop floor of Liberty's if you please.'

At the memory Alice shook her head in wonder. If anyone had said to her that her baby would arrive in full view of a floor full of customers she'd have screamed in horror, but when the time comes, the time comes; you don't get to pick and choose.

'What I'm trying to say is there are times in life when you have no control, you just have to make the best of it and stop worrying,' Dot finished.

'And you're saying this is one of those times?'

'I am,' Dot confirmed. 'You're doing a fine job. Why don't you come down the shop a bit early with Arthur and I'll collect him from you there before you start your afternoon shift. Beatrice would love to meet your lad, I'm sure. Everyone loves a baby.'

'Do you think so?' Alice asked, brightening at the suggestion.

'If *she* doesn't *we* all will. It's worth a try. Pop in half an hour before lunchtime when it's quiet and she'll be all over him,' Dot said.

As Alice listened to her landlady thud up the stairs to get ready for work, she finished her own cup of tea and stood up full of fresh resolve. She still wasn't quite convinced that she was doing enough for Arthur, but Dot had just given her a very good idea of how to try and get off to a better start with her new manager.

Chapter Five

Clutching the handle of Arthur's pram, Alice felt relaxed as she walked down Argyll Street towards Liberty's later that day. The sun was shining and even though she had needed a scarf to keep out the April chill, Alice could smell spring in the air.

There were definitely more people in the capital since Christmas and they were all largely American soldiers, known as GIs. They weren't hard to spot, what with their well-cut uniforms and the way they moved slowly along the street with their hands in their pockets, a far cry from any British soldier – or even civilian, Alice thought with a wry smile. She had no idea how long they would be in the country, but she found their presence reassuring. It made her feel as if there were more of them in the war together, and that could mean that one day her beloved Luke might be returned to her.

The thought gave Alice a sense of hope she hadn't felt since Arthur's birth, and she found herself quickening her step towards her second home. Despite Arthur's sudden entrance there she hadn't brought him back to the store since. Consequently, today felt like something of a celebration and she was looking forward to showing off her darling boy.

Peering into the pram she was delighted to see her son was wide awake and smiling up at her. These were the moments she felt happiest, when it was just her and Arthur locked in their own private little world, the two of them against everyone else.

As if reading her mind Arthur gurgled and stretched out his arm, trying to reach for his mother. Alice smiled and stopped to plant a kiss on her son's forehead, earning herself a tut and a rebuke from the person behind as they collided with her. Swinging around to apologise, Alice's heart sank as she came face-to-face with Mrs Claremont. So much for the chance of a perfect new start.

'Alice.' Mrs Claremont grimaced as she rubbed her leg. 'Don't you know better than to just stop in the middle of the street?'

'Sorry,' Alice said, aghast, 'I didn't think.'

'Clearly,' Mrs Claremont grumbled, straightening up and casting a glance in Arthur's direction. 'Is this your son?'

'Yes,' Alice said proudly. 'We were just on our way to Liberty's.'

'You're not due in until later today,' Mrs Claremont said, narrowing her eyes.

'I know. But Dot suggested I bring Arthur in a little earlier to show him off to everyone.'

Mrs Claremont looked at Alice in undisguised horror. 'Not on the shop floor?'

'Yes – why not?' Alice asked, bewildered.

'Because it is a place of business,' Mrs Claremont hissed, her cheeks pinking with anger. 'It is not appropriate to bring a child into a working environment.'

Alice was astonished. 'He's a baby,' she protested. 'I don't understand why you don't want me to bring a baby into the shop?'

Mrs Claremont opened her mouth to say something and then seemed to think better of it. She glanced down at her watch before looking at Alice again. 'Mrs Milwood, it strikes me we have perhaps got off on the wrong foot. Do you have time for a cup of tea?'

This was not what Alice had been anticipating. 'All right,' she agreed.

Just ten minutes later and the two women and Arthur, now fast asleep, were settled in a café around the corner in Carnaby Street. As Alice poured the tea out into the two cups and added a dash of milk, Mrs Claremont began to speak. 'Mrs Milwood, I appreciate that my way is rather different to that of Mrs Canning and that might be difficult for you.'

Alice glanced at her new manager over her teacup, and saw that behind the bluster there was a hint of nervousness around her eyes. 'Yes, but that's not necessarily a problem,' she said carefully.

'I know that I can come off as being a bit abrasive,' Mrs Claremont continued as though Alice hadn't spoken, 'but to me hard work is one of the most important things we can do in our lives.'

'I agree,' Alice said firmly. 'That's why I wanted to bring Arthur into the store to meet you, Mrs Claremont. To show you just why I work so hard, and to show you why Liberty's means so much to me.'

Mrs Claremont waved Alice's words away. 'I don't need to see your child to know that you value hard work, Mrs Milwood. But let me ask you this: have you ever seen any male members of staff bring their offspring into the store?'

A look of horror passed across Alice's face as she set her cup down. 'Of course not. But babies are women's work.'

'Exactly,' Mrs Claremont said emphatically. 'And now, thanks to this war, we women are being asked to take on men's roles until they come home. So many out there think we're not up to the task and we have to show them otherwise. Now, as fabric manager at Liberty's I want to show Mrs Canning, Mr Button and the entire Liberty board and family just how well we can do here without the menfolk. We must work harder than hard, Mrs Milwood, and every penny we bring in counts towards our success. That's what the family will look for during these times of war – how much money we make. I want our department to be the very best at Liberty, and for that we must rely on ourselves, Mrs Milwood, just as we do when it comes to raising our children.'

'But what's that got to do with me bringing Arthur in?'

'Because it shows weakness, Mrs Milwood, and as a lone parent the one thing you can't afford to be is weak.'

'I'm not sure that's true,' Alice replied doubtfully.

Mrs Claremont jabbed at the table with her forefinger. 'Trust me when I say that it is. Like you, I had to raise my two children alone after their father was killed in the last war, and like you, I had no family or friends to help me. I know you'll do whatever it takes to feed and clothe your child – provide for him as both mother and father. That's why I run a tight ship. Because I have an unfaltering belief in hard work and discipline, particularly in times of war like this.'

'I understand,' Alice said, taking another sip of her scalding hot tea. 'It must have been hard for you when your husband died. Were your children very old? Do they remember him?'

Mrs Claremont smiled wistfully. 'They were four and six and they adored him as I did. We were lost for a time – I did things I never thought I'd do to provide for my family. But my children were my world,' she said fiercely.

Alice nodded at the sentiment as she topped up their cups with more tea. Judging from Mrs Claremont's tone, Alice didn't think she should ask more.

'Sadly, I hardly see them now of course. Briony is in the FANY and Tom is serving in the army, so it's just me in a little flat in Kilburn all alone,' Mrs Claremont finished.

'You must miss them.'

'I do,' Mrs Claremont replied wistfully. 'But I'm used to it now, I suppose. They moved down to Devon to be with my sister about ten years after their father died.'

Alice paused for a moment to look properly at the woman sitting opposite her. The aggressive, hard mask Mrs Claremont always seemed to wear had slipped just a little and Alice saw a lone tear roll down the older woman's cheek. 'Still, I imagine holidays must have been fun in Devon. And wonderful for the children to have all that fresh air,' Alice said brightly, trying to take the sting out of what she could tell was still a very upsetting situation for her new superior.

Mrs Claremont smiled gratefully. 'Yes, it was, and much better for them really to be in the countryside.'

'I often wonder whether Arthur would be better off in the countryside,' Alice mused. 'Even though I grew up here, London's hardly the best place to raise a family. But I could never leave Liberty's. For me this job is a way of life and Liberty's is the family home.'

'What are you talking about? I mean I love Liberty's, of course, Mrs Milwood, but there are other stores and other jobs.'

Alice leaned back in her chair and grinned at the chance to reveal to her new boss just how special Liberty's was. 'The staff here, well, we're like family, especially the girls in fabrics. We've all grown so close, and we've been through so much together. I would be lost without them, especially now Arthur's here. They're always there ready to help me out whenever I need.'

As Arthur let out a little cry in his pram, Alice bent down to pick him up. 'I'm delighted we had this chat, Mrs Claremont. I'm sure we'll be a great team.'

But Mrs Claremont said nothing; instead she got to her feet, left a handful of coins on the table for her tea and swept out of the café. As Alice watched her superior disappear she had the strangest feeling that she had said something to upset her new boss, but for the life of her couldn't think what.

Chapter Six

Thanks to the new dresses Dot had lovingly taken in for her, Mrs Claremont felt Alice was suitably dressed for the shop floor. As she served all her favourite customers she felt a happiness pass through her that she hadn't felt for some time.

By the time Rose rang down for her, to say that it was time for her afternoon meeting, Alice felt relaxed and confident. She made her way upstairs through the maze of cramped corridors that led to Mr Button's office, where the store manager, Mrs Claremont and Flo welcomed her inside the wood-panelled office.

'Take a seat,' Mr Button said, gesturing to the empty chair besides Mrs Claremont.

'Mrs Claremont and I have been talking about utility fabric and the clothing that will come into stores from the summer, Mrs Milwood,' Flo began with an air of authority Alice hadn't seen before.

Nodding, Alice remembered Mrs Claremont's speech in the café earlier that day and gave Flo and Mr Button what she hoped was a professional smile of understanding. Utility clothing was a subject that had been discussed in the papers for some time. The government wanted to cut back even further on waste in a bid to help the war effort and so had suggested that as well as food and clothing rationing, any new clothes that were produced from now on would have to conform to certain restrictions such as skirts only being a certain length and jacket lapels a maximum width.

'It means that we have to know the weight per yard, the degree of shrinkage and so on,' Mr Button said. 'The Board of Trade is being very strict.'

'Naturally customers and retailers are worried that this means drab clothing but at Liberty's we want to show everyone that won't be the case at all,' Flo added.

'Yes of course,' Alice replied.

'With utility clothing fast on the approach we need to give our very best customers the choice and quality they deserve so we want to ensure all our utility fabric is available in as many prints as possible to keep variety,' Mrs Claremont put in.

'And make sure each fabric is special,' Alice offered, seeing what Mrs Claremont was getting at.

'That's it exactly,' Mr Button said, steepling his fingers as he leaned forward, resting his elbows on his desk. 'The problem, as I was explaining to Mrs Claremont, is that some of our agents aren't keen to make a special feature of our prints. Although they're behind the utility scheme, some of our retailers can't grasp why we're creating our famous prints especially for utility clothing patterns. Many say it's a lot of effort for nothing.'

Flo leafed through the paperwork before her. 'So many that we have spoken to recently think that now the Americans are in the war effort, rationing and so on won't last much longer and that these utility fabrics and garments won't even make it on to the shop floors. Mr Button and I want to get the stores that stock our goods—'

'Our agents,' Alice interrupted.

'That's right,' Flo nodded. 'We want to get the stores that stock our goods to really understand, like and back this scheme.'

Alice frowned as she regarded her superiors. 'But according to the trade press, the government wants to roll out utility clothing by June.'

'That's right.' Flo nodded again. 'It's well known that the Board of Trade is working with a team of designers who are coming up with their own interpretation of functional fashion with designs for blouses, top coats and dresses.'

'Gone are the days of shoppers visiting us twice a year after the Paris shows,' Mr Button said wistfully. 'This is the future and we must embrace it. People shop differently now.'

'Mr Button is right.' Flo pushed a copy of the *Picture Post* across the desk towards Alice. 'As you can see, Deborah Kerr is wearing utility clothes complete with new skirt and lapel widths. If it's good enough for Hollywood royalty, it's good enough for Liberty's.'

Alice peered at the picture and felt a swell of admiration for the star. Anyone with reservations about utility clothing would surely take one look at this picture and realise that fashion could be both beautiful and practical. Dressed in a tweed coat and headscarf, the actress looked a million dollars.

'Obviously designers are waiting for the final restrictions on collar widths, pleats and so on, but this should give you a good idea of what we can expect utility clothing to look like,' Mr Button said.

'And how our customers can recreate these looks using utility patterns and our very special Liberty fabrics,' Flo added. 'There is of course no restriction on design or colour and we want everyone to know that at Liberty's you can find your own personal style.'

Alice could see the wisdom in the way they were approaching this sudden change in fashion, and how they could help customers get behind the idea. 'How can fabrics help?'

Flo glanced down at her notebook. 'There are a couple of things we would like to do. Firstly Mr Button and I think it's best to hold an event here within the store that will raise awareness of the utility scheme and just how much fun you can still have with clothes, whether old or new.'

Alice nodded; she would put her thinking cap on immediately and come up with something.

'However,' Mr Button said, interrupting her thoughts, 'what we really need you to do is go down to Bath and visit one of our agents, Jolly's, there. We know you have built up some marvellous relationships with our agents across the country over the years, Alice. Consequently, we think you're the one to wax lyrical about why they should be putting our prints at the forefront of their displays.'

'But surely that's a job for Mrs Claremont as head of department?' Alice frowned, turning to her new department manger but finding Mrs Claremont's expression blank as she gazed resolutely at the floor.

'We would rather like to send you,' Mr Button said, his eyes twinkling. 'You would only need to stay for one night, and of course we'll put you up. We need someone who knows the stock and knows our agents. You have a wonderful relationship with Mrs Downing who runs the Jolly's drapery department, I understand?'

'Well, yes, though we haven't spoken in a while.'

'A minor detail, Alice. You're excellent with people – isn't that right, Mrs Claremont?'

'Hmm,' Mrs Claremont replied non-committally.

Alice thought for a moment. She would love the opportunity to visit the agents; she hadn't done so since war broke out. Not only that, Mr Button was right: she did have an excellent relationship with the head of drapery in Jolly's; of all things, the two had bonded over the fact they had both brought up their sisters.

'There's just one issue,' Alice said. 'Can I bring Arthur?'

Mrs Claremont tutted under her breath and Alice felt irritated as she turned to face Flo and Mr Button square on.

'We were rather hoping that you would agree to let Mrs Hanson look after him for the evening,' Mr Button replied, his copper eyes roaming over her face hesitantly. 'I have taken the liberty of discussing this with her and she has agreed as long as you don't mind.'

'Dot really doesn't mind?' Alice whistled. 'It's a big ask.'

Mr Button smiled. 'I rather think Dorothy will enjoy it. I have never seen her look more content than I have when she's settled in the kitchen bottle-feeding Arthur.'

Alice leaned back in her chair. She hadn't left Arthur once since he had been born. It had been hard enough leaving him to come to work yesterday. Was she really ready to leave him overnight? Just the thought of spending a night away from him made her feel queasy. Only – smoothing a lock of hair that had escaped from her chignon – she knew without doubt this wasn't a request. Women were doing more for this war than they had ever imagined, and if it wasn't for Arthur she had no doubt that she would be in the services doing whatever she could for her country. She glanced across at Mrs Claremont, and saw her give a nod of encouragement: it was time to be brave.

'I would be delighted,' she said gravely. 'Thank you for thinking of me.'

'You're quite welcome,' Mr Button said, getting to his feet and signalling that the meeting was over. 'You'll go on the last Saturday of this month. Although the trip isn't very long, there are of course so many problems with train travel, and speed restrictions, that parts of the line will be slow. I suggest you leave on the first train although Mrs Downing won't be expecting you until the afternoon.'

'Very good, Mr Button,' Alice said, getting to her feet. 'And thank you all again for the opportunity.'

'It was Mr Button's idea,' Mrs Claremont replied stiffly. 'He feels that you are the best person for this job. You're fortunate to have someone like Mrs Hanson on hand to help you with your son.'

Alice nodded in agreement; she knew how lucky she was and she wasn't about to make a mistake. 'I can assure you I will give the job my all,' she said as she turned to walk out of the door.

'We know you will, Mrs Milwood,' Flo said with an air of confidence. 'We can't wait to hear how you get on.'

Flashing a smile at her friend, Alice returned to the shop floor feeling elated. This was her chance to shine and she was determined not to let the Liberty family or herself down.

Chapter Seven

There was no other way to describe it, Alice thought as she clambered aboard the crowded Tube carriage at Oxford Circus, she was downright exhausted. As a GI got up to offer her a seat, Alice thought she might pass out with gratitude when she sat down. It had been just over a week since she had returned to her job, and during that time she had been working her fingers to the bone, determined to prove her worth to Mrs Claremont.

Following their conversation in the café last week, Alice, much to her surprise, found she was almost enjoying the extra challenge. Her working days were different now than they had been as not only had she become responsible for organising the break times of each staff member, something that had traditionally always been done by Flo, but she had also volunteered to keep an eye on Rose. At first, Alice had been worried as to how Rose would cope with it all; however, she had taken it all in her stride and appeared to be adjusting well to life back in the store, even if it was only for two days a week.

Still, Alice thought as the train arrived at the Elephant and Castle, for the moment things were going well, even if she was shattered. But none of that mattered now: the only thing Alice wanted in that moment was a strong cup of tea and a good long cuddle with her son.

Slipping her key into the faded black wooden door, she unlocked it with practised ease. Once inside, she all but threw her coat and bag on to the floor in her rush to see

Arthur. Although she was getting used to time away from him, every moment spent apart seemed like an eternity.

'Hello, I'm home,' she cried, padding down the corridor to the kitchen in the half-light, aware that she and Dot would have to start getting ready for blackout in a few moments. She heard the quiet chatter of voices and quickened her pace. Dot was obviously talking to Arthur, so perhaps he was still wide awake following his afternoon nap.

She was about to rush straight to the cot and revel in the sweet, warm smell of her son, when the sight of a familiar petite woman sitting at the table caught her by surprise.

'Joy!' she hissed. 'What the hell are you doing here?'

Alice's sister swung around, a smile plastered across her angular face, her blue eyes dancing with delight as she got up to greet her sister. 'There you are. I was just passing and thought how nice it would be to come and say hello to you and little Anthony.'

'Your nephew's name is Arthur,' Alice said, trying to keep the annoyance out of her voice as Joy wrapped her arms around her older sister.

Wriggling free from her sister's embrace, Alice stepped back to take a look at her sister. 'So what brings you all the way out here? We're a long way from Claridge's.'

'Oh, Joy don't work up Claridge's any more, do you, love?' Dot said by way of explanation as she placed Arthur into Alice's arms and turned back to the kettle to make a pot of tea. 'She's got herself a new job now.'

'That true?' Alice asked bluntly. 'What happened at Claridge's?'

Joy waved away Alice's concerns as she reached out a finger to stroke Arthur's chin as if he were a cat rather than a baby. 'Oh, it wasn't right for me. So I'm working at Mayfair House now.'

47

Alice let out a low whistle as Arthur waved his chubby fists in the air and smiled at his mother. 'That fancy hotel all the film stars stay in?'

'That's the one,' Joy said with a lazy smile as she leaned against the table. 'We see a lot of them GIs as well.'

'I thought they all hung about up the Savoy?' Dot quizzed.

Alice looked at Dot in surprise. 'How do you know that?'

Dot's eyes twinkled. 'You'd be surprised what you pick up when you listen, Alice Milwood.'

'Anyway,' Joy said impatiently, clearly keen to bring the conversation around to herself again. 'I thought it was high time I paid you and Arthur a visit.'

'Well, it's lovely to see you,' Alice said brightly, getting ready to show her sister out. 'We'll perhaps come and see you at your digs, Joy, when you're a bit more settled.'

At the mention of digs Joy's face flushed bright red. Her reaction wasn't lost on Alice and in a funny way she felt a sense of relief. Her younger sister always had an ulterior motive and it looked as if they were finally about to discover what it actually was.

'The thing is ...' Joy began hesitantly. 'I haven't actually got any digs at the moment.'

Alice felt a flash of annoyance. Here it was: the real reason for her sister's unexpected visit. 'What happened? You were only in the last ones five minutes.'

'It wasn't my fault,' Joy protested, looking at Alice pleadingly, which only served to deepen Alice's anger. How many times had she heard those four little words from her sister's mouth?

'What happened, Joy?' she said again, this time through gritted teeth as she turned around to set Arthur back down.

Joy rolled her large blue eyes. 'Oh, it was something and nothing. The landlord thought I'd been stealing from the other lodgers.'

'And had you?' Alice asked, getting straight to the point.

'Of course not! I told you at Christmas I'm not like that any more, Alice.'

'You'll forgive me if I don't believe you,' Alice replied, hands on hips as she eyed her sister with suspicion.

'You never do.' Joy replied, unable to keep the hurt out of her voice. 'You've never put a foot wrong in all your life, yet you always judge me.'

'Don't be so ridiculous! You were nicked by the police last year for pick-pocketing so don't act as though I'm barking up the wrong tree. Between you and Dad, Joy, I reckon I've spent half my life down the nick getting one or the other of you out of trouble.'

Joy took a step towards her sister, her eyes full of determination. 'All I'm saying is – is it too much to expect your own sister to believe in you?'

'When that sister is you, Joy Harris, then yes it is,' Alice hissed.

Dot took a step between the sisters and pushed them gently apart with her hands. 'Look at the two of you. You're both grown women, not a pair of little kids. Now calm down for Arthur's sake if not your own.'

Turning to her landlady, eyes still glowing with anger, Alice gave an imperceptible nod of her head and walked over to the range. She took a deep breath and looked at her sister. 'So what is it you want?' she asked, doing her best to keep her voice even.

Joy looked cautiously at Dot before glancing back at her sister. 'What I was hoping is that I could perhaps stay with you for a bit. Just until I get myself sorted,' she added quickly.

At that Alice snorted with laughter. 'You must be joking. I haven't got time to police your behaviour. I've got a job and child to raise alone. I don't need the grief and I certainly wouldn't wish it on Dot.'

'Please, Alice,' Joy said in a wheedling tone. 'I promise I won't be any trouble.'

'And how many times have I heard that?' Alice replied with a firm shake of her head. 'No, I'm sorry, I'll help you find somewhere else but you can't stay here, there's no room. And besides, aren't we a bit far for you to travel into work?'

'Not on the Tube,' Joy protested. 'The thing is I don't have any money until I get my first week's wages. Nobody will take me.'

As Alice's eyes drifted to the overstuffed suitcase propped up by the doorway a fresh round of fury pulsed through her. Joy had assumed she would help her out. Well, this time she was too tired to deal with her sister's antics.

'And whose fault's that?' Alice snapped. 'If you hadn't gone thieving at your last place then maybe you wouldn't be in this mess.'

'And how many more times have I got to say it wasn't me,' Joy yelled so loud she caused Arthur to grumble in his cot. 'Alice, I'm begging you. I promise I've turned over a new leaf. This new job's a proper fresh start for me, I really want to make it work.'

There was a pause then as Alice turned to look at Dot, who was observing the exchange from the pantry. The landlady knew Joy of old, but instead of the unforgiving glance Alice was expecting, she saw a look of helplessness in her eyes.

'Look,' Alice said, turning back to face her sister. 'It's not that I don't want to believe you, Joy; trust me, nothing would give me greater pleasure than to see you make something of yourself – settle down, find a nice fella, have a family. But I just can't trust you.'

'Can't you give me a chance?' Joy tried again, her cheeks reddening with the effort of begging. 'If I make a mistake then I'll go, no questions asked and no bother neither.'

At that it was Dot's turn to roar with laughter. 'Get on, you're Jimmy Harris's daughter, you don't know how to do anything without bother. No matter what your sister says, Joy, your Alice is just the same in that regard.'

'Oi!' the sisters chorused in protest, before exchanging a smile.

Alice sighed as she looked at her sister. Joy was her flesh and blood; she had a duty to take care of her, didn't she? 'What do you think?' she called to Dot. 'Can we put her up for a bit?'

Dot peered around the pantry door holding a tin of peaches – Alice knew better than to question where they had come from. 'I suppose so. She's family, Alice; you have to say yes to family, more's the pity. She can go in Mary's old room for a bit until she gets herself sorted. But I warn you, lady' – she turned to Joy and narrowed her eyes – 'there'll be no trouble here or you're out.'

'And no taking advantage neither,' Alice pointed out sharply. 'The moment you get your wages you pay Dot your bed and board immediately, no excuses or I'll kick you out myself.'

'Deal.' Joy smiled, unclipping her long blonde hair and hugging her sister in one fluid movement. 'You won't regret it, Alice, I promise.'

As Alice breathed in the scent of her sister's cheap perfume, she already felt a pang of regret. Trouble usually had a way of finding Joy, and she couldn't help wondering just how long it would be before it made its way to her again.

Chapter Eight

Unusually for Alice she arrived at Liberty's in a bad mood. Not only had she not got to bed until after midnight as she had suddenly remembered she needed to wash Arthur's nappies, but she had also been disturbed by Joy moving her things about as she settled into the room next door. Then it had struck her that today was Luke's thirtieth birthday.

As she helped Mrs Claremont finish her morning checks before the floorwalker, whom everyone called Dreary Deirde, arrived, Alice found her mind was still filled with Luke. She wondered where he was, what he was doing and if he was celebrating the milestone in any way at all. All too easily, memories of the last birthday they had spent together flooded her mind. Luke had turned twenty-seven and they had taken the train to Margate. There they had gone for a picnic as the April weather was unusually glorious and they had spent the day on the sands watching the tide come in and out, making plans for the rest of their lives. It had been simple and romantic: a wonderful way to celebrate. Just the thought of it made Alice want to break down and cry for her lost love. As she furiously tidied away a stash of needles, she imagined what it would be like to stab one of these through Hitler's heart, just as if he were a pin cushion.

'Mrs Milwood, I don't know what's wrong with you this morning but I would be grateful if you would alter your face by the time customers arrive,' Mrs Claremont said crisply, cutting through her thoughts.

'Sorry,' Alice said meekly, feeling anything but.

'Everything all right?' Mrs Claremont enquired, her tone gentler.

Alice looked at her in surprise. Mrs Claremont never showed the slightest interest in her well-being – or her personal life come to that. 'I'm fine, thank you.'

'Are you sure?' Mrs Claremont pressed, her grey eyes seemingly filled with concern.

'Well – not really,' Alice said with a sigh, relieved at the prospect of unburdening herself. 'My sister moved in with Mrs Hanson and me last night and let's just say I have mixed emotions about it all. And on top of that, today is my husband's birthday. I suppose I didn't sleep very well with so much on my mind.'

'I see,' Mrs Claremont said, lips pursed. 'I can quite understand how you have a lot to think about, but I expect you to remain professional and leave your home life at the door, Mrs Milwood. If you're not feeling up to dealing with customers this morning, may I suggest you spend some time going through our paperwork and ensuring the stockroom is tidy until you feel more able to cope with the shop floor.'

About to open her mouth to protest, Alice thought better of it. Mrs Claremont might be right, she wasn't much good on the shop floor at the moment, but the last thing she wanted to do was spend any more time in the stockroom losing out on valuable commission.

'I'll be fine, thank you, Mrs Claremont,' she said firmly.

Before Mrs Claremont could protest, Alice made her way across the shop floor towards one of her regular customers and started to serve her.

Sneaking a glance at Mary, the two exchanged weary smiles – there was no denying it, life in fabrics just wasn't the same as it used to be. The department had once been a

53

place of great joy and friendship but in the ten days since Alice had returned she couldn't help feeling as though something was lacking in the place. It was a dreadful shame, not just because she had always seen Liberty's as her second home, but also because she had a feeling life at her first home was about to become quite turbulent. She knew Joy wouldn't be staying forever, and she also knew her sister had promised that she was going to turn over a new leaf. However, the simple truth was that Alice didn't believe her and she knew it would only be a matter of time before Joy returned to her old ways. She was just like their father – unable to help herself, no matter how hard she tried.

Just then, Alice glanced up and saw Rose walking down the stairs with Mr Button by her side. The sight of them together gladdened her heart. It was such a pleasure having Rose back at Liberty's and she moved quickly across the floor to greet them.

'You two are a sight for sore eyes this morning.' She beamed. 'What can we do for you?'

As her eyes scanned Rose's appearance, she was delighted to see that her old friend looked more like her old self. There was colour to her cheeks and she had even managed to pin up her long auburn hair in a slightly messy knot, giving her a glamorous look.

Mr Button grinned at Alice, before nudging Rose. 'We're looking for reinforcements.'

'Sounds suspicious, sir,' Mary added as she sidled up alongside. Alice couldn't resist a smile at the way Mary still sounded as if she were in the army when she was addressing anyone more senior than her.

The store manager laughed as he released his arm from Rose's and rocked slightly on his heels with merriment. 'Not at all. This is Rose's passion project.'

'Yes, but Mr Button here has been extremely supportive,' Rose began, only for the echo of Mrs Claremont's footsteps to drown out the rest of what she was saying.

'What's all this?' she asked briskly.

'As Mrs Harper was just saying, Mrs Claremont,' Mr Button explained, 'she has some rather exciting news.'

Alice turned to Rose and realised the colour in her cheeks was down to excitement. 'Go on,' she coaxed.

'We're going to open the crypt up after hours so we can offer first-aid events to the public,' Rose said. 'I'm going to be running them. We're going to explain to people what to do in an emergency, how to do mouth to mouth, how to dress a wound – that sort of thing.'

'That's wonderful!' Alice clapped her hands in delight. 'That will be so good for the community.'

'What a marvellous idea,' Mary agreed. 'I know the Red Cross will be thrilled. How can we help?'

Rose beamed at them. 'I hoped you would all help me out. There's only so much I can do being virtually blind, but I spoke to the Red Cross this afternoon, and you're right, Mary, they all think it's a marvellous idea and have offered to come and run talks so the theme is a bit different each time we do it. I've got another appointment at Guy's Hospital next week and thought I would see if some of the staff that helped me after my accident would like to be involved.'

'Well, we would love to be part of it,' Alice said immediately, thinking the idea was inspired.

'Of course we would,' Mary echoed warmly. 'And what a wonderful idea to invite staff from Guy's too. I bet if I spoke to David about this he might have some more ideas on what we should include for these evenings. Do we need training?'

Rose nodded. 'The Red Cross and the St John's Ambulance all offer training courses so they will be coming to help. All we need to do now is spread the word.'

At that the girls smiled with excitement; only Mrs Claremont remained stony-faced. 'Are we sure this is such a good idea?'

Everyone turned and looked at her in surprise. 'Why ever not?'

'Do we really want all and sundry traipsing through our glorious store after hours?' Mrs Claremont said tightly. 'Don't misunderstand me, I think the initiative is marvellous, but is this what our dear founder Arthur Lasenby Liberty would want for his precious store? And what about our customers? They expect a certain standard when they shop in Liberty's. They don't want to hobnob with the great unwashed. Don't forget profit really should be at the heart of all we do, especially when we are struggling to make money and survive in these uncertain times, like every other store.'

Alice's jaw dropped in shock. Was this really what the new fabric manager thought? She glanced across at Rose and saw the younger girl's face had fallen like a stone. Alice knew Rose loved nothing more than helping people and to see her idea trampled on so cruelly was devastating.

Seemingly reading her mind, Mr Button stepped in to protest. 'As you quite rightly say, Mrs Claremont, there is a war on,' he began, his tone gentle yet firm. 'And I am also sure I don't need to remind you that it is vital we, the British people, pull together.'

'Well, quite, but I don't see—' she began only for Mr Button to cut her off.

'And I think you'll find that Arthur Liberty was rather supportive of collaborations. Teamwork, Mrs Claremont, is at the very heart of all we do at Liberty's and I think you would do well to remember that. Now, I think Mrs Harper's idea is a marvellous one and I expect you all to support her. Not only is it good for the morale of staff but it also means we can help others in our community too. With Mr Hitler and now Japan gunning firmly for our blood it's vital we are all as informed as possible, wouldn't you agree, Mrs Claremont?'

Alice sneaked a glance at her boss and was delighted to see the older woman had the good grace to look a little ashamed. Her usual tidy bun was slightly ruffled and an embarrassed flush had crept up her neck.

'Yes of course, Mr Button,' she replied, quickly recovering her composure. 'Do let us know how we can assist. When are you hoping to hold the first event, Mrs Harper?'

'Wednesday next week, after my appointment at the hospital,' Rose replied eagerly. 'I've already got someone from the St John's Ambulance coming. In the meantime I've got to go through all our first-aid kits and ensure they're all up to scratch and then tell as many people as possible.'

'We can help with that,' Mary said quickly. 'We'll alert all our customers and ask them to tell their friends and family too.'

'Oh, would you?' Rose asked brightly. 'That would be wonderful.'

'And I'll make sure the other departments down here know as well,' Alice added.

'Thank you, ladies,' Mr Button said. 'I know that this promises to be a great Liberty's initiative.'

With that the duo slipped off across the floor, Mr Button guiding Rose gently back up the stairs towards the office.

'What a thoroughly ridiculous idea,' Mrs Claremont snapped the moment they were out of earshot. 'We should be concentrating on building up the business, not giving in to sentimentality. When I was in gifts we never would have had time to get involved in something so ludicrous.'

Alice felt a flash of fury and was about to open her mouth and roar at Mrs Claremont when she felt Mary lay a gentle hand on her forearm. Mary gave her a shake of the head as if urging caution. 'Oh look, Mrs Perkins is back,' she said cheerily. 'Alice, I bet she wants to talk to you about how to make baby clothes again. You know you're the master at that sort of thing.'

Knowing Mary was doing her best to distract her, Alice smiled gratefully at her friend and made her way to greet her customer. As she observed Mrs Claremont rifling through paperwork out of the corner of her eye, Alice bit back her frustration. Why was her new manager going out of her way to be difficult?

Chapter Nine

Over the course of the next week Alice found, much to her surprise, that she was enjoying having her sister around. Not only did Joy appear to be toeing the line and respecting her and Dot's wishes but she was working hard, helping to look after Arthur and had even offered to show Alice's friends some support by joining her tonight for the first of Rose's St John's Ambulance training nights. Alice wasn't sure how long Joy could keep this change of character up, but Alice was determined to make the most of it.

Together with Mary, Dot and Flo, they had worked tirelessly to ensure that Rose's event that night was a success, and she was keeping her fingers and toes crossed this would be the start of greater things to come for her friend after all the hardships she had endured. Only as she hurried down to the crypt she felt a wave of horror as she saw Rose sitting forlornly in a chair by the fireplace all alone, head in her hands.

'Rose, what's wrong?' Alice asked, hurrying to her side.

'It's just a bit pointless, isn't it?' Rose replied, lifting her head and looking through her friend.

'What's pointless, sweetheart?' Alice asked, clasping her friend's hands.

'All this.' Rose shrugged, gesturing in the direction of the rows of chairs and various medical kits that had been set up on a table at the front of the room. 'You can try and prepare as much as you like for disaster but if something bad's going to happen there's nothing you can do about it.'

Alice tried to ignore the alarm spreading through her as fast as butter melted on hot toast. Rose was usually so optimistic; there had to be a reason for her downturn in mood. 'Has something happened to Tommy? Is that why you're feeling so low?'

At the mention of her husband, Rose shook her head. 'No, as far as I know Tommy's fine. Or at least he was the last time I heard from him a couple of weeks ago.'

'You know what it's like,' Alice tried encouragingly. 'Sometimes it's impossible for them to get a letter out to us, but you know he's thinking of you all the time. Look at how he tried to get compassionate leave last year after you became ill.'

'Poisoned, you mean,' Rose snapped, her blue eyes suddenly alive with fury.

Alice sprang back in surprise; she had never heard Rose talk like this before. 'Darlin', I thought you'd forgiven Mrs M. for that and were moving on. Besides, some of your eyesight's coming back now. Who knows when you'll get the rest of it back?'

'*If* I get the rest of it back,' Rose corrected. Her gaze had returned to the floor. 'I went to Guy's today. Doctors say it's unlikely I'll ever see properly again.'

'What?' Alice gasped, fear thudding through her body. 'What are you talking about?'

'The doctors say this has gone on too long now for me to get my sight back,' Rose snapped angrily. 'Methanol poisoning is usually temporary and passes quickly, if it's going to pass at all.'

Worry surged through Alice and she took a closer look at her friend's face. Gone was Rose's girlish hope and youthful air of naivety. Worry lines had deepened across her forehead and a few strands of grey had suddenly appeared in her auburn hair. Alice didn't know what to do or say to make her friend feel better. It was so unfair. All she could do was pull Rose into her arms. Sometimes words weren't the best medicine, it was a simple action that was required.

'Come on, we've got people coming for this event,' Alice said eventually, releasing her friend. 'They'll be expecting a show and you don't want to let Liberty's or yourself down. This first-aid night is a brilliant idea – you've got a real chance to show other people what to do in a crisis.'

Nodding, Rose got to her feet and reached for the long white cane she always carried. 'Yes, I suppose we must carry on,' she said listlessly.

Just then Mary and Flo walked through the doors of the crypt armed with boxes.

'Rose, where shall we put all this lot?' Flo asked. Only the top of her head was visible above the box of bandages.

'Here, let me help.' Alice rushed to relieve the girls of some of their load.

'Oooh, thank you,' Flo sighed with relief as she followed Alice towards the front of the room and laid everything down there. 'What's all this anyway?'

'Just equipment the St John's Ambulance has let us borrow,' Rose said in a monotonous tone.

'Blimey!' Alice raised an eyebrow. 'We'll all be trained nurses after tonight then!'

Rose shrugged her shoulders and turned away, causing Mary and Flo to exchange puzzled looks with Alice.

Just as Flo was about to say something, Alice heard the sound of footsteps on the stairs. 'Oh, look, ladies, the first of our visitors have arrived. Flo, can you give me a hand to show them to their seats?'

Once the visitors had been settled and the guests from the St John's Ambulance had been welcomed, Rose, aided by Mary, walked to the front and beamed at everyone. It was a good turnout, Alice thought, as she waited for Rose to begin. Including the volunteers they made for about twenty-five, and Alice was delighted to see that as well as Malcolm and her sister, Aggie had turned up to lend her support and was sitting quietly at the back next to Joy.

'Hello, everyone, and welcome to this very first Liberty's emergency first-aid training evening,' Rose began hesitantly, clutching her white cane for all it was worth. 'It's a pleasure to have you all here and I hope you'll all learn something worthwhile.'

As Rose paused there was a round of applause, and Alice felt the room rooting for her friend.

'As you can see from this white stick, I'm almost completely blind,' Rose began in earnest, her gaze now lifting from the floor towards the small crowd. 'I'm very passionate about this project because I believe that if I had been surrounded by people who had been familiar with basic first-aid knowledge, my sight could have been saved. And so, without further ado,' she continued, 'I will now hand you over to our very capable volunteers.'

With that, Rose took a step back with the help of Mary, and the volunteers from the St John's Ambulance began their talk.

'Did you hear that? Flo gasped incredulously as she rounded on Alice. 'She blames us!'

'No, she doesn't. She had some bad news from the doctors at Guy's today. They say it's unlikely she'll get her sight back now and I think the truth of the situation must have hit her hard.'

Flo said in a quiet voice, 'Maybe this news has made her think about her blindness differently now she knows it's not temporary.'

Alice thought for a moment. The way Rose had spoken moments earlier had thrown her.

'Do you honestly think so?' she asked eventually.

'You heard her: she believes that if she had been sur-rounded by people who knew basic first aid she could have had her eyesight saved,' Flo replied evenly. 'We were the ones who were with her when she went blind.'

There was a brief round of applause then as the vol-unteers started handing out apparatus and encouraging people to get into groups. As Mary, Malcolm, Aggie and Joy joined Alice and Flo to make up a group of their own, Alice pounced. 'Do you think Rose blames us for losing her eyesight?'

'Hey come on now, love,' Malcolm said, laying a hand on Alice's forearm consolingly. 'She would never think that. She loves the bones of you girls.'

'Yes,' Mary added in a clipped tone. 'Whatever gave you that idea?'

'I don't know. I just feel so wretched about it all.'

'But not as wretched as Rose will be,' Mary said. 'We need to help her.'

'If she does blame us, she may not want our help,' Flo said in an exasperated tone. 'What does Tommy say? Has he been in touch?'

Malcolm nodded. 'He has. He keeps offering to try and come back on compassionate leave but Rose still won't have it. Her mother keeps writing 'n' all, offering to see if the ATS will let her come home for a bit, but Rose refuses.'

Alice shook her head in disbelief. 'Silly girl. It would give her a lift to see her loved ones – and you too, Malcolm.'

Rose's father smiled kindly at Alice, and subconsciously rubbed the leg that had been badly injured during the last war and caused him to limp. 'That's as may be, but it's Rose's decision. All I can do is hope she changes her mind.'

'Maybe she will now her situation has changed,' Flo mused.

Joy shrugged. 'Or maybe she needs to stop being treated like an invalid you're all worried about.'

As everyone's eyes swivelled towards Joy, Alice saw that far from being sarcastic, Joy was being serious. 'What do you mean?'

'I just mean that Rose is still Rose. All right, she doesn't have her eyesight and, don't get me wrong, that's terrible. But she is still your friend. Maybe if you take the kid gloves off, she might not feel like she was so different.'

There was a pause as everyone digested what Joy had said. Alice had to admit her sister had a point, and was just about to say as much when Malcolm spoke. 'Perhaps. I think it would help if she felt she had more support at work though, Flo. It didn't help that your new fabric manager told her last week that she wouldn't get behind these events.'

At the mention of her direct supervisor Alice glowered. 'I see she isn't here tonight, despite what Mr Button said.'

Flo sighed, frustration written across her face. 'I encouraged her to come but she said that being a member of the WVS she was more than familiar with first-aid procedures and there would be no benefit to her being in the store after closing time.'

'She has some very strange ideas,' Alice hissed.

'I think we can all agree that although Mrs Claremont is a fan of hard work, teamwork is *not* a theory she subscribes to,' Mary added.

'No, it isn't.' Flo assented. 'It never has been; she's always worked hard but puts her own needs above those of anyone else. I had hoped that when she replaced me in fabrics that would change; the department has always been built on camaraderie but that seems to have fallen by the wayside. I saw you girls weren't even allowed to talk the other day on the shop floor in between serving customers.'

Alice made a face. 'She says it looks bad if we're gossiping.'

Flo roared with laughter. 'It's what makes the department special! Customers feel as though they're with friends rather than in some nameless store. I wish she would understand that.'

'My word,' Joy exclaimed, 'that was heartfelt, Flo. You sound like my supervisor at Mayfair House. She says she's always so swamped with paperwork she never gets to see any part of the hotel other than her office.'

'I know the feeling,' Flo said glumly. 'And it doesn't help when jobsworths like Mrs Claremont make my life harder by not filling in their own paperwork.'

'Why not?' Alice quizzed. 'She gave me a lecture recently about how we had to be better than men and show we were more than capable as women of doing their jobs, how we had to be self-reliant. How does not doing her job properly prove that?'

Flo sighed. 'She says that men wouldn't be asked to do the things we are asking her to do – especially when they aren't technically the manager of that department.'

Alice frowned. 'How do you mean?'

'I probably shouldn't say this, but Mrs Claremont's position isn't permanent at the moment,' Flo admitted in hushed tones. 'Mr Button knows she's a hard worker but he's giving her a trial.'

'So that means the position of fabric manager is up for grabs?' Alice asked excitedly.

'Well, yes,' Flo replied doubtfully, 'but, Alice, we need someone in that role full-time – unless they're exceptional.'

'Then I'll be exceptional!' Alice said determinedly. 'I'm going to show you what I can do when I go to Bath next Saturday.'

Flo frowned. 'There's no need to go overboard, Alice. You have enough to do; we can sort things out with Mrs Claremont in time.'

'Well, I hope you can, Flo,' said Mary. 'That woman is making our lives a misery on the shop floor. I was half thinking of going to the war office and asking for another job alongside Liberty's and my Red Cross work so I only have to be in the department part-time.'

'Haven't you been called up yet?' Joy asked incredulously.

Mary shook her head. 'No, I'm listed as Malcolm's carer so it's unlikely.'

'Something I'm grateful to you for, Mary love,' Malcolm said fervently. 'What about you, Joy? Haven't you received your papers yet? It's terrible you young girls being dragged in to fight like this.'

'No, I haven't,' Joy said with a smug smile. 'Rumour has it if you work in a posh hotel then they probably won't make you do anything else as you're seen to be helping out the posh folk that make all the important war decisions.'

At the knowing statement the girls roared with laughter. 'That can't be true,' Aggie snorted.

'It blinkin' well is,' Joy insisted. 'Posh nobs need some-one to wait on 'em.'

'Where did you get this from, Joy?' Alice chuckled.

Joy eyed her sister crossly. 'I'm not making it up. Anyway, I have got something else I want to talk to you about.'

'If it's another joke like the last one, I think we'd all like to hear it,' Flo said.

Rolling her eyes, Joy ignored the sarcasm. 'Actually I wanted to invite you girls to tea at Mayfair House. Perhaps one weekend after you get back from Bath, Alice?'

Alice gasped in amazement. 'That's a lovely offer, Joy, but we can't afford that.'

'I get a discount being staff so it won't cost that much. It's a way of celebrating my new job. Come on, it'll be fun, and it might cheer Rose up too. What do you say?'

As Alice cast a glance towards Rose, she saw how the girl was still nervously gripping her stick across the other side of the room. These past few months had taken their toll on all of them; it would be lovely to enjoy such a fancy treat. Looking back at her friends she caught the excited expressions on Flo and Mary's faces. 'I think we all say yes, Joy, if it's really no trouble,' she said. Perhaps this would be what the doctor ordered, and just the thing to lift Rose's spirits too.

Chapter Ten

The train to Bath was cramped and crowded as it snaked its way through the grimy streets of London and out into the lush green countryside of the West Country. Finding a seat next to a GI who was poring over *The Times* crossword, Alice sat with her thoughts. It had been heartbreaking saying goodbye to Arthur, and Dot had almost had to shove her out of the door when the time came. She knew it wasn't for long, but the idea of leaving her child felt so wrong, it was as though someone had severed her right arm.

As she gazed out of the window feeling forlorn, Alice tried to relax. She had always loved taking the train to Bath when she joined the Liberty buyer, Mr Charleston, on his visits to the Jolly's agents. Diligently she would take notes while he talked and afterwards he would treat her to a Sally Lunn bun. But then of course war had broken out and he, along with much of the male workforce, had been called up. Now, buyers weren't really needed as there was scarcely anything for people to purchase, so visits to agents around the country were rare, and usually carried out by a senior saleswoman or department head.

Looking down at the plain gold band on her ring finger, Alice twisted it idly as she realised that never in a million years would she have predicted that she would have to be both mother and father to her boy – especially after she had worked tirelessly to ensure her son would grow up in the warm, loving and contented family that she never did.

As the late April sunshine hit the golden stone build-ings, Alice revelled in her first glimpse of the city as she gathered her belongings and prepared to step off the train. For some reason Alice had always felt very at home in Bath, finding something comforting about the sight of the countryside and hills perched high above the city itself. Naturally it was a world away from London but Alice had always felt the city had a lot in common with the capital, what with its beautiful architecture, smart shops and repu-tation for entertainment.

While she looked at the crowds of GIs laughing good-naturedly with one another as they stood back to let her off the train, Alice couldn't help wondering if that's why they were headed to Bath. Perhaps it was unfair, but there was something about the slow way they moved, their laconic speech, the cut of their uniforms and their generally easy manner that made her think they just didn't work as hard as British soldiers. She was forever hearing stories about lazy Yanks from customers who came into the shop, and, as pleasant as many of them seemed, she couldn't help wondering if they lived up to their reputation.

Pushing her way through the small crowd that had gath-ered by the stone steps, Alice realised there was no time to think about that now as she glanced up at the large station clock. It was almost noon, the train had taken longer than she'd expected, and now there was just an hour before her meeting with Mrs Downing.

Still, as the station wasn't too far from Jolly's she knew she would still have time to go over exactly what she wanted to say as she strolled up to the store. In all honesty, although Alice knew that Mr Button and Mrs Claremont were concerned that some of the Liberty's agents would be reluctant to embrace utility fabric and clothing, she couldn't imagine Mrs Downing would give her any problems. The woman had always been so supportive of anything to do with Liberty's in the past, always professing to adore the lace and silks they routinely kept in stock.

With the sunshine warming her back Alice enjoyed the change in scenery. There were no bombed-out ruins or heaps of rubble lining the streets. In fact, in Bath it was almost possible to pretend war didn't exist. Walking through the Georgian streets the sights and sounds of a city bustling with life made Alice feel as if London was a million miles away.

Jolly's department store was affectionately known to the locals as the Old Lady of Milsom Street. As Alice approached she was pleased to see that the window displays boasted Liberty prints, and felt a shiver of hope that her task this afternoon would be relatively straightforward.

Stepping back to get a proper look at the centrepiece of the store's window display, Alice didn't see the young GI behind her, and managed to send the poor man flying.

'Oh my days,' she cried, spinning around in horror to find the GI sprawled on the pavement surrounded by his shopping bags. 'I'm so sorry!'

'That's quite all right, ma'am,' he replied, politely tipping his cap as he scrambled to his feet.

'Here, let me help you,' Alice babbled as she reached out to help the man and his bags up.

From his position on the ground the man looked up in amusement at Alice's offer to lift him up. 'I think I can manage, ma'am.'

Ignoring his protestations Alice bent over to collect his bags. 'I really am so sorry.'

'There's no harm done, ma'am. It was my fault; I should have been watching where I was going.'

'No,' Alice insisted. 'It's very sweet of you to try and make out you were at fault but really the blame is mine. Are you hurt at all?'

The man laughed. 'It was just a bump to the knee. In the military we get that all the time.'

Alice laughed too as she looked at the man before her. Tall with chocolate-brown hair, matching eyes and a wide-open face, Alice was surprised at how charming and polite he appeared to be. Taking a moment to admire the uniform that fitted his body like a glove, Alice could see why so many Englishwomen were drawn to the Americans who had descended on to their land.

'Ma'am,' the man said gently, cutting across Alice's train of thought. 'Could I trouble you for my bags back please?'

'Sorry?' Alice asked, feeling wrong-footed.

'My shopping.' The man smiled, pointing to the bags in Alice's hands. 'That you were kind enough to pick up for me.'

'Oh God! Sorry! Yes, here you go.' She held out the bags for the GI to take.

'Thank you, ma'am. You have a good day now.'

'Yes, you too,' she said, watching in stupefied silence as he walked down the road, tipping his cap once more as he waved goodbye.

An hour later and Alice's attempts at injuring a member of the US Military were forgotten as she sat in Mrs Downing's office, surrounded by Liberty print guard books and cups of tea.

From the moment she had arrived, Ivy Downing had welcomed Alice with open arms. She had demanded the latest news from Liberty's along with every detail about Arthur – facts Alice was more than happy to provide. In fact the two women were so consumed with gossip it took them a good hour before they were able to get down to the business of work.

'I must say that the quality and the range of prints on offer in utility fabrics really are exceptional,' Mrs Downing breathed, running her fingers over one of Alice's favourite designs, a blue floral print based on nerines.

'I know. I don't know how they do it but the fellas down in Merton print works are a godsend.'

Mrs Downing smiled as she gazed down at the print. 'It feels like a luxury, doesn't it, to have anything nice during this blasted war.'

Alice nodded. She understood only too well. The guilt that she – along with everyone else – felt at having even one nice thing when their brave boys on the front line were withstanding a torment she couldn't understand, was considerable.

'How has the war been treating you?' Alice asked.

'Oh, the same as everyone else.' Mrs Downing sighed. 'The problem for us in Jolly's is that we suffered during the depression so we were already on the back foot.'

'But the store is so beautiful,' Alice said admiringly as she peered out of the office window that looked out on to the shop floor. From her position opposite Mrs Downing she could see the store's trading motif, a peacock, depicted in a mosaic all the way along the ground floor. Above it stood a huge sweeping staircase that was so grand it would, Alice thought, give the one at Liberty's a run for its money,.

'Yes it is. Obviously with rationing it's getting harder and harder to make everything as beautiful as we want it. But I really think Liberty's are on to something with these fabrics and I will ensure they take pride of place in our store.'

'Oh, Mrs Downing, I can't thank you enough,' Alice gasped, clasping her hands together with joy, 'you've made my day.'

'Not at all, dear.' The drapery manager smiled as she handed Alice back the guard book. 'You just keep sending the fabric our way and I'll do the rest.'

With that Alice got to her feet and allowed Mrs Downing to show her out of her office.

'Do you have time for a tour of the store before you go home?'

Alice's face flushed with pleasure. 'Yes please. I'm staying tonight so in no rush to get the train.'

Mrs Downing clamped an elegant hand around Alice's forearm excitedly. 'You should have said. Would you like to come out with us later? A few of us are going to the Assembly Rooms – you could join us.'

'Only if it's no trouble,' Alice said, excited at the thought of an evening out. 'I don't want to intrude.'

'That's the last thing you'll be doing! It will be our pleasure to welcome you to the fold. Besides, with you working at Liberty's you're practically family and it will be our treat to show off our city.'

'Well, if you're sure, perhaps I could see you after tea?' Alice suggested. She could hardly believe how successfully her day was turning out.

Mrs Downing beamed in delight. 'Perfect. I shall come and collect you at your bed and breakfast later on.'

'I'll look forward to it!' Alice replied.

Chapter Eleven

The room Alice had been given in the bed and breakfast was beautiful, right at the top of a Georgian townhouse near Pulteney Bridge; she could see across the rooftops of the city and out on to the countryside beyond.

Feeling a sudden pang of delight at the possibility of a few hours' uninterrupted sleep, Alice was beginning to see the one upside of a night away from her son. As she checked her wristwatch she saw it was almost eight. With just a few minutes before Mrs Downing called on her, Alice began rifling through her suitcase. She was half hoping someone had magically placed an elegant evening gown in there instead of the plain green tea dress that had been mended so many times it was more thread than fabric. Alice put it on and glanced at her reflection in the mirror. It was hardly high couture, she thought, tugging the dress this way and that, but it was the best she could do. Reaching for her dark green wool cardigan, she made her way downstairs and was delighted to see Mrs Downing was already waiting for her in the lobby. Spotting the Jolly's matriarch sitting elegantly in her Liberty-print blouse and skirt, Alice felt instantly dowdy and foolish – she should have thought to have brought her own Liberty-print outfits, but had only brought the one she had worn down on the train for their meeting.

'Mrs Downing, you look lovely.' Alice smiled warmly as she greeted her new friend.

'Thank you, dear,' Mrs Downing replied, smoothing an imaginary crease out of her skirt. 'I thought I'd wear this in your honour. Oh, and while we're at it, please call me Ivy while we're not at work – this evening is meant to be fun.'

With that, Mrs Downing led the way outside into a night bathed in moonlight. 'We're all meeting in the Assembly Rooms. Have you been there before?'

'No. I've heard of it though.'

'I should hope so! Jane Austen used to write about it in her books.'

'I've never read Jane Austen,' Alice admitted, feeling slightly guilty.

Mrs Downing smiled. 'Well, you'll want to after tonight.'

Thoughts of Mary flashed into Alice's mind. She would have had her own debutante ball all those years ago – would it have been as grand as the balls held in the Assembly Rooms?

Crossing the road, she walked into the stone building and gasped in delight. The word beautiful didn't do the place justice, Alice thought as she took in the fine art on the walls, the stone pillars and crystal chandeliers that hung from the vaulted ceilings. It all reeked of grandeur.

Weaving her way through the elegantly dressed clientele, Mrs Downing explained that the building was laid out in a U shape with the tearoom and the ballroom – which was where they were heading – right at the end. As they entered the ballroom Alice let out another gasp of delight. This room was even more decadent, with five cut-glass chandeliers, the same high vaulted ceilings and even a balcony for guests to look over and admire the dancing.

'You can almost picture the balls Jane Austen wrote about,' Mrs Downing whispered dreamily.

'Quite,' Alice replied as she took in the band playing in the corner and the crowded dance floor full of uniformed RAF officers and their American counterparts all dancing the night away.

'We're just through here.' Mrs Downing guided Alice towards a small round table where two other girls were already sitting. 'I don't think you've met Millie and Doreen, have you?'

'Nice to meet you.' Alice smiled as she shook hands with each of the girls, sat down next to Mrs Downing and quickly took in the girls' appearance. They were both around the same age as her and looked incredibly glamorous. Millie's long dark hair had been expertly styled into a victory roll that flattered her angular cheekbones and dark eyes, while Doreen's auburn locks had been cut into a very elegant bob with a fringe that framed her green eyes.

'And you,' Millie trilled. 'We thought you might like these,' she said, pushing two glasses of port and lemon across the table. 'One of those GIs got them in for us earlier.'

Mrs Downing raised her own glass and grinned. 'I hope you girls haven't been chasing Americans again.'

'Just Millie.' Doreen laughed, giving her friend a playful nudge. 'You know very well I'm spoken for, Ivy.'

'Doreen's fella's an engineer,' Mrs Downing explained. 'Works over near Neath, isn't that right?'

Doreen blushed at the mention of her sweetheart. 'We've been courting over three years now. We met when I went up to Cardiff for the day and he spilled tea on me.'

'More likely you did it yourself,' Millie cackled. 'He's a looker, your Fred.'

'Are you spoken for, Alice?' Doreen asked, ignoring her friend's giggles.

Alice nodded. 'Yes, my husband's in the RAF. He's been missing almost eight months now though.'

Doreen's hands flew to her mouth. 'Oh, I'm sorry.'

Waving her concern away, Alice smiled at the redhead. 'You weren't to know. I think about him every day and hope and pray that today's the day he'll be found. It's what gets me through the pain.'

'It's all you can do sometimes,' Mrs Downing offered knowledgeably. 'Both my sons are overseas fighting somewhere and I light a candle for them every Sunday, praying they'll be returned to me when this blasted war is over.'

'But until then, we have to focus on living our own lives,' Millie said gently. 'We don't know when this war will be over.'

'Or if,' Doreen muttered darkly.

'And what better place to live our lives while we can than here?' Millie added, ignoring her friend's gloom.

Alice nodded in agreement. 'My friends at home all say the same. Though we don't go out anywhere as grand as this.'

Doreen's eyebrows waggled. 'You're not serious? We all thought you Liberty girls would be living the high life up the West End.'

'Yes, when the Marks and Spencer's head office were all evacuated here for a bit, they used to moan something rotten there was nowhere to go out like London,' Millie chimed in.

A giggle escaped from Alice's lips. 'Well, I don't know where the girls from Marks's were going, but I can tell you us Liberty girls like a port and lemon just like you Jolly's girls. We just stick to the pub or the cinema – very rarely do we go to a dance like this, unless it's one of Liberty's, of course. But since war broke out events at Liberty's are few and far between.'

'It's the same at Jolly's,' Mrs Downing said sadly. 'Mind you, we don't usually come here, do we, girls? But there's a special dance on in honour of all the GIs that are here visiting officers at Charmy Down, and Millie's cousin is married to one of them, so that's why we're here.'

At that the band struck up a lively tune Alice recognised as the jive and Millie looked at Doreen pleadingly. 'Will you dance? I've been learning all the steps to this one.'

Her friend rolled her eyes, but Alice could tell she was equally keen to get on the floor. 'Go on then.'

The girls walked on to the dance floor, which was now swollen with British and American officers and their partners, leaving Alice sitting alongside Mrs Downing. Alice couldn't help smiling as she watched the Americans twisting, shaking and moving their hips to the unrelenting thud of the beat. It was quite a sight: the well-turned-out Yanks in their smart-fitting uniforms teaching the British steps that they had never heard of. As the Americans moved their bodies effortlessly to the music, the British struggled with the loose fluidity of the steps, but their unrelenting desire to prove themselves willing and above all else polite meant they had a good go at mirroring the Americans' moves, even if they did look as if they'd rather be at the dentist's having a tooth out.

As the band stood up to take a bow, the British stood and clapped politely, moving only their hands, whereas by contrast the Americans whooped, whistled and cheered, calling for more.

'For heaven's sakes,' Mrs Downing grumbled. 'What on earth do they do if they think something's really good?'

Alice smirked and said nothing. She rather liked the Americans' overzealous approach, finding it a refreshing change from the traditional stiff upper lip of war-weary Brits. As she joined in to applaud the band, who were now taking a well-earned rest, her eyes strayed to a GI hovering at the corner of the dance floor. There was something familiar about him, but for the life of her she couldn't work out what. Suddenly the man turned his head and Alice gasped as she recognised him as the GI she'd knocked over earlier.

'Will you excuse me, Alice dear?' Mrs Downing asked, getting to her feet. 'I must just nip to the ladies'.'

'Yes, of course,' Alice replied, grateful for the distraction as she stood up to let the woman pass.

As Mrs Downing walked swiftly away, Alice turned back to her drink. Only as she reached out for it, she jumped as she suddenly realised that the man she had just been staring at was now standing at the foot of her table.

Tipping his cap, he beamed at Alice. 'Hello again.'

'Hello,' Alice mumbled, feeling her cheeks flush with embarrassment. 'How are the bumps and scrapes?'

'Not too bad, thank you.' He lifted a glass of dark-coloured liquid. 'Nothing one of your English pints hasn't cured.'

Alice smiled at the sing-song lilt of his accent. 'Glad to hear it.'

'Can I get you a drink?' he asked, gesturing to her glass.

'That's very kind of you but I've plenty left in this one,' Alice said evenly.

The GI nodded. 'I guess I asked for that,' he said, giving her a half-smile, before looking at her hopefully once more. 'Could I sit down?'

'As long as you're not too long. My friends will be back very soon,' Alice replied. She knew she sounded hoity-toity but the truth was his friendliness was making her nervous and when all was said and done she was a married woman.

'Fair enough.' He grinned again, holding out his hand for her to shake. 'I'm Jack Capewell, staff sergeant in the US Army.'

'Alice Milwood,' she replied, unable to resist his easy manner. 'Deputy fabric manager at Liberty's.'

As Jack shook his head, Alice felt a jolt of happiness at being able to explain all about the shop she loved. 'It's a beautiful store that sells all manner of arts and crafts. It was founded by a chap called Arthur Liberty who loved working with artists, designers and architects. Now we sell only the most beautiful of clothes, rugs and homewares in the most beautiful building you've ever seen.'

'Really?' Jack raised an eyebrow. 'Sounds like one very special department store. I should come pay it a visit.'

'You should,' Alice said delightedly, pleased her enthusiasm for Liberty's had rubbed off on someone else.'

'I'd have to tell my sister all about it. She loves anything with a bit of glamour,' Jack said.

'Sounds just like my sister!'

Jack chinked his glass against Alice's own. 'We'll have to exchange stories, see who got the rawest deal.'

'I can tell you now, it'll be me,' she laughed. 'So are you stationed in London or Bath?'

'London,' Jack replied. 'Just down for the weekend meeting with your fine British officers. They're treating us to a night out here in these very fine and elegant rooms.'

'Me too.' Alice raised her voice slightly over the roar of approval as the band took to their seats again. 'I mean, I live in London not Bath. I'm here visiting work colleagues too.'

A smile played on Jack's lips. 'We really do have a lot in common. Would you like to tell me all about it over the next dance?'

It was all Alice could do not to giggle at the obviousness of his chat-up line. 'We've a name for lads like you up in London, but I'm too polite to say! What I will say instead is that it's very kind of you to ask me, but I'm spoken for,' she finished kindly, gesturing to the plain gold wedding band on her ring finger.

Jack had the good grace to look crestfallen. 'Ma'am, I am so sorry, I meant no offence.'

'None taken,' Alice replied as he stood up. 'It was nice meeting you.'

'And you, Mrs Milwood,' Jack said softly, tipping his cap once more as he left her alone.

Watching his retreating back, Alice ignored the brief stirring she felt in the pit of her stomach. She wasn't sure if it was the Assembly Rooms, the romantic city of Bath or the fact she was out somewhere new with new people but she suddenly felt very much alive.

Chapter Twelve

Alice couldn't remember the last time she had enjoyed herself so much. After declining Jack's invitation to waltz the night away she had eventually allowed herself to be propelled on to the dance floor, first by Millie, then Doreen, and even Mrs Downing herself as they danced the foxtrot and an American dance Alice hadn't heard of before: the jive.

By half past ten she was spent, and Alice begged the girls for mercy, pleading tiredness as they whirled and twirled her around the dance floor. Eventually they gave in and Alice, grateful for the breather, sat down and enjoyed the rest of the port and lemon the girls had given her when she arrived.

Taking a long sip of her drink Alice looked back towards the packed dance floor and found herself astounded at the energy people had. The band was in full swing and the dancers seemingly just getting into their stride while she herself felt ready for bed.

Catching herself yawning Alice placed a quick hand in front of her mouth and felt a pang of guilt, before realising that actually there was no need. She was, after all, a mother with a young baby and a job; it was no surprise she was tired. Mrs Downing had already left half an hour ago, but Alice, determined to show some Liberty spirit, had soldiered on with the other girls. Yet, looking at her watch once more, she knew all she wanted was her bed. Her digs in Laura Place weren't that far away and she had promised the landlady she would be home well before midnight when the locks would be firmly placed on the door. Pulling her coat on, she saw Doreen and Millie giving a couple of GIs the run-around with their own version of the jive and gave them a wave goodbye.

They would hardly notice she was gone, Alice thought, stifling another yawn as she ventured out into the moonlit night, grateful that it would help guide her home in a strange town. Pausing for just a moment to gaze up at the sky, she felt a sudden chill at the bright light. Alice remembered only too well how she and the rest of London used to feel sheer terror when the moon was so big and the night so clear, as they knew that would mean only one thing: hours of devastation.

Rounding the corner, Alice felt a sudden urge to get back to her digs as quickly as possible and quickened her pace only to see Jack loitering on the corner, lit cigarette in his right hand.

'What are you doing out here?' she asked.

She was rewarded with a grin. 'I needed some air. All that dancing, while it's fun 'n' all, it's not really my thing. I prefer the quiet life.'

'Me too,' Alice admitted. 'Always have.'

Jack looked at her in surprise. 'Can I walk you someplace?'

'Oh, I'm fine, thank you,' Alice replied quickly.

'No, really,' Jack replied. 'Back where I come from it's not right to let a woman walk home alone. My mom would beat me black and blue!'

Alice couldn't help herself and giggled at his accent. There was something so warm and comforting about it; she felt she could listen to it all day.

'I really shouldn't,' she said hesitantly. 'I'm not sure my husband would like it.'

'Ma'am,' Jack said firmly. 'If you were my wife and a member of the military offered to walk you home in the dark, I would consider it a personal favour. Now please allow me to escort you.'

'All right,' Alice relented. 'I'm not far away, I've digs in the centre.'

'Well, that's just perfect,' he said cheerfully as they strolled companionably along the road. 'That means I can get back here and nobody will be any the wiser.'

'Will anybody miss you?' Alice asked as they walked down the hill, the brilliant moonlight continuing to light the way.

Jack shrugged. 'Nobody that matters.'

As the pair turned into Broad Street, Alice found herself admiring the architecture once again. The bright moonlight bathed the Bath stone in a light so white and pure it made the buildings seem almost ethereal.

'It's a beautiful city, ain't it?' Jack remarked, reading her mind.

'Have you ever been here before?' Alice asked.

Jack shook his head. 'Not before today. I'd heard about it back in the States of course.'

'Really?' Alice sounded incredulous.

A laugh escaped from Jack's lips. 'Your gorgeous cities are famous, even to a farm boy like me. We don't all think the world begins and ends in America.'

'I thought all you Americans thought your country was the best in the world,' Alice teased.

'You Brits sure as hell say what you mean, don't you?'

'Sorry, I didn't mean to be rude,' Alice replied, feeling embarrassed.

Jack chuckled. 'And you sure as hell all apologise easy enough.'

Alice paused to round on Jack. 'And you Yanks go at everything like a bull in a china shop. No doubt you'll be going at Hitler the same way.'

'Hey?' Jack looked at her quizzically, his tanned skin illuminated in the moonlight. 'What's all this? I'm only kidding around.'

Alice felt suddenly wrong-footed. She too had only been teasing but she had a feeling it had all come out wrong. Wearily, she ran a hand over her face. She was too tired to fall out with American soldiers tonight, or indeed any other night. All she really wanted to do was go home.

'How about we forget it?' Jack said charitably, correctly interpreting her feelings once more. 'It's late and I'm sure you're as tired as I am.'

'Thank you,' Alice said gratefully. 'Sorry.'

Jack laughed again as they continued down the hill. 'You need to stop apologising.'

'Sorry,' Alice said automatically before shaking her head despairingly at herself. 'I'm not going to say another word.'

'Now that would be kind of a shame,' Jack said warmly.

Alice was about to tell him off for his cheek when a low eerie strumming sound above caught her attention. 'Did you hear that?' she asked, stopping in the middle of the street to cock her ear towards the sky.

'Hear what?'

Just then two large bangs erupted overhead.

'That!' Alice cried, turning her head in time to see a line of flares drop up ahead lighting the city as brightly as if it was daylight.

'Germans,' Jack said grimly.

'Here? They can't be bombing Bath. It must be Bristol – there's nothing here worth targeting.'

'I'm telling you now, it's the Jerries,' Jack roared, just as the piercing wail of the air-raid siren sliced through the air.

'We need to find shelter.' Alice looked desperately around for anything that might point them in the direction of a public shelter. But the streets seemed eerily empty.

'Come on.' Jack grabbed her hand and pulled her down the road.

'Where are we going?' Alice cried.

But Jack's reply was impossible to make out above the low whine of the Luftwaffe, the shape of the raiders now clearly visible overhead.

Of course Alice had been caught in a raid before but this felt different. When the bombs fell in London almost daily, she and the rest of the Liberty girls had become experts at taking refuge and thought nothing of whiling away the time with a good book or some knitting. But now she was a mother; her son already had a father missing. An instinct for survival kicked in as Alice let go of Jack's hand and charged ahead, pounding down the street in what she hoped was the direction of Laura Place, praying that the digs she was staying in could offer salvation.

'Alice!' Jack cried above the din. 'Wait up!'

But Alice wasn't waiting for anyone, she was fixated on only one thing: ensuring her son had one parent who remained alive.

Chapter Thirteen

As Alice ran towards Argyle Street, trying to make sense of the chaos around her, she felt as if she was going to be sick. The eerily quiet streets of moments earlier were gone and in their place teams of uniformed volunteers from the Civil Defence League were trying to stop the fires already surging through Bath's precious buildings from spiralling perilously out of control.

From her position near the River Avon, Alice could see bright orange flames ripping through the heart of houses that had stood for centuries. The sheer heat of the blaze was overwhelming, and she instinctively shielded her face as she heard Jack's footsteps come to a halt behind her.

'Are you OK?' Jack cried.

Alice nodded. 'You?'

'Fine, but we need to find shelter now. Alice honey, I'm not sure we can even get to your lodgings.'

'Then let's just find shelter where we can.'

At that, the noisy drone of the aircraft roared ominously overhead. Glancing up, Alice was horrified to see the twin-engine Heinkel now flying perilously low along the street, heading in one direction only: straight towards her. As the plane got nearer and nearer Alice tried to move but she couldn't. It was as though her legs wouldn't listen to her brain. Instead she found herself mesmerised, gazing at the plane audaciously flying so close to the ground she could make out the face of the pilot.

Heart in her mouth, Alice watched the plane suddenly fire its machine guns at will, aiming for the volunteer fire crew. Like a line of dominoes she saw the firemen fall to the ground. At the sight, Alice felt sick, but no matter how much she wanted to, she couldn't take her eyes from the pilot responsible for such destruction. A sudden, indescribable rage filled her very core. And as she looked up at him in the plane, carrying out the orders of the dictator who stood for nothing but evil, she found herself opening her mouth and screaming in fury.

'Nazi scum!' she shrieked. 'You murdering filth!'

But her voice was lost in the wind Alice's outburst, and as the plane continued along its course, she saw it was now just feet away from her as it neared the fountain at the centre of the street. Alice knew she should get out of the way but she was so consumed with rage for all the pain and suffering these Jerries had caused she found she couldn't move. About to open her mouth and scream again, for her, for Luke, for all the lives that had been taken too soon, she felt a pair of arms grip her firmly around her waist and without warning she was flying through the air only to land with a thud in the doorway of a sports shop on top of Jack. The plane suddenly stopped firing and the drone grew quieter as it flew away.

Once she realised her life was no longer in immediate danger, Alice became acutely aware she was lying face down on top of a man.

'I'm so sorry,' she gasped, sitting upright.

'Entirely my fault,' Jack replied, sitting bolt upright next to her. 'You were so busy cursing at the Germans, I had to act fast. The last thing I wanted was for you to go the same way as those firemen.'

At the mention of the emergency service volunteers who had so unceremoniously lost their lives, Alice hung her head in sorrow. 'We should go and see if we can help any of them. There may be some that are injured.'

'And maybe some that need messages sent to their families,' Jack finished, his tone sombre.

With the planes gone, silence echoed all around them, apart from the sound of the cricket bats that hung in the window, swinging in the breeze.

For the next few hours Alice and Jack worked side by side as they helped clear the wreckage, giving notes to messenger boys who cycled across the city carrying news of loved ones, and administering tea, first aid and words of comfort to those that needed it. The air was heavily scented with the stench of burnt wood, and thick dust from the blasts filled the skies.

Word spread fast that the Germans had dropped a heavy load of hate on the south of the city, destroying entire streets and wiping out families with an avalanche of bombs.

But of course it wasn't just Jack and Alice dispensing aid. The moment the all-clear siren sounded teams of WVS volunteers arrived ready to serve tea to the newly homeless, while wardens roamed the streets checking on the welfare of residents.

By the time dawn broke, Alice was done in, and when a lady from the WVS offered her and Jack a cup of tea and a blanket each, she wanted to kiss her.

'Quite the night huh?' Jack said, leaning his head against the pillars of the Argyle Street church.

'You could say that,' Alice replied wearily, the early morning breeze whipping around her neck. 'It's not what I was expecting.'

'Me either.' Jack winced as he took a sip of his tea. 'How the hell do you Brits drink this stuff?'

'Very easily.' Alice gulped down the warm liquid, enjoying the instant relief.

'I guess it's an acquired taste.'

'You never did make it back to the Assembly Rooms,' Alice said suddenly. 'Will you be in trouble?'

Jack shook his head. 'There was a raid on and I did my part. What about you? We don't even know if your digs were bombed out.'

Alice pointed towards a house across the street. 'It's still there. I ought to go and get my things, try and work out how I'm getting back to London. Someone told me the station had been hit so I can't imagine it'll be easy to get a train home.'

'Husband waiting for you?'

'No, but my son will be.' Alice replied sadly, tugging the blanket tightly around her. 'My husband's in the RAF and is missing. He's never met our baby son,' she found herself blurting.

'Jeez. That's terrible. Alice, I'm so sorry,' Jack said, his face earnest. 'Does that mean you're raising your boy all alone?'

Alice nodded, her face grim. 'Just like thousands of other women across the country whose men are away serving.'

Jack eyed her carefully. 'Not quite the same though, is it?' he offered, painfully aware that the words regarding Alice's missing husband were better left unsaid.

'No, not quite,' she answered, allowing herself to look into this man's eyes for the first time since they had left the dance hall. She hadn't meant to tell him her life story, but there was something about Jack that made her feel relaxed and Alice felt strangely drawn to him. She had seen the way he worked all night, never once stopping to rest or take a break. He had been full of kind words for the children who had been bombed out of their homes or become separated from their mothers. He had even taken care to round up all the stray cats and dogs roaming the streets, before handing them to a vet manning a temporary pet rescue centre. For some reason Alice felt she could tell Jack almost anything, and what's more she wanted to know everything about him too.

'What's your life back home like?' she asked.

Jack raised an eyebrow. 'Quiet. Nothing like this.'

'I'd hope not for your sake,' Alice quipped.

Offering the rest of his tea to Alice, she gratefully accepted and wrapped her hands around the tin mug for warmth as Jack settled back against the pillar. 'I'm a farmer back in Montana, a state in the north-west of America.'

'What kind of farming do you do? I'm born and bred in London, I don't know one end of a blade of grass from the other!'

Jack laughed. 'That wouldn't necessarily be a problem. I'm a cattle farmer. My daddy was a cattle farmer, and before that my daddy's daddy.'

'A family farm,' Alice said brightly. 'Must be nice seeing all those open fields and breathing in the fresh air every day. I often wonder if me and Arthur – that's my son – wouldn't be better off in the countryside somewhere. A city's no place to bring up a kid, is it?'

'I don't think so.' Jack shook his head before gratefully accepting a slice of bread and butter from a WVS volunteer. 'I couldn't imagine raising my boy anywhere else.'

Alice raised her eyebrows in surprise. 'You never said you have a family.'

'I don't,' Jack said gruffly. 'I have a son – Jack Junior. He's five.'

'I'm sorry. It must be hard for you and your wife to be apart.'

'My wife and I have been apart for too long as it is,' he replied sadly, his eyes downcast. 'My Marilyn died in a farming accident when Jack just turned one, and since that day I've been both mama and papa to that boy.'

Alice's mouth fell open. 'Oh Jack, I'm so sorry. I swear I'm always putting my filthy great feet where I shouldn't.'

'How could you have known?' Jack said, his warm chocolate eyes meeting hers. 'But I like to talk about her, it keeps her memory alive for me.'

'I know what you mean. I'm the same with my Luke. A lot of my friends are too frightened to mention him in case it upsets me, but I would rather talk about him; that way I can believe he's coming home.'

'Do you think he will come back then?' Jack asked bluntly.

Alice paused. For so long she had been convinced that he would return, but lately she had to admit there was a part of her that was starting to believe he wouldn't and that actually he was dead. 'I hope he will,' she said eventually. 'Sometimes in this war, all you can do is hope.'

'That's what I told my boy before I left,' Jack replied, rubbing a grimy hand across his face. 'He was so upset about me leaving, he thought England was on the other side of the world.'

'It almost is,' Alice said over the rumble of another WVS truck bringing in urgent supplies. 'Where is your son now?'

Jack's face lit up at the chance to talk about his boy. 'He's with my sister, Gracie, on the farm. She's got twin boys of her own that are a little older than Jack Junior so she knows what she's doing.'

'I can imagine,' Alice said drily. 'Has her own husband joined up too?'

Jack nodded. 'Eric's serving in the US Navy, scaring poor Gracie senseless, of course, but it's like I said, we're all in this thing together now. The sooner we all step up, do what's right, the sooner we can all get back to normality.'

Alice took another sip of her tea and said nothing. She wasn't sure she knew what normal looked like any more, but here in this moment she felt a strange connection to this handsome foreigner who knew a little of her pain.

'It must be strange for you being so far from home in a strange country,' she said eventually.

'It's nice here.' Jack smiled. 'You Brits are very hospitable.'

'So I've heard.' Alice smirked. 'You GIs are finding a girl on every corner.'

Jack blushed. 'Not all of us are like that. I've always been a one-woman kind of guy. Me and Marilyn were childhood sweethearts.'

'I'm sorry,' she replied softly.

Then before she could change her mind, Alice leaned over and clasped Jack's cool hand in her own to offer comfort. If he seemed surprised he didn't show it, as he placed his other hand on top of Alice's and squeezed. 'Thank you,' he replied.

Alice was about to reply when an ARP warden tapped her on the shoulder. 'Sorry to interrupt but just thought you should know there's a mobile canteen now offering breakfast. You two look like you could use a meal.'

Removing his hand from Alice's, Jack got to his feet. 'That's the best offer I've had all day. Will you join me, ma'am?'

As he gallantly stretched his hand out towards Alice to help her up, she gratefully accepted. Walking beside him across the street towards the van, the steam from the tea urn clearly visible in the early morning air, Alice tried to remember the last time she had enjoyed breakfast with a man who wasn't her four-month-old son.

Chapter Fourteen

By the time Alice returned home on Sunday night, she was exhausted. Following her breakfast she had collected her belongings from her lodgings, and then with Jack's help, and after saying a hurried and emotional goodbye to him, had begun the long journey home. Sadly, Alice had been right. There had been no trains, following the brutal explosions on the railway line and nearby gas works, so she had gratefully accepted a lift from one of Jack's colleagues who was driving back to London that day.

Many people from the city had been terrified Hitler would strike again that Sunday night and so had fled to the country the moment dawn broke. Alice couldn't honestly say she blamed them. Having survived a year of almost nightly bombings in London she could understand their fear only too well. However, that meant the roads out of Bath were busier than usual with extra cars and buses in search of sanctuary.

As the car rumbled slowly along the roads, Alice found herself reflecting on the previous night and how stupid she had been to put her own life in jeopardy when she had Arthur to think about. How could she, as a mother, have been daft enough to roar insults at those Nazis when they were just yards away? They could so easily have killed her with just one of the bullets from the machine guns. Alice didn't know what had possessed her. She had been so consumed by rage, so filled with a desire to let these people know just what they were destroying, that all sense and reason had vanished from her mind. By the time she got back, she was ready to sink straight into bed, but as Dot was waiting up for her with Arthur she had been forced to tell her all about the devastating attack on Bath. Naturally Dot had been shocked at all she had been through and offered to gather the Liberty girls together. Alice smiled appreciatively at the gesture, but all she wanted to do was hold her son close, which is just what she did all night and most of the next day too.

Now, it was Tuesday evening and as the carriage clock on the mantel struck six thirty precisely Alice heard the sound of the key in the door.

'Only me,' Dot called.

'Hello, only you,' Alice replied, simultaneously kissing Arthur who was snoozing on her lap and feeling pleased her landlady was home. She was tired of her own company, finding her mind had been filled with thoughts of the weekend. Not only had she been continually cursing herself for placing herself in danger, she had been plagued by thoughts of Jack. He had been so easy to talk to, and the fact they were both bringing up their children alone had made her feel close to him in a way she hadn't felt close to anyone in a long time. But with Dot home she was grateful for the distraction and wanted nothing more than a natter about her landlady's day at the WVS and an early night.

Only as Dot walked into the kitchen with a smile as wide as her face, Alice could see that was the last thing that was likely to happen. Not only was the scent of vinegar-soaked fish and chips filling the room, but behind her, all wearing grins equally as large, were Flo, Aggie, Mary, Rose and Joy.

'Impromptu Liberty Girls and Friends Night,' Dot said, dumping the bag on the table. 'We thought it might be nice for you to have a bit of company after all you've been through.'

Mary sighed. 'Yes, it sounds as though you had a bugger of a time.'

'Dot says you worked through the night, sweetheart,' Aggie ventured, taking a seat.

'You must be shattered,' Flo added.

'Just a bit,' Alice replied, feeling weary at the girls' questions, yet oddly touched they had come all the way over to see her.

Inhaling her son's sweet, soft scent she felt a pang of sorrow. To think there had been a possibility she would never see her gorgeous boy again. As if reading her mind, Arthur shuffled himself in his mother's arms and threw his pudgy arms around her neck, earning a collective gasp of delight from the Liberty girls and a fresh round of tears from Alice.

'Where did you get the money for the chipper?' Alice asked, wiping the tears from her face and turning to Dot.

The landlady tapped her nose knowingly. 'Ask no questions and all that. Thought you deserved a treat so I had a word with my mate Mickey Dennis who runs the chippy on Walworth Road. Let's just say he was happy to oblige.'

'I'm not asking.' Alice chuckled, the aroma of the chips already making her tummy rumble.

Joy sat on the other side of her and gazed at her sister, her eyes filled with concern. 'Do you want to talk about what happened in Bath? Dot says you barely said two words about it,' she asked kindly, before adding worriedly: 'But not if you don't want to. I don't want to pressure you.'

Alice smiled. There were times Joy completely took her breath away. On impulse she leaned over to kiss her sister's cheek and was surprised when Joy caught her by the wrist and turned to whisper in her ear: 'I'm so glad you're all right. Despite everything between us, I would be lost without you.'

Joy let go and turned away to stare at the floor, and for a moment Alice wondered if she had dreamed the exchange. Only glancing down at her wrist and spotting a small fingernail indentation, she knew it was true, and Alice couldn't have been more touched.

She went to open her mouth to reply, to tell everyone what had happened, but then an image of the pilot in her sightline flashed into her mind. Letting out a small shudder, Alice realised the last thing she wanted was to relive the events of Saturday night. 'Thanks for the concern, girls, but I'm tired. And if I'm honest, no, I don't want to talk about it. You remember what every night of the Blitz was like? Well, it was like that, only for the first time I didn't make it to a shelter and I helped clear up the wreckage.'

'I don't know how you did it,' Aggie persisted. 'I mean, you must have been terrified. I don't know what I would have done. I'd have given up, I think.'

Rose nodded, clutching her cane. 'Me too. But then, being blind 'n' all, Hitler's band of merry men could have wiped me right out.'

Aggie agreed. 'Oh Rose, you poor thing, I don't know how you get through the days. I find it hard enough. I'm sick of this war and all the trouble it brings.'

'I don't know myself sometimes.' Rose shrugged. 'Sometimes I think a bomb would be a blessing – put me out of my misery.'

'For goodness' sake, you two,' Flo sighed impatiently. 'Alice is fine – she survived, didn't she? And you two going on about how you think you wouldn't cope isn't helping.

I've got news for you all: we none of us like our lives at the moment. War's horrible, but we're surviving and that should be celebrated.'

Dot smiled and got to her feet. 'Well said, Flo. Come on you lot, this is a celebration. We're meant to be cheering Alice up not bringing her down. Now, Joy, how about you come and help me dish these chips out. And no nicking the scraps either when my back's turned.'

Grumbling under her breath, Joy did as Dot asked, leaving Alice alone with her friends.

'So what shall we talk about?' Mary asked brightly. 'The weather?'

Alice laughed. 'It has been quite warm for April. But I think I'd rather hear about Liberty. Why don't you tell me how Mrs Claremont has been?'

'Angry,' Flo remarked directly. 'She went into Mr Button's office on Saturday afternoon and said it should have been her that went to Bath instead of you.'

'Silly woman.' Aggie sniffed. 'She should be grateful she didn't have to deal with those bombs. What a thing to say.'

Flo shrugged. 'I think Alice will be waiting a long time for praise. Mrs Claremont's moods seem to go from bad to worse. I don't know what's wrong with her. She's always upset about something at the moment.'

'But she never said a word to me. In fact in that meeting she said she wanted me to go!' Alice gasped incredulously.

'Well, something must have changed her mind as she went in all guns blazing and said that as the manager—'

'Temporary manager,' Alice corrected, cutting Flo off.

'As temporary manager, she should be making relationships,' Flo clarified with a nod, her chestnut curls working their way loose from the chignon she had been wearing all day.

'Oh, let's talk about something else,' Dot said, her arms now laden with plates of fish and chips.

'Gladly,' Joy added from behind her. 'I'm sick of hearing about the bleedin' woman.'

'All right, Joy,' Alice said sharply, covering her son's ears before helping herself to a plate from Dot's hand. 'There's no need for language.'

Joy said nothing as she took a seat opposite Mary and helped herself to some chips. 'Has anyone got anything else they want to talk about?' Alice tried again. 'Rose, any news from Tommy?'

Rose gave a sharp nod of her head. 'He wrote last week. Still going on about trying to get compassionate leave.'

Alice put down her fork and stared at her friend. 'Why don't you say yes? I'm sure he'd love to see you, and it would do you good too. You haven't seen him since …'

'Since I went blind,' Rose replied bluntly.

To Alice's surprise, Joy leaned over and rubbed Rose's back comfortingly. 'Alice was just trying to be kind,' she pointed out. 'There's no need to snap.'

Rose turned to Joy and gave her a watery smile before lifting her chin, her eyes searching for Alice. 'Sorry, Alice.'

'That's all right,' Alice said hesitantly. 'I was just trying to say that it might give you comfort. Heaven knows I'd love to hear from my Luke.'

Flo looked up from her own plate, a chip halfway to her mouth. 'I feel the same. Sometimes I can go weeks without hearing from my Neil, never mind imagine when I'm going to see him again.'

'I had a sweetheart at sea once,' Joy piped up. 'I'm still waiting for him to write to me.'

'When was the last time you saw or heard from him?' Alice asked, her tone disbelieving.

'Erm, last August?' Joy said.

The girls roared with laughter, not altogether unkindly. 'I think that's code for "This is finished, Joy",' Alice said as the laughter subsided.

'What a swine,' Joy gasped, seemingly not in the least bit offended. 'I bet you're right. Well, that's the last time I sit with anyone in the back row of the pictures.'

Dot rolled her eyes. 'Anyone else?' she asked, looking pleadingly. 'OK, my turn then. Edwin's asked me if I'll go with him to Margate for the weekend when the weather picks up.'

'Ooh, that sounds nice,' Alice said. 'Are you going?'

Dot winked. ''Course I am! He's paying. I've told him separate beds though, no funny business – I'm too old for all that carry-on.'

Aggie chuckled. 'I should be fortunate to be asked at my age. Count yourself lucky, Dorothy.'

'As an old bird, I count myself very lucky, Aggie, and thankfully Edwin does too.'

'Oh, give over, Dot, you're young enough to be my mother,' Alice teased.

'And you're young enough to be put across the back of my knee, lady!'

As the girls giggled at the exchange, they carried on eating their fish and chips, savouring the treat.

'So is there a reason for this unexpected weekend away?' Alice asked.

Dot set her plate down and folded her hands in her lap. Alice was immediately concerned; she could see the worry etched across her friend's face. 'Well, there is something that's troubling me about it,' she began hesitantly. 'He keeps mentioning how the two of us aren't getting any younger—'

'Romantic!' Joy sniggered, earning herself a glare from Alice.

'And he keeps dropping hints that we should get married,' Dot finished, ignoring Joy's jibe.

'Blimey!' Alice exclaimed. 'I thought you were happy rubbing along as you are.'

Dot sniffed. 'We are; well, at least I thought we were. In truth I'm not sure I want to get married again, girls. My George' – her eyes strayed to the striped creamer that he had gifted her when they wed, which took pride of place on the kitchen dresser – 'was my husband. I don't think I want another.'

'You don't think George would think you were being disloyal, do you?' Alice cried.

'I don't know,' Dot admitted in a small voice, 'I just know that much as I love Edwin, I don't know if I want to marry him – not yet. Anyway,' she went on, her voice falsely bright, 'he ain't even asked me yet so I'm probably worrying about nothing.'

'And if there's one thing I know it's that you don't worry about things that haven't happened yet,' Flo said sagely.

Alice nodded. 'It was thoughts like that I clung to when the bombs were falling in Bath. My first thought was staying alive for Arthur's sake – imagine how terrible it would be if he had to grow up with one parent missing in action and another killed during a bombing raid.'

'But that didn't happen, did it?' Dot said gently.

'Yes, we should all be grateful for the little things we've got in life,' Rose replied in a bored tone.

Alice opened her mouth to say something but, to her surprise and relief, saw Joy had laid a comforting hand on her friend's arm. 'Well, your experience in Bath should make us all think how short and precious life is. We should grab every opportunity with both hands, because you just never know when that chance is going to be taken away from you.'

At that the girls nodded, cheered by Joy's sentiments, but Alice was surprised to find that her thoughts had turned to Jack and how sad it would be if she didn't grab with both hands an opportunity to see him again.

Chapter Fifteen

First thing on Wednesday morning, Alice found herself walking through Liberty's labyrinth of corridors towards Mr Button's office. After a good night's sleep and a gossip with her girls, she felt ready now to tell him about her meeting with Mrs Downing. She felt pleased she had positive news about her visit to Bath. After all, she and Mrs Downing had become firm friends by the end of the night, something which had not only surprised and delighted her, but she was sure would be good for business between Liberty's and Jolly's going forwards.

'Come in,' Mr Button called as soon as she knocked at his door.

'Hello, sir.' Alice smiled as she walked inside.

Mr Button returned her smile and stood up, gesturing for her to take a seat. 'My dear, how the devil are you?' he asked earnestly. 'I did tell Dorothy to let you know that you didn't have to work today if you didn't feel up to it – you had quite a night in Bath.'

Alice nodded. 'You could say that, sir, and yes, Dot did give me the message, thank you, but I wanted to come in today and let you know how well I got on at Jolly's.'

'Very good.' Mr Button nodded, sitting down once more. 'I'm sure it was a great success. I spoke with Madeleine Marshall, the store manager, this morning on the telephone and it seems the girls in the department thought you were wonderful. Professional and full of knowledge about the Liberty's brand. Of course I expected nothing less, it's why I wanted to send you, but it was nice to have it confirmed.'

Alice felt a flush of pleasure at the praise. 'We all got along very well. Mrs Downing was kind enough to take me out dancing for the evening with some of the girls from the store. It was wonderful.'

As Alice finished speaking she looked at her store manager for encouragement, but found his face was grave. 'Is everything all right?' she asked cautiously.

'I think there's something you should know,' Mr Button began, steepling his fingers together and leaning across the desk. 'Saturday night wasn't the only attack on the city. The Germans returned on Sunday night as well and wreaked more devastation.'

'Oh my days!' Alice exclaimed, her hands balling into fists. 'How bad was it?'

'Very bad.' Mr Button shook his head in sorrow. 'Over the two nights, the south-east of the city was all but destroyed, killing hundreds of residents in their homes.'

'I had no idea! I could see it was bad – incendiaries lit up the city like it was Christmas – but I didn't know so much was devastated.'

'Mrs Marshall said the damage was worse on Sunday night. The Germans came back to finish the job, doing their best to decimate the city as a whole; they failed, of course, but not without causing some serious damage. The Regina Hotel, the Assembly Rooms all flattened,' Mr Button replied grimly. 'I'm sure you saw in the news the British attack on Lübeck last month. It's thought the attack on Exeter earlier in the week and now Bath is Hitler's revenge.'

Alice's hands flew to her mouth in shock. To think she had been whirling away the night with new friends just days earlier. A chill ran up her spine as an image of the pilot she had seen in his plane flooded her mind: the evil in his eyes lighting up his entire face like the incendiary he had no doubt dropped. How could such hate exist in the world? With this unrelenting war raging across the globe, what sort of hope was there for her son or indeed for any child born in these dreadful times?

'Are you all right, Alice?' Mr Button asked, his voice rich with concern. 'You've gone quite pale.'

Nodding quickly, Alice took a deep breath to steady herself. 'Fine, thank you. I'll get back to work if I may.'

'Yes of course,' Mr Button said softly. 'We can talk more later.'

With that Alice got up and walked towards the door. Only, resting her hand on the door handle, a thought suddenly entered her mind. 'Mr Button, sir, you said you spoke to the store manager, Mrs Marshall?'

'That's right,' Mr Button replied, briefly glancing up from his paperwork.

'Was there a reason you didn't speak to Mrs Downing?'

There was a pause then as Mr Button shifted uncomfortably in his chair. 'My dear, I was rather hoping not to have to share this with you until it had been confirmed, but it seems that Mrs Downing was killed in the raids on Saturday evening. We aren't sure but as she lives in the Kingsmead area of the city, which was badly hit, and nobody has seen her since ... I'm sorry.'

A wave of nausea flooded her body. Surely not Mrs Downing? Alice gripped the brass door handle tightly, desperately trying to find the right words to say but nothing came out.

'Alice dear, why don't you go and have a cup of tea in the staffroom and return to the shop floor when you're feeling more stable. I shall let Mrs Claremont know.'

'No!' Alice said firmly, coming to her senses. 'No, that's very kind of you, Mr Button, but I think it's best I get down to the shop floor. Mrs Downing would have expected nothing less.'

'If you're sure,' Mr Button said softly, admiration for his deputy fabric manager written across his face.

'I'm more than sure,' Alice said determinedly. 'Jerry won't stop us living our lives any more than he already has.'

Despite Alice's brave words in Mr Button's office she found it difficult to concentrate and spent the rest of the day in a daze as she thought of nothing but Mrs Downing. She wondered if her new friend had suffered or, worse, was still alive somewhere, buried beneath a mound of rubble, every breath as painful and panicked as the last. As she served each customer she was painfully aware of Mrs Claremont's eyes boring into her, and felt her supervisor was just waiting for her to make a mistake. Alice realised the fabric manager would know all about what had happened in Bath and thought it was telling she hadn't reached out to offer an ounce of compassion. Alice was determined not to give Mrs Claremont the satisfaction of visibly struggling with her emotions and so plastered a smile on her face and hoped the day would soon be over.

Thankfully, Alice's silent prayers were answered. The moment floor walker Dreary Deirdre completed the last of her evening checks, Alice bolted upstairs to the staffroom, pulled on her coat and fled. Bursting out of the back entrance on to the street, she found the evening still filled with light. She didn't even say goodbye to Mary; all she wanted to do was get home, hold her son and never let him go.

Hurrying down Kingly Street she rounded the corner in the direction of the Tube, so lost in thought she almost didn't hear a man calling her name.

Whipping her head around in the direction of the sound, she came face-to-face with none other than Jack Capewell.

'What are you doing here?' Alice gasped.

'Looking for you, actually. I didn't want to bother you while you were working so I was waiting out front.'

Alice smiled apologetically. 'The staff entrance is around the back. This entrance is for customers only.'

'Ah.' Jack rocked back and forth on his heels, seemingly wrong-footed.

At the sight of him looking so unsure, Alice's heart went out to him. 'What can I do for you?' she asked kindly.

'I just wanted to see how you were doing after the weekend, is all.'

'Oh, that's kind,' she replied in a posh accent she didn't recognise. She looked at him properly then and saw he looked as tired she felt. 'To be honest, I've had better days,' she admitted, returning to her usual South London tones.

'Me too,' he replied. 'You hear about the second night of bombing?'

Alice jerked her head towards the store. 'My boss told me. He'd got word from the manager of the store I visited.'

'I wasn't sure,' Jack replied stiffly. 'I just thought I'd see if you had heard and were OK?

'One of the ladies I was with that night was killed,' Alice blurted. 'I've been thinking about it all day, feeling sick. We weren't great friends or anything but I can't stop thinking about her. I keep wondering if I could have protected her – maybe if I'd spoken to her for longer, danced with her more, if I'd walked home with her …' As her voice trailed off, Jack stepped forward and placed a comforting hand on her shoulder. Alice looked up into his eyes, which were filled with nothing but kindness, and felt her own hand float on top of his. The simple touch of his large, heavy palm was a salve to the pain she had been feeling all day.

'You can't allow your mind to go there,' he said softly. 'You start down that path and you're opening yourself to nothing but torment. The Germans are to blame for this – nobody else.'

'I know you're right,' she replied, a hint of wistfulness to her tone. 'I did that when I first got news of Luke's disappearance; it nearly sent me doolally. I can't do it again.'

'And nor should you. You and I know better than any-one how hard it is when you lose someone. You blame yourself, you wish you'd done things differently – cheated the outcome somehow. But it never works, Alice, you have to say goodbye and the best way of honouring those we loved and lost is to keep living our own lives – live the very best lives we can, while we can.'

As the evening sun warmed her face, Alice turned her gaze from Jack and looked up at the sky. He was right: nobody knew how long they had left on this earth; they owed it to themselves and each other to make the most of it.

'I didn't just come here to see if you were all right,' Jack went on, cutting across her thoughts. 'I wanted to talk to you about something else.'

Alice frowned as she saw a flash of hesitation pass across his features. 'What is it?'

A cough escaped his lips as Jack seemingly tried to for-mulate what he wanted to say. 'I wanted to ask if we could be friends. I know you're married 'n' all, and I don't want to get in the way of that. But hell, Alice, I really like you and I think you really like me. We've already been through quite a bit together – what do you say?'

The hesitation had disappeared from his features and been replaced by hope. Instinctively she knew there was only one answer she could give. For some reason she was drawn to this man, and she wanted to get to know him better. In a world filled with so much pain, the idea of a friendship with someone who understood her very soul called out to her. 'I'd like that,' she said quietly. 'I'd like that very much.'

Chapter Sixteen

As April turned into May, the warm spring sunshine gave everyone, including Alice, a much needed lift. Dressing herself and then Arthur, as she got ready for work one Friday morning, she felt a flush of happiness as he looked at her with his twinkling bright eyes, and smiled at her properly. This new, unprompted gesture took Alice's breath away, as she realised that no matter what else was happening in the world, her boy was growing up just as he should be.

As she sat, the morning light flooding through the room, she felt joy flood through her. Resting her head gently against her son's, she inhaled his sweet baby smell and felt happier and lighter somehow for the first time since the raid in Bath. Not only were things working out well at work since her visit, with Jolly's ringing almost daily to find out about how much utility print fabric they could stock, life had also taken an unexpected turn thanks to her friendship with Jack. It had been two weeks now since he had found her outside Liberty's and so far they had enjoyed tea in the Lyons Corner House and gone to the pictures at the Coronet. She had even gone for a dance at one of the American Army's Red Cross clubs.

Tonight, however, Alice had asked Jack over for tea, promising to impress him with a Woolton Pie and prove that rationing didn't mean the Brits couldn't eat good food with a meagre allowance.

But that was all a lot later and, checking her wristwatch, she groaned inwardly as she saw she was running late.

Scooping Arthur up into her arms, she planted a kiss on his chubby cheeks and tried to ignore the rising sense of guilt she always felt when she had to leave him with Dot. Instead she consoled herself with the fact that there was no choice if she wanted to provide for her boy.

Arthur had been grumbling for most of the week and, after several sleepless nights, she had a feeling he was about to start teething. Walking him down the stairs, she was ready to tell Dot just that, but jumped back in surprise at the sight of her landlady dressed in her hat and coat. Had Dot forgotten about looking after Arthur for the day?

'Where are you going?' she demanded, a frantic edge to her voice.

'Work, you silly mare,' Dot scolded, 'where else would I be going at half past seven in the morning?'

Alarm flooded through Alice as she clutched hold of Arthur. 'No, it's my day for work today. I always work Fridays, you know that.'

Dot sighed as she straightened her hat. 'Yes, but Beatrice said she wanted to change our shifts up. She told me she'd discussed it with you last week. You're going in tomorrow morning.'

'That's not true! Mrs Claremont never said a word to me about changing my days. I've got to get into work now.'

'Are you sure, darlin'?' Dot eyed her carefully. 'You've been ever so busy of late. Did you forget the conversation she had with you? Beatrice was ever so detailed about it.'

'I bet she was,' Alice fumed. 'Because she was making it all up. Dot, I'm late as it is.'

Dot rested her only good leather bag on the tiny table in the hallway and regarded Alice thoughtfully. 'So you're sure Beatrice never spoke to you?'

'No!' Alice felt like crying. 'What the hell am I going to do if you're going to work?'

There was a pause then as Dot pursed her lips and seemed to consider the situation. 'How about I go in now and straighten things out with Beatrice and Edwin?'

'But I can't stay here!' Alice was panicking. 'I'll get the sack.'

''Course you won't,' Dot said firmly. 'There's clearly been a mix-up and I'll sort it out. Now, trust your Auntie Dot, get back inside and look after your son today. Besides, you're making Woolton Pie tonight for all of us and lover boy – it's just as well you're not at work.'

Alice couldn't miss the faintly barbed tone in Dot's voice at the mention of Jack. Although she hadn't come right out and condemned the relationship when Alice explained to her she had made a new friend and would be inviting him around for dinner, she could tell her landlady didn't approve.

Before Alice could protest, Dot turned to leave, when she suddenly stopped. 'I just want to say that with every-thing that's happened in the last few weeks, it's nice you've found a bit of happiness. Life's short, Alice, you don't need me to tell you that,' she said gently as she opened the door. 'I just wanted to let you know I'm only teasing. Really I'm pleased you've found someone who makes you smile.'

As Alice listened to the familiar click-clack of Dot's foot-steps disappearing along the pavement, she smiled. Her landlady always meant well – unlike her boss, she thought, feeling a swell of panic rise within her. Beatrice Claremont was organised, she was meticulous with the paperwork each day and although she didn't have the natural rapport with the customers that Flo had, she did know the ins and outs of their stock levels and she didn't make mistakes with the staff-ing rotas. It was a mystery how this could have happened.

Glancing back down at Arthur she thought for a second. His gummy smile was almost tempting her to stay behind, and if she was honest with herself there was nothing else she would rather do, but there had to be another way. Hearing the sounds of Joy moving about upstairs, Alice had a brainwave. She set Arthur down in his makeshift cot in the kitchen then fled up the stairs and rapped on her sister's door.

'What time are you working today, Joy?' she called.

'I'm not,' came the reply. 'I've got a day off.'

A surge of relief flooded through Alice. 'I need you to watch Arthur for me for a couple of hours.'

Alice heard Joy stalking across the floor. 'I'm sorry, what?' she replied in surprise.

Alice did her best to look contrite. She hated asking Joy for anything, always sure it would cost her far more than the original favour in the long run, but this morning she had no choice, and besides, Joy had been behaving herself of late. Perhaps she was up to the challenge. 'Could you watch Arthur for me this morning?' she said in a begging tone. 'There's been a mix-up at work.'

Joy slipped her a curious glance before nodding. 'All right,' she said, doing up the belt of her dressing gown tightly around her waist. 'But I've got to be off by two.'

'I thought you said you had the day off?'

'I do, but I'm taking Rose out for the afternoon. She's got a half-day,' Joy replied matter-of-factly.

Narrowing her eyes, Alice looked at her sister in disbelief. 'What do you mean you're going out with Rose?'

'I mean we fixed it up last week. We're going shopping up west.'

'But you're not friends with Rose,' Alice spluttered.

'Who says?' Joy shrugged. 'Rose is great fun. I told you, you just have to see beyond the blindness. She's still your friend, Alice, only now she's mine too.'

For the first time in a long time Alice was speechless. There were so many questions whirling around in her head, she didn't know where to start. But hearing the clock in the hallway chime eight, she knew there was no time to carry on the conversation now either. 'We'll talk about it later. So can you take care of Arthur until lunchtime?'

'Of course. It will be my pleasure.'

'And will you be here tonight for tea?'

Joy clapped her hands together in delight. 'Ah yes, your new friend's coming round. I'll be here. I can't wait to meet him.'

The way Joy used the term 'new friend' as though it was something sordid made Alice swell with fury but, instead of tearing into Joy as she usually would, she smiled sweetly. 'Good,' she said through gritted teeth. 'I'm looking forward to it.'

With that, she ran down the stairs, closely followed by Joy. As her sister picked Arthur up, Alice issued a list of instructions that she knew Joy wouldn't pay any heed to. Eventually, all but shoved out of the door, Alice left for work, wondering how on earth she was going to tell Beatrice Claremont she had caught her out.

As it turned out she didn't have to. When Alice arrived on the shop floor she discovered that Mrs Claremont was in meetings all day.

'I thought you'd have been in earlier,' Mary mused as she finished balancing her sales book from her position by the cash register.

Alice wrinkled her nose in confusion. 'Why?'

'Well, with you being in charge today?'

'What?' Alice gasped.

'Yes. Mrs C. told us last night you would be taking charge for the day as she's up against it,' Mary sighed. 'I was hoping that meant you would be promoted permanently so you would have been in a bit sooner.'

Alice shook her head in shock. She couldn't believe what she was hearing – this apparent mistake had gone from bad to worse. On the way in Alice had wondered if she was being ridiculous thinking Mrs Claremont had created this situation on purpose. But what if she was right? Was there a way to find out just what Mrs Claremont had been up to?

'Mrs Claremont told Dot I had the day off and asked her to work today leaving me without anyone to care for Arthur,' Alice said cautiously.

Mary's mouth fell open in surprise. 'Are you quite sure?'

'As sure as you are that Mrs Claremont said I would be in charge,' Alice continued. 'Did she mention anything about Dot coming in today?'

As Mary shook her head, Alice felt a fresh wave of uncertainty flood through her. 'Mary, do you think that Mrs Claremont deliberately told Dot to come in so I'd have to stay at home?'

'Surely you can't believe that?' Mary gasped incredulously.

Alice shrugged. 'I'm not sure. On the surface it makes no sense at all but Mrs Claremont is meticulous with her organisation; she wouldn't make a mistake like this. I've had to leave Arthur with Joy and that's only for the morning as she's dashing off at lunchtime to take Rose out.'

'Sorry, what did you just say? I'm not sure which of those two statements surprises me more: the fact you've been forced to leave Arthur with your sister or the fact your sister is taking Rose out – since when did they become so close?'

A deep sigh escaped from Alice's lips. This morning had started off so positively and yet within the space of a few hours her world had been upended again. 'I can't think about any of that now. I need to go and speak with the girls from Jolly's, check they're happy with everything.'

Mary smiled sympathetically. 'Have you spoken to them since the funeral?'

Alice nodded. 'They seem fine. It was a beautiful service apparently – well, as beautiful as a service can be under the circumstances.'

Even now, three weeks after the bombings, Alice still found the events of the raid hard to come to terms with. Mrs Downing's body had been identified a few days after the Saturday night raid, and buried in a communal grave with another 246 others on May 1st.

As Mary opened her mouth to offer some words of comfort, Alice saw Mrs Claremont walk across the floor. If she was surprised to see Alice she didn't show it.

'Glad to see you're here on time,' she remarked drily.

'No reason for me not to be is there, Mrs Claremont?' Alice simpered. 'I'm afraid I do need to be away by lunchtime though, as we discussed last week.'

Mrs Claremont's face clouded over with confusion. '"Discussed last week"? I'm sorry, my dear, I have no idea what you're referring to. However, if the simple fact of the matter is that you cannot organise your working life because of personal considerations then I'm afraid I shall have no choice but to let Mr Button know.'

Alice raised an eyebrow. Clearly Dot hadn't got to Mr Button yet, but she wasn't about to let the opportunity to put her superior right slide. 'Oh but, Mrs Claremont,' she replied in an innocent tone, 'I rather think we discussed it at the same time as you and I talked about me looking after things here while you would be in meetings. I said that unfortunately I wouldn't be able to stay all day, what with Dot coming in as well. I'm sure you remember?'

As Mrs Claremont shifted on the spot, clearly uncomfortable, Alice knew that her instincts had been proved right: this was no mistake; for some reason she couldn't quite fathom, this had been deliberately planned.

'Yes of course, Mrs Milwood, it's all coming back to me now,' she said eventually.

'I'm so pleased.' Alice smiled, feeling a glow of satisfaction. 'I would hate to cause you any trouble.'

Chapter Seventeen

By the time Jack knocked on the door of the Bell Street terrace, Alice was exhausted, overwrought and anxious. Not only had she spent most of the morning trying to avoid a row with Mrs Claremont but she only got home just in time before Rose and Joy put on their hats and coats and scarpered, without so much as a hello between them.

After they had disappeared through the front door like a pair of whirling dervishes, Alice had checked on her son, who thankfully was sleeping soundly in his cot. She had half wondered about joining him, until she remembered that she had to feed the proverbial five thousand that night and so she had sprung into action and busied herself making Woolton Pie.

When she heard the rap at the door, she was just in the middle of applying the last of the rouge she had managed to eke out since before the outbreak of war. Startled, she raced down the stairs only to find Dot welcoming Jack inside with open arms.

'I can't tell you, Mr Capewell, how nice it is to finally have a real live GI in our home,' Alice heard Dot say in a strangely polite tone.

'Not at all, ma'am, it's a real pleasure to be here,' Jack replied in his usual easy manner. 'And please do accept these chocolates as a thank you for inviting me.'

'Oh my days,' Dot said loudly, almost falling out of character. 'Mr Capewell, you shouldn't have. I can't remember the last time we had chocolates this fine.'

Or at all, Alice thought drily. It was high time she rescued Jack.

'There you are,' she called in greeting from the foot of the stairs, 'Sorry, I was just getting ready but I see Dot's been making you welcome.'

'She certainly has,' Jack said graciously, giving Alice a half-bow, half-smile.

Alice glanced at her landlady in surprise. She could see that despite Dot's misgivings about welcoming a GI into her home, she was quite taken with Jack already.

She was just about to show Jack into the kitchen and suggest a glass of beer that she had managed to get from under the counter when she had picked up her week's butter rations, when another rap at the door prevented her.

'You get that,' Dot said, all but shooing her away. 'I'll take care of Mr Capewell.'

'Really, ma'am, it's just Jack.'

As Dot threw her head back with a high-pitched, tinkly laugh, Alice didn't know whether to laugh or cry at her landlady's behaviour. Deciding that Jack was a big enough boy who could look after himself, she answered the front door and smiled as she saw Flo and Mary either side of Mr Button and Aggie.

'Welcome, welcome,' she smiled, relief flooding through her that everyone had arrived. 'Dot,' she called loudly, 'Mr Button is here, along with Mary, Flo and Aggie too.'

As Alice took her guests' coats, and Mr Button ventured through to the kitchen, Flo shot her an awkward glance while Mary wasted no time in her candour. 'Why are you being so bally strange?'

'Jack's here,' Alice whispered, 'and Dot's quite taken with him.'

At the explanation the girls broke into guffaws of laughter while Alice did her best to shush them. 'You know

119

these GIs. They're charming British women left, right and centre.'

'Well, let's just hope Mr Button can keep her on course,' Mary remarked. 'Or we'll all be in trouble.'

Shaking her head with mirth, Alice followed the group into the kitchen and was delighted to see Jack introducing himself to everyone.

'Have you had a good day?' she asked him.

'Can't complain. We've been busy working on exercises – or drills as you might call them over here.'

'Definitely drills,' Mary chimed in.

'Mary used to be in the ATS,' Flo clarified. 'She's our army expert.'

At the praise, Mary coloured. 'Hardly,' she snorted.

Jack looked at her with admiration in his eyes. 'Mary, no – if I may call you that. My God, to have served your country in the way you have is incredible.'

At the defence, Mary smiled. 'That's very kind of you, Mr Capewell, but I'm certain that when I was in the ATS we never encountered anything like the danger you magnificent boys encounter on a daily basis.'

Jack held his hands up. 'Can I just ask what's with all this Mr Capewell business? It's Jack. Please can you all call me that? I feel as if I'm meeting my bank manager any time I hear the term "Mr".'

At that the group laughed and, seeing how relaxed everyone was, Alice got to work pouring drinks for everyone. Only, reaching for the glasses, she realised that there were still two who were missing.

'Anyone seen Rose and Joy?' she quizzed.

Dot frowned. 'Rose promised me she would be here well before Jack was due.'

'So did Joy,' Alice fumed.

'I'm sure they won't be long,' Flo said consolingly. 'It's nice they've become friends.'

'Yes, you can't have too many friends during wartime,' Aggie simpered, turning to Jack. 'Wouldn't you agree, Mr Capewell— Oh, I'm sorry, Jack.'

As she let out a delicate laugh Flo and Alice exchanged looks. It seemed Dot wasn't the only one taken with the GI.

'You're quite right.' Jack smiled politely at Aggie. 'Friends are very important.'

'Even if the relationship is thoroughly unexpected,' Mary added, raising an eyebrow.

Alice wasn't sure if she meant Jack and Aggie, Jack and Dot, Jack and her or Rose and Joy.

'I thought that,' Flo said, taking the glass of beer Alice poured for her. 'How on earth have they become so friendly?'

Alice shrugged. 'I don't know and to be honest I don't want to know, just as long as Joy's not leading Rose astray.'

'She wouldn't be doing that, would she?' Flo asked. 'Joy's turned over a new leaf since she's been living with you.'

'Perhaps we'll get to the bottom of it over afternoon tea on Sunday,' Mary offered.

'That's right.' Dot grinned. 'I'd forgotten we were going to her fancy hotel.'

Jack smiled back at her. 'That sounds nice.'

'Yes, I'm rather jealous myself.' Mr Button was keen to join in. 'I wonder if there's a spare seat for me.'

Dot patted his hand. 'There isn't, love. Some things we have to keep separate.'

Alice didn't miss the pointed barb, and glancing at Mr Button and the way he returned to his drink she had a feeling he understood just what Dot meant as well.

Alice said nothing, instead she pulled the Woolton Pie from the oven and chuckled at the way her friends oohed and ahhed as she set it down.

She was just about to start slicing it up when the sound of screaming made her jump. Peering into the front room, she could see that the noise was coming from her son, and she rushed to his side.

Looking down into his face, she couldn't miss the look of anguish in Arthur's eyes or the way one of his cheeks was bright red. It was obvious he had another tooth coming through, and, scooping him into her arms, she did her best to soothe him, while peering over her shoulder into the doorway to apologise to her guests. 'I'm so sorry: he's teething. I'll just take him upstairs.'

'Poor little bugger.' Dot raised her voice over the noise. 'He's had a hard few days. That tooth's been coming through for a while.'

'I know,' said Alice. 'I won't be long, I'll just see if I can settle him.'

'Want me to do anything?' Dot called to Alice's retreating back.

'No thanks, I'll be fine.'

Reaching the bedroom she shared with her son, she perched on the narrow single bed and rocked her baby to sleep.

'I know, darlin',' she said in a soothing tone, offering him her finger to nibble on, 'it won't be forever.'

As Arthur clamped down hard on her finger, Alice resisted the urge to swear in agony in front of her son.

'Hi,' came a voice.

Swinging around she saw Jack leaning in the doorway.

'Sorry, I didn't mean to interrupt, I just wondered if there was something I could do.'

'That's kind of you. I don't think there's anything any of us can do; poor little boy's just got to sit it out like we all had to.'

Jack crossed the floor towards her and peered over her shoulder to get a better look at Arthur. 'Well, hey there, little man. You're not going to chew your mama's fingers to pieces now, are ya?'

'I've a feeling he's going to do just that,' Alice moaned as her son bit painfully down on her finger once more.

'Here, mind if I try something?' Jack offered, reaching down to take Arthur from Alice's arms.

'No, course not,' she replied, feeling doubtful.

Watching her new friend take her son in his arms, she felt a pang of worry. Just how much did Jack know about children?

As he smiled down at her son she was relieved to see Arthur didn't start crying immediately and so she stood up, ready to see what Jack would try next.

'Now this is a little trick I used on my boy when he was Arthur's age,' he murmured, reaching into his pocket for a crust of bread.

'What on earth are you going to do with that?' Alice gasped, looking in horror at the rather tough-looking crust.

'Trust me, works every time, and it will save your fingers.' He gently pushed the crust into Arthur's mouth.

To her surprise Arthur didn't scream or cry at the offering of stale bread; instead he gnawed quite happily with relief instantly flooding across his chubby face.

'However did you learn to do that?' she demanded in a loud whisper.

Jack smiled as he continued to gently rock the baby in his arms. 'I told you: I used to do that for my boy. My mama taught me – old family remedy, you might say.'

'I could have done with this a week ago. You could have saved me from bruised fingers and several sleepless nights!'

'All part of the service, ma'am,' Jack chuckled as Arthur chewed on the bread.

'You're a natural with kids,' Alice found herself saying. 'You must really miss your boy.'

'Every single day.'

Alice nodded and looked back at her son. She hated being away from Arthur. The thought of it was too much to bear, yet Jack had to live with that pain constantly.

Glancing up at him and seeing the joy in his face as he held her son in his arms, she knew she couldn't do anything to take away the agony of being apart from his child. However, it was possible that she and Arthur could help make his time away from his own family at least a little easier to bear.

With Jack's help, Arthur quickly settled and by the time Alice returned downstairs, she was delighted to find Dot had taken matters into her own hands and served everyone already. 'Have you left enough for Joy and Rose?'

'Bugger 'em,' Dot snapped. 'They knew what time tea was. It's gone half past eight now, if we leave it any longer we'll be eating our breakfast.'

'I'm happy to wait if we're not all here,' Jack said kindly. 'I mean I don't want to put anyone out.'

'No, Dot's right.' Alice was firm. 'They were due an hour and a half ago.'

'I agree,' Mary said, playing with the stem of her glass. 'We all made an effort to be punctual; I don't see why we should wait any longer.'

'Well, if you're sure, I won't say no,' Jack said. 'Alice has talked about this wonderful pie for the past two weeks and I can't wait to try it.'

At that the table broke into laugher, leaving Jack looking more than a little confused. 'What did I say?' he asked.

'Sorry, son,' Mr Button chuckled. 'I just don't think anyone has ever said they couldn't wait to try Woolton Pie before.'

'Dot sniffed. 'It's certainly a dish we have a lot.'

'But Alice's is legendary,' Flo offered loyally.

'Well, now I'm intrigued,' Jack said, picking up his fork in his right hand, much to the amazement of the group.

'Oi! We might be on rations in this country but manners cost nothing,' Dot said, pointing to his knife with her forefinger.

Startled, Jack gazed at Alice for help. 'What have I done wrong?'

'Your knife,' she said. 'We don't eat with just a fork in England.'

'Oh.' Jack looked around and immediately spotted his mistake. 'I'm sorry, I didn't mean to cause offence. It's just in the States we don't use our knives unless it's for a steak or something like that.'

At the mention of the word steak, Alice felt her eyes glaze over with what she was sure was a mix of lust and envy. She couldn't remember the last time she had enjoyed red meat, let alone a steak.

'No harm done, Jack,' Mr Button said kindly. 'I've no doubt that if I spent time in your fine country I'd make the odd mistake here and there too.'

'You'd know to bloody use a knife and fork, though, wouldn't you,' Dot muttered in a stage whisper.

At that everyone erupted into laughter again, and Alice felt a swell of happiness as she looked at the faces surrounding her. This moment was almost perfect, she thought contentedly, until she realised that someone was missing from the table: Luke. As another round of laughter passed around the table, Alice allowed the happy sound to wash over her and did her best to join in. Some moments were never truly perfect.

Chapter Eighteen

The following Sunday Alice found herself walking through the streets of Belgravia in the pouring rain as she made her way towards Mayfair House. Her best black court shoes were so worn she had needed to put cardboard in them, and she hobbled down the streets with Arthur sleeping soundly in his pram, feeling for all the world as if she didn't belong.

Although Alice knew that parts of Belgravia had been bombed, this particular street with its stonewashed buildings, so tall and elegant with their matching front doors complete with boot scrapers, looked as if they had hardly been touched by the atrocities Hitler had wrought. And if it hadn't been for the holes in the stone walls where the metal railings used to be, Alice could have been forgiven for thinking that war didn't exist in this particular corner of England at all.

Gingerly she rounded the corner and continued to gawp at her surroundings. She had only ever been to Belgravia once before and that was when she was a child. Her father had brought her and Joy to one of these posh houses where they had enjoyed tea with a very smartly dressed woman who spoke with a broad South London accent just like them. Alice hadn't a clue what or who she was, but going by the smile on her father's face, not to the mention the rather large bag of cash he'd been carrying as they left, the woman worked for him in some way or another.

Spotting the opulent red-bricked building which she knew to be the hotel, Alice hurried towards the entrance where she had arranged to meet everyone. Joy's invitation to afternoon tea at her new workplace was a nice gesture and Alice was determined that the afternoon would be a success.

'Where've you been?' Dot demanded, tapping her watch. 'You were supposed to have been here ten minutes ago.'

'Yes, come on, we're starving,' Flo grumbled. 'I deliberately didn't eat breakfast or lunch in preparation for this.'

'It's true, she didn't,' Aggie said, straightening her grey felt hat. 'She said she didn't want to spoil her appetite.'

Dot raised an eyebrow. 'You can't blame Alice for that, Flo.'

Flo rolled her eyes. 'Perhaps not, but I can try.'

'Hear that,' Aggie whispered in a stage whisper to Dot. 'She's grumpy because she didn't eat.'

'They never listen to their elders,' Dot replied with a wink, before nudging Alice. 'This one's the same.'

Alice and Flo exchanged looks of mock despair before Alice spoke. 'I'm sorry, it took me ages to get Arthur off to sleep.' She peered gingerly into the pram, afraid the sudden chatter of voices might have disturbed her son. 'Do you really think it's all right that I've brought him? I mean this place is a bit hoity-toity, ain't it? I can't imagine they take too kindly to children here.'

'Oh, they won't,' Mary said authoritatively as she turned up the collar of the army greatcoat she still wore to keep out the rain. 'Children should always be bally well seen and bally well never heard.'

Alarm passed across Alice's face. 'You see. I shouldn't have come.'

'But what I was trying to say, if you'd let me finish, is that these hotels are always very accommodating to their guests so you mustn't worry.'

'And what if Arthur cries?' Alice said fretfully.

'Then one of us will take him outside so he doesn't disturb the other diners,' Flo said kindly. 'Really, Alice, you mustn't worry so much. I know it's not ideal but this isn't the problem you think it's going to be.'

'All right,' Alice sighed, still feeling reluctant. 'Shall we?'

'About bloody time,' Dot grumbled, leading the little group through the double doors that were quickly opened by a uniformed doorman.

Stepping inside, Alice felt all the more conscious of the cardboard in her shoes. She wasn't usually so unconfident – after all, years at Liberty's where she'd hobnobbed with royalty from across the world had given her good training, but she was aware that she was always the one serving them not the other way around. Now here she was in this very grand hotel feeling like a fish out of water.

The first thing Alice noticed was the beautiful scent of freesias wafting through the air, then she saw the glittering chandeliers, as beautiful as the ones that used to grace the Assembly Rooms. Feeling a pang of regret as she thought of that fateful night, Alice glanced quickly down and took in the white marble floor, which gleamed like the Liberty silk that had made her wedding dress. Elsewhere, gold-framed pictures of lands that Alice had never seen and would likely never see graced the walls, while a rich red carpet that looked as though it was as thick as the mattress she slept in clad the huge wooden staircase that led to the floors above.

'It's beautiful,' Mary breathed. 'I haven't been here since Cynthia's debutante ball ten years ago. It was a frightful gas – jolly good cream cakes as I remember.'

'Well, it looks as though we're about to sample some for ourselves.' Flo grinned. 'There's Joy.'

Alice smiled gratefully at her sister, who was beautifully turned out in a pair of black trousers – many women were wearing them these days – along with a gorgeous silk blouse; Alice recognised it as an old Liberty print.

'Hello, girls, we're just through here!' Joy ushered them all inside to the dining room.

Alice brought up the rear, her jaw dropping as she took in the fact that this room was even grander than reception. White linen tablecloths adorned the thirty or so tables while five more chandeliers hung from the ceiling. At the back of the room, a team of smartly dressed men and women wearing a uniform of black seemed to keep magically reappearing with trays filled with so much delicious-looking food Alice was sure her mouth wasn't just watering, but dribbling.

Joy led them to a table by the window and they all sat down. 'I thought we would all have the traditional afternoon tea so I ordered already – I hope that was all right?' she said, appearing suddenly nervous as she straightened the serviette on her lap.

'That was very kind of you, Joy,' Mary said sincerely as she closed her menu. The waiter arrived with their tea and she continued: 'I must say it all looks rather splendid, doesn't it?'

'How the other half live,' Dot marvelled as she took a sip of the tea the waiter had just poured.

Joy made a face before she leaned over the table and began to whisper: 'It can be a bit bloody annoying when you come in here and see all this lot eating like kings while the rest of us are on scraps.'

'It makes you wonder how they do it,' Rose grumbled. 'I mean why doesn't the government stop them or something?'

Dot guffawed and slapped the table. 'Because half the government is in here, love! Still,' she continued, helping herself to more tea from the pot the waiter had left on the table, 'for once we can enjoy a slice of the good life as well. Very nice of you, Joy, I must say, to organise all this for us. You sure you're not going to get in no trouble for it?'

Joy shook her head. 'It's my pleasure. The way you girls have welcomed me into your home and your hearts – well, I want to say thank you.'

'We're very glad you found us,' Rose said in a kinder tone that Alice thought sounded much more like her old friend. 'You've brightened up our lives.'

'Being here, despite what you were saying about the way the other half live, Dot,' Mary ventured, 'well, it does at least feel as if we've got an afternoon off from the war, doesn't it? We're just a group of rather fine ladies taking tea.'

'You're right,' Rose agreed. 'I do in fact feel rather fine sitting here.'

Mary grinned. 'It's as though we could be Liberty customers for once.'

'Oh no, we'll never be that posh.' Alice chuckled as the waiter returned with a platter of sandwiches piled high on a tiered stand. They looked and smelled delicious, with delicate cucumber sliced between perfect triangles of white bread, while on the tier below stood a selection of salmon, ham, egg and cheese all sliced with the same care and precision.

'Ham!' Flo screeched. 'When was the last time you saw ham?'

'Or salmon?' Mary breathed admiringly. 'When did any of us ever see salmon?'

There was a brief silence then as the girls simply gazed in wonder at the spread before them, each unable to believe that such luxurious foods still existed in the world.

'Let's not stand on ceremony then,' Dot said, holding up her delicate china plate and filling it with a sandwich of each variety. 'Oh my days! That's beautiful. Never in my life have I eaten something so delicious.'

Mary laughed at the obvious pleasure on the matriarch's face. 'I'd have thought Mr Button would have been bringing you to places like this all the time, as he's manager of Liberty's.'

Dot made a face. 'I've not seen much of Edwin these days. He's always so busy at work. I half wondered if he'd gone off me!'

'I don't think so,' Flo said sadly. 'We're just horribly short-staffed at the minute. I swear that's the only reason I got the deputy manager's job, because I was the only one of the department managers that didn't have a family at home to rush back for.'

Aggie shook her head in despair as she helped herself to another cucumber sandwich. 'Do you see how she puts herself down, every chance she gets?'

'I'm not,' Flo protested, turning to her aunt, 'I'm just being realistic.'

'And I keep telling you that you need to have more self-belief. You're more than good enough for that role, so start believing in yourself.'

Flo was just about to open her mouth to reply, when she saw her aunt clutch her chest. 'You all right, Aggie?' she asked, her face flushed with worry.

'Fine, love.' Aggie waved Flo's concerns away. 'Just a bit of cucumber gone down the wrong hole, I think.'

Joy was immediately on her feet and pouring a glass of water. 'Here,' she said gently, pressing the glass into Aggie's hand. 'Drink this slowly, you'll feel much better. That blasted cucumber's always catching in people's throats.'

'Thanks, love,' Aggie whispered gratefully.

As the older woman took a sip, the rest of the girls looked on in alarm.

'Will you all get back to your butties, girls,' Aggie hissed. 'I feel like a zoo exhibit the way you're all staring!'

'Sorry,' Flo whispered before turning to everyone else. 'What were we talking about?'

'Staffing,' Mary put in. 'And the lack of it. I was just about to say that being short-staffed can't be a new thing, can it? I mean the men went off to war a couple of years ago.'

'Yes but now women have been conscripted a lot of our girls have gone part-time or have been called up themselves,' Flo explained as she continued to shoot her aunt anxious looks. 'It's only married women or carers, or some lucky few that haven't been.'

'Well, I haven't been called up yet,' Mary sighed. 'I can only think it's because of my discharge from the ATS. I'm glad I joined the Red Cross last Christmas though; it's made me feel as though I'm doing a bit more. And Rose's Red Cross talk the other week has been very inspiring. I can't wait until it becomes a regular event.'

At that the girls all nodded their heads. 'It was a lovely idea of yours, Rose,' Flo murmured. 'What made you think of it?'

Rose shrugged, barely glancing up from her plate of sandwiches. 'I just felt it was something we should be doing, but I've decided not to bother organising any more. I've one final one in a few weeks then that'll be it. I mean, let's face it,' she said, letting out a hollow laugh, 'I don't think the public like a permanent reminder in front of them of what happens if you don't get the help you need in time.'

'Rose, you can't give up on the talks,' Mary persisted. 'It was a brilliant idea, and all of Liberty's was behind you.'

'Apart from Mrs Claremont,' Rose said listlessly, 'and perhaps she was right. No, sorry, my mind's made up. I've spoken to Mr Button and he said if I don't feel up to it I don't have to do it.'

With that Rose returned to her sandwiches, leaving the rest of the girls unsure what to say next.

'Have you heard much from David, Mary?' Flo asked, changing the subject.

'Not since last week. He said he was preparing to move overseas but wouldn't say where.'

'Of course not,' Dot said. 'And what about his sister, Mabel?'

A flash of anger passed across Mary's features before she spoke. 'He didn't bring her up. I think he knows I don't like to hear or talk about her.'

'We none of us do,' Aggie murmured in agreement. She still looked a little pale after her sandwich incident. 'It breaks my heart every time I think about what she got up to with my former brother-in-law. At least Mabel Matravers is under lock and key though, unlike Bill Wilson. He won't let this go without a fight, I'm telling you, girls, so watch your backs.'

Flo laid a comforting hand on top of her aunt's. 'And I keep telling you my father's not coming anywhere near us; you know he won't risk going back inside. Aggie, you have to relax, he's long gone.'

'Flo's right,' Mary said softly. 'Besides, if he's cross with anyone it'll be Mrs Matravers. According to David's last letter she's trying to atone for her sins and has provided police with details of his last known address and those of his friends.'

'Well, that'll certainly have my old man gunning for her,' Flo muttered, her cheeks pinking with anger.

'Still, I should have thought David needs to talk to someone about all this,' Dot pointed out reasonably, 'and you are his intended, darlin'. I know it's uncomfortable to listen to him go on about his sister, but it's probably just as painful for him to talk about it as it is for you to hear it.'

'And no doubt he's worried about that niece of his,' Aggie added. 'Flo tells me Mrs Matravers had her little girl in prison.'

Mary gave a curt nod of her head. 'That's right – Emma. She was born in March I think, though she's being looked after by the state at the moment, something else David's not happy about. It's all such a mess.'

'Have you thought any more about setting a date?' Flo asked.

Mary shook her head. 'David mentioned something in his last letter about us bringing it forward but I would still rather wait. I still want to marry in peacetime.'

'Whenever that'll be,' Dot snorted.

Alice wiped her mouth with her serviette. 'Dot's right, Mary. We don't know when this war's going to be over. The last one was four years long, for crying out loud. We're three years in already.'

'But the Americans are here in their droves,' Mary protested. 'Surely now it'll be over in months with their help?'

'And money,' Dot added sagely.

'Look around you now – the place is swarming with them,' Aggie added.

'They're always here, as you can see,' Joy added, gesturing at the room. 'Usually complaining about the British weather and the terrible food.'

'Bloody cheek!' Dot grumbled. 'There's no rationing for them with their food parcels and whatnot from America. Let 'em whinge, I say.'

At that, the table guffawed with laughter.

'Now, that's not true. They're ever so well-mannered and polite,' Joy said. 'One offered me some nylons when I was waitressing in here yesterday.'

Alice raised an eyebrow. 'Tell him you don't want his nylons. I've told you before, we don't want no trouble.'

'Joy can go out with a GI if she wants – she's not married or engaged. Surely if anyone's entitled to a bit of fun it's Joy?' Rose muttered darkly, pushing her plate away.

'Thank you, Rose,' Joy said gratefully before raising an eyebrow at her sister. 'Anyway, talk about pot and kettle. What about your own GI?'

Alice felt a flush of colour creep up her neck. 'He's not my GI, as you put it. He's a friend.'

'And a very nice friend 'n' all,' Dot put in, taking a large bite of her egg sandwich and sending crumbs everywhere. 'He seems a proper gentleman.'

'Oooh yes.' Aggie smiled. 'A lovely man.'

'He is a lovely man,' Alice said hotly. 'A real family man and he misses his son dreadfully.'

Flo looked at Alice, her eyes full of sympathy. 'I can't believe he's widowed so young. What is he – our age?'

'Thirty,' Alice replied.

'Oh, same age as Luke,' Joy pointed out.

Alice glared at her sister. 'What is it you're trying to say?'

'Nothing.' Joy shrugged, helping herself to another sandwich. 'Just making an observation, that's all.'

Alice narrowed her eyes. 'As long as that's all it is.'

'What else would it be?' Joy protested in mock innocence.

'I think he's jolly good fun,' Mary said firmly. 'And I think you were lucky to have bumped into him in Bath.'

'Literally!' Flo laughed.

As the other girls joined in, only Rose remained silent.

'Rose? Are you all right?' Alice asked gently.

'Why does everyone keep asking me that?' she snapped. 'I just wish you'd stop going on about how good these GIs are. They won't save us. What about support for our precious boys fighting for all they're worth, living on scraps like the rest of us? These glamour-puss Americans are swooping in at the eleventh hour and taking all the glory when it's our boys that have been putting their lives on the line for the past three years. Don't tell me you don't know what I mean, Alice. Look at your Luke – still missing in action.'

Alice's jaw dropped in shock at Rose's sudden outburst. 'I try not to think about it like that,' she said honestly. 'I think that the Americans' involvement is a good thing – anything that helps bring Luke home more quickly.'

'Sorry,' Rose said in a tight voice as she got to her feet. 'I'm just a bit tired, I'll go and splash a little water on my face.'

Watching Rose clutch her stick as she walked gingerly to the bathroom, Alice felt a flood of despair creep through her bones. Her old friend was vanishing right before her eyes and she was at a loss to know how to help.

Chapter Nineteen

Once Rose had disappeared from view, Alice rounded on the rest of the table. 'Have you noticed the change in Rose? She hasn't been herself for weeks now.'

'I've thought that too,' Flo agreed as she brushed the sandwich crumbs from her lap. 'I've never seen her so upset.'

Mary pushed her plate away. 'She's been a bit out of sorts for a while,' she said in a small voice. 'I think she's really missing Tommy and the news about her sight has hit her hard. At home, she's always biting either my head off or Malcolm's.'

'That's not like her,' Alice replied thoughtfully.

Mary looked uncomfortable as she nodded. 'It's not. I mean I know I can't imagine what it's like to lose your sight, but I can't help thinking that she had clung to the fact that this blindness might be temporary. Now she knows that's unlikely it's as though she's angry with the entire world and isn't afraid to show it.'

'That poor girl,' Flo added, biting her lip.

'She is a poor girl,' Aggie ventured. 'Imagine how you might feel if you lost your sight. I think she's right to feel a bit angry – she's grieving, remember, only this time it's not for a person it's for who she was.'

'We need to do more for her,' Dot said. 'Take her mind off things. Perhaps I'll see if she wants to help me up the WVS. She might not be able to see well enough to sew herself but she's such a good teacher she can show some of those that can't stitch for toffee a thing or two.'

'I'm worried about the fact she's given up on these first-aid nights.' Mary frowned. 'I think it would be good for her to carry on with them and I know the Red Cross will want her to.'

Alice put down her serviette and stood up. 'I'll go and talk to her – tell her that we're all here for her.'

'No, let me,' Joy said suddenly, resting her hand on top of her sister's. 'I'm not as close to her as you girls are; we don't have the same history. She might find it easier to talk to me.'

Alice looked doubtful. 'I'm not sure, Joy, Rose needs to be handled gently. She's been through a lot.'

Joy narrowed her eyes in annoyance. 'I know that – we have become quite friendly of late. You're all going on about her blindness as though there's nothing more to her than that. She's still a young woman with thoughts, feelings and dreams – it might do you lot some good to think about that.'

A flicker of guilt passed across Alice's face as she realised to her surprise how right her sister was.

'Oh, let her try,' Dot put in sagely. 'She's right; Rose might open up a bit more.'

'All right,' Alice agreed reluctantly, 'but be gentle, Joy!'

'What do you take me for?' Joy said, rolling her eyes.

As Joy walked across the room the girls said nothing until she was gone. 'Do you really think she was the best person to send?' Mary wailed.

Flo shrugged. 'She can't do any worse than us. Rose barely says two words to me at work these days.'

As the waiter replaced the tray of finger sandwiches with a plate teetering with cakes, Alice found herself licking her lips in anticipation.

'And what about you Alice?' Mary asked as she helped herself to a delicious-looking carrot cake. 'How are you? I remember after the bombing in Whitstable last year I felt a bit out of sorts for a while.'

'Fine.' Alice shrugged, still not wanting to talk about it. The memory was too raw.

'Come on, let's leave our worries at the door now,' Aggie said at last. 'This is supposed to be an afternoon where we enjoy ourselves, so let's try and have a good time, eh?'

'You're right, sorry,' Flo sighed. Then she noticed Aggie was still rubbing her chest. 'You're not still bothered by that cucumber sandwich, are you?'

'I'm getting terrible indigestion at the moment.'

Flo raised an eyebrow. 'Might help if you got a good night's sleep.'

'What on earth's sleep got to do with indigestion?' Aggie said in an exasperated tone. 'Honestly, Flo, you do fuss.'

At that moment Arthur opened his eyes and grinned at the table, causing all the women to coo and beg Alice for a cuddle.

'You're doing ever so well at holding down a job and bringing up Arthur all the while worrying about Luke,' Flo said admiringly as she took Arthur from Dot and rocked him gently in her arms.

'That's right,' Mary agreed. 'I don't think I could do it.'

Alice rolled her eyes. 'You could do it in your sleep, Mary Holmes-Fotherington.'

Flo chuckled. 'So what we're saying is that us Liberty girls are extraordinary and we couldn't manage without one another.'

'Too right.' Dot smiled, raising her cup of tea. 'Here's to the Liberty girls.'

'The Liberty girls,' the little group cried as they clinked their cups against each other's.

'What's all this?' Joy said from behind her, her arm linked through Rose's.

Alice blinked in surprise. Joy had only been with Rose for about ten minutes and yet she had done something the other girls hadn't managed in weeks: put a smile on their friend's face.

As Joy sat back down, Alice found herself smiling warmly at her sister. 'We were just having a little celebration toast. To us girls.'

'About time,' Joy teased. 'When I left you lot were carrying on like it was a wake not a tea party.'

The girls laughed then, and as Flo handed Arthur back, Alice was delighted to see that Rose was also joining in with the giggles.

'I think it's probably time for me to go,' Alice said reluctantly as she glanced down at her son. 'He's been so good up until now, I don't want to spoil it for everyone else.'

'He's been wonderful.' Mary beamed, leaning across to stroke Arthur's cheek with her forefinger. 'What did I tell you? Nobody here has batted an eyelid, have they?'

Alice glanced around the room. Mary was right; nobody had been remotely interested in their little party all afternoon. Even so, she didn't want to ruin it now.

'We've made light work of the food so I think it's time we all left,' Dot said, surveying the empty plates and cake stand that now bore only a few crumbs.

'It's been wonderful though,' Flo exclaimed. 'What a treat, thank you so much for inviting us, Joy.'

'It's nothing,' Joy said as she signalled to the waiter for the bill. Immediately the chit was placed in front of her and Alice reached across to have a look at the amount, only for her sister to slap her hand away.

'Today is on me.' She reached into her bag for her purse.

'Absolutely not,' Mary exclaimed. 'That's very generous of you but even with your staff discount it's an expensive treat for you to shoulder alone. We insist on paying our way.'

'Yes of course, Joy,' Rose said immediately.

'It's a lovely gesture, darlin',' Dot said admiringly, 'but you can't afford it.'

Joy's eyes flashed with pride and determination. 'Not at all. You girls have all been so good to me, and I want to say thank you – properly. I've been making plenty in tips and, besides, my staff discount really is incredibly generous so it will hardly cost me a penny. I insist.'

With that Joy opened her purse and laid out a variety of notes and coins on the table.

'That's incredibly generous of you,' Mary repeated as they gathered their coats.

'Yes, Joy, you really must let us take you out for something next time,' Flo insisted.

'Though it might not be as grand as Mayfair House,' Rose teased.

Dot chuckled. 'Or even a Lyons Corner House.'

Together the girls left the hotel to a chorus of thank yous from the staff and Alice found herself at the back of the group, pushing Arthur in his pram as they sauntered through the Belgravia streets towards home. Excited chatter buzzed between them at the unexpected treat but it was only Alice who was silent, her mind racing to places she didn't want it to go. Yes, there was no denying the fact that her sister had been extremely kind, but Alice had seen just how much money had been stuffed into Joy's purse and she knew fine well that sort of cash didn't come through tips alone. She glanced up at Joy striding ahead, her arm still linked through Rose's, and felt alarm bells ring. Joy was up to something, Alice knew it, and she was determined to find out exactly what.

Chapter Twenty

It wasn't until the following evening that Alice found time to talk to her sister about the large sum of money she'd seen in her purse. In between feeding Arthur, washing nappies and attempting to run up a couple of new romper suits from an old pair of trousers that were beyond mending, she had spent the day stewing over Joy, trying to think of a logical reason as to why Joy was carrying so much cash, but each time she drew a blank.

As the clock struck five she heard the sound of a key in the lock, and Alice felt her resolve build as she knew she was finally going to get the chance to find out what was going on.

'Hello,' Joy called, her voice echoing down to the kitchen. 'Cor, I've had a bugger of a day – me dogs are killing me.'

'I've made tea,' Alice shouted. 'Why don't you come in and tell me all about it.'

'Ooh, you're a lifesaver.' Joy sighed as she hobbled into the kitchen in threadbare stockings and collapsed into the chair nearest the window.

Alice filled a cup to the brim and pushed it across the table towards Joy. 'Tough day then?'

'You could say that,' Joy grumbled. 'We had a load of GIs in again – all guests of a local dignitary. All I've done all day is fetch and flippin' carry.'

'Isn't that your job?'

'I suppose.' Joy sniffed, reaching for the tea. 'I'm just a bit tired of being called "baby".'

Alice chuckled at her sister's indignation. She had always been a drama queen and could see that despite her best efforts to change there were still some quirks that remained.

'I wanted to talk to you actually,' Alice began hesitantly.

'What about? Do you want me to look after Arthur for you tonight? Only I can't, I'm sorry, I'm off out.'

'No, nothing like that.' Alice shook her head. 'Where are you going anyway? Somewhere nice?'

'Just the pictures with some of the girls from work,' Joy said hurriedly. 'I've got to get back up the West End sharpish. I only came back to change.'

With that Joy leaned forward to set her cup down, only for Alice to lay her hand warningly on her sister's forearm. 'Before you go, there's something I want to talk about.'

'Will it take long?' Joy whined. 'I'm going to be late as it is.'

Alice folded her arms. 'No, I don't think so. I've just got a question for you – shouldn't take you too long to answer it.'

As Joy pulled up the sleeve of her dress to check the time, Alice felt a flash of horror. She had never seen that watch before and, judging by the gold band and mother-of-pearl face, it was expensive.

'New watch?'

'No, I've had it ages. An old flame gave it to me – you remember Trevor Hayes, don't you?'

'Flash Fat Trevor from down the Lane?' Alice scoffed. 'Ran the stables at the end? How could I forget? He was that bent he couldn't lie straight at night.'

'It was all a long time ago, Alice,' Joy fumed as she got to her feet. 'I've moved on from that.'

There was a pause as Alice regarded her sister: shuffling from foot to foot, her cheeks red with sudden anger and that intense gaze in her eyes. Alice knew her sister only looked that agitated when she had something to hide.

'Have you really moved on from that, Joy?' Alice asked softly. 'Only I'm beginning to think there's something you're not telling me.'

'Like what?' Joy snapped. 'I've done nothing but bend over backwards to show you I've changed since I moved in. I've looked after Arthur, I've helped you with Rose, I've tried to show you I want to move on but you can't forget the past, can you? You want to label me as the naughty little sister no matter what I do.'

'I can forget the past,' Alice said evenly. 'I can even forgive. All I want is to see you happy and settled.'

'And that's all I want.' Joy held Alice's gaze. 'I've done nothing wrong.'

'Then where did you get all that money?'

Joy paled. 'I don't know what you're on about. I haven't got any money.'

'I saw it,' Alice fired back, feeling suddenly very tired. 'When you went to pay for the afternoon tea, you opened your purse and I saw you had several notes stuffed in there.'

'That was my wages! I'd just got paid!'

The indignation on Joy's face was almost funny, Alice thought as she looked her sister up and down. She recognised the look of old. It was the same look her sister had worn whenever she was caught with her hand in the biscuit tin, when she'd been arrested by the police for pickpocketing and when Hannah, Flash Fat Trevor's wife, had caught the two of them indulging in a bit of how's your father. Joy only ever wore that look when she'd been up to no good and both she and Joy knew it.

'Just tell me,' Alice said, her tone weary now. 'We both know you're lying. I don't have the time for it and apparently you don't either if you're off out tonight, so just save it and tell me what's going on.'

Joy opened and closed her mouth like a goldfish, clearly searching for the right thing to say. Realising her sister wasn't going to confess, Alice felt the rage inside her burn even brighter.

'When you moved into this house, I told you that you had to behave,' she began, her voice taking on a dangerous, steely edge. 'I told you that I didn't want my son to grow up like we did – exposed to the petty behaviour of a petty criminal. I wanted better for him than that. You promised me you would behave yourself, that you'd changed. You haven't changed, Joy, you're a chip off our dad's old block and you bloody well know it. Now sling your hook because I've had enough.'

Without even waiting for a reply, Alice turned her back and started to wash up the tea things.

'You don't know what it's like,' Joy wailed. 'You've never put a foot wrong in your life.'

'Oh, is this the part where you tell me how misjudged you are, how tough you've had it?' Alice rolled her eyes; she'd heard it all before. 'How about you think about someone else, eh? You ever think about how tough I had it? Taking care of you, putting food on the table while you went out thieving left, right and centre. Things were hard for me 'n' all, Joy, but I never turned to crime. I'd seen enough of that in my childhood: I didn't want to see it in adulthood as well.'

Joy slumped back in the kitchen chair. As she rubbed her hands over her face Alice thought how old she looked all of a sudden. Her hair, which had once been full of bounce, seemed more brittle and there were extra lines around her eyes and mouth.

'I'm sorry,' she said eventually. 'It was a one-off.'

'Whose was the cash?' Alice asked. 'And the watch? And this time no more lies Jey.'

'A customer's,' Joy replied quietly, her gaze fixed to the parquet floor. 'Her bag was hanging on the back of the chair while I was waiting on her at dinner a few weeks ago. She'd left it open and I know how rich she is. I knew she wouldn't miss what I took, but to me it was life-changing. I mean that's how I treated you all to afternoon tea – we all benefited.'

Although Alice had suspected this was what had happened, hearing the truth out loud made her wince with horror. 'We've all benefited? We've all benefited from you being a thief? Is that really what you're trying to say?'

'No, sorry,' Joy said, backtracking immediately. 'I just meant that I didn't want to keep it all for me. I wanted you all to have a nice time as a thank you.'

'The invitation was nice enough! Us girls were happy to pay our way, you know that – we always have. You said you could get us a healthy staff discount and that was enough for us. You had no need to go thieving, Joy, but you've never had a need, you do it because you like it, because you think it makes you closer to Jimmy.'

There was a pause then as Joy seemed to think before she spoke. 'You're right,' she said in a small voice, 'I've just been finding it hard lately. I miss him. Dad wrote to me recently.'

Alice stared at her sister in surprise. She hadn't had a letter from their father in years and assumed that although Joy and her father were closer than she and Jimmy had ever been, their father had abandoned her too.

'What did he want?' Alice's tone was unrelenting.

'Not much. I wrote to him after I lost my job up Claridge's; he told me that I had natural talents and I could be Queen of South London if I wanted. He said I should forget the hotel work and concentrate on what I'm good at. I suppose his words stuck.'

Alice rolled her eyes in disgust. Their father had always known how to pull Joy's strings. 'Offer to introduce you to some people that could help you, did he?' she snapped, folding her arms as she stared knowingly at her sister. 'Then suggest he receive a finder's fee?'

Joy's face flushed. 'Something like that,' she mumbled. 'He was just trying to help me. I know you don't approve of him but I don't know why you always have to see only the bad in him.'

'Because he is bad through and through,' Alice hissed. 'When will you get it into your thick skull that our father is best left well alone? You'll never change. I *knew* I shouldn't have given you a second chance.'

Joy was on her feet now. 'Please don't throw me out. Please give me another chance,' she begged.

'It's just more lies,' Alice said, shaking her head. 'Look, I understand why you want to keep in touch with Jimmy – just because I want nothing more to do with him doesn't mean you shouldn't if that's what you want. But it's the lies I can't cope with, especially now I've got a son to think about.'

'But honestly, really I mean it this time. I was stupid – I regretted it the moment I did it. Please don't throw me out – I've nowhere else to go.' As Joy fell silent Alice looked at her sister and caught something in her eyes that immediately transported her back to their childhood. In an instant she remembered the way her father had suddenly disappeared and how she had been left to raise Joy all alone. That first night, Joy hadn't stopped sobbing; she had adored their father and wanted him to come back. Then on the second night, when Joy realised her father was never coming back, she had sobbed that she was going to end up all alone, that her mother was dead, their father had gone, and it had taken Alice several hours of promising that she wasn't going to leave as well before she could get Joy to calm down. With a sigh, Alice realised that she couldn't abandon her sister to fend for herself now any more than she could have done when she was a child. Her sister had her faults but Alice wasn't going to turn her back on her in the way their father had done. She would always do her best to set Joy on the right path, no matter what.

Chapter Twenty-One

The following morning Alice was surprised to find that Joy seemed to have found a new resolve. Not only had she set about making a pot of tea for everyone rather than just herself, but she had ironed Alice's work clothes and even swept the hearth.

The effect wasn't lost on Dot, who raised an eyebrow but knew better than to ask questions – and Alice knew better than to offer any answers. If Joy really had turned over a new leaf then it would take more than a pot of tea to prove it, but in the meantime, it was a treat to see she had made an effort.

Alice herself had a long day ahead of her. Not only did she have a full day on the shop floor but she also desperately needed to think of some ideas to showcase Liberty's commitment to utility clothing and fabric. She thought back to the recent article she had read in *Vogue*. The magazine had promoted this new movement, and declared it unfashionable to be fashionable, instead insisting everyone get behind the government's Make Do and Mend campaign.

She wondered if she could go to the Liberty library and find inspiration on one of her afternoons off. And if she couldn't, well, being surrounded by the history of the store she loved was a nice way to pass the time.

Arriving at work, Alice resolved to ask Mr Button or Flo when she might be granted access and made her way deftly towards fabrics. With the scent of the polished floorboards filling her nostrils, Alice breathed in deeply; she loved this time in the morning when it was just her, the staff and their beautiful shop. Only, nearing the department, she was alarmed to hear the sounds of raised voices. Pausing underneath the chandelier that hung from the atrium, she could make out the sounds of Mrs Claremont and Mary arguing about something.

She wondered if she ought to stay where she was or go straight to her department, but checking her watch she saw that the doors would be flung open to the customers in a matter of moments. If either Mrs Claremont or Mary were caught carrying on like that while customers were on the shop floor they would both be for the high jump and Alice knew she would have to intervene.

Hurrying towards fabrics she soon saw the culprits. Leaning over the cash register, red-cheeked and angry, the two women looked as if they were spoiling for a fight rather than an opportunity to help customers with patterns.

'All I'm saying is, there's a good way of dealing with people,' Mary was saying impatiently, 'and the way you spoke to my customer yesterday was not the best way of dealing with the situation.'

Mrs Claremont drew herself up to her full height. 'Your customer?' she replied indignantly. '*Your* customer? I am head of this department, Miss Holmes-Fotherington, and as such every customer is *my* customer. If I feel they need to be directed in a different fashion, it is my duty to do what you cannot.'

'Your duty!' Mary gasped loudly, her hands shaking with rage by her sides. 'Your duty will see us lose customers rather than keep them.'

Alice had heard enough. Rather than the argument petering out, Alice thought it looked as if it was about to become a full-scale brawl.

'Ladies,' she hissed. 'The shop is about to open. Whatever is all this about?'

At the sound of Alice's voice Mary and Mrs Claremont fell silent, instead continuing their row by looking daggers at one another.

'Miss Holmes-Fotherington here believes it's perfectly acceptable to devote hours, and I do mean hours, to one customer,' Mrs Claremont said eventually, her voice dangerously low.

Alice looked at the woman. It was hard to find any sympathy for Mrs Claremont's argument simply because she looked so furious. And the fact was Alice agreed with Mary entirely – indeed, would have done even if Mary weren't her friend. One of the things that made Liberty's so special was the fact that they devoted such time to their customers, encouraging them to browse, look around, enjoy the beauty of the wares on offer without hurrying them along. Mrs Claremont had worked at Liberty's long enough to know that, so why she was being so difficult with Mary?

'I think you've both said enough,' Alice snapped as she heard the sound of the doors opening. 'We have worked hard to build up a good reputation in this department and I won't have it ruined by you two because you don't know how to behave on the shop floor.'

'Excuse me, madam,' Mrs Claremont blurted, 'I rather think you've forgotten who you're talking to.'

'And I rather think you've forgotten where you are,' Alice replied coldly. 'Now enough, both of you. What on earth would Mr Button say, or indeed Mr Liberty himself if he could see you both now?'

With that Alice turned away from the women and focused her attention on what she was good at: serving. As the rest of the day passed, Alice found her nerves becoming increasingly frazzled. Mrs Claremont and Mary barely spoke to one another all day and the atmosphere wasn't lost on their usual customers, who didn't linger and chat as they usually did.

By closing time Alice was more than ready to go home, and felt that a night with a screaming Arthur, who was still teething, would be preferable to a day spent with her boss and her friend.

'We've had a busy day's takings, haven't we?' Alice said, doing her best to strike up a conversation between the warring women as she reached for the sales books and leafed through the figures.

'Indeed, Mrs Milwood,' Mrs Claremont replied in a pompous tone, 'notwithstanding the fact that a few of us have had our differences today.'

Mary glanced up from the packets of needles she was tidying and looked Mrs Claremont straight in the eye. 'I don't have any differences.'

'And I certainly don't,' Mrs Claremont said in a pompous tone. 'Because I've settled them – with Mr Button's help of course.'

Unable to help herself, Alice exchanged a nervous glance with Mary before she spoke. 'What do you mean?'

'I mean it's high time this department started performing as I wish,' Mrs Claremont said, plucking an imaginary piece of fluff from her jacket. 'I've spoken to Mr Button at great length this afternoon about my concerns. I've said that I feel the friendship within this group may be challenging the future of fabrics and that it should remain off the shop floor rather than on it.'

Mary took a step towards her boss. 'Mrs Claremont, you know that my prime concern has always been this department—'

'I know that,' Mrs Claremont snapped, cutting Mary off. 'But Mr Button and I agree it might be best for everyone if there were some changes. That's why, Miss Holmes-Fotherington, you will be working in carpets. It'll be good for you to experience life in other departments. You start tomorrow.'

Chapter Twenty-Two

The moment Alice stepped into the infamous Rainbow Corner one lunchtime the following week, she felt a flutter of excitement, all thoughts of the problems at her workplace temporarily forgotten. She had of course heard the rumours that the renowned GI Club on the corner of Shaftesbury Avenue, provided by the American Red Cross for servicemen serving far from home, was a den of iniquity designed to corrupt British society, but to Alice it seemed more like a fairy-tale.

Open twenty-four hours a day, not only was there a barber's, laundry and doughnut stand in the basement, there were also rooms where servicemen could enjoy an hour's sleep before heading back on the train to wherever they were being posted.

Glancing up at Jack, Alice saw him smile and clap his fellow soldiers on the back as they weaved their way through the crowds. As they walked over to the other side of the club, Alice looked around and saw people eating what looked to be giant sandwiches filled with some kind of meat and cheese, grease dribbling down their chins as they tucked in. The scent of fried food filled the air and Alice's stomach rumbled appreciatively – what was this place?

'Here we go.' Jack smiled, pushing her gently towards what looked like a giant piece of machinery.

She turned to him perplexed. 'What is this?'

Jack roared with laughter. 'Honey, this is a soda fountain and let me tell you it doesn't get better than this.'

Reaching for a glass he filled it to the brim with a fizzing brown liquid and handed it to her expectantly.

Peering at it in concern, Alice took a sniff. It smelled unexpectedly sweet and it looked revolting. Looking back at Jack she could see the excitement in his eyes as he encouraged her to take a sip.

Reluctantly Alice held the glass to her lips and swallowed. As the sparkling liquid travelled down her throat it was all she could do not to gag. It was so sweet, so sickly, and what was that taste?

'What is that?' she asked, grimacing.

'That is Coca-Cola,' he said triumphantly.

'And you drink this?' she asked incredulously.

'All the time.' He sighed. 'It's a real taste of home.'

Alice peered at the glass again, holding it aloft as if it contained all the mysteries of the world. 'I think I'd rather have a port and lemon.'

Jack took the glass from her and laughed again. 'You're a real tonic, Alice Milwood, you know that, right?'

'I could do with a gin and tonic after the morning I've had,' she muttered under her breath.

'That bad, hey?' Jack asked as he steered her towards a leather booth and invited her to take a seat.

Alice sighed and leaned back. When Jack had called in earlier to see if she was free at lunchtime she had been only too happy to say yes. It had been a week since Mary's move to carpets and to say the atmosphere was tense in the fabric department was an understatement.

Since Mary's departure Mrs Claremont had been even worse, bossing staff about and issuing demands such as even earlier start and finish times so they could all have extra staff training. It was a problem Alice was not only desperate to understand but desperate to solve too. She had been tempted to talk to Mr Button, but she knew that he had enough to cope with as they were shockingly under-staffed. She didn't want to trouble him unless she had to, but there seemed to be some new problem every day.

Only this morning Mrs Claremont had said that the way the department's files were stacked needed attention, and insisted that Alice, as the department's deputy, was the one to run a training session. That, coupled with the fact that Alice really missed her friend, made her working life a very miserable experience indeed.

'You could say that,' she sighed. 'It's just everything at work is changing, and not necessarily for the better.'

'You know, I think what you all need is a day out to ease your troubles.'

Alice looked at him blankly. 'How do you mean?'

'Well, it sounds like you girls are all having a tough time at the moment. What about a day out or something – take your mind off things?'

'We can't have a day out!' Alice spluttered. 'There's a war on, and I'm a mother for a start.'

'So?' Jack shrugged, gulping down a mouthful of Coke. 'That mean you can't have any fun?'

'Well, no,' Alice began, 'but it's not possible.'

'I don't see why not. What about a Sunday in some park that you know of? One not too far away? The weather's getting warmer – it might cheer you all up, and if Arthur's anything like Jack Junior, I bet he'd love the chance to play in the park.'

As he finished speaking, Alice glanced at her watch. 'I'd better be getting back, but thank you, Jack. I'll have a think about your idea.'

'I'll walk you out,' he replied as Alice got to her feet.

Alice slipped on her coat. 'If you're sure it's no trouble.'

'It's not a trouble, it's a pleasure,' he said warmly as they walked out of the club and on to the sunshine-filled street.

'What else do you have planned for the day?' she asked.

'I've got a meeting with my CO,' Jack replied as they strolled along Haymarket and up towards Soho. 'There's a chance I might be moving out of London.'

Alice stopped abruptly. The shock of his announcement rocked her. 'I thought you were here permanently?'

Jack shrugged. 'I thought so too. But it's possible they'll move me elsewhere. Nothing's definite yet,' he finished before his smile turned playful. 'Why, you gonna miss me?'

Alice felt a flush creep up her cheeks at being caught out. 'And the rest, Jack Capewell,' she said quickly, picking up the pace as she walked along the street. 'I'm too busy with a son and a job to miss you.'

'Well, I'll miss you,' he said, hurrying alongside her. 'Your friendship has become very important to me.'

At the confession Alice felt herself bristle. She couldn't have feelings for men who weren't her husband; it wasn't right. But then the thought of a world without Jack in it hit her as hard. Though she could never admit it, like Jack, their friendship had come to mean a lot to her.

Rounding the corner and reaching the top of Argyll Street, she was suddenly aware of Jack pulling her towards him. At the feel of his strong arms wrapped firmly around her, she allowed herself just for a second to breathe in the rich, heady scent of his cologne and rest her head on his shoulder. 'I mean it, Alice,' he whispered softly in her ear, just loudly enough for her to hear above the roar of London street life. 'I know I shouldn't say it, I know it's complicated, but you mean the world to me.'

The heartfelt honesty of his words shocked her. Jack shouldn't feel like this. And though she wanted to tell him that she felt the same way, she just couldn't. Reluctantly wrenching herself free from his embrace, she fixed her gaze on him. 'Where you come from it might be all right to accost women in the street,' she said half-teasingly, 'but in England it's not what we do.'

Jack took a step back and dipped his head by way of apology. 'Sorry, ma'am, forgot where I was for just a second there.'

'Make sure it doesn't happen again,' she said in a clipped tone but with a grin on her face so he knew she wasn't wholly serious.

'You can count on it,' he said. 'Will I see you and Arthur at the weekend?'

'Perhaps,' she replied, giving him another brilliant smile as she turned to walk back to work.

She had barely put one foot in front of the other when her heart sank at the sight of the woman before her. There, barely a couple of feet away, was Mrs Claremont, a smug smile on her face.

Alice felt herself growing hot at her boss's scrutiny. Just what exactly did she think she'd seen? Whatever it was, Alice wasn't about to give her superior the satisfaction of trying to find out. Instead, she carried on walking back towards the store and smiled as she passed her boss.

'Lovely day, isn't it,' she remarked.

'Lovelier for some than for others,' Mrs Claremont smirked. 'Does your husband know you're going around canoodling with strange GIs?'

It was as if a mist had descended as Alice felt a white-hot fury rise within. She rounded on her boss. 'And what business is it of yours?'

Mrs Claremont glared at Alice. 'If you're bringing this store into disrepute with your immoral behaviour, not to mention my department, then it's got everything to do with me.'

'How dare you,' Alice said, her voice dangerously quiet. 'I would never bring Liberty's reputation into question, you know how much I value my position here.'

'That's not the way it looked to me!'

Alice shook her head sadly. She had hoped that following their conversation in the café all those weeks ago they might somehow reach a new level of understanding. She had thought that it would be possible to show Mrs Claremont the real joy of being part of the Liberty family, but her new boss had shown no interest – and Alice was tired.

'When we had that chat in the café and you said you'd been left alone and had nobody to help you raise your children, I felt sorry for you. I thought it was a travesty, something nobody deserved, but now I can see why you ended up that way – you drove people away with your bitterness.'

As Alice finished, Mrs Claremont stood looking aghast, opening and closing her mouth like a fish, until she recovered her composure. 'You'll regret talking to me like that, Alice Milwood. I'll make sure you pay, make no mistake.'

Chapter Twenty-Three

Back at work, Alice continued with the rest of her afternoon's duties and tried to push all thoughts of her altercation with Mrs Claremont from her mind.

If she was honest Alice knew the woman would have every right to have her sacked or moved for insubordination. But then again, she thought, quietly seething as she served one of her regulars, she had been strongly provoked and she doubted there was a court in the land that wouldn't agree.

When she wasn't serving she turned her mind to Jack's news. As if she couldn't feel any worse at the idea of losing her job, the idea of losing her friend left her feeling broken. It surprised her how quickly Jack had become a part of her life and how much he meant to her. Although they had only been friends for about a month, Jack had fast become the first person she wanted to talk to each day and she enjoyed his company far more than she cared to admit. Deep down she knew her feelings for him weren't appropriate and she had a sneaking suspicion that was why she had overreacted to Mrs Claremont's attempts to rattle her.

Still, she thought with a sigh as she reached for a roll of fabric and began cutting it into a pattern ready for one of her customers to collect later, it had happened now. What would be would be, and in the meantime, there was still Jack's idea of a day out, which the more she came to think about it the more she thought it could be just the thing to restore all their spirits.

Glancing around the shop floor, she saw Mrs Claremont still hadn't returned from lunch and as they were quiet she decided to go and talk to Mr Button about taking a loan out against the Liberty holiday fund for the day trip. Perhaps, if she could persuade the store manager, they could travel somewhere for the day, or at the very least treat themselves to a lunch?

Walking up the wooden staircase she never tired of admiring, thanks to its uniquely carved panels and intricately designed woodwork, Alice make her way to the store manager's office.

Seeing Rose sitting at her old desk, Alice was surprised to find she felt nervous around her old friend. 'Hello, Rose, is Mr Button in?'

Rose frowned at the sound of Alice's voice. 'He is, but he's had Mrs Claremont in with him all afternoon. Their voices have been raised – and I've heard your name mentioned quite a bit. What have you done?'

'Said something I shouldn't.' Alice sighed as she stood over her friend's desk and fiddled with one of her paperclips.

'Yes, well, we've all done that, I suppose,' Rose replied, not unkindly. 'Do you want me to see if he'll see you?'

'No, that's all right,' Alice replied, her tone resigned. 'Unless Flo's about? I could talk to her.'

Rose grimaced. 'She's in the meeting too.'

At that Alice's face fell and she said nothing.

Rose offered her friend a ghost of a smile. 'I'm sure whatever it is isn't that bad.'

'I think it might be,' Alice whispered.

Before she could say anything else, the door to Mr Button's office opened and Mrs Claremont and Flo walked out.

At the sight of Alice, Mrs Claremont stood by the doorjamb and smirked, while Flo looked as if she wanted the ground to swallow her up whole.

'Alice, perhaps it's best if you, er ...' Her voice trailed off as Mr Button appeared behind them all, his hands clutching a file.

As soon as he saw Alice, Mr Button's face became grave. 'Mrs Milwood, I wonder if you could step into my office please?'

His tone brooked no argument and she followed him inside, ignoring the look of delight that passed across Mrs Claremont's face.

'I expect you know what this is about,' Mr Button said, sitting behind his desk but not inviting Alice to do the same.

Alice nodded her head sheepishly. 'Yes, sir. My insubordination.'

'Quite right,' Mr Button said, his tone softer now. 'What on earth were you thinking of? You are one of the most well-respected, well-liked members of staff we have. Why on earth did you speak to Mrs Claremont like that?'

Alice lifted her chin to look Mr Button directly in the eye. She regretted what she had done, but she wasn't sorry. 'Because she said some things that weren't very pleasant, sir. I lost my temper.'

Mr Button eyed her coldly. Steepling his hands together, he leaned across the table. 'You do realise that I've spent the past two hours listening to Mrs Claremont tear you to shreds. She wants you sacked. I had to draft Flo in to help calm things down.'

Alice said nothing for a moment. She could understand why Mrs Claremont would feel like that, but what was troubling her more was her department manager's attitude. After their talk in the café, she'd truly believed they might be able to bond over their struggles in life, but in actual fact it seemed that since then Mrs Claremont was going out of her way to make life more difficult, not just for Alice but the department as a whole – it was something Alice was no closer to understanding. Opening her mouth to say as much, she promptly closed it again. Something told her that Mr Button had heard enough moans and groans for one afternoon; what he needed most now was an apology.

'I'm sorry, sir,' Alice said sincerely. 'I accept whatever punishment you wish to send my way. It's no more than I deserve.'

'It *is* no more than you deserve,' Mr Button agreed, unclasping his fingers and leaning back in his chair. 'However, I also know that Mrs Claremont more than likely brought it on herself. Things are not shaping up as I wanted in fabrics.'

'Oh?' Alice looked at him hopefully.

'But you have walked right into her hands.' Mr Button gave an angry shake of his head. 'And now I am faced with a very difficult decision. However, Flo and I managed to have a private conversation after Mrs Claremont brought this to our attention and we have come up with a solution we both feel is fair.'

Alice's heart banged against her chest as loudly as a drum as she waited to find out her fate.

'Flo and I feel that rather than have you sacked, it's better you are demoted and become a sales assistant once more,' he said. 'Mrs Claremont has requested that her deputy in gifts moves across to fabrics and becomes her deputy in fabrics. As a result Jean Rushmore will now take over your role and you will, I'm afraid, receive a decrease in wages as a result.'

Alice's jaw fell in shock. To lose the job she adored, not to mention the salary that went with it, all because of one careless mistake, seemed an awful cross to bear. Yet at least she still had a job, and that in itself was something to be thankful for. She might not like it, but at least she would be able to feed and clothe her child and really that was the only thing that mattered.

'Thank you, sir,' she managed eventually. 'I'm sorry I let you and Flo down.'

Mr Button offered Alice a small smile. 'I'm sure that you had your reasons for your response to Mrs Claremont, but I have to set an example, Alice. I have to show that insubordination will not be tolerated and I cannot reward this kind of behaviour, no matter how well deserved your caustic tongue might have been.'

Nodding, Alice did her best to return Mr Button's smile. She knew he would have fought tooth and nail for her to remain in the department and she ought to be grateful.

'I appreciate that, sir. I'll make the best of the situation and I won't let you down again,' she said meekly.

'I know you won't.' His tone was kindly. 'And I also know that this will be difficult. I want you to know that you have my full support, Alice, along with the board of course. We all think you're a wonderful staff member, loyal, dedicated and hard-working. You know our customers better than they know themselves. I want to help you succeed, Alice, you just need to give me a reason to. Now, is there anything else?'

Thoughts of the money she had wanted to borrow for a day out flashed into her mind but she knew she could hardly ask for that now.

'No thank you, sir. I'll just get back to work,' she said sadly, preparing to return to the shop floor with her tail very much between her legs.

Chapter Twenty-Four

As the gentle breeze whipped around Alice's neck, she basked in the warmth of the June sunshine that beat down against her face and smiled. Jack had been right: a day out was just what the doctor ordered.

A few days had passed since Alice had been demoted, and although every day had been tough she was just grateful to have a job. It was this gratitude that helped Alice deal with the fact she now spent many of her shift hours in the stockroom rather than the shop floor. This not only meant the job itself was less interesting but that Alice lost out on vital commission.

When Dot had heard about what had happened she was furious and wiped the floor with Mr Button on her behalf. However, he told her much the same thing as he had told Alice, which was that he naturally hadn't wanted to demote Alice but his hands were tied. Dot was furious and told him that she wouldn't be going away for the weekend with him after all – before asking if she could borrow from the company's holiday fund for a loan to treat the girls to lunch in the park.

Apparently the roar of laughter that came from his office could be heard on the floor below in carpets, according to Mary, as he readily agreed to Dot's cheek.

Which was how on a fine Sunday afternoon in early June, Alice together with Flo, Mary, Rose, Dot and of course Arthur found themselves lying in Hampstead Heath, sunning themselves without a care in the world.

'Alice, is there any more tea in that flask?' Dot asked from her position down on the grass.

'It's blistering,' Mary squawked in amazement. 'Surely you'd rather have a nice cold drink instead?'

'Tea cools you down,' Dot replied, eyes firmly clamped shut. 'So less moaning and more supping, if you please.'

Alice chuckled and wordlessly poured her landlady out another cup. Dot propped herself up on her elbows to drink it and the look of pleasure on her face as the scorching liquid trickled down her throat was evident for all to see.

'I dunno how you can drink that on a day like this,' Flo wondered as she peered up at the cloudless blue sky, the warm sunshine making everything in the park seem as if it were bursting with colour.

'You've got to take your cuppa breaks when you can,' Dot muttered. 'And since Beatrice caught me with a brew in the stockroom the other day my tea breaks have been severely curtailed.'

Flo pulled a face. 'I thought we weren't talking about her today.'

'We're not. I think Dot just wanted to get her off her chest,' Mary said hurriedly before changing the subject. 'It's a shame Aggie couldn't make it today.'

'I know.' Flo sighed, the brim of her sunhat falling in front of her face. 'She had a rotten night's sleep again last night and generally just feels awful. I told her to get some rest.'

'Has she not been up the doctor's yet?' Dot enquired.

Flo shook her head. 'Says it's a waste of money, that there's nothing wrong with her that sleep won't cure.'

'Well, a decent night's kip is a cure-all, but she wants to get that indigestion looked at.' Dot frowned. 'She looked ever so pale at that afternoon tea the other week.'

'And she still seems so worried about your dad turning up,' Mary ventured. 'Surely she can see that it's very unlikely.'

Flo shrugged. 'You saw for yourself what she was like about it. She won't listen to reason.'

'Perhaps I'll pop in on her this week,' Dot offered. 'See if I can persuade her to visit the doc at the very least.'

Flo looked at the matriarch, her eyes filled with gratitude. 'Would you really? Oh, thank you! That would be a weight off.'

'My pleasure, darlin'.'

There was a silence then as all the girls revelled in the warmth of the sun. But it wasn't long before the conversation soon returned to Liberty's with Mary breaking the silence first.

'So, Dot, Alice said Mrs Claremont had rather a go at you yesterday. Is that true?'

Dot raised an eyebrow. 'She tried. Said I'd stacked the fabrics the wrong way but we've always made what we can of the Rayon section – even now with what little we have left. I would have put her in her place but, Mary, you've moaned so much about being in carpets I thought a tongue-lashing off our esteemed boss would be better than being amongst the dusty old rugs you keep grumbling about.'

'It's not that bad is it?' Flo asked, aghast.

Quickly, Mary shook her head, 'No, it's just I miss you girls and of course it's all so different.'

'Boring different?' Alice asked.

Mary grimaced. 'We get fewer customers, that's true. And of course I don't know quite so much about carpets as I do about fabrics. And, well, Mr Brown-Smythe is of course a marvel, I mean what he doesn't know about Persian history could be written on the back of a stamp—'

'But what you're saying is you'd rather watch paint dry than keep working in carpets,' Dot said, cutting Mary off and getting to the heart of the matter.

The girls burst out laughing as Mary nodded. 'Afraid so. I just feel I don't belong there.'

There was a pause then as the girls considered what Mary had said above the calls of children playing bat and ball behind them.

'I know what you mean,' said Flo eventually. 'I still don't think I should be doing Mrs Matravers' job.'

'Don't be silly,' Alice said in a surprisingly firm tone. 'You're doing very well.'

'Hardly! I nearly messed up a fabric order from Jenner's in Edinburgh the other day. Thankfully Mrs Claremont was able to put me straight, but if she hadn't I'd have really been in trouble.'

'Well, that's what staff are for,' Mary pointed out, not unreasonably, as she helped herself to a cup of tea from the flask. 'To help you out. You're deputy store manager, Flo, you can't possibly do everything.'

'I know,' she sighed, casting her gaze out across the lake, 'but it was a mistake I made with my old department. I mean, I could be forgiven for getting something wrong in jewellery but fabrics ...'

As her voice trailed off, Alice placed Arthur on the rug she had brought for him to lie on and leaned over to squeeze her friend's hand. 'I've said it before, and I'll say it again, you're doing brilliantly.'

'Exactly,' Mary offered. 'I mean Mr Button hasn't said anything, has he?'

'And we all know he would say if he had a problem, Flo,' Alice said knowingly.

'Sorry, girls, you're right. I'm worrying too much. I think I must be missing Neil.'

'Hardly surprising.' Alice replied. 'You're newly-weds; it's only natural to want to be together.'

'Quite right,' Rose agreed, running her fingers absent-mindedly across the grass. 'I had a letter from Tommy last week. He's still saying that he'll try again for compassionate leave.'

'Oh, Rose, let him,' Mary said almost pleadingly. 'He wants to be with you.'

'No!' Rose replied sharply. 'Me and Joy both agree—'

'Joy?' Alice interrupted.

Rose looked up defiantly. 'Joy has been very supportive lately. She says I have to learn how to cope on my own. That you never know what's around the corner.'

'Oh, like Joy would know,' Alice scoffed. 'She doesn't cope on her own. She always comes cap in hand to me.'

'I think you're being very unfair,' Rose said stiffly. 'Joy has really been trying lately. She had her reasons for stealing when she was younger, what with you being so poor.'

Alice couldn't help herself and let out a roar of laughter so loud that she woke Arthur. She spoke over his cry of disapproval. 'That what she told you? She also tell you how she used to go looting through people's belongings when they was blitzed out of their homes even though she had a full-time job 'n' all?'

'She never did that,' Rose said fiercely.

'And what would you know?' Alice replied almost jeeringly. 'I've known Joy a lot longer than you, darlin', I know what she's capable of.'

For a moment Alice wondered if Rose would flounce off in disgust, but instead she just stared at her. 'And I suppose you're such a brilliant judge of character,' she said quietly.

'What do you mean?' Alice asked.

'I mean I don't know why you're lecturing me about who I choose to mix with when you want to take a look in the mirror,' Rose finished almost triumphantly. 'Ask anyone – we all agree.'

Alice turned to the rest of her friends questioningly, only for them to look away, preferring to sit in uncomfortable silence. 'What is it you all agree about?' she asked, forcing her tone to remain even.

Taking a deep breath, Mary was the first to swing around and face her. 'What we mean is that we're not sure it's a good idea for you to be spending so much time with Jack.'

'That's right,' Flo put in kindly. 'Don't misunderstand me, we all think he's a lovely man, but it's not right that you're together so much.'

'We're not together so much,' Alice scoffed.

'You are, love,' Dot offered. 'You and Arthur are out with him every chance you get. Whether it's walks up Regent's Park or trips out to that club of his, it's like you've found Arthur another father when he's not had a chance to know his real dad.'

'And that's my fault?' Alice gasped incredulously.

'We know it's not your fault, Alice,' Mary ventured, getting up from her place on the rug to come and sit beside her friend. 'And we know there's nothing inappropriate between the two of you—'

'Nothing at all,' Flo cut in.

'We just don't want you to get hurt. I mean, he's already told you that his CO wants to send him elsewhere at some point,' Mary continued.

'You're already grieving for one lost fella,' Dot said softly, 'we'd hate to see you mourning two.'

The girls fell silent then as Alice looked at each of her friends in wonder. This was obviously something they had spent a great deal of time thinking about, and worse, discussing behind her back. The last thing she wanted was people gossiping about her, even if they were her friends.

'But we're just friends. We've been through so much together in such a short time. We both know the pain of raising children alone,' Alice said in a quiet voice. 'We understand each other.'

'But would Luke understand if he came back tomorrow?' Rose asked bluntly. 'Sorry, Alice, but you need to face up to the truth.'

Alice looked away. She had a funny feeling that Luke wouldn't understand, and no matter how much she told herself that the bond she and Jack shared was purely platonic, she wasn't sure Luke would see it that way. And if she was being honest with herself, she wasn't entirely sure that it was. The first person she thought about after Arthur was always Jack, and the first person she wanted to tell any news to was always Jack. The girls were right; she was beginning to see Jack as some sort of father and husband figure and she knew that wasn't right.

She sighed unhappily. 'I need to put an end to it, don't I?'

'You don't need to stop,' Mary said kindly. 'Perhaps just see a bit less of him.'

'That's right,' Dot offered. 'Treat him like I treat Edwin.'

At that the girls broke into unexpected laughter.

'You and Mr Button are courting,' Flo protested.

'I still don't see him all the time.' Dot sniffed. 'I show him who's boss. Take this weekend. I should have gone away with him, but, "Oh no," I said, "Edwin, I'm going out with the girls for the day."'

'True,' Flo agreed, 'but that was after he told you he had to work this weekend because we need to do a stocktake.'

Dot coloured. 'That may be true, but I still told him.'

Alice gave her landlady a playful nudge. 'I don't know why you can't just admit how smitten you are with him.

171

The world won't catch alight, you know, if you admit that you, Dorothy Hanson, née Banwell, have feelings.'

'You and Mr Button are made for each other. If he asks you to marry him you should say yes!' Mary cheered.

Dot bristled at the word marriage. 'I will not! We're happy as we are.'

Flo smiled. 'But you could be so much happier.'

'Just give in to it, Dot. It's hard enough to find happiness with this war on,' Mary coaxed.

'I am happy,' Dot exclaimed, sitting up and throwing the dregs of her tea across the grass. 'But I also know heartache, and I also know the danger of making poor decisions.' She turned to Alice and gave her a kind smile. 'Look, love, we all like Jack and we would none of us think there's something improper between you—'

'We know how loyal you are to Luke,' Mary added.

'Just think about what we've said. We don't want you hurt again, especially when there's not just you to think about but Arthur too,' Dot finished, getting to her feet. 'Now, who's joining me for a promenade down The Spanicurals?'

As Alice watched her landlady, flanked by Mary, Flo and Rose, she leaned over towards her son and planted a kiss on each of his cheeks – her friends had given her food for thought but Arthur would always come first.

The rest of the afternoon passed in a perfect blur as the friends took it in turns to stroll, nap, read and chatter all while the sun beat down.

But when the sun began to dip it was time to make their way home. Thankfully the journey back to the Elephant and Castle didn't take as long as anyone expected but it was clear Arthur had just about had enough by the little grumbling noises he made on the Tube all the way home.

'I'll take him straight up,' Alice said as she unlocked the door and peeled off her jacket.

'I'll get the kettle on,' Dot said, following Alice inside.

As Alice began to walk up the stairs towards her bedroom, the sound of a sharp knock at the front door made her and Dot jump.

'Who the hell's that? Dot exclaimed.

'Mr Button?' Alice suggested, as whoever it was rapped at the front door once more.

'It better not be,' Dot grumbled. 'I look a right state. You go, Alice, and let me sort myself out a minute.'

'What about Arthur?'

'I'll sort him.'

Rolling her eyes, Alice handed her son over to her landlady. Once the coast was clear, Alice pulled open the door and gasped in shock at the sight before her. There, standing on the step was a man who at first glance appeared to be several years older than her but – she saw as she peered closer – was actually about her own age.

Tall, with olive skin, he looked tired but happy and Alice could see he had nothing but the RAF uniform he stood up in.

Alice's hands flew to her mouth as she realised who it was. 'Luke?'

Nodding, he held his arms open and Alice fell straight into them, inhaling the scent of musk, citrus and something that was purely and undoubtedly her husband.

'Oh Alice,' he whispered in her ear, 'my love, I thought I'd never see you again.'

At the sound of her husband's heartfelt words, Alice tried to reply, only she couldn't. The lump in her throat was so large and Luke's arms were wrapped so tightly around her that she couldn't speak. She had missed him so much, and there had been times when she had feared he was dead, that she would never see him again. But now here he was. Her husband, living, breathing and very much by her side. It was all she had ever wanted. Transported by the moment, all she could do was stand on the doorstep and lose herself in the arms of the man she hadn't been sure she would ever see again.

Chapter Twenty-Five

The first thing Luke wanted to do once he had finally let go of his wife was meet his child. As Alice led him upstairs to the room she and Arthur shared, she couldn't stop looking at him, afraid that if she took her eyes off Luke for a second he would disappear.

It was obvious Luke felt the same way. The way he gripped Alice's hand, refusing to let go, along with the looks of love he kept shooting her way, made her melt inside. He had changed. His once handsome face was now gaunt and lined and he'd lost half his bodyweight; the once perfectly fitting blue RAF uniform, where he had proudly displayed his stripes, hung from him as if he were a skeleton. Then there was his right leg; he was visibly in pain, judging by the way he limped through the house, but at this moment Alice didn't have the heart to ask him what had happened. All she wanted to do was introduce him to their precious son and, judging by the smile on Luke's face, it was clear it was all he wanted too.

Tiptoeing into the room, Alice snapped on the bedside light and together they peered over the cot to find Arthur wide awake and happily gurgling away at the sight of his beloved mother.

'Hello, beautiful.' She bent down to scoop up his warm, tiny body. 'Arthur, this is your father.'

As Alice passed Arthur to Luke, she couldn't miss the wave of emotion that passed across his face. 'Arthur?' he whispered, before exchanging a look of wonder with Alice. 'Is this really him? This is our son?'

'This is him. He's all ours, Luke.'

Luke gasped, turning his attention back to his son and gently dropping a kiss on to his forehead. 'How did we make something so beautiful?'

At that Alice smiled, and even Arthur joined in with the joke, grinning excitedly up at the man holding him with such pride in his arms. 'I have no idea.'

'I just can't believe it,' Luke croaked. 'All the while I was away I couldn't stop thinking about you and our child. There were times I wondered if I would ever see you again, if we would ever be a family ...' There was a pause then while Luke collected himself, as if he wanted to get his words exactly right. 'This moment, this boy, us: it's all I've ever wanted, Alice. It's like a fairy-tale. And to think I've already missed so much ...'

As Luke's voice trailed off, Alice wrapped her arms around her husband and her son, revelling in the simple joy of being a family. 'Then let's make sure it never happens again,' she whispered in the half-light. 'Let's make sure we stay together forever.'

Luke said nothing, and simply buried his face in his wife's hair, the tears that soaked the top of her scalp telling Alice just how much he agreed.

An hour later and Luke had not only enjoyed a slice of Dot's seemingly never-ending supply of carrot cake but he had had a bath, and was dressed in some of his old clothes. As he sat at the kitchen table, next to Alice, holding his baby son in his arms, she could see he was as smitten as she was with their child.

'Are you feeling all right now, Luke?' Dot asked gently. 'Can we get you anything?'

Luke wrapped his one free hand around his wife and pulled Alice in closer, kissing the top of her head. 'I've got everything I need right here.'

'Can you tell us how you got here?' Alice asked dreamily, 'or is it all a bit too raw for you? I still can't believe you're here – that if I close my eyes you won't disappear.'

Luke smiled. 'I'm not going anywhere.'

'So what happened?' Dot pressed, clearly desperate for answers.

Handing his son back to Alice, Luke sat upright and took a deep breath. 'I was sent on a bombing raid near Boulogne with a group of other bombers. We were all lined up when the bomber next to ours dropped his load and ended up taking out our wing and engine.'

'Oh my days!' Dot gasped.

Alice shot her landlady a warning glance. 'Then what happened?'

'We knew our aircraft was in trouble,' Luke continued. 'So we bailed out, but we were fired at by the enemy as we landed. I was shot in the leg, but unlike everyone else in the plane I survived.'

'Were the Jerries close then?' Dot asked.

Luke nodded. 'I could see I was in a forest not far from Boulogne and I knew the enemy wouldn't be far away so I ran as fast as I could. The last thing I wanted was to end up a prisoner.'

Alice nodded. She had secretly read up on the plight of prisoners of war after she had received the letter from the Air Ministry alerting her to the fact Luke was missing and discovered horror stories of men who were worked to death or starved – the Jerries were cruel, everyone knew that, and Alice could quite understand why Luke would want to try and make his escape, no matter how much it hurt him to do so.

'I didn't have any supplies so I walked for five days without food until I found a farmer,' Luke continued matter-of-factly. 'I was so happy to see another human being I almost wept with relief, but instead I got out my RAF-issue phrase book and asked him for help.'

'Then what?' Dot demanded. 'If you made it to safety why did it take you so long to get back?'

'Good question,' Luke replied, rewarding Dot with the long, lazy smile that made Alice's heart sing. 'Luckily for me the farmer was a member of the French Resistance and so he sheltered me, but we had to wait for someone to help me get across the English Channel. I stayed with the farmer – Pierre – for months, helping on the land, all the while dreaming of home. I began to wonder if I would ever get back at all, but eventually Pierre told me that he could smuggle me aboard a gunboat bound for Dartmouth, along with several other men who had escaped capture.'

'Anything could have happened,' Alice said, horrified at the thought of her precious husband in so much danger. 'You must have been terrified.'

'I was, yes,' Luke admitted. 'But I knew it was my only chance of escape. The gunboat was so crowded; we were all packed in like sardines. And it was frightening being at sea at the dead of night. But I couldn't stay on the farm any longer.'

'Did they know about the Resistance's operation then?' Dot asked, her face a picture of alarm.

Luke nodded slowly; Alice couldn't help notice how his hands trembled under the table as he answered Dot's question. 'They knew that the Resistance smuggled Allied servicemen overseas, but they didn't know the routes they used. What was hard was seeing the Channel every day, and knowing that I was separated from my wife and my child by just a few miles of water. I wondered what the hell you were thinking, but didn't dare risk writing in case my letter fell into enemy hands or got the farmer and any of the people trying to help me in trouble ...'

As Luke trailed off, Alice wrapped her arms around her husband, the tears falling freely now she knew he was safe. 'I can't believe you made it home.'

'There were times I wondered if I ever would,' Luke murmured as he leaned towards her and planted yet another kiss into her hair.

'So where did you get the RAF togs from?' Dot asked, gesturing to the uniform Luke was wearing.

'The Resistance had arranged for our boat to be met by someone from the Air Ministry and we were taken to the closest RAF base in Hampshire where we bathed and were given clean uniforms.'

'And did someone examine that leg?' Alice asked gently.

Luke looked down at his right leg, which was stretched out stiffly in front of him. 'Pierre did a wonderful job of getting the bullet out but because it was left for a few days, doctors think I may have suffered nerve damage.'

'Will it get better?' she asked.

'I hope so.' Luke smiled weakly. 'I'm signed off at the moment though, and the RAF say it could be a while before I'm fit for duty, so if you'll have me, I could use a place to stay.'

Alice looked at him incredulously. She had been terrified of asking how long he was back for, but now the answer had surprised her. 'You mean you're here for a while?'

Luke nodded. 'Yes, until I'm declared fit, which could be weeks.'

A broad smile lit up Dot's face as she got up to clear the tea things. 'You stay here as long as you like, darlin'. You two take my bedroom; it's the only one with a proper-sized double. Makes more sense for a family to be in it.'

'Don't be silly, Dot,' Alice gasped. 'You can't go giving up your room for us.'

'Nonsense, darlin',' Dot said firmly. 'Your Luke's home, and that's the best news many of us have had in weeks. We should celebrate.'

'Oh, I don't know,' Alice said doubtfully. 'Luke needs time to recuperate.'

'Don't be daft.' Luke grinned. 'Dot's right: we're all together again now and a family. I want to tell the world.'

Chapter Twenty-Six

News of Luke's return had flown around Liberty's like wildfire. When Alice came back to work first thing on Friday morning – Mr Button had kindly given her a few days off – she was inundated with questions.

The only one who wasn't impressed at Alice's news was Mrs Claremont, who had simply told her that now her husband was back Alice would be able to work that bit harder as she had even more support at home. At any other time, her boss's words might have upset her, but Alice was too overjoyed with life to worry about anything Mrs Claremont could say. For now all she could think about was that her husband was home, safe and sound, and together with Arthur the three of them would be a family, at least for a little while.

Just then a tap on her shoulder startled her and she jumped back in surprise to find the new deputy fabric manager, Jean Rushmore, looking down at her. Alice got to her feet. 'Everything all right?'

'Oh, um, yes, it's fine, Mrs Milwood,' Jean replied nervously. 'I just wanted to come and introduce myself properly, only we've never had the chance really until now.'

Alice found herself smiling at the dark-haired younger girl as she offered her a hand to shake. Alice knew from the routine gossip that Jean was a quiet but dependable staff member, and Alice also knew it wasn't Jean's fault that she had taken her job. 'I'm very pleased to meet you properly. If there's anything I can help you with, just let me know.'

Jean's face immediately broke into a relieved smile. 'I'm so glad you said that, Mrs Milwood. I was worried what you would think of me.'

'There's nothing for you to worry about,' Alice said kindly. 'None of this is your fault and I would hate for you to feel bad. Tell me, I know I've seen you about the store but I don't know much about you. Have you worked at Liberty's long?'

'Two years.' Jean smiled, her cat-like hazel eyes lighting up her heart-shaped face. 'I got taken on by Mrs Claremont on my twenty-first birthday, when the store was crying out for staff after war broke out. It was the best present of my life.'

Alice returned the grin. She could well understand how Jean felt; Liberty's got under your skin. 'You must have learned a lot by now.'

'I don't know about that,' Jean replied, with a hint of a West Country accent. 'I know everything Mrs Claremont has taught me.'

'Then I'm sure she's told you everything you need to know,' Alice replied diplomatically. 'Are you from London? Only I thought I could detect an accent.'

'Cornwall.' Jean smiled. 'I thought I'd done my best to dampen down my accent. Mrs Claremont said customers wouldn't like it.'

Alice pursed her lips and said nothing. She could only imagine just what the new fabric manager had been telling her. 'You've a lovely accent,' she insisted. 'It's nice to hear something a bit different. What brought you up this way? Family, was it?'

Jean shook her head. 'No, me and my sister just wanted to see the big city so we moved up. Anyway, I'd better get back to my paperwork or Mrs C. will have my guts for garters.'

With that Jean beat a hasty retreat and Alice couldn't help wondering what on earth had really brought her all the way to London. After all, people didn't move great distances like that without good reason. Still, she thought, getting to her feet, who didn't have skeletons in their closet? She certainly did, and she wouldn't want them getting out. Although Percy Wilmington had known of Alice's heritage, he had assured her that he was the only one at Liberty's aside from the family that did know, and that was only because he had grown up just outside Bermondsey. Nobody else would think twice, he had assured her, and he had been proved right, as nobody ever mentioned Alice's past – something she was grateful for. So lost was she in thought that it took her a moment to recognise Jack beaming down at her and when she did, she almost jumped two feet high in the air. 'Oh my days!' she gasped. 'You scared me witless.'

Jack chuckled. 'So sorry, ma'am. Are you OK?'

'I'm fine,' Alice breathed, still clutching her chest with a hand full of needle packets. 'What are you doing here anyway? I thought Fridays were spent training in Surrey?'

'They are, but I've the afternoon off and thought I'd see if you'd like to come see a movie with me when you get off work.'

A flicker of confusion passed across Alice's face at the term 'movie'. 'Oh, you mean a film.'

'Yes, exactly,' Jack said, rolling his eyes. 'So anyways, you wanna see something with me? Or shall we do something with Arthur instead?'

Alice bit her lip. With all the joy surrounding Luke's return, as dreadful as it sounded, she had forgotten about Jack.

Glancing around the busy shop floor, she beckoned him over to the window where it was a bit quieter. 'I've got something to tell you,' she said hesitantly.

'Go on,' Jack replied, his voice even.

Alice looked at the floor. She knew she had to tell him, he was her friend, he would be thrilled for her – of course he would – but she also knew that Luke's return would change things between them. 'The thing is … the thing is Luke's come back,' she said quickly.

'Alice, that's wonderful,' he gasped, looking for all the world as though he meant it. 'I'm so happy for you guys. Did he say what had happened to him?'

'He was shot down by the Jerries. Then the Resistance helped him across the Channel, but it took a while, you know, and of course he's injured.'

'You must be delighted to have him home,' Jack cried. But his smile didn't quite reach his eyes.

Alice nodded enthusiastically. 'I'm thrilled. Arthur's got his dad home.'

'And you guys can be a family again!'

'Until he goes back to the RAF.'

Jack frowned. 'He's talking about that already? I thought you said he was injured?'

'He is. But he won't rest until he's back on active duty.'

'Well, that may never happen.'

'But it might,' Alice snapped, before her face softened. The last thing she wanted was to fall out with Jack. 'I'm sorry, I didn't mean to snap, it's just been a lot to think about.'

'Of course.' Jack nodded in understanding as he gazed intently into her eyes. 'I guess that means you can't come to the movies with me tonight?'

Alice shook her head, her eyes no longer able to meet his.

'Or any night?' he said, his tone full of knowing.

She gave another small shake of her head. 'I'm sorry,' she whispered.

Jack reached for one of her hands and clasped it with both of his strong ones. At the feel of his flesh against hers she let out a gasp of surprise; his touch still had the power to take her breath away. 'Don't be sorry,' he whispered, bending down to kiss her lightly on the cheek. 'I'm happy for you. I'll see you around.'

With that he turned on his heel and walked out of the store without a backwards glance, leaving Alice feeling emptier than she ever had before.

Once Liberty's shut up shop for the night, Alice made her way to the pleating room where Dot had set everything up for a small party for the Liberty girls and Joy. Wandering through the maze of corridors and across the little bridge that connected Kingly Street with East India House, Alice remembered how she and the girls had spent several nights here before Arthur was born, sewing and gossiping. It seemed a long time ago.

Still, she thought, pushing open the door and finding almost all of their guests had already arrived, that was all in the past. Now Luke was home, it was time to look forwards not back.

Watching her husband now, chinking his pint glass against Mr Button's as he held tightly on to his son, Alice felt a surge of warmth. This was what she had wanted for so long; now it was finally here and it was time to celebrate.

Mr Button grinned at Luke. 'I remember when I came home from the last war. It took me a while to find my feet. I imagine it will be the same for you too, Luke.'

'Yes, although I haven't got much time to find my feet,' Luke replied. 'I need to be on the mend as soon as possible. I've got to get back on active service.'

Alice was just about to say something when someone else beat her to it. 'Oh, not this again,' Joy sighed as she sidled up next to Alice. 'Luke, honestly, you're like a broken bleedin' record. Just enjoy a bit of time off, would you?'

At the sight of her sister, Luke's face hardened. 'And what the hell would you know about it? You're frightened to death of a bit of hard graft – always have been, always will be.'

'Luke, that's enough,' Alice cautioned. 'Joy was only joking, weren't you?'

''Course. Have a day off, will you, Luke?' With that Joy rolled her eyes, knocked her ginger ale back in one and went off in search of another drink.

'Sorry,' Luke sighed. 'I shouldn't have spoken to her like that. I'll apologise later. There's just something about Joy that brings out the worst in me; we've never got on.'

Dot smiled. 'Don't worry about it, darlin', she has that effect on all of us.'

'True,' Alice ventured. 'Though she has been trying lately.'

'That she has,' Dot agreed, raising an eyebrow and earning herself a round of laughter in the process.

Just then the sight of Mary, Rose and Flo walking into the pleating room lifted Alice's spirits and she waved them over. They hadn't had a chance to meet Luke yet and she was looking forward to showing him off.

'Luke,' Alice beamed as the girls drew closer. 'I'd like you to meet my very good friends: Mary, Flo and Rose.'

'Very pleased to meet you.' Luke shook each of their hands. 'Am I right in thinking one of you helped Alice deliver my son?'

Mary put her hand up shyly. 'That was me, though I must say I couldn't have done it without Mr Button – he was absolutely marvellous.'

'Now, now,' Mr Button said, waving away the compliment.

'Nonsense,' Flo offered loyally. 'You were both a wonder that day.'

'Yes, I'd have been no help at all,' Rose said bluntly. 'What with me not being able to see a thing.'

There was an awkward pause then as everyone glanced at Rose and wondered how best to respond. Fortunately Dot stepped in and raised her glass. 'I think we can all agree everyone was wonderful, and everyone' – she nudged Rose good-naturedly – 'has been very helpful to Alice over the last few months.'

Alice nodded eagerly. 'I'd have been lost without you all.'

'Which is why I'd like to raise a toast to all you Liberty girls.' Luke grinned. 'Knowing Alice here had you all to help take care of her made being apart so much easier. I knew you would never let her down.'

'And we never will either,' Dot added, chinking her glass against the others. 'Here's to Luke's homecoming and to us Liberty girls.'

'To Luke and Liberty's,' everyone chorused.

Alice basked in the delight of being surrounded by so many of their friends, but as her eyes drank in the love and laughter in the room, she realised that there was one very dear friend missing: Jack.

Chapter Twenty-Seven

When Alice woke the following morning she turned over to find Arthur sleeping on one side of the bed and Luke fast asleep on the other. She couldn't help smiling at the scene, before she wordlessly got dressed in the dark, not daring to raise the blackout blinds in case she woke her husband. Scooping up her still-sleeping son, she held her close to him as she padded out of the room and down the stairs.

As Alice approached the kitchen she heard the sound of voices and she was surprised to find Flo and Dot sitting at the table. Armed with a pot of tea and heads bent low, they clearly hadn't heard Alice enter and she wondered if she ought to tiptoe away. However, Arthur had other ideas and opened his mouth to let the world know he was finally awake.

'Morning, darlin',' said Dot smiling wanly. 'You three sleep all right?'

'We did – even Arthur was out like a light.' Alice moved hesitantly towards the table. 'Flo, are you all right? I don't want to intrude.'

Flo lifted her head, her red-rimmed eyes as obvious as the fact she had barely slept all night. 'You're not,' she croaked. 'I came to see you both actually, but Dot said to let you sleep as you'd been getting precious little lately.'

Grimacing, all Alice could do was shrug. It was the truth and the price you paid for being a mum. 'What is it, love? What's going on?'

'It's Aggie,' Flo said tonelessly. 'She's dead.'

Alice's jaw dropped open in shock as she turned to Dot for clarification.

'It's true, love,' Dot murmured, her eyes pooling uncharacteristically with tears. 'Flo says she had a heart attack last night. She'd gone to see *Blithe Spirit* – you know that Noël Coward thing over at St James's Theatre? I encouraged her to have a night out when I popped in on her the other day. She was looking forward to it, reckoned it would give her a lift.'

'Oh Flo,' Alice exclaimed, 'I'm so sorry. How did you find out?'

'Her mate Rita told me,' Flo said monotonously. 'She tried to find me last night to let me know but of course I was out myself. Poor Aggie, she was all alone. I should have been there for her.'

'Come on now,' Dot said gruffly as tears began to pour like rivers down Flo's cheeks. 'Aggie was not all alone, she had Rita with her for a start, and she'd hardly have expected you to have been there all the time, you did enough for her as it was.'

'Aggie just hadn't been herself since Dad turned up on my wedding day. She was so nervous all the time, though she did her best to keep it hidden. I can't help wondering what would have happened if he hadn't turned up out of the blue like that. Maybe, if Aggie's nerves hadn't been so frayed, she would still be here now,' Flo said, as if Dot hadn't spoken.

'Flo, love, you can't think like that,' Alice said kindly. 'That's the last thing Aggie would have wanted.'

Flo dipped her head. 'I just keep thinking what if. What if I hadn't gone out? What if I'd let Dad give me away after all? What if I'd spent more time at home rather than spending every hour I could at work, worrying about my new job and getting everything right? Then I might have seen something was wrong with her.'

At that, Flo's shoulders heaved as great sobs coursed through her body and Alice looked at Dot in despair. She could tell there was nothing either one of them could say that would make her feel better, but one thing was clear, Flo was not fit to go into work today and nor was she fit to be alone.

'Do you mind holding Arthur while I get washed and dressed?' Alice asked Dot as she handed her landlady her son. 'I'll go with Flo and help her.'

Flo waved her hands at Alice. 'You don't have to do that. I'll be fine. I've got to finalise an order for Beath's over in Canterbury today.'

Dot snorted in disgust as she cradled the baby. 'Well, you can forget that, lady. You're going straight home. I'll clear it with Edwin and someone else can sort the order out.'

'And I'm coming to help you,' Alice said firmly. 'We can sort everything out together.'

'But who'll look after Arthur for the rest of the day?' Dot asked. 'You can't take a baby up to Islington and start dealing with hospitals and paperwork, never mind what else.'

'Luke,' Alice replied firmly. 'I'm sure he won't mind.'

'Sure he won't mind what?' Luke said gruffly as he walked through the door. Hair mussed up and day-old stubble covering his face, he looked like a little boy lost, Alice thought as she watched him sink down into the hard kitchen chair and devour in almost one gulp the tea that Dot poured out for him.

'Taking care of Arthur.' Alice smiled, perching on the chair next to his. The morning sunshine streamed into the kitchen now, giving Luke's hair a golden glow. 'Just for a couple of hours. Flo's aunt has just passed away and she needs some help.'

Luke nodded at Flo. 'I'm very sorry for your loss, love,' he said, before turning to Alice. 'But I don't see why that means I have to look after Arthur.'

'Well, it's just like Dot said,' Alice said, feeling uncomfortable under Luke's glare. 'I'll be too busy to look after Arthur properly, and as you're here I thought you wouldn't mind.'

There was a pause then as Luke took another gulp of tea. 'Taking care of kids is woman's work, Alice. It's bad enough I can't fight for my country at the moment, never mind being insulted further by being asked to take on a woman's job as well,' he snapped, slamming his cup down so hard the dregs of brown liquid sloshed on to the table. 'For once in your life, Alice, will you think about someone besides yourself? Life does not revolve around you and Liberty's.'

Alice jumped at the severity of his words. 'Luke, I'm sorry,' she began, 'I didn't mean to upset you. Of course I'll look after Arthur – I'm sorry.'

But Luke was already on his feet. 'Forget it,' he grumbled, reaching for the paper and helping himself to the last of the tea from the pot. 'I'm going back to bed.'

With that Luke limped back up the stairs and left Alice feeling stupid. 'I'm so sorry,' she said to the girls, her cheeks flushed with embarrassment. 'You shouldn't have had to see that, and it's my fault; I don't know what I was thinking.'

Dot reached an arm around Alice's shoulders. 'Don't be silly. He's probably just tired.'

'It was a nice idea,' Flo sniffed, reaching behind her for the coat she had left on the back of her chair. 'But I'd better get back; there's so much to sort out.'

'Nonsense,' Alice said fiercely. 'You've hardly slept; you're not fit to go anywhere. Why don't you have forty winks on the settee, and when Joy gets up I'll ask her to look after Arthur for a couple of hours.'

'That a good idea?' Dot asked. 'Joy and Rose were out later than us last night.'

A small sigh escaped Alice's lips; she had forgotten that. 'In that case,' she said in a tone that brooked no argument, 'I'll bring Arthur with us. But first, Flo, you need to rest.'

As Dot and Flo stared helplessly at her, Alice refused to back down. Her friend needed her help and she wasn't about to shy away from that. Once it was clear that there was to be no disagreement, she went upstairs to tell Luke.

Gently pushing open the door, she felt a stab of relief to see her husband propped up in bed holding the paper.

'Just wanted to let you know I'll be taking Arthur with me up to north London today,' she said, perching on the end of the bed.

'Good,' Luke muttered as he continued to read.

'I'll try not to be too late back,' she continued, trying to catch his eye, but Luke's face was glued to the headlines.

'So I'll see you later,' she said.

'Don't forget Chris is coming tonight so we'll need tea before we go out to the pub?'

A frown crossed Alice's face. 'Your brother Chris? But I thought he wasn't coming at all? I mean he didn't arrive for your party last night.'

Her voice trailed off as Luke put the paper down and met her gaze with disdain. 'I told you last night, Alice, that Chris sent a telegram saying he wouldn't be able to make it to the party but that he would come the following day.'

For a moment Alice felt stricken. She was sure she would have remembered if Luke had told her something so important, yet she couldn't recall him mentioning anything at all. She was about to say as much when the warning glance in Luke's eyes made it clear it was better she kept quiet.

'Yes, of course you did.' Alice smiled in what she hoped was a reassuring fashion. 'Do you know what time he'll be here?'

Luke scratched his chin. 'About five, I think. He's staying at the bed and breakfast on Walworth Road so at least you'll not have a bed to make up for him.'

'No, of course,' Alice said, wondering where on earth she would have put Chris had he wanted a bed. 'I'll be back in time. I think we've got enough in to make cheese jacket potatoes.'

'That'll be great, love,' Luke said, picking up his paper. 'Thanks.'

Getting up to leave him to it, she suddenly stopped. 'What are you doing today, darlin'?'

'Just a few errands,' he said over the top of his paper. 'The medical officer is coming over next week and I want to talk to him about my rehabilitation, so I'll be practising my exercise drills trying to get the leg stronger.'

'Anything I can help you with?' Alice offered.

Luke shook his head, his eyes suddenly brimming with excitement as he put his paper down. 'That's very nice of you but it's me that's got to put in all the work. The sooner I'm mended the sooner I can get out of here and back to fighting Hitler.'

Alice nodded in understanding. 'All right then, see you later.'

As she walked out of the door and back down the stairs towards Arthur and her friends it suddenly crossed her mind that it was only when Luke talked about going back to the RAF that he really seemed to come alive.

Chapter Twenty-Eight

By the time Alice returned from helping her friend in Islington she was shattered. Despite the relatively late start, she, Flo and a thankfully sleepy Arthur had endured a long and busy day organising Aggie's affairs. Not for the first time she found herself marvelling at the strength of her friend.

Like Alice, Flo had grown up with a good-for-nothing criminal for a father, and, also like Alice, she was determined her own future wouldn't be damaged because of his ways. The only tears Flo had shed had been the ones around Dot and Alice's kitchen table, and it seemed that after her nap on the settee her resolve had returned.

Together the pair had sorted, signed, collected and written to all of Flo's relatives to let them know of Aggie's demise. As if sensing the gravity of the situation, Arthur had been on his best behaviour, not even uttering a gurgle, never mind a scream, something Alice was eternally grateful for.

Now, as she opened the front door and wheeled her son in through to the hallway, all she wanted to do was sit down in the parlour with a very large cup of tea.

'Alice, love, is that you?' Luke's voice called. 'Look who's here.'

With a stab of regret, Alice remembered Chris was coming and she was now going to have to make supper for them all. Removing Arthur from his pram she plastered on her best smile as she walked into the parlour.

'Chris! Hello!' she exclaimed, allowing him to envelop her and her son in a hug.

Just like Luke, Chris was tall with olive skin, but he was stockier than his older brother and his face was less angular, giving him something of a softer appearance.

'Alice, my darlin', how are you, sweetheart?' He beamed, about to squeeze her harder before Arthur's cries alerted him to the fact he was hugging two people not one. 'And this here's my nephew. My God, Alice, he's a beaut – looks nothing like you, Luke my boy!'

'Get away with you.' Luke chuckled good-naturedly, waving away his brother's insults with his half-drunk beer bottle. 'I thought we'd get fish and chips in tonight – Chris's paying.'

'Yes, thought it would save you the bother of cooking, especially when this great lazy lummox has been sitting on his backside all day.' Chris prodded his brother cheekily in the ribs, earning himself a swipe around the head.

Alice couldn't help laughing. She hadn't seen Chris for about two years – his work as a parish vicar near Swansea kept him busy – and she had forgotten how much she enjoyed his easy manner.

'How's the B and B?' she asked over the casual insults.

'Fine, thank you! 'Course, I'd rather have stayed here with Luke so I could keep an eye on him.'

Luke arched an eyebrow. 'And you could have done if Alice's sister wasn't here.'

'Now, now, Luke,' Dot called warningly as she bustled in from the hallway. 'We'll have none of that. Family's family.'

Chris took a sip of his beer and nodded before he spoke. 'Quite right. Dot, it's a pleasure to see you again.'

'And you. Always said you had better manners than that Luke.'

At that everyone roared with laughter. 'Told you.' Chris chuckled, hands in his pockets.

'How was work today?' Alice asked. 'Was Mr Button all right about Flo?'

Dot frowned as she noticed the half-empty beer bottle in Luke's hand but didn't comment on it. ''Course he was. You know Edwin, soft as snow. Said she shouldn't rush back. Old Beatrice has volunteered herself, hasn't she, to help out in the office and the silly fool's only said yes.'

A look of alarm passed over Alice's face as she digested this piece of news. 'Typical Beatrice, getting her feet under the table.'

'I'd be lying if I said the same thought hadn't crossed my own mind. Honestly, Liberty's just don't seem the same these days,' Dot sighed as she sank into the remaining chair.

Alice nodded. 'I know. Flo was saying the same thing.'

'I thought you loved your job?' Chris looked at her quizzically.

'Yes, you seemed to last night – surrounded by all your Liberty family,' Luke said in a tone she couldn't quite read.

'I do love it,' Alice replied, choosing to ignore her husband for the moment. 'But we've got a new boss, and she's made some changes. The new girl she's brought in, Jean, knows next to nothing about fabrics, though I'll confess she does seem nice enough. As for Mary, she's miserable as sin in carpets.'

'Cor, it all goes on up Liberty's, doesn't it?' Chris marvelled.

'And don't we know it.' Luke said, laughing along with his brother.

Dot nodded. 'You're not wrong there. Anyway, I've invited Mary for supper; she'll be here in a minute. I think she needed cheering up; she's not exactly having an easy time of it at Rose's neither, what with Rose's mood swings.'

'Mood swings?' Alice quizzed.

'You must have noticed. I swear the happiest I see that girl these days is when she's out with your Joy. Anyway, I'll give you a hand with the supper, Alice.'

Chris got to his feet. 'Actually I said I'd treat us all up the chipper.'

'Oooh, lovely.' Dot beamed. 'You can come again. Alice, go and give him a hand, why don't you? The poor lad'll never carry all that on his own.'

'You sure you don't mind?' Luke asked as Alice stood up.

Chris shook his head. ''Course not. As long as you don't mind me stealing Alice for a bit.'

'Take her.' Luke grinned, taking another sip of his beer.

Out on Bell Street, Alice and Chris sauntered down the road together, a warm summer evening breeze blowing between them. The longer evenings were a real treat for them all. With the nightly air-raid sirens seemingly a thing of the past, kids played out on the street, couples walked hand in hand through the parks and everyone seemed to be a good deal happier, despite the fact that more and more was becoming rationed. The cruellest cut back had been soap rationing back in February, but recently Joy had come home from work with a face like thunder. She had spouted on about a new law that said all hotel and restaurant meals mustn't cost any more than five shillings per customer and couldn't be any more than three courses. While Alice balked at the fact that anyone could eat more than one course during this time of austerity, it seemed that many of Mayfair House's customers were furious and wrongly taking it out on the staff.

'Penny for them,' Chris said, bringing Alice back to the here and now.

She grinned up at him. 'I was just thinking how nice the weather is now – gives us a bit of cheer with this war.'

'I was thinking only the same thing last week. I'd spent all day writing a sermon and it was lovely to come out of the vicarage into bright sunshine.'

His positivity was refreshing, especially when everyone at work seemed so miserable. 'How's Barbara?'

Chris's face lit up. Barbara and he had got married at the same time as she and Luke, and it was clear to everyone who knew the couple how they worshipped one another. 'She's very well. Sends her love, of course, and is sorry she couldn't come down as well, but the journey's a bit much for the kids.'

Alice understood only too well. Coping with one small baby was enough of a challenge, never mind two young boys under the age of five. 'It was good of you to come down from Wales on your own. I know Luke's thrilled to have you here.'

'I am too.' Chris beamed as they turned the corner into Walworth Road. 'I thought he was dead – I won't lie to you. When I got that telegram to say he was alive, well, it was like all my Christmases had come at once. I couldn't believe it.'

'Neither could I. I still can't. For so long now, I've been used to it being just me and Arthur; now Luke's here too and we're a family – a proper family, I mean.'

Chris nodded. 'Behaving himself though, is he?'

'How do you mean?' Alice bristled at the question.

'I don't mean nothing by it. Just that he doesn't seem quite his usual self. Bit grumpy, bit on edge. But then I suppose his leg's giving him a lot of gyp.'

'That and he can't wait to get back to the RAF,' Alice said grimly.

Chris stopped in the middle of the street. 'You can't be serious. He's been missing for goodness knows how long and now he wants to get back to fighting again?'

'Wants to defeat the Jerries single-handed.'

There was a silence as Chris digested this. 'Bloody stupid boy,' he seethed. 'He should be grateful he's not only back in one piece but that he's got you and a lovely baby to come back to.'

'True. But I suppose it's natural for him to want to get back to doing what he loves – and of course he does love his country too.'

'We all do,' Chris said proudly as they arrived at the fish and chip shop. 'But we all try and make time to appreciate what we have as well. I'll try and have a word with him while I'm here, Alice. Knock a bit of sense into him.'

Chapter Twenty-Nine

Flo was noticeably absent from Liberty's some ten days later when Mr Button called an emergency staff briefing before the store opened. Everyone from all the departments gathered under the chandelier in the atrium and Alice struggled to hide her disgust as she watched Mrs Claremont stand proudly alongside Mr Button, as his right-hand woman.

'Now, as you know, we are proud to have many special friends here at Liberty's,' Mr Button began, rocking backwards and forwards on his heels as he caught everyone's attention. 'And one of our very special friends is Princess Valentina.'

At the mention of the Russian princess's name the crowd let out a little gasp of excitement. The princess was a firm favourite amongst the staff, particularly as she had single-handedly saved their Christmas party last year. Rose nudged Alice excitedly in the ribs, and the two grinned delightedly at Mary.

'She will be here after lunch today,' Mr Button said, cutting through the noise. 'And I want you to ensure she receives the finest of Liberty welcomes.'

With that Mr Button walked back up the stairs, closely followed by Mrs Claremont whispering relentlessly in his ear.

'Well, I wasn't expecting that,' Mary said as everyone returned to their departments. 'Flo will be sorry she's not here.'

'So will Joy.' Rose sighed. 'She loves Russian royalty.'

Alice snorted in exasperation. She was getting fed up of the way Rose and Joy were seemingly joined at the hip. 'Why would Joy be here? She doesn't work at Liberty's.'

'I'm only saying it would have been nice for her,' Rose replied sulkily. 'She deserves a treat after all she's been through.'

Alice glanced at Mary, who looked as blank as she did. 'What do you mean "all she's been through"?' Alice asked warily.

'Just that she's had an old friend get in touch, that's all,' Rose replied. 'She says she's from her past and she's a bit worried.'

'Did she say who it was?' Alice demanded.

Rose coloured at Alice's tone. 'I think she said her name was Shirley.'

Shock coursed through Alice's veins at the sound of a name she hadn't heard in a long time. Shirley Allbright was trouble with a capital T and an old pal of their father's who had taken Joy under her shoplifting wing. Now it seemed that after eighteen months the woman was not only out of prison but determined to drag Joy back down to her level.

'Thanks, Rose,' Alice said eventually, aware that both she and Mary were gawping at her. 'I'll talk to her, give her a bit of support.'

'I think you should,' Rose said stiffly. 'She's finding it hard enough with Luke at home now.'

'Rose!' Mary scolded. 'That's a dreadful thing to say. Luke's only been back five minutes and already you're helping Joy find fault with him.'

Alice held her hand up and smiled at Mary. 'That's enough. Thanks, Mary, but it's no secret Joy and Luke have never seen eye to eye. I hoped that things would be different now; it certainly seems to me Luke's done nothing but be civil to Joy but she obviously sees it differently.'

Alice's words seemed to make Rose squirm. 'Look, I'm not saying Joy's a saint,' she began, 'I just think she puts on this tough front and actually she's quite fragile inside.'

'Aren't we all,' Mary muttered.

'She's coming along to the last of the first-aid nights tonight,' Rose said, ignoring Mary's barb. 'Maybe talk to her then?'

'All right,' Alice ventured, seeing Mrs Claremont re-appear on the stairs. 'Leave it with me, Rose.'

Back in her department she spent much of the morning ensuring that the princess's preferred fabrics were all out on display for her to admire, even bringing up the few scraps they kept back in the stockroom that were too small for anyone to do anything with.

By the time she'd finished stowing them under the counter she saw the princess was on her way towards the department. Watching her walk in that stately way of hers, black hair swinging over her shoulders, Alice found she was almost dizzy with excitement as Mrs Claremont rushed to greet her.

'What can we show you?' she asked, practically falling over herself to curtsey before the princess.

Princess Valentina smiled coolly at Mrs Claremont and looked around. 'Where is Miss Wilson? She runs the fabric department, yes?'

Mrs Claremont shook her head. 'I'm afraid not any longer. I'm in charge now.'

A flicker of confusion passed across the princess's face. 'I see. But what about Mrs Milwood behind the counter?'

At the mention of her name, Alice beamed at the princess, and was about to speak, only for Mrs Claremont to interrupt her. 'Not any longer. Now, can I just say that I'm not sure what we are going to show you as most of our fabric is utility?'

'Please,' the princess snorted as she brushed past Mrs Claremont and Jean. 'Alice here knows I love to look at all the fabrics. Now, Mrs Milwood, what have you got for me?'

Alice smiled. 'Mrs Claremont is right, we don't have much but I did take the liberty of bringing up some of this lovely 1930s floral teal print.'

Mrs Claremont hissed in her ear. 'A princess doesn't want to see the old tat we have to sell on ration.'

At the use of the word 'tat' it was all Alice could do not to gasp in shock. 'Of course I would,' Princess Valentina said firmly. 'Mrs Milwood knows I adore all prints.'

With that Alice marched her over to the latest rolls of fabric and admired them together, with Valentina itching to buy something suitable for a siren suit.

After an hour the princess bade Alice a fond farewell. 'Thank you, my dear, a pleasure as always.'

'You're more than welcome, your highness,' Alice said warmly. 'It's always such a treat for us when you visit.'

The princess paused then, as if she was wondering if she ought to speak. 'Alice, what has happened to this department?' she said finally once Mrs Claremont was out of earshot. 'Where is your other friend, Miss Holmes-Fotherington? And why is this awful woman in charge? Things are not the same!'

'I know,' Alice said softly, keen to try and calm Valentina down. 'I'm so sorry you found us this way.'

The princess reached down to clasp Alice's hands. 'No, it is I who am sorry for you, Alice. Your precious fabric department has lost its soul.'

That night there was standing room only for Rose's final first-aid training and it was just the tonic Alice needed after Valentina's visit. Customers, people from neighbouring businesses, as well as residents who had apparently travelled across London were ready to learn how to save a life and Alice was thrilled for her friend. With a turnout this big, Alice had high hopes it might give Rose a much needed boost in confidence and convince her that the first-aid nights needed to be a regular thing.

Watching her now up on the stage chatting to the Red Cross volunteer who was organising the talk, Alice felt pleased that, even though Rose was not herself at the moment, something was going right.

Rose clapped her hands together for attention; she welcomed everyone to the event and then introduced the guest speaker. As Alice continued to listen she became aware of someone taking a seat beside her. Turning to look at the latecomer, she realised it was Joy.

Alice's calm evaporated at the sight of her sister as she remembered what Rose had told her earlier. She knew she couldn't put off talking to Joy any longer. 'Can I have a word with you?' she whispered.

Joy jumped in surprise. 'Now? I've only just arrived.'

'It's important,' Alice hissed, getting to her feet.

The sisters made their way out to the staff entrance with Joy grumbling under her breath. The sunshine was still gloriously warm, but Alice felt a shiver run down her spine at the thought of what she was going to have to say to Joy.

'Is it true?' she demanded, getting straight to the point. 'Has Shirley Allbright been in touch with you?'

'How do you know about that?'

'Rose told me. She was worried about you. Is it true?' Alice snapped.

'Yes, it's true,' Joy replied almost smugly. 'So what?'

Alice couldn't believe what she was hearing. '"So what"?' she hissed, grabbing her little sister by the shoulder and shaking her. '*So what?* That old cow nearly landed you in prison, you stupid girl. What the hell are you doing hanging about with her again?'

Joy's nostrils flared with rage at Alice's outburst. 'It's none of your business. I can be friends with who I like.'

'Not Shirley Allbright you can't, she's nothing but trouble,' Alice thundered, and then gasped in realisation. 'That was why you were nicking them purses and that watch at work, wasn't it? You wanted to impress Shirley.'

Joy's cheeks flamed with colour at being caught out. 'It wasn't like that.'

'Then what was it like?' Alice asked, hands on hips, this time refusing to be fobbed off.

'She's just got out of prison. Needed some help getting back on her feet,' Joy said matter-of-factly. 'I've only done the odd job for her.'

'The odd job?' Alice echoed in disbelief.

'That's right,' Joy replied, oblivious to her sister's tone. 'And now I've told her that it's over. I won't be doing any more for her.'

Alice shook her head in disbelief. After all the progress her sister had made, she hated to think of Joy returning to her old ways. 'Sweetheart,' she tried again. 'This isn't going to get Dad to love you any more, you know. Don't think that he's going to hear from Shirley how well you're still doing at thieving – it's not going to make him come back. You have to understand that.'

Joy screwed her face up with anger. 'Alice, it's not like that, I keep telling you. I know Dad's long gone – he's not interested in either of us, never has been. It's just about respect, ain't it? Shirley's an old mate of Dad's. We may not like her but, well, she's down on her luck and you have to look out for your own – you know all about that, you'd do anything for your Liberty girls.'

'No, Joy, I would never do anything like that for my girls,' Alice said impatiently. 'And more importantly they would never ask me to either. Look, aside from the incident with the purse you've been doing so well and it's been a pleasure to see you turn your life around. Surely you don't want to go back to your old ways?'

'It's about loyalty, Alice. I have changed, I am different, I've just got to help Shirley out.'

Alice let out a sigh of despair. 'I warned you that I wouldn't tolerate you getting up to your old tricks again. Any more funny business, I said, and you'd be out on your ear.'

Panic crossed Joy's face. 'Now come on, Alleycat, don't be like that. I'm just doing a mate a favour.'

The use of her childhood nickname wasn't enough to make her change her mind. 'And I'm doing my son a favour. I don't want him having the same upbringing we did, Joy.' Alice thundered. I don't want to worry about what trouble will be brought home to my door every night and I don't want my child worrying about that either. Now, I'm sorry, but if you're knocking about with Shirley Allbright you'll have to go. I mean it this time: I want you out of the house first thing in the morning.'

Chapter Thirty

'What the hell's going on?' Dot cried, bursting into the kitchen.

'You might well ask,' Alice replied furiously, as she continued to gather armfuls of clothes and scoop them into a crate.

'I am asking,' the landlady said, her tone unyielding, as she leaned against the door frame and watched Alice continue to sift and pack. 'It's just gone six in the morning and the place looks like the Blitz.'

'I'm not telling anyone anything,' Joy said, her tone calm, from her position at the kitchen table. With her hands in her lap and a steaming cup of tea beside her, she didn't look the least bit bothered by what her sister was doing.

Sensing she wasn't going to get an answer, Dot walked across the room and took the crate from Alice's hands. 'Well, someone had better tell me soon because I'm not being denied my beauty sleep for no good reason,' she hissed as the sound of heavy footsteps echoed on the stairs. 'And by the sounds of it I'm not the only one that's been woken up at the crack of dawn.'

Sure enough, Luke ventured into the kitchen, his eyes struggling to adjust to the harsh kitchen light that illuminated the otherwise blacked-out room. 'Alice, what are you doing?' he asked, bleary-eyed.

'What should have been done weeks ago,' said Alice, continuing to put things in the crate. 'Kicking Joy out.'

Dot looked at each of the sisters in wide-eyed astonishment. 'What do you mean? What's happened?'

'I'd rather not say,' Alice said, shooting her sister a warning look. 'But what I will say is she was warned and she ignored me.'

Joy rolled her eyes. 'Not this again. Alice, I've told you I'm not having anything more to do with Shirley.'

'Not Shirley Allbright?' Luke sighed, helping himself to a cup of tea from the pot that stood on the table. 'Come on, Joy, I thought you'd left her behind a long time ago.'

'And what would you know about it?' Joy snapped. 'Shirley's had a hard life, not that you'd understand that. You've always looked down your nose at me and Alice, coming from fancy Scottish stock.'

Luke scratched his head as he tried to wake up. 'Joy, I don't know where you think I come from – my parents are hardly laird and lady of the manor. I was raised in a tenement in Aberdeen but I still knew better than to knock about with the Shirley Allbrights of this world.'

'Luke's right,' Dot said, pulling out a chair. 'She's always been a bloody pain in the 'arris. I remember when she nicked all the washing off me line one summer.'

'Oh come on, Dot, she was only having a laugh,' Joy protested.

'Only having a laugh? I caught the cheeky cow trying to sell my bloomers down the Lane the next day!'

'And that's exactly my point,' Alice said, drumming her forefinger on the table for emphasis. 'You were warned I wouldn't tolerate your old tricks and I meant what I said last night: I want you out.'

Joy ran a hand through her messed-up curls. 'And where am I supposed to go?'

'Work? You told me a lot of the girls live in; well, you can do the same.'

'Come on.' Joy scoffed. 'You can't expect me to live in a tiny hotel room. And besides, who will help you out with Arthur? I've been babysitting a lot for you these days. You won't have me on tap like you have been.'

There was silence then as Alice digested what Joy had just said. She made a good point; she had been a godsend of late with Arthur and best of all her son seemed to like his aunt. Still, she thought, shaking her head, it was obvious Joy had not turned over a new leaf and she couldn't risk the poor influence she would have over her son.

Suddenly Luke's voice broke the silence. 'I'll take care of him when needs be.'

Alice looked at her husband in grateful surprise. 'You will?'

'Of course.' Luke shrugged. 'He is my son and, like you, I don't want him exposed to bad behaviour,' he continued, looking pointedly at Joy. 'I know what I said before about caring for children being woman's work, but, well, we're all making sacrifices with this war, aren't we? I don't mind taking my turn.'

'Oh Luke,' Alice cried, pausing from her mission to gather up Joy's belongings to throw her arms around her husband's neck. 'That's the sweetest thing you've ever said.'

'Get away,' he laughed, pushing Alice from him. 'I'm just doing what's right, that's all. And now there really is no reason for your sister to stay, especially when she can't follow our rules while she's under our roof.'

With that Joy got to her feet and leered at Luke. 'You've always hated me! I bet my sister kicking me out the door is like Christmas come early for you.'

'No, Joy,' Luke said, meeting her angry gaze. 'I get no pleasure from this whatsoever, but I agree with my wife: until you can behave you'll have to go.'

Fuming, Joy turned to Dot, who was watching the action agog. 'And what do you say about all this? This is actually *your* house, not this pair's.'

Helping herself to a cup of tea, Dot's eyes didn't leave Joy's. 'Don't try and bring me into this, darlin',' she said evenly. 'I'm not stupid enough to get in the middle. For what it's worth though, I think Alice is right. You was warned when you got here what'd happen if you brought any trouble to the door, and I know Shirley Allbright's nothing but trouble. Now, I don't know what's gone on and, to be honest, I don't want to know, but I will say that if you're hanging about with her then chances are you're not going about behaving like a nun yourself, so I think we'll all be better off if you sling your hook.'

'What if I said I was sorry?' Joy tried again, her voice pleading. 'Please, Alice, please help me?'

'It's no good, Joy,' Alice said firmly as she glanced quickly at Luke. His small nod of encouragement spurred her on. 'I can't risk you bringing trouble here again.'

With that Joy sprang like a cat from her chair and scooped up the crate Alice had been throwing stuff into. 'I'd sooner starve on the street than come to you for anything.'

As she flounced out of the room, Alice sank into the chair feeling weary. 'Well, that went well,' she said, smiling weakly at Luke.

He wrapped his arms around her and pulled her in close. 'You've done the right thing, love. I'm proud of you; I know it's not easy.'

Alice squeezed him tight. 'Thanks for standing up for me.'

'Anytime,' Luke said softly. 'And I know I haven't been the easiest fella in the world to live with since I got back but I meant what I said. I will help out with Arthur more. I'm not too proud to take care of my own son.'

With the words she had longed to hear out in the open, Alice felt warm tears of relief trickle down her face. The last few months had been overwhelming and now she had the love and support she longed for. Was it down to Chris? she wondered. Had he managed to have the word with Luke that he promised?

'You know what else isn't easy?' she said eventually as she wiped away the last of her tears.

She felt Luke shake his head against her shoulder. 'Going to a funeral after all this. Aggie's being buried today and I've volunteered us both up there before the ceremony starts to help with the wake.'

Luke kissed the top of her head. 'It's a good job I love you, Alice Milwood.'

Later that afternoon, Alice along with Mary, Flo, Rose and Dot found themselves standing in Aggie's front room around a piano, just as they had six months earlier for Flo's wedding. Today, however, the girls were there to pay their respects to Agatha Taylor.

The ceremony and burial had gone without a hitch thanks to Flo's tireless organisation, but it was clear that the event had taken its toll. The dark shadows under her eyes revealed Flo hadn't been sleeping as well as she should, while her fingernails were chewed to the quick.

Now the wake was in full swing, and although Flo wanted to do right by her aunt, Alice could also see that she just wanted to crawl into bed and sleep. Without saying a word, she pushed past the throngs of people and found just what she was looking for: a large bottle of unopened port.

Uncorking the bottle, she gave it a good sniff to check it hadn't been tampered with and then poured five generous measures. Laying them on a tea tray she found by the old butler sink, Alice carried the medicine back into the front room and gestured for each of the girls to take a glass.

'Here's to Aggie,' Alice said, holding her glass for a toast.

'And all who sailed in her.' Flo giggled while the others looked at her blankly. 'Sorry,' she said sheepishly, 'it was just something daft Aggie always used to say.'

Dot linked her arm through Flo's and gave her a comforting squeeze. 'There's nothing as queer as folk, and Aggie was as queer and wonderful as they came.'

'Awfully kind as well,' Mary pointed out. 'She would do anything for anyone. Didn't you say, Flo, she was helping out with the WVS and the Civil Defence League?'

Flo nodded. 'And she recently applied to work on the buses.'

'She put us all to shame,' Mary said wistfully. 'I've signed up to join the Women's Auxiliary Police Corps in my spare time. David's furious.'

Dot peered at Mary over her glasses. 'Why? That's a very brave thing to do.'

'He says it's stupid. That we're getting married and all I should be thinking about is creating a family for us. Honestly, since his sister was imprisoned it's all he can talk about.'

'I suppose it's understandable,' Rose reasoned. 'I mean, he must feel all alone now and want to create that with you. After all, family is so important, isn't it, Alice?'

The barb in Rose's tone wasn't lost on Alice. 'Yes it is, Rose, it's extremely important. That's why I like to ensure my loved ones are not in any danger.'

'Come on now, you two,' Dot snapped. 'This isn't the time or the place to get into what's gone on with Joy. Rose, I appreciate Joy is your friend but this wasn't easy for Alice.'

Rose let out a hollow laugh. 'You girls always stick up for one another and it's always me left out in the cold. I should have known it would be no different now.'

'What are you talking about, Rose?' Flo asked in bewilderment. 'We've always tried to be there for you.'

'I have to say she's right, darlin',' Dot put in. 'I know you're hurting over your eyesight, and believe me I understand why, but don't you think all this moodiness has to stop?'

'Moody?' Rose gasped. 'Is that what you think I am? Moody?'

'Well, perhaps not moody,' Dot began, doing her best to backtrack.

'Oh no, Dot,' Rose fired, 'call a spade a shovel, why don't you? Well, I'm sorry for being a burden. Trust me, I won't be troubling you so much in the future. Not only have I called time on the first-aid nights, I've also cut my hours down. I'm only going to be working one day a week now so luckily for you lot you'll now be seeing less of me and my moods.'

Leaving the girls speechless, Rose turned away and stalked across to the other side of the room.

'Would you Adam and Eve it?' Dot said finally. 'What on earth is up with that girl?'

Flo shook her head. 'I don't know, but it seems as though she's getting worse not better.'

'It's as though anything we say upsets her,' Alice wailed. 'I just don't know how to help her.'

'I don't myself,' Dot muttered sadly, 'but I know we need to try.'

Just then, a young man approached Flo. Alice knew he was called Eddie, and had employed Aggie to sing in the pub.

'Will you come and sing us a song, love?' he asked.

Flo smiled but shook her head. 'No thanks, Eddie. Aggie was the singer not me.'

'But you've a lovely voice,' Eddie persisted. 'Aggie always said so. Come on, for her sake.'

'Go on, love,' Dot coaxed. 'We'll all join in.'

'Yes, that's a lovely idea. Why don't you sing "We'll Meet Again"? That's a nice one,' Mary suggested.

'All right,' Flo said, colouring with embarrassment. She followed Eddie over to the piano and everyone gave a little cheer.

'Thank you,' she said to the crowd. 'This was one of Aggie's favourites. All join in if you can.'

As Eddie struck up the familiar melody, Flo's voice wafted out across the room pure and true. It struck Alice that nobody was joining in because Flo's voice was so melodic that she could quite possibly give Vera Lynn a run for her money. By the time Flo had finished there was barely a dry eye in the house and Alice was astonished to find her own cheeks were wet with tears. Dabbing them with the back of her sleeve, she told herself she was weeping because it was Aggie's funeral. Yet, deep down, she knew that when Flo had been singing about seeing one another again, one sunshine-filled day, thoughts of Jack had entered her mind.

As the last notes of the song faded away, Alice felt wretched as she realised she was hoping that the two of them hadn't had their last day in the sun.

Chapter Thirty-One

Despite the warm June weather, Alice found herself feeling bleak the day after Aggie's funeral. Not only was it nearly time to say goodbye to Chris, who was returning to his parish and of course his family in Wales after two weeks away from them, but the news made for horrifying reading. The papers were full of reports that gas was being used to kill Jews the Germans had sent east, and the country was in a state of concern over what Hitler would do next.

'The man is pure evil,' Luke said fiercely as he jabbed his forefinger at the newspaper, with the latest headline revealing more German atrocities. 'We have to stop him. This isn't right.'

'None of it's right,' Dot said sadly. 'I mean, have you ever heard anything like it? Gas to kill folk for being Jewish.'

'And that's why I've got to get back out there,' Luke said. 'I've got to talk to the medical officer and get him to let me start flying again.'

Alice wrinkled her nose in concern as she took a bite of toast. 'But love, your medical officer said last week you might have a way to go yet with your leg. Why not focus on the exercises you've been given – you'll get back to war soon enough. '

Luke glowered at his wife. 'Do you really think it's that simple? That I can just do my exercises and forget about the others who are still fighting?' He paused for a moment to take a deep breath before he spoke again. 'Alice, men I served with, were friends with, have died. Why can't you understand that I need to get back out there? It's where I belong.'

'I'm sorry,' she whispered, feeling chastised. She was about to say something else, to try and find another way to reach him, when the sound of someone rapping at the door caught her attention. 'I'll go,' she said.

Opening the door her face broke into a broad smile at the sight of Chris.

Chris nodded as he walked into the house. 'Certainly is me. Tomorrow I'll be back with the family.'

'But we'll still be seeing you later to say goodbye?'

'Of course.' Chris squeezed her shoulder. 'I'm not going anywhere without a send-off.'

'Hello, mate,' Luke said brightly, all trace of his anger gone completely. 'What shall we do today?'

Chris nodded his thanks as Dot poured him a cup of tea. 'How about we go for a walk up Regent's Park and then call in the King's Head for a pint – for old times' sake?'

'Good idea,' Luke replied. 'I'll just get my coat.'

Alice felt a surge of alarm. 'But you said you'd look after Arthur this morning,' she said. 'I've got work and Dot's going up the WVS.'

Luke shrugged his shoulders. 'Sorry, love.'

'But you said you'd help,' Alice replied impatiently, earning herself a look of reproach from Luke.

'And I said I can't,' he hissed.

'Come on, Luke,' Chris said, laying a hand on his brother's shoulder. 'I help out with the kids all the time; it's the way of things now.'

'That might be so,' Luke said, whirling round to face his brother, his face contorted with anger. 'But I'll look after him when I can, not when it suits my wife. I might have a gammy leg and not be fit enough to serve my country, but I'm still head of this family and what I say goes.'

Turning back to Alice he shoved his hands in his pockets and stood up straight. 'I'll be back later.'

With that he pushed past his brother, who mouthed an apologetic sorry before joining Luke. As the front door slammed shut, Alice whirled around in despair. 'Am I going mad? He did say when Joy got her marching orders that he'd help out, didn't he? He said he'd look after Arthur.'

Dot gave a curt nod of her head as she began to clear away the breakfast things. 'That he did, love. But I tell you now, there's no sense arguing with a fella when they get like this. You're better off waiting 'til later when he's a bit calmer.'

'But what the hell am I supposed to do in the meantime?' Alice wailed. 'I can't miss work again, I'm walking a thin line as it is now I've been demoted.'

'That might not be the case for too long, mind,' Dot said. 'Edwin heard all about what Princess Valentina said to you. She's one of our best customers and old Beatrice was dragged over hot coals.'

'I didn't know that,' Alice gasped in surprise. 'What did he say?'

Dot grinned and tapped her nose. 'Can't tell you. Loose lips and all that, even if Edwin is unofficially my other half. But what I will say is that you ain't the only one on a tight rope. Now, how about I ask Doris next door if she'll cover me down the WVS this morning and then I can take Arthur for you.'

Relief flooded through Alice. 'Would you really do that for me?'

''Course I would. There may be a war on, but half the battles in this country are waged on the home front with us women first in line for duty. Leave him with me, love, and get yourself ready.'

Alice didn't need telling twice. She got ready at break-neck speed, kissed Dot and then Arthur goodbye, and hurried to the Tube.

It seemed fate was on her side for just as she stepped on to the platform a train thundered alongside her and she boarded immediately.

As the train sped away, she leaned her head against the window and started to think about her life. It felt as though she was surrounded by problems and, much as she hated to admit it, Luke was one of the biggest. How funny, she thought, that just a few weeks ago she spent every waking moment dreaming of his return. But now he was here, there were times she wished he wasn't. She hated to admit it but he had changed so much since he had been away at war and his moods were so erratic. More often than not she felt afraid to open her mouth as she fretted over how Luke might react. Look at how he had responded that morning when she had asked him to look after his own son while she went out to work – something he had promised to start doing.

She wasn't wholly unsympathetic, she could appreciate that it must be difficult for men returning from battle to adjust, especially when they were injured or had been held captive. But did that mean they had to be so difficult all the time? And why couldn't they understand that those who had been left behind had endured just as tough a time, albeit in a different way? You only had to look at the bombed-out buildings that surrounded them to see that. Alice hated herself for thinking it but a part of her wished she could go back in time to when it was just her, Dot and Arthur – life had been so simple then.

As the Tube pulled into Oxford Circus and she joined the throng of workers spilling out of the Underground into bright sunshine, Alice's heart felt heavy. From the moment she met Luke she had known that he believed love should be like a fairy-tale. He always said his parents had never had a cross word and insisted he didn't believe in rows either. Before war broke out and Luke left for the RAF they had enjoyed an idyllic relationship – Alice could count on one hand the number of cross words they had exchanged over the years. But since Luke had returned, it felt as if they were locked in a private battle of their own, and Alice was at her wits' end trying to work out how to fix it.

Feeling helpless, Alice pushed thoughts of her marriage from her mind. It seemed too big a problem to deal with at that moment, but was it possible she could do something to change the shape of her working life? Walking down the street she thought about Valentina's words. The princess had been so disappointed with the department, and not because of the lack of fabric on offer but because of the way it was run. What if there was some way to incentivise Mrs Claremont? Alice knew she didn't lust after the fabric the way she, Flo, Dot and Mary used to do, but there were other things that Mrs Claremont enjoyed, one of which was success. Could she persuade her boss to radiate enthusiasm in the way the department needed and in turn have customers cooing over fabric just as they used to? She remembered her plan to go to the Liberty library for inspiration: she had to try and come up with a winning idea to revolutionise the department's fortunes and boost the sales of utility print and clothing and so far she was stumped.

But later that morning, as she listened to Mrs Claremont and Jean talk about sales targets, she felt less than inspired.

'Nobody knows more than I do,' Mrs Claremont began, 'that it's not easy in these times of war to encourage people to part with their hard-earned money and rations, but we do need to make an effort, girls.'

'I've been thinking, Mrs Claremont,' Jean said nervously as she reached for the guest book that had been left on the counter. 'The Liberty customer is different. They want beauty, a taste of the good life, and that's what Liberty's brings them.'

Alice glanced at her in surprise. She may not know about sewing, Alice realised, but she did seem to understand the Liberty customer in a way Mrs Claremont did not, even though she was only young. Clearly Jean was determined.

'What about it?' Mrs Claremont barked. 'We sell utility fabric now. That is not beautiful to customers, it's functional.'

Yet despite the rebuke in their boss's tone, Jean refused to be put off. 'I was thinking that there must be a way to try and tap into that.'

Mrs Claremont rolled her eyes. 'How on earth do you suggest we do that? To me it's simple: we push them to ensure they spend all of their coupons here and encourage them to tell their friends to do the same.'

Alice thought for a moment, the kernel of an idea forming in her mind. 'What if we showed the women just how inspirational utility fabric can be?' she began. 'What if we offered a prize for the most creative outfit made with Liberty fabric? You know, a leather handbag or something that we have plenty of in stock for the woman that can create the most attractive outfit?'

Mrs Claremont shot Alice a withering stare. 'I have never heard of anything so ridiculous, Mrs Milwood. How would customers make their utility outfits attractive? We may be selling our own prints but customers still can't have pleats or turn-ups or even a collar that's any more than half an inch. How would they make it attractive?'

'By encouraging them to use what's already in their wardrobes,' Alice said triumphantly. 'They may not be able to put pleats into a skirt, but once they've made a utility-pattern dress with one of our utility prints they can accessorise it with a bag, a hat, scarf or shoes already in their own collection. They'll tell their friends about it and we'll pick up more traffic through the doors that way, which will feed into other departments such as hats which aren't reliant on ration coupons.'

'Oh my days! That's brilliant,' squawked Jean, gazing at Alice in wonder.

'We could even get on the back of the Make Do and Mend campaign,' Alice continued, warming to her theme. 'There are hundreds of groups springing up around the country teaching women how to sew; we could run a group like that here – a sort of community stitching night.'

Jean clapped her hands together excitedly. 'Everyone will be talking about the store. What do you think, Mrs Claremont?'

The fabric manager walked back around the counter and shoved the guest book under the cash register. 'I think that this idea is cheap and has no place in Liberty's. Mrs Milwood, it strikes me that you need more time for reflection – the stockroom needs tidying again.'

Alice opened her mouth to say something, but a sudden look of anguish that flashed across her boss's features stopped her. Was all this bull and bluster a front? If so, why?

Feeling wrong-footed, Alice wordlessly made her way to the basement. She was tempted to argue the point, but thought better of it. The moment she opened her mouth she should have known Mrs Claremont would find fault.

Flicking on the light switch, she began to sort through the latest delivery. Oddly, though, Alice found she wasn't put off by the fact Mrs Claremont had poured cold water all over her idea; if anything she was encouraged. Liberty's was her very own home away from home; she would do all she could to save the place she loved no matter how many obstacles were placed in her way.

Chapter Thirty-Two

At lunchtime Alice made her way up the stairs to the staff-room, and smiled as she saw Mary and Flo hunched over one of the tables, devouring their sandwiches.

'You two are a sight for sore eyes.' Alice flung herself into a chair next to Mary.

'Tough morning?' Flo sympathised.

Alice rubbed her eyes. 'Yes, you could say that.'

'Anything you'd like to discuss?' Mary asked, taking another bite of her paste sandwich. 'A problem shared ... '

'... is a problem I'd have to relive.' Alice grimaced as she reached into her own bag for the slice of leftover vegetable pie she had brought in from last night's supper. 'Let's talk about you two. How's carpets, Mary?'

Mary rolled her eyes. 'Dreadful. I hardly know a thing about rugs, Persian or otherwise.'

Flo sighed. 'Well, Mr Button is going to call a meeting later on before we all go home. He wants everyone to put forward ideas for their departments to boost business. It was something they used to do at Bourne and Hollingsworth all the time apparently.'

'Seems a good idea,' Alice said, taking a bite of her pie. 'I'll have another think this afternoon in the stockroom, given Mrs Claremont shot down my first idea this morning to boost utility sales.'

'What was it?' Mary asked.

Alice shrugged. 'I just said we ought to encourage customers to get creative with utility fabric by holding a competition for the best dressed or something. You know, customers could become inventive with things they already own to accessorise and so on.'

'We could hold a fashion parade to pick the winner!' Mary said excitedly. 'It would be such a draw.'

'That is a good idea, girls.' Flo grinned excitedly. 'Make sure you're first to raise your hands later on tonight.'

'I will,' Alice beamed. 'How are you anyway, Flo? How's the glamour of life upstairs?'

Flo rolled her eyes. 'Not brilliant. There's a mistake with a Beath's order and I'm going through a backlog of paperwork to try and fix it.'

'Ouch,' Alice said sympathetically.

Flo brightened. 'But I do have some good news.'

'Go on,' Mary coaxed, finishing her sandwich.

Flo looked proudly at her friends. 'I have been asked to sing regularly in the Lamb and Flag.'

'What?' Alice gasped. 'The pub around the corner from yours where Aggie used to sing? That's wonderful!'

'My word, you'll be in ENSA next,' Mary exclaimed. 'What's brought all this on? I thought you always refused Aggie's requests to sing with her?'

'Aggie's death,' Flo said sadly. 'I miss her, girls. She was so much more than my aunt; she was like a mother to me. She would have loved me to have done this, and so I'm doing it for her.'

Alice clasped her friend's hand. 'This is so wonderful. It's nice to hear a bit of good news. So, when do you start?'

'Yes, we'll come and give you some support on your first night,' Mary said excitedly. 'We'll bang on the tables, give you a standing ovation – that sort of thing.'

Flo laughed at her friends' enthusiasm. 'Next Wednesday. Then if that goes well I said I'd sing regularly one or two nights a week.'

'Well, you can count us in.' Alice beamed. 'Even if I have to bring Arthur, we'll be there with bells on.'

After lunch Alice returned to the fabric department and was delighted to find that Mrs Claremont didn't want to send her back to the stockroom. Instead she was allowed to serve her regular and favourite customers with Jean, and she was pleased to find the younger girl was taking an interest in the fabrics they displayed.

'I just want to say I thought your idea was ever so good earlier,' Jean said shyly.

'Thank you. I've worked in this department a long time now and like to think I know the customers better than I know myself.'

'And that's why, between you and me, I think it's daft I've been promoted above you,' Jean said in hushed tones as Mrs Claremont served another customer. 'I don't know nothing about fabrics.'

Alice shrugged her shoulders. 'That's just the way it is for now. But I'll help you. Didn't you learn anything about fabric from your mother?'

Jean shook her head. 'My mum ain't into things like that. To be honest, me and my sister Bessie left home at fifteen and came to London, so I didn't learn much.'

'And where do you and your sister live now?'

'Me and Bess are in lodgings over Queen's Park way. But my sister sometimes has her sweetheart round who I'm not that keen on so I try and stay out of their way as much as I can.'

Shooting her a sideways glance Alice couldn't miss the look of sadness that passed across the younger girl's face and felt a flash of pity for her.

'Well, maybe you should come out with us Liberty girls one night,' Alice said charitably. 'Mrs Canning's going to start singing in a pub near Islington. We said we'd go along and give her some encouragement on her first night next week.'

'Really?' Jean gasped, her green eyes alight with gratitude and surprise. 'I'd like that, thank you.'

'You're welcome.' Alice smiled, and then saw Mrs Claremont walking across the floor towards them. 'Now back to work before we're for it with Madam.'

The rest of the afternoon passed without incident and by the time the store closed and everyone had assembled to hear Mr Button's announcement, Alice felt a surge of excitement. Despite Mrs Claremont's reluctance to encourage her idea, Alice was going to suggest it anyway.

Everyone gathered under the atrium's chandelier and there was a buzz of anticipation as Mr Button brought them all to order, with Flo standing ably beside him, arms full of notepaper as she took her rightful place. As Mr Button cleared his throat, Alice sneaked a sideways glance at Mrs Claremont and smirked. She looked furious that she was no longer standing beside Mr Button, and Alice couldn't help feeling a glow of satisfaction that she no longer had Mr Button's ear.

'Evening, everyone,' he said warmly. 'Thank you so much for staying on an extra five minutes. I know you all want to get home and enjoy this lovely weather we're having.'

At that there was a murmur of appreciation. The weather had been particularly glorious in London of late, and the thought of outdoor walks in the fresh air without the worry of blackout appealed to everyone.

'However, as you know, at Liberty's we welcome your involvement, your thoughts and your ideas,' Mr Button continued, rocking backwards and forwards on his heels as he always did when addressing the staff like this. 'With this in mind, we want you to come up with some ideas for your own departments to really drive our customers through the door. We know there's a war on, we know there's not an awful lot of choice in stock—'

'Unless you're in the leather goods department,' some bright spark called, earning himself a laugh from the crowd.

'There is that.' Mr Button chuckled, joining in with the long-time joke that the only reason Liberty's was surviving was because the leather goods department had overbought before the war. 'But you know your own departments better than we do and the Liberty family along with the board all feel that it's you who will know what your customers want better than us behind the scenes all day. So, does anyone have anything? No pressure, I know you'll want to go away and think about this, but perhaps there's something that has been on your mind for a while that you would like to see implemented.'

As Mr Button drew his speech to a close, Alice glanced at Flo who gave her a nod of encouragement. Raising her hand in the air, she was astonished to find Mrs Claremont immediately snatched her hand down only to raise her own.

'Ah yes, Mrs Claremont,' Mr Button called over the sea of heads. 'Do you have an idea?'

'I do, sir, yes.' Mrs Claremont nodded, her eyes fixed firmly on Mr Button. 'I think we should consider holding a competition for the most inventive outfit created with Liberty's utility fabric.'

Alice's jaw dropped open in shock. She wanted to protest; only Mrs Claremont was still talking. 'I thought we could encourage women to perhaps accessorise outfits with their own scarves, shoes or pins, and of course many of these items can be bought off ration such as hats, which will drive people to the store and into other departments.'

Mr Button scratched his chin thoughtfully, while Alice gazed at Flo, feeling bereft. 'It is a good idea,' Mr Button said eventually. 'In fact it's a marvellous idea. We could hold a fashion parade for all our contestants and their wonderful outfits, just as Paris couturiers did before the war!' His voice was filled with excitement as he warmed to his theme. 'It would allow customers to tell all their friends and people might start buying all their utility fabric here.'

'Precisely,' Mrs Claremont said smugly.

'Well, bravo to you, Mrs Claremont,' Mr Button said, giving her a round of applause and encouraging everyone else to do the same. 'What an inspired idea. Come to my office first thing in the morning and we'll come up with a plan for you to put into action. Mrs Milwood, Miss Rushmore, you're very lucky to have a superior such as Mrs Claremont, you can learn a lot from her. Now, anyone else?'

As the suggestions came in thick and fast, Alice couldn't tear her eyes from Mrs Claremont. 'How could you do that?' she hissed eventually.

'Do what?' came the innocent reply.

'You know fine well what,' Alice growled. 'That was my idea.'

Mrs Claremont turned to her and paused. As Alice met her boss's gaze she couldn't ignore the fact that Mrs Claremont's hands were trembling. The look of defiance she had worn just moments earlier was now replaced by something that looked a little like fear. Was Mrs Claremont regretting her action? Was she about to apologise? If so Alice ought to do the decent thing and at least make it easy for her.

'Look, Mrs Claremont,' Alice began evenly, 'I'm sure you have some good ideas of your own. Let's just talk to Mr Button about some of your suggestions too.'

But any sign of remorse disappeared. Mrs Claremont snapped, 'In case you hadn't noticed, Mrs Milwood, I'm afraid that both out there on the streets and inside this store it's every woman for herself – and that idea of yours is now mine.'

Chapter Thirty-Three

When Alice got home she was so full of anger all she wanted to do was drown her sorrows in tea and whine with Dot. But of course it was Chris's last night before he left to go back to Wales the following morning, and so she knew she would have to plaster on the very brightest of smiles for the brother-in-law she was so fond of.

After a quiet journey home Alice was delighted to find Dot balancing Arthur on her knee as she enjoyed what looked like a riotous game of twenty-one with Chris and Luke.

'My round again,' she said, helping herself to the coins on the table.

Alice chuckled as she joined them. 'Oh my days! You ain't playing cards with Dot, are you? She'll clean you out.'

'So I'm beginning to realise.' Chris laughed, shuffling the pack.

Only Luke raised an eyebrow. 'Now, now, she'll break soon and when she does, I'll clean up.'

'Never in this world,' Dot said confidently, picking up the hand Chris had dealt her and showing it to Arthur for approval. 'What do you say? Another winner? 'Course it is.'

Leaving them to it, Alice went to make herself the cup of tea she longed for.

'You couldn't make me one of them, could you, love?' Luke called. 'Actually, forget that, can I have a beer instead?'

'Hang on,' she replied, walking over to the pantry. Reaching down for one of the bottles that they kept in crates, she was surprised to find there were only a handful left. She was sure that last week there had been at least two crates' worth and she had told Luke that they would have to last a long time. Beer, like everything else, was scarce and she'd only managed to get hold of this because she'd given Wise Albert, one of the stallholders down the Lane, a couple of her old maternity dresses that no longer fitted for his wife.

Trying to disguise her displeasure, she placed a bottle down in front of each of the men.

'Why are you looking like that?' Luke asked.

'Like what?' Alice replied.

Luke gave a small shake of his head. 'You know what.'

'I don't,' Alice replied. 'I'm just a bit tired after work, that's all.'

'That a dig, is it?' Luke asked laying his cards on the table, only for Chris to tug warningly at his sleeve.

'Come on, mate, what are you starting trouble for? Alice didn't mean anything by it other than she's probably dead on her feet from being stood up in the shop all day.'

Shooting his brother a menacing glare, Luke turned back to Alice. 'And that's my point, isn't it, love? You're the one out there grafting and I'm the one shirking my responsibilities, not taking care of my family.'

Opening his beer, he took a long gulp of the brown liquid, his eyes fixed on Alice. 'Well, admit it,' he said, setting the bottle down with a thud on the table.

Alice sighed as she glanced at Dot, who was resolutely staring at her cards. After the day she had endured she really didn't want a row with Luke; all she wanted was a quiet night and the chance to say a decent goodbye to Chris before he disappeared to the bed and breakfast he had been staying in.

'That's not what I meant at all. I know you look after us, support us, that my wages would be nothing without the money you bring in from the RAF,' Alice said, her eyes filled with what she hoped was kindness as she did her best to placate him. 'Please, Luke, I'm sorry.'

Taking another sip of the beer, Luke's face relented. 'No, it's me that should be sorry. I'm being silly. Now come here and give us a kiss.'

Walking over to her husband, Alice allowed his arms to snake around her waist and, for a moment, enjoyed the quiet along with the feeling of a row successfully avoided. Then: 'Well, I'd better get dinner on.'

Chris was on his feet. 'No, no, no, I insist on treating you all.'

Alice, Luke and Dot looked at him in surprise. 'Whatever for?' Luke asked. 'Alice doesn't mind – do you, Alice?'

Shaking her head, Alice smiled at her brother-in-law. 'It's a lovely idea, but it won't take me long. I managed to get a bit of rabbit for us all yesterday.'

Chris held his hands up. 'I don't want to be a pain, Alice, truly I don't, but the thing is I don't like rabbit. I know you can't be choosy when there's a war on but I do draw the line at rabbit. I put it down to the fact we've too many of them at home darting about the fields. The boys have adopted one as a pet – Flopsy, they've called her.'

Luke roared with laughter as he finished his beer. 'You've gone soft, lad. You always were a soppy sod.'

'And you, older brother of mine, were always tough as old boots. Or at least you were until our family dog croaked it.'

'I was nine!' Luke protested. 'Rover was my best mate.'

'All I'm saying is if the cap fits ...' Chris shrugged, slipping his brother a wink. 'Thing is, what I'd really like is fish and chips again. The chipper up our way's closed down and I don't have a clue when I might get a haddock roll again.'

'Well, if that's what you want.' Alice reached for the coat she had just taken off. 'I'll come and give you a hand again. It'll be like old times.'

At that they both laughed, and even Arthur joined in for good measure. 'Don't get fobbed off with the first batch,' Dot warned, standing up, Arthur still in her arms. 'They're always shoddy; they use up the old potatoes first. Hang on for the second batch. I'll look after this fella, Alice.'

'Thanks. I've a feeling he might need changing.'

'I don't have a feeling, I know he does,' Dot replied candidly. 'He stinks.'

Alice turned and followed Chris out. 'Want anything, Luke?' she called as she reached the door.

He lifted his empty beer bottle. 'Just another couple of these if you pass a pub, love? I don't know how we've got through so many. Must be Chris.'

Biting down her fury, Alice merely nodded. Only as she stepped out into the warm evening air she felt so angry she couldn't resist letting off a bit of steam with Chris.

'What the hell is he playing at?'

'What do you mean?'

'I mean the drinking,' Alice said, storming off down the road. 'You must have noticed.'

Hurrying to keep pace, Chris shook his head. 'He's all right. He's just a bit fed up.'

'But we can't afford for him to drink like that,' Alice hissed. 'I don't think he knows the lengths we all go to to get things round here. It doesn't grow on trees, you know; most of it's bartered for and we look the other way.'

She stopped suddenly and rounded on her brother-in-law. As she looked into the caramel eyes that were identical to her husband's she found all trace of anger instantly disappeared.

233

Instead all she felt was concern for the husband she was sure was struggling to come to terms with his new life. 'I'm sorry. I'm just worried about Luke. He's not himself. He wants to get back on active service, I understand that, but it's the mood swings, Chris, I just can't handle them.'

'What do you mean?' Chris asked, his voice even.

'You must have noticed,' Alice said as a gust of wind lifted her skirt and pressed it back against her thighs. 'He's not himself. One minute he's so kind, so loving and can't help out enough; the next thing I know, the Luke of old has been replaced by this hard, unloving stranger I just don't recognise. I don't know what to do any more. I don't know how to help him.'

A flash of discomfort crossed Chris's face. 'I think you're worrying too much. Just give Luke a bit of time.'

'But how much time should I give him?' Alice pressed urgently. 'Has he said anything to you?'

Chris eyed her warily. 'What do you mean?'

'Just if there's anything else bothering him? Come on, Chris, you're his brother, you know him better than anyone. If he's in trouble or needs my help I want to help him. He's my husband; I love him.'

'Well, maybe he doesn't deserve your love,' Chris muttered angrily.

Alice stared at him in shock. 'What did you say?'

'Nothing. Forget I spoke,' Chris said hurriedly. He carried on walking, leaving Alice trailing behind.

'What did you mean?' she called again, almost running now to keep pace with him. 'Why would you say something like that?'

'I didn't say anything. I was just being stupid.'

Alice felt like screaming with frustration. 'Chris, if you know something, please just tell me. I want to help my husband.'

At that Chris stopped so suddenly Alice only just managed to stop herself crashing into the back of him. 'Maybe you're not the one to help him,' he said.

'Why are you talking in riddles? Why wouldn't I be the one to help him? He's hurt, injured in the line of duty, spent months locked away in some French farmhouse desperate for freedom – he needs me.'

'No, Alice,' Chris said, rubbing his face in despair. 'That's the thing. Because while I love my brother it's killing me seeing you break your back working all the hours God sends when Luke's not been honest with you.'

'What do you mean?' she gasped.

Chris lifted his chin and fixed his gaze determinedly on his sister-in-law. 'The thing is, everything Luke told you about being shot down, recovering and being rescued by the French Resistance is true. What's not true is why it took so long for him to get back. The fact he could have come home a lot sooner. The fact is he didn't want to.'

'Why?' Alice whispered, dread pulsing through her body.

'Because he was having an affair,' Chris said with searing honesty. 'He fell in love with another woman.'

As the words hung in the air, Alice thought she might be sick. How could this be true? It was impossible that Luke would betray her like that. They adored each other, had done ever since that day she had been a farthing short at the cinema.

Despite the warmth of the evening Alice felt suddenly cold. Her teeth were chattering and her arms and legs were covered in goosebumps.

'There must have been a mistake,' she said eventually, her voice shaking. 'You've got hold of the wrong end of the stick. Luke wouldn't do that. His family are everything to him. Besides,' she continued, desperately clinging to the shred of hope she had left, 'he knew I was pregnant. He would never deliberately stay away all that time without meeting his son.' There was a silence, then: 'Say it's a mistake. Say you're wrong.'

But the moment Alice looked into Chris's eyes and saw the mix of despair, sorrow and anger, she knew that there was no mistake. Her Luke was no longer her Luke. Everything that had been done could now never be undone.

In that moment she found her heart hardening, almost instantly. She had been strung along long enough, doing all she could for her child, for her husband – her family – while Luke left her thinking he was dead, when instead he had been busy making hay while the sun shone.

'Who is she?' she asked, her voice flinty and unyielding.

'Alice, what good will it do?'

'Tell me,' she snarled. 'I want to know everything.'

Chris took a deep breath before he spoke. 'Her name is Hélène. She helped rescue him. They fell in love and he was convinced he could spend the rest of his life with her out in France, helping the Resistance and overthrowing the occupation.'

'So why didn't he?' she asked through gritted teeth.

'They had a row, I believe. I'm not sure what about. I think she wanted to get married—'

'"Married"?' Alice echoed in disbelief.

'I think that made him come to his senses. He realised what he had done, how worried you must be, how he was missing out on getting to know his child, and of course fighting for his own country – the country he loves. So he came home.'

'And when did he tell you this?' Alice asked bitterly.

'The day I arrived,' Chris admitted. 'I think it was a relief to let it all out and, well, being a vicar, I think he was looking for me to forgive him. Luke's never been good with secrets; I'm sure that's why he's been drinking so much, and why his moods have been so erratic. He's a mess.'

'Do you think he still loves her?' Alice said fiercely, getting straight to the point.

Chris shook his head and squeezed her hands. 'He never really did, Alice love. It's always been you. This Hélène was just a distraction.'

The feel of Chris's skin against her own was like a salve to the pain in her soul. She felt as though the bottom had been ripped out of her world and, just at that moment, the kindness in Chris's touch was the only thing holding it all together.

Chapter Thirty-Four

It had been four days since Chris had returned home and Alice's world had been shattered. Since his departure, there were times Alice wondered how on earth she had managed to carry on as normal. The moment her brother-in-law dropped his bombshell she had begun to look at Luke with fresh eyes. It was as though he were a stranger. The man she had married would never have dreamed of having an affair, much less a relationship so strong that he would pretend to be missing in action while his wife delivered their child alone.

It wasn't just the betrayal, Alice reminded herself. It was the way he had thought so little of her and the family they were bringing into the world. The selfishness he had shown beggared belief and there were times Alice would find herself thinking she must have dreamed the whole thing: the reality was just too ridiculous.

Yet no matter how rotten she felt about it all inside, she had no idea how to talk to Luke about it. So life carried on. He still asked her to pass the salt, or make him a cup of tea. And of course he continued to refuse to look after Arthur one day, then the next tell her she was the most gorgeous woman in the world and he was the luckiest man alive.

The truth was Alice had become rather numb to it all. She knew she ought to be screaming, shouting, even hurling plates at Luke for his betrayal, but she didn't feel anything. For months, while he had been missing, she had lain awake at night, Arthur snoring soundly beside her, fretting that he was dead. Now in a funny way Luke did feel dead to her and she had no idea what to do or what to say. They were married, they had taken vows, for richer, for poorer, in sickness and in health – she couldn't just walk away. If truth were told she wasn't sure she wanted to. How would she manage without him? *Could* she even manage without him? For so long Luke had cared for her; even when he wasn't by her side, it was the gentle strength in his letters that had propped her up and kept her going. Alice knew she put on a hard front, she had to and still would when pushed, it was the only way to survive, but inside she was softer than she liked to admit.

Sitting in the Liberty staffroom during her well-earned tea break, her mind was in overdrive as she pondered yet again what Luke had done. For all the pain he had caused, she couldn't ignore the fact that he had returned to her side. Then of course there was Arthur to consider. She had always wanted an entirely different childhood for her own family than the one she had endured. Didn't she owe it to Arthur to give him the chance of a normal upbringing, no matter what happened between her and Luke?

Getting to her feet to wash her teacup in the little sink at the back of the room, she caught her reflection in the mirror. She seemed to have aged a hundred years. Grey shadows hung under her eyes, and wrinkles, too deep to be kindly described as laughter lines, gave her skin a leathery, worn appearance. She needed a good night's sleep, she decided. There was to be no more tossing and turning beside Luke while he slept like the dead. No, she had made her bed and she would lie in it. She had chosen to keep this secret to herself, having decided that, for the moment, it was better for all concerned if it were swept under the carpet. Therefore she would have to forget about it – but how best to do that she wasn't sure. At that moment an image of

Jack's smiling face came unbidden into her mind and she felt a physical pain so sharp it was as though she had been cut with a knife. She hadn't realised how much she missed her friend until now.

The door to the staffroom opened and Flo walked in. 'Just the woman,' she called cheerily. 'I've been looking for you.'

'Oh?' Alice replied listlessly, not even bothering to turn and look at her friend.

'Yes. Mr Button wants to talk about the fashion parade.'

Alice let out a hollow laugh. Up until the other day she'd thought Mrs Claremont's betrayal was the worst thing she had to worry about. How funny that now she could hardly bring herself to care. 'Can you say I'm busy? I think it might stick in my craw to pretend to be interested in this when the idea was stolen from right under my nose.'

Flo shook her head, her hair bouncing on her shoulders. 'I know it's awful. I would have said something to Mr Button if you'd let me. He's so pleased with her and it's just not right. She wants hanging for this.'

'Well, I'm hoping that if we give her enough rope that's exactly what she'll do,' Alice muttered, squeezing the wet dishcloth out and leaving it out on the side to dry before finally turning to face Flo.

'I think we're all hoping that,' Flo murmured before catching sight of Alice. 'Christ, you look awful.'

'Thanks,' Alice muttered sarcastically.

Flo took a step towards her, her face lined with sympathy. 'Sorry, love. Are you feeling all right?'

'Fine. Probably just a bit tired. Arthur's teething again.'

'Anything I can do?'

Alice returned her friend's smile as best she could and shook her head. She couldn't stand anyone being nice to her at the moment; she thought it might break her. 'Dot's actually taken Arthur down to see her sister in Canterbury today, seeing as she's honorary grandma. She's staying for two nights so I'm hoping I might get a bit of rest, though it's killing me being without him.'

'Well, there is an upside – this means you'll be able to come to my first show tonight. I'm terrified.'

'I hadn't forgotten,' Alice lied. 'I've asked Jean too.'

'Why?' Flo asked, unable to help herself.

'She's all right really, you know. Just young, for the good of Liberty's we have to show her the error of Mrs Claremont's ways.'

'And we can start with this fashion parade meeting,' Flo said firmly. 'In Mr B.'s office at three. Besides, it won't take a genius for him to see it was your idea not hers the moment you start talking. Mrs Claremont doesn't know the first thing about fabrics, whereas you do.'

With that Flo rushed back to her office and Alice returned to the shop floor. Flo's words had given her a lift. It was true, she thought, Mrs Claremont knew nothing about the world of fabrics, and, worse still, didn't want to learn. Flo was right: it would soon become highly apparent she had stolen the idea.

As her gaze wandered over to the till, Alice's heart skipped a beat. There was a man standing patiently behind the counter.

'Jack,' she said softly, hurrying across the floor towards him. 'What are you doing here?'

Jack greeted her with an apologetic smile. 'Sorry, Alice. I didn't mean to disturb you at work.'

'That's all right. What can I do for you?'

'Be my friend again,' he said, looking at her pleadingly. 'Look, I get it, your husband's home now, and I know it's not proper for you to spend time with me, a single man. But we formed a bond that night in Bath and I can't just forget that – or you. I miss our friendship, and I wondered if there was any way we could be friends again? If you say no, I'll go, of course I will, but I had to ask.'

As Alice stared into his chocolate eyes, she found herself melting. She had missed him more than she cared to admit, and now he was here standing in front of her, Alice knew she couldn't turn him away a second time; after Chris's revelation she needed a friend more than ever. She might be a married woman, she might have responsibilities, but if she had learned anything since the outbreak of war it was that you had to grab happiness where you could.

'Yes, Jack,' she said with a steely resolve, 'we can be friends again.'

Chapter Thirty-Five

'Where is it you're going?' Luke asked from the kitchen table as he watched Alice slide on her best black shoes.

'I told you,' Alice replied stiffly, 'north London. Flo's got a gig singing and she's nervous.'

'But I don't see why that means you have to go out. Dot's taken Arthur; we've got the place to ourselves.'

At this he shot her a lascivious wink and it was all Alice could do to keep her cheese on toast down. 'I won't be late,' was all she offered instead.

'Why don't I come with you?' he said suddenly, leaping to his feet. 'You know, that way I can walk you there and walk you back.'

Alice looked at him in surprise, her coat hanging half off. 'You would really come out to north London for the night?'

Luke gave her a wide smile. 'For my wife I would do anything,' he said slowly. 'Besides, it might be fun. Let me get my shoes on.'

'All right,' she said, turning back to the mirror to check her appearance. She glanced at him via the reflection as he laced up his shoes and found she wasn't altogether sure how she felt about him joining her. None of the other girls would be bringing their other halves, but then, she thought sadly, none of the other girls had husbands or boy-friends this side of the water. She should be glad that Luke was showing an interest in her life – and besides, hadn't she decided that no matter what had happened their vows were too important to give up on, even if the "for better, for worse" part seemed particularly hard to bear right now?

'Right, ready.' He smiled, offering her his arm. 'And can I just say, my love, that you look beautiful tonight?'

At the compliment Alice flushed with confusion. She was so used to demonising Luke in her head these days that the moment he was nice to her she felt wrong-footed. 'Thank you,' she managed eventually.

As they strolled through the streets towards the Tube, the warm summer night like a balm to Alice's soul, she began to relax. She hoped she would start to forgive Luke in time, that the betrayal would start to hurt a bit less. Perhaps tonight was the perfect way to start to rebuild their marriage.

It didn't take long for them to arrive. The Lamb and Flag was a traditional pub on the corner of a tree-lined street. Pushing the door open, clouds of cigarette smoke greeted Alice before she saw a handful of people clustered around the bar. Through the smoke she could just about make out Flo, dressed in a black high-necked knee-length dress and bright red court shoes. Alice grinned. With her hair pinned in face-framing loose waves, her friend looked gorgeous, and it was a delight to see after the sadness that had enshrouded her over the past weeks.

Alice caught Flo's eye as she looked up from chatting to the pianist and rushed over to greet her.

'Luke, I didn't know you were coming,' Flo exclaimed after wrapping Alice in a warm hug.

'I didn't know myself until an hour ago. You don't mind that I'm here?'

'No! The more people to cheer me on the better. I'm terrified.'

'Well, you've no reason to be,' Alice said, patting her hand, 'you've got a lovely voice. You should be proud of yourself.'

At that Flo made a face. 'I am, but Neil's not. I got a let-ter this morning: he doesn't want me singing in the pub.'

'Why not?' Alice demanded.

Flo rolled her eyes. 'He doesn't think it's appropriate.'

'I can see what he means,' Luke said evenly. 'I suppose he feels it's not quite right for a married woman.'

At Luke's statement both Alice and Flo looked daggers at him.

'What?' he cried, holding his hands up in defence. 'I'm sure you're right, Alice, Flo does have a great voice, I'm just saying I can see Neil's point.'

'Neil's not here though, is he?' Flo said bitterly. 'And although I appreciate him fighting for our country, he doesn't understand what life is like back home. Aggie's just died, I'm all alone, I need something else to think about, to help me deal with the grief, and I want to honour my aunt in a way she would have been proud of.'

As Flo finished, Alice was alarmed to see tears start to well and she wrapped an arm around her friend. 'Don't you go upsetting yourself. You do what you think will make you happy, and you're due on that stage in a few minutes so take a deep breath and then knock 'em dead. Don't think about Neil right now, love.'

'All right.' Flo offered Alice a watery smile. 'The others are all over at that table in the corner by the way.'

Following Flo's gaze Alice saw Mary chatting with Jean, and on the other side Rose deep in conversation with some-one who looked like her sister. Alice bristled with anger; what on earth was Joy doing here?

'Before you start I think Rose brought her along hoping you two would make up,' Flo said in hushed tones. 'Give it a try, eh? For me?'

She felt Luke place a comforting hand on her shoulder. 'Yes, go on, love. I'm not Joy's biggest fan, but she is your sister. It's not right the two of you aren't talking. Perhaps she's learned her lesson.'

Alice bit back the urge to scream. She felt as if too much was being asked of her at the moment. However, this was Flo's night, not hers, and she wanted to support her friend.

'I'll do what I can,' she said, her tone clipped.

'That's all I can ask,' Flo replied kindly as she turned back to the piano player.

With Luke by her side, Alice weaved her way through the tables and waved at her friends in greeting.

'Alice, you made it.' Mary beamed. 'And you brought Luke. Hello, sir.'

'Hello. Girls, what can I get you?'

As everyone started to give Luke their drink orders, Alice glanced at her sister. She seemed to have lost a little weight, judging by the way the cardigan hung limply from her shoulders, but other than that she looked fine. Tired, perhaps.

'I didn't know you would be here when Rose invited me,' Joy said sulkily, stubbing out her cigarette in the ashtray on the table.

'I only just found out myself *you* would be here,' Alice replied smoothly, smiling her thanks at Luke as he slipped past her to get to the bar.

'Now, now, you two, we don't want any trouble,' Mary warned, eyeing each of the sisters cautiously.

'Yes, I hoped you two might make up,' Rose offered.

'But you should have warned me, Rose,' Joy complained.

Rose shrugged. 'All you would have done is try to get out of it. Besides, you're my best friend. You've done so much for me in recent weeks, I wanted to do something nice for you.'

Alice and Mary exchanged looks of surprise. Just how close had Rose and Joy become and what exactly was it

246

that Joy had done for her lately? Quickly Alice ran her eyes over Rose. There was something different about her but she couldn't tell what it was. The clothes hadn't changed, and neither had the hair or the glasses she still insisted on wearing. But there was definitely an air about her that was different. It was the way she was holding herself, Alice realised. Rose seemed more confident somehow, no longer apologetic for who she was.

Joy looked at Rose in a way Alice had never seen before. There was genuine affection in her sister's eyes as she leaned over to clasp Rose's hand. 'And I'm grateful, but Alice has made her feelings perfectly clear.'.

'I have,' Alice agreed. 'I told you what I wouldn't put up with, and you ignored me.'

'You refused to listen to me,' Joy whined. 'You just don't understand.'

Alice held her hand up. 'I understand all right. I've always understood. What I won't do is tolerate your behaviour.' She paused then, and pinched the bridge of her nose. The last thing she wanted tonight was a row with her sister; she had to control the situation before it took control of her. She thought back to the shock news Chris had delivered only a few days ago. Sometimes you had no idea what was around the corner, and with Joy being the only family she had left, she wondered if she ought to try and make up with her. 'Look Joy, you're my sister and I love you,' she said in softer tones. 'I will always love you. I may not agree with everything you do but I will always be there for you. I would like to repair our relationship if possible.'

'Does that mean I can move back in?' Joy asked brightly. 'The digs at Mayfair House are horrible.'

'No. I can't ignore what's happened and I won't have you under my roof again.'

Joy's face fell and Alice watched in surprise as she turned to glance at Rose, who gave her a nod of encouragement.

'All right,' she said at last. 'I can accept that.'

'Good.' Alice smiled. 'I'm pleased.'

Luke returned, carrying a tray laden with drinks. 'What did I miss?' he asked, doling out the glasses.

'Alice and Joy have made up,' Mary said in delight. 'Isn't it wonderful?'

'She's not moving back in, is she?' Luke asked bluntly. Alice shook her head. He grinned. 'Then it's wonderful.'

'I don't suppose you sew, do you?' Jean asked suddenly.

'What on earth are you on about now?' Alice asked.

Jean coloured slightly. 'I just thought that now you and your sister are friends again she might want to help out with our community stitching nights.'

'I can sew,' Joy replied doubtfully as she turned to Alice. 'What are community stitching nights?'

Quickly Alice outlined the plan, earning herself a look of reproach from Luke. 'Well, it's a fine idea, but does this mean you'll be spending another night away from me? You've got a son to take care of, in case you'd forgotten.'

'I haven't forgotten. It's why I've been excused fire-watch duty. If I can't find someone to take care of him, I'll bring him with me,' she said firmly. 'Mr Button doesn't mind.'

''Course he doesn't.' Mary chuckled. 'You did give birth to the child in the store.'

'In fact, it might not be a bad idea to get children in with their mums,' Jean said thoughtfully. 'We had a few in on that final first-aid night and they all get so involved.'

'It's a shame you only wanted to do two, Rose, they are so popular and you seemed to really enjoy them,' Mary said sadly. 'Is there anything we can say to get you to change your mind?'

With a firm shake of her head Rose gazed at the floor and Alice could see just how little their friend wanted to talk about it.

'It would be a great way to get kids to learn how to sew,' Jean added, returning to the subject. 'They'll have skills for life then.'

'Rather than be reliant on help for life,' Mary muttered wryly, thinking of her own privileged background.

'All right, count me in,' Joy said happily. 'As long as that's all right with you, Alice?'

Alice couldn't help smiling at her sister. Despite everything she had missed her. 'It's all right with me.'

Everyone raised their glasses then to toast Joy and Alice but Luke refused to join in.

'What's wrong?' Alice hissed in his ear as she glanced around nervously at the girls.

'I can't believe you're going to spend another evening apart from me,' he said angrily. 'We're married, Alice, that should mean something to you. Well, I've had enough, I forbid you to get involved.'

'Don't be so stupid,' Joy scoffed. 'You can't tell Alice what to do.'

'Joy, stay out of it,' Alice said warningly before turning back to her husband. 'Luke, this is work, it's all hands on deck. I'm afraid I do have to do this.'

At that moment Flo started to sing and everyone clapped and cheered while Luke slammed his glass down on the table. 'There are times I don't know why I came back at all,' he spat.

Anger flooded through Alice. After everything Luke had done, all the lies he had told, he had the nerve to sit there and say that. She opened her mouth to unleash her feelings but caught sight of Flo singing her heart out and knew she couldn't. She didn't want to detract from her friend's big night.

Looking back at her husband she shook her head in despair. 'I'm sorry you feel that way.'

'So am I,' he snapped, standing up and storming out of the pub without a backward glance.

Wordlessly Alice turned her attentions back to her friend. Flo had a natural, raw talent and looked for all the world as if she belonged on that stage. Alice hoped she wouldn't allow Neil to take this opportunity away from her. But then, Alice thought sadly, the thing about marriage was once you had made your bed, you very much had to lie in it.

Chapter Thirty-Six

Creeping out of bed as dawn broke, Alice was surprised to find Luke wasn't beside her. She quickly padded down the stairs to the kitchen, where she found Luke standing by the range in a threadbare dressing gown still far too big for him, making a pot of tea.

'What are you doing?' she asked, unable to keep the surprise from her voice.

'Peace offering,' he said glumly. 'I behaved horribly last night and wonder if you can ever forgive me.'

As Luke set the steaming cup down on the kitchen table for her, Alice gasped in surprise as he presented her with a round of toast complete with a scraping of butter. The National Loaf was somewhat tasteless and scarce, but the rare sight of breakfast freshly prepared by her husband made it seem as if it had come out of the Ritz.

'Don't think this gets you off the hook that easily,' she grumbled, taking a large bite. 'You embarrassed me in front of my mates and left me to come home alone.'

Luke looked contrite as he sat in the chair opposite, leaned forward and squeezed her hand. 'I really am sorry, Alice. I don't know what came over me.'

'Too much drink, I should think,' she said wryly, raising her eyebrow at the stench of his breath.

'I had one too many at one of the pubs up the road after I left you. Drowning my sorrows.' He leaned back and scratched his chin thoughtfully. 'Look, I do understand you have to work.'

'Good,' Alice said curtly. 'Because I said I'd help get the ball rolling with the fashion parade so I'll be back late.' Luke nodded as she took another bite of her toast. 'When does your medical officer visit again?'

'He came yesterday,' Luke looked sheepish. 'Said I'm a long way from being ready to go back to active service.'

Alice dropped the toast on her plate and reached forward to take her husband's hand. 'Luke, why didn't you tell me? I could have helped you.'

Letting out a bitter laugh, Luke looked into her blue eyes. 'How, Alice? With the best will in the world, how could you have helped me?'

Alice considered her husband's response. 'I could at least have listened,' she said eventually. 'I'd have understood.'

'Would you?' Luke sighed. 'Because half the time I'm not sure *I* understand. I mean where's the sense in wanting to go back into a war? I already nearly lost my life once, why am I in such a rush to go and do it again?'

'Because you love your country,' she said fiercely. 'Because you want to fight for our way of life to continue. Because you've seen what's happened to those poor Jews and know it's not right.'

There was a pause then as Luke offered Alice a weak smile. 'I appreciate you trying to help, love, but I think this is something I have to work out for myself. Besides, I don't want to burden you, it's not fair.'

'I'm your wife,' Alice said evenly. 'If you can't talk to me who can you talk to?'

Luke's gaze dropped to the floor. 'It's not that simple. I know you and Arthur have been here fighting your own war on the home front, and that things have been difficult for you in a way I could never understand, but I promised myself that when I came home I wouldn't talk about the horrors I'd seen. A lot of blokes were the same. We none of us wanted to taint our marriages by bringing that stuff back with us.'

Luke lifted his chin to meet Alice's eyes and she saw a glimpse of the person she knew of old. His eyes were filled with a heady mix of pain, determination and protectiveness and she felt her heart go out to him.

She took his hand again and gently squeezed it. 'Maybe you should try,' she urged softly. 'Luke, you don't need to protect me. Perhaps you should try telling me a bit about what life was really like for you in France.'

There was a pause then, as Luke gave a tiny nod of his head. 'All right. Maybe it's time.'

Alice held her breath, bracing herself for the truth as Luke began to speak.

'When I was trapped over there all I could think about was you and our child. I thought about what I was missing out on, what a waste of life it was that I was cocooned in this hell not knowing if I would ever get out. It devastated me, Alice, but I slowly learned to rely on myself. It was the only way I could get through it all,' he said looking her straight in the eye.

As Luke finished talking Alice felt a burst of anger at the lies that spilled so easily from his mouth. 'I can't imagine how terrible it was for you,' she said slowly. 'All alone like that, not able to get in touch with me to even let me know you were alive.'

'It really was awful. I look back now and I don't know how I survived it.' Luke's eyes took on a wistful expression. 'It was the thought of you and our child that helped me cope through those long, dark days … Oh, I'm going out with an old pal tonight, did I mention it?'

Alice shook her head, wrong-footed by the change of subject.

'Yes, Ralph Patterson,' Luke ventured. 'We trained together and he's been injured too. Though he's well now and just been put on admin duty. We bumped into each other last week and he suggested a pint.'

'All right,' Alice said evenly. 'Have a nice night.'

Pushing her plate of half-eaten toast away she got to her feet and looked at her husband. As her eyes roamed over his familiar face it suddenly hit her that she had no idea if he was telling the truth. Was he really going for a drink with his friend or was he up to something else? And that was the biggest problem of all, she thought sadly. While she might be doing her best to forgive him, to want to try again, the trust in their marriage had been broken. Turning her back on him, she walked up the stairs to get ready for work,

'Aren't you going to finish your toast?' Luke called.

'No thanks,' she shouted back. 'I've had enough.'

From the moment Alice arrived at Liberty's that morning she was rushed off her feet. The department was inundated with customers thanks to the competition posters that had gone up and the announcements in the press. At lunchtime Flo dragged her down to the stockroom.

'What on earth's up with you?' Alice grumbled after being manhandled. 'You haven't had another letter from Neil, have you?'

Flo shook her head. 'Nothing like that.'

'Well, then what is it? Mrs Claremont will have my guts for garters if she catches me gossiping down here, even if it is with the deputy store manager.'

But Flo said nothing; she just looked stricken.

'What is it?' Alice tried again, more gently this time.

'I've made a mistake,' Flo whispered, her eyes wide with despair. 'A big one.'

Alice rested her hand on Flo's forearm as she encouraged her to continue.

'One of our agents, Beath's – over in Canterbury, you know – has been on the phone. There's been a problem with an order they placed with me. They've received two hundred rolls of utility fabric and say they only ordered twenty but we've charged them for two hundred. I know they ordered twenty, but somehow I've written two hundred.'

'All right, Flo, calm down,' Alice soothed. 'Could there have been another order form? Something that came later?'

Flo shook her head. 'I've looked everywhere. I think I must have been going mad. It happened when I came back to work after Aggie died, but the delivery only went out the other day, on my day off. My mind can't have been on the job. I'm so ashamed.'

'Come on now, there's no need for all these tears. What do Beath's want?' Alice asked.

'They've done it. They've sent the hundred and eighty rolls back and demanded a refund, which of course I've actioned, but to lose that amount of money in order is dreadful.' Flo wailed. 'They say they'd never have ordered that amount and I know that.'

Alice pinched the bridge of her nose as she tried to think. This was so unlike Flo; she never made mistakes like this. 'What are you going to do?' she asked.

Flo shrugged. 'What can I do? I'm going to have to own up and tell Mr Button. A mistake like this is very bad for business.'

Alice nodded. 'I think that's the best thing. The sooner you tell him the sooner he can help you fix it.'

'But I could get the sack!' Tears were pricking Flo's eyes now. 'And then what?'

'You're not going to get the sack,' Alice said firmly. 'Just tell him the truth and I'm sure he'll understand.'

'I don't think he will. I think he's going to be furious.'

'Sadly, my love, I don't think you've got a choice. Come on, do it now – once it's done you don't have to think about it. You can tell me everything during your tea break.'

'If I'm still here,' Flo replied dolefully.

'Go!' Alice said, shooing her friend up the stairs in front of her.

Reaching the top Alice's heart sank as she came face-to-face with Mrs Claremont.

'Seems to be your day for gossiping, Mrs Milwood,' she said in a steely tone. 'You've had another visitor while you've been down here. He's disappeared into gifts but I imagine he'll drift back here soon enough.'

'Do you know who it was?' Alice asked. She really wasn't in the mood to talk to Luke, particularly not at work.

'I'm not your social secretary, Mrs Milwood,' Mrs Claremont snapped. 'I've no idea who he was.'

'Excuse me Mrs Claremont,' Flo began, 'but I needed to speak to Mrs Milwood on urgent business regarding the fashion parade. Our first stitching event is tomorrow; I assume you will be in attendance as acting head of the department?'

Mrs Claremont drew herself up to her full height and shook her head. 'Unfortunately, I have a prior engagement. I will be on hand during the day should anyone have concerns.'

'I see,' Flo said, giving her a withering stare. 'That's a shame.'

With that Flo swept past Mrs Claremont, leaving Alice to follow suit. Walking back across the floor towards the cash register, she saw the department was empty apart from one man.

At the sight of him, her heart leapt. 'Jack?'

'Alice, there you are. How are you?'

'I'm well. You?' she replied, cautiously moving towards him.

Jack beamed at her, and the sight of his familiar smile made her melt inside. 'I just wanted to drop by and see if you were busy tonight?'

'Tonight?' Alice echoed. 'Why?'

'I thought you might like to see a movie. *Gone with the Wind* is on and I've never gotten around to seeing it.'

Alice raised an eyebrow in surprise. 'I can't believe you've never seen it. It's wonderful.'

'Does that mean you'd like to go with me? I'll throw in a drink at the Rainbow Corner. Not Coke again, I promise.'

Alice chuckled as she thought for a moment. She had told Jack the two of them could be friends, and not only was Luke out for the night but Arthur was still away with Dot. Where was the harm in spending a couple of hours with a handsome GI?

'All right. I finish at half past five today. Do you want to meet me after work?'

'Perfect,' he said, clapping his hands together in delight.

Watching him leave, Alice felt her pulse race at the thought of spending another evening with Jack. No matter how hard she tried to tell herself that Jack was only a friend, she knew her emotions were sending her into dangerously deep waters.

Chapter Thirty-Seven

As Alice walked out of the staff door, Jack was waiting for her. The sight of him in his GI uniform was the tonic she needed after a hellish day and she couldn't wait to escape from her life with a few hours in his company.

'Right on time!' He beamed, tapping his watch.

'Well, I know you military men are sticklers for time-keeping,' she said as they began walking along Kingly Street together.

'That and I don't like to keep a lady waiting.' Jack chuckled. 'Now how about a proper drink first? I thought we could go to the pub rather than Rainbow Corner.'

They were outside the King's Head; Alice looked long-ingly at the door. 'Yes please. If I'm honest, I could really do with a port and lemon.'

'Then your wish is my command,' Jack said, holding open the door for her.

He escorted her to a table by the window, helped her off with her jacket and then went to the bar. Moments later he returned with a pint and a suspiciously large glass of port.

'I hope you're not trying to get me drunk, Jack Capewell,' she said teasingly, eyeing the glass.

'Not at all, ma'am! You just looked like a lady in need.'

Alice took a sip and allowed the liquor to trickle down her throat. The warmth of the port immediately began to take the edge off her day and so she took another sip, enjoying the relaxed feeling that spread between her shoulders.

'I needed that,' she said eventually, setting her glass back down on the stained wooden table.

'So I see,' Jack remarked wryly, taking a sip of his own drink. 'What's happened today?'

Alice rolled her eyes. 'Where to start? But before we get into all that, tell me about you. How have you been?'

'Fine. I'm being put in charge of a new unit so I'll be sticking around London a while longer.'

'That's good news! Are you pleased?'

'I am now you and I are friends again,' Jack replied bashfully. 'The truth is I sorta don't have anyone else to spend time with.'

'What about all your friends in the army?'

Jack winced. 'They're great guys, but when you're the boss, you're not really pals with anyone.'

'I understand. Flo said she had to keep a distance when she was made up to deputy store manager. Mind you, I never saw anything different about her.'

'How is Flo?'

Grimacing, Alice wondered just how much she should say. Taking another gulp of her drink, she decided to come right out with it. 'The short story is that Flo made a mistake and this afternoon she was demoted.'

'What?' Jack gasped. 'Just like that? What did she do?'

'Got an order wrong. I won't go into it all, but suffice to say it was a colossal mistake and Flo is now back on the shop floor and she's devastated to have let people down.'

'Poor Flo,' Jack said earnestly. 'Is she all right?'

Alice nodded. 'I saw her at tea break in the canteen and she said that in a funny way it was a relief. She hated being in charge really and missed the shop floor.'

'So at least she's back with customers then?'

'She is,' Alice confirmed, folding her hands in her lap to stop herself drinking her port too quickly. 'And she's back in fabrics too, plus we've got the store's utility fabric fashion parade for her to throw herself into.'

As Jack raised an inquisitive eyebrow Alice told him about the store's latest plans.

'That's great,' he said when Alice had finished.

Alice sighed. 'It is for me, but not so great for Flo. She used to run fabrics, now she's just a run-of-the-mill shop assistant, while Mrs Claremont, who knows next to nothing about fabrics, continues to kill the department.'

Jack looked confused. 'But your fashion parade at the end of the month must be helping you guys along?'

'It is,' Alice ventured. 'But Mrs Claremont had nothing to do with it. In fact she won't even come along to our first stitching night to get things moving.'

'What did she suggest it for then if she didn't want to get involved?' Jack asked, looking perplexed.

'She didn't!' Alice thundered. 'It was my idea and she took the credit for it.'

Jack shook his head in astonishment. 'And I thought the military had it bad with some shady characters. My, my, your Liberty's is like a movie.'

'Speaking of which,' Alice said finishing her drink. 'Shall we get going?'

Together the two of them strolled through the streets towards Leicester Square. It was another warm, sunny night and Alice allowed herself to bask in the sunshine after spending all day inside. Before long they reached the cinema itself; Jack paid for the tickets and she followed him inside. They were just in time.

Alice lost herself in the story, enjoying every moment of Rhett and Scarlett's romance being played out on the big screen. However, her long and difficult day at Liberty's combined with the warmth of the theatre made her fall asleep; she woke only when Jack shook her.

'Oh my days!' she gasped, coming to. 'I can't believe I fell asleep.'

Jack helped her on with her jacket. 'That's all right. It's a long movie. Besides, you seemed so comfortable on my shoulder I didn't want to wake you.'

Alice flushed bright red. 'I'm so sorry,' she whispered.

'You don't need to be.' He chuckled. 'Your snoring was only faint.'

'No!' she gasped. Her hands flew to her mouth in horror before she realised Jack was joking. 'You swine,' she giggled, playfully swatting him with her right hand.

'Hey, easy now!'

As they walked outside, Jack asked. 'What do you feel like doing now?'

Glancing at her watch, Alice felt another flush of horror. 'I'd better get back, I've an early start in the morning to help get everything set up for our stitching night. I'm sorry.'

At the announcement, Jack's face fell, before he managed to recover himself. 'No problem. Let me walk you to the Tube.'

Together they sauntered in no particular hurry back through Leicester Square.

'How's Jack Junior?' Alice asked as the evening breeze whipped around her neck.

'He's fine. He wrote me last week, says he's been out riding.'

Alice made an impressed face. 'He'll be rounding up the cattle for you by the time you get back. A real-life cowboy.'

'That's what worries me,' Jack replied sadly. 'I feel like I'm missing out on so much.'

'I know what you mean. Arthur has only been away a couple of days with Dot but I've missed him terribly. I can't imagine how difficult it must be for you.'

'It's one of the hardest things I've ever had to do. The thought of this war never ending, and me never seeing my son again, are the only things in the world that truly terrify me.'

'They get under your skin, don't they, children? I'd be lost without Arthur.'

'I expect you and Luke are thinking about having another baby now he's home,' Jack ventured.

There was a pause then as Alice stopped to look at him. Neither one of them had mentioned Luke so far that evening, and now that his name was out there it felt strange to Alice, almost as if he were an intruder getting in the way of their evening.

'I don't know,' she said honestly. 'The way things are at the moment, I just don't know.'

Jack narrowed his eyes in concern. 'What's wrong?'

The worry etched across Jack's face tugged at Alice's heart. She thought she had done so well at keeping Luke's affair a secret, but with Jack standing there, offering her a shoulder to cry on, she knew she was undone and could no longer carry this burden alone.

'Luke had an affair,' Alice blurted. 'His brother Chris told me. That was why he was away so long. He wasn't fighting for his life; he could have returned a lot earlier. Instead he was having an affair with a French Resistance fighter, all while I was back here worrying to death about whether he was alive or dead and raising our son alone.'

As she broke off, Alice was aware that tears of anger were now streaming down her face. Saying the words aloud really brought it home to her just how much of a fool Luke had taken her for.

Sensing Alice needed help, Jack reached for her hand and guided her to a nearby bench. 'Alice, honey, you gotta take a breath.'

Nodding, Alice inhaled deeply and tried to calm down. 'Sorry,' she said eventually. 'I didn't mean to tell you all that. I haven't told anyone.'

'Nothing to be sorry for,' he said softly, still holding her hand. 'We all need someone to talk to. When my wife died, I refused to talk to anyone about it. I said goodbye at her funeral, went back to work the next day. A year later, I'm sobbing like a child into my baby son's hair.'

At the confession, Alice's heart went out to the GI sitting beside her. 'You must have been devastated when she died.'

'I was. But I didn't talk to nobody, I couldn't, I had to be strong for my son.'

Alice recognised the truth of Jack's words. That was precisely why she had kept this secret to herself, because her son had to come first.

'Does Luke know that you know?' he asked.

Shaking her head, Alice gazed down at her lap. 'I'm too afraid of what I'll say. I'm so angry with him, so disappointed.'

'I get that. Really I do. I mean I don't know the guy but my feeling is that you deserve a lot better, honey.'

As Alice lifted her head and looked into Jack's chocolate eyes, she saw such tenderness, she thought she might cry.

'Alice, what I'm about to say next, I would never say if you hadn't told me what you just did about Luke. But, well, I figure I may as well take my chances.'

'No, you don't have to say anything. I should be getting back.' Alice tugged her hand free and got to her feet.

'I love you,' Jack blurted as she started to walk away.

She whirled around to face him, her face contorted with tears. 'No, no don't say that. Don't spoil our friendship.'

Jack was on his feet in an instant and gripped hold of Alice's arms. 'I have to finish this now I've started. Alice

Milwood, I think I fell in love with you the moment you collided with me outside Jolly's. You deserve the world, you're bright, you're funny and you have such a huge heart. The way you worked tirelessly to help those people that were hurt, my God, if I didn't know it before I sure knew it then … After Marilyn died I never thought I would find anyone to love again, but you are everything to me.'

With that he gathered her in his arms, bent down and kissed her tenderly. Alice felt as if she had come home. His mouth was so soft, so loving, the feel of his lips against hers filled her with such intensity of emotion, that she felt truly adored in a way she never had before. For a moment, Alice lost herself in the power of that one kiss. But then, as if someone had poured a bucket of cold water right over her, an image of Luke flashed into her mind and she jerked away.

'Alice, what's wrong?' Jack asked, his face filled with concern.

'I'm s-sorry,' she stammered, her face aghast. 'We shouldn't have done that.'

Jack reached for her again but Alice took a step back and shook her head. 'No. I'm married, Jack. I told you about Luke's affair because I felt I could talk to you. We should never have done this.'

There was a pause then as Jack fixed his gaze on her. 'I'm sorry, honey, I just … I love you.'

The way Jack was looking at her now was all too much. She felt woolly-headed. Her voice was trembling but her words were firm. 'I love my husband, Jack. I'm sorry, but Luke is my future. No matter what he's done, we made vows together; I can't ignore them. Please, we can't see each other again.'

Then without a backwards glance, Alice fled for home, determined to push the memory of the sweetest kiss firmly from her mind.

Chapter Thirty-Eight

The day of the community sewing evening Alice woke to find the heavens had opened, with the grey skies and soggy weather only serving to echo the Liberty girl's feelings of despair.

When Alice had got home, she'd felt consumed with guilt and planned to tell Luke just how much she loved him. But he hadn't returned, and she had fallen asleep in the easy chair by the hearth in the kitchen and woken cold and stiff in the early hours. Trudging up the stairs to bed she found that Luke was home and snoring softly in the bed they shared, and she clambered in next to him, full of remorse over her own betrayal. No matter what Luke had done, she had to take responsibility for her own actions and knew that no matter what, her heart and her duty had belonged to her husband from the moment she made her vows in church.

Arriving at Liberty's she ran up the stairs to the staff-room, only to find Flo peeling off her wet coat with a face like thunder.

'What's wrong with you?' Alice asked, taking off her own jacket and hanging it up to dry.

'I was on firewatch duty last night,' Flo grumbled. 'Not only am I wet through and cold but I'm too tired to sift through the filing cabinets full of orders Mrs Claremont wants me to go through.'

'Why has she got you doing that?' Alice quizzed.

Flo shrugged her shoulders as she traipsed down the stairs behind Alice. 'Because she wants to show me that she and Jean are still in charge, I suppose.'

Alice frowned. 'You know Jean's all right, Flo. She recognises that she doesn't know much about fabrics but she's keen to learn.'

Remaining silent, Flo merely pursed her lips as she pushed her way through the doors and walked out on to the shop floor where, surprisingly, Jean was all alone and looked flustered as she pulled paperwork apart all over the cutting table.

'Jean, are you all right?' Alice asked cautiously.

Whirling around red-faced, Jean shook her head. 'No! I'm not all right. Mrs Claremont is in a meeting with Mr Button and she says that we've got a VIP coming in and I've got to show her all her favourite stock. Only trouble is there's no sales record here so how am I supposed to find out what she likes?'

Alice rested a hand on Jean's shoulder and guided her away from the cutting table towards Flo. 'Firstly, calm down, Jean. This is not the end of the world. Who's the VIP?'

'Lady Milton-Browne,' Jean wailed. 'I've never even heard of her, and neither have the other girls.'

Flo grinned. 'Lady Milton-Browne is one of our most high-profile VIPs. She's also not really a lady.'

Jean's eyebrows shot up. 'Then who is she?'

'She's really the film star Betty Fawcett. Lady Milton-Browne is a nickname we give her so she doesn't get mobbed by adoring fans when she visits.'

At the revelation, Jean's hands flew to her mouth. 'Oh my days! Betty Fawcett's wonderful. Why didn't Mrs Claremont tell me?'

'Probably because she didn't know herself,' Alice said wryly. 'Look, there's nothing to worry about. We usually take her down to the crypt and sit her down with a cup of tea and all the old guard books – Betty loves the Tana Lawn in particular – then she normally goes off and buys a couple of scarves.'

Flo chuckled. 'So you should stop tearing the place up looking for her sales records ...'

'... and instead focus on your abilities to brew up,' Alice added.

Immediately Jean relaxed and broke into relieved laughter. Just then Mrs Claremont appeared on the shop floor.

'What's going on here?' she barked. 'We're due to open any second.'

'Yes, Mrs Claremont,' Jean said, suitably chastened, while Flo and Alice rearranged their faces.

'That's better,' Mrs Claremont said smugly. 'Now, Mrs Canning, why aren't you sorting through paperwork as instructed? And Mrs Milwood, I want you on hand to answer Lady Milton-Browne's questions. She is an esteemed peer of the realm and as such we must look after her.'

'Of course, Mrs Claremont,' Alice replied evenly, hiding her smirk.

'Jean will be looking after her ladyship,' Mrs Claremont pronounced authoritatively. 'I take it you've studied her sales record and can present her with all she needs?'

Jean nodded. 'Absolutely.'

'Very well. I shall be upstairs with Mr Button should you need me. We are finalising arrangements for tonight's sewing evening. As you know I can't be in attendance, but Miss Rushmore will be on hand should you need her.'

As Mrs Claremont disappeared across the shop floor, Alice, Jean and Flo burst into laughter.

'Oh girls,' Flo said, wiping her eyes with the back of her hand. 'If this wasn't so sad, it would be funny. I cannot believe our department is being run by someone so clueless.'

'But at least you're here now,' Jean mumbled, her green eyes filled with gratitude. 'You know what you're doing.'

Alice and Flo exchanged knowing looks before Alice spoke. 'We do, and we'll make sure you have everything you need to ensure the visit with Betty is a success.'

'But first things first.' Flo winked. 'Why don't you go and make us a cuppa and we'll have it while we sort through this lot.'

Two hours later and Betty Fawcett was doing just as Flo and Alice expected: sitting in the crypt devouring a pot of tea and Liberty's guard books with equal gusto.

'Oh my, this is just gorgeous,' she said, pointing to a pretty navy peacock print.

'They are, aren't they?' Jean managed as Alice gave her a nudge.

'Designed by Liberty's,' Alice offered as Jean remained mute.

'I guess you don't have any of this?' Betty asked, her heart-shaped face full of hope.

Alice shook her head sadly. 'It's rationed, but there may be some scarves in the print.'

Betty clapped her hands delightedly. 'You girls know just how to look after me.'

'We try.' Alice grinned, pouring another cup of tea out for Betty while simultaneously kicking Jean under the table.

Ever since Betty had arrived Jean had been starstruck and barely able to open her mouth to speak. Alice had to admit that with her long red hair, blue eyes, alabaster skin and fine delicate features, Betty was a beauty, but she was also just a woman like them, even turning her hand to the war effort by helping out with the WVS.

She was a breath of fresh air, and Alice had hoped Jean might rise to the challenge of dealing with her, but it was clear the young girl was daunted and afraid the gaps in her knowledge would show. As a result, she had hardly said a word and had left Alice to pick up the slack while Flo manned the shop floor.

Alice was just about to suggest they all make their way over to scarves, where Betty would be able to admire the Voysey print, when Mrs Claremont appeared, her face full of excitement.

'Hello, Lady Milton-Browne.' She beamed, curtseying. 'I'm Beatrice Claremont. It's a pleasure to have you here.'

Betty looked up at her and smiled. 'And it's nice to meet you. But really, dear, there's no need to curtsey.'

Mrs Claremont's cheeks flushed with pleasure. 'That's very kind of you, your ladyship.'

'And there's no need to keep calling me that either,' Betty replied, puzzled. 'You do know I only use that name for appointments. Plain Betty is just fine.'

Confusion passed across Mrs Claremont's face before she recovered herself. 'Very good. Well, as long as you're getting everything you need.'

'I'm being looked after very well,' Betty replied with a grin. 'Shame I haven't been able to spend as much time with Flo as I'd like. She's so knowledgeable about the prints, along with Alice. We love to natter about 'em.'

At the slight, Mrs Claremont bristled. 'I can assure you that Miss Rushmore and I are more than capable of looking after your needs. Mrs Canning is indisposed, shall we say, and no longer manager of the department.'

Betty's face fell. 'Oh, that is a shame. Who's manager now then?'

'Well, I am.' Mrs Claremont smiled tightly. 'And I am happy to help you with whatever you need.'

'All right then,' Betty said, jabbing at the guard book. 'What can you tell me about this pink peony print?'

Mrs Claremont looked flustered at the question and nervously checked her watch. 'Mrs Milwood can help you with any queries you may have, I'm sure. Now, if you'll excuse me I'm rather late for a meeting. A pleasure to have met you, Lady, er, Betty.'

Once Mrs Claremont had gone, Betty smacked the table with delight and threw her head back with laughter. 'That woman knows less than I do about Liberty fabrics. Why on earth is she in charge and not Flo?'

'That's a long story.' Alice sighed, reaching for the guard book. 'Now why don't we get you across to the scarf department, see if we can't find you something nice to accessorise that new utility outfit.'

'Good idea.' Betty followed Alice and Jean up the stairs towards the shop floor. 'What's this?' she asked, pausing in the stairwell to look at one of the posters about the upcoming fashion parade Alice had tacked to the wall.

'Something to help get our customers involved in Liberty prints,' Alice said. 'We want to get the country sewing and looking lovely in our fabric so we're holding a parade and inviting people to learn to sew with our stitching nights. The first one's tonight in our crypt.'

Betty nodded approvingly. 'What a brilliant idea. Who's judging it?'

At the question Alice's jaw dropped as she realised nobody had given any thought as to who would judge the contest. Reading Alice's expression, Betty smiled. 'How about I judge it?'

'Oh no, we could never ask you to do that,' Jean gasped.

'Jean's right,' Alice agreed. 'You're so busy, but it's a very kind offer.'

Betty shook her head. 'Not at all. I'd love to come along and judge all the wonderful creations. I bet you'll get lots of women participating. Besides, you need someone who knows what they're on about and while it may take me a while to learn my lines, I do know my Liberty prints.'

'Well, if you're sure.' Alice was hardly able to believe her luck.

'I'm more than sure,' Betty said forcefully. 'Stick my name up on them posters; I'll be there in a heartbeat to make you and Liberty's proud.'

Chapter Thirty-Nine

Later on, Alice recounted the story of Betty's involvement to the rest of the Liberty girls, once they were all together at the stitching night, revelling in their delighted faces.

'I can't get over it,' Flo exclaimed. 'This fashion parade's going to be a real hit.'

'You're not kidding!' Dot beamed, who together with Arthur had come straight to Liberty's the moment she had stepped off the train.

'You've done ever so well,' Mary said admiringly. 'Perhaps we could raise money with a whip-round on the night for those that were bombed out in Bath as well.'

'That's a wonderful idea,' Jean enthused. 'You Liberty girls always seem to know just what to do.'

Alice chuckled as she bounced her baby son gently on her knee. She had missed him more than she thought possible, and now he was back in her arms she wasn't sure she ever wanted to let him go.

'It all depends who you ask,' Dot said knowingly. 'Still, looks like you've done well with this first community stitch night, girls. The place is a sell-out.'

As Alice glanced around the crypt, the venue for the stitch nights, she saw Dot was right. She had been fretting all day that people wouldn't come, but women had been queuing at the door all desperate to learn how to make something wonderful with Liberty fabric, and take part in the fashion parade at the end of July.

So far it was going well. Jean was demonstrating how to follow a pattern to the twenty or so women gathered around her. Alice and Flo believed it would be good practice for the new girl to show off what little she did know, giving her a much needed confidence boost. Afterwards, Alice and Dot were going to take over with a basic stitching session to get everyone started, while Flo and Mary would be on refreshment duty. The only one missing was Rose, who said that as the stitch night was happening on a day she didn't work that meant she didn't have to come.

'You know we ought to make you something lovely, Mary,' Flo said suddenly.

'For me? Why?' she asked perplexed.

'Well, you'll be getting married soon.' Flo sounded excited. 'Perhaps we ought to think about making you a dress.'

Alice smiled wistfully. 'I remember my own dress. It was beautiful, a dropped waist and high neckline with full sleeves and veil to match. I felt every bit as gorgeous as Princess Valentina.'

'I remember the day you chose the fabric – had to be persuaded you were worthy of something so beautiful,' Dot said with a smile.

'What was it?' Mary asked.

'A gorgeous Liberty silk,' Alice murmured. 'Even with the discount and the fact I was allowed to buy it at wholesale price it seemed a fortune. Luke paid for it in the end.'

That wedding dress had been a symbol of their love and all they meant to each other. She still had it now, hanging in the back of her wardrobe, where it was gathering dust. But she would never part with it; the dress was something she would always cherish.

Mary shrugged, her face the opposite of a blushing bride. 'I don't know if and when he'll get leave, and I'm not sure he wants to marry me just for me, if you know what I mean.'

Alice wrinkled her nose in confusion. 'I don't know what you *can* mean. What other reason could he have for wanting to marry you other than because he wants to be with you?'

'I think a lot of it's because he wants to adopt baby Emma,' Mary said, her tone wary.

'Mrs Matravers' baby?' Alice asked in surprise.

Nodding, Mary traced a finger in the pattern of the Tana Lawn that lay stretched out in front of her. 'Yes. He feels guilty that she's being raised in care when we would be perfectly capable of giving her a home. And then of course, in time, Mrs Matravers would be able to see her when she was released from prison.'

Alice let out a low whistle. 'That's a tall order. How do you feel about that?'

Mary met Alice's gaze, her green eyes tortured. 'I just don't know. Obviously I feel for the child, but it's such a lot to take on. Part of me believes it might be better for her if she never had anything to do with Mrs Matravers and could grow up far away from a life of crime.'

'Mary, surely you can't mean that,' Flo protested.

'I bet you she does,' Jean said, having caught the tail end of the conversation. 'My dad was a drinker and Mum – well, Mum had better things to do. I couldn't wait to leave.' As her voice trailed off, Alice's heart went out to the girl. She looked broken, but Alice knew better than to pry. Some secrets were better left unsaid.

In an effort to change the subject, Flo put down the pattern book she had been flicking through. 'Things going all right with Luke now then?'

Alice bristled. 'Whatever makes you think they weren't all right before?'

'Well, just the way he was the other night in the pub. Neither one of you looked very happy,' Flo said quickly. 'Sorry, I don't mean to cause any offence.'

Alice did her best to soften her expression. 'Sorry. It's been difficult since Luke came back. I suppose we've both had to adjust.'

''Course it has,' Mary exclaimed sympathetically. 'Luke's had to deal with getting to know his son, an injury and being on sick leave from the RAF.'

'Perhaps he needs something different to take his mind off things?' Mary said thoughtfully. 'Would he consider joining the Home Guard, do you think? Just temporarily, until he's strong enough to get back in the RAF active duty. They're always looking for people.'

'That's a good idea!' Alice said. For the first time in a long time she felt a flash of hope. 'Perhaps if he was with some like-minded souls he might feel a bit more hopeful himself.'

'Settling down is bound to take time,' Dot mused, before she fixed her gaze on Alice pointedly. 'Have you talked to Jack about this?'

At the mention of his name, Alice coloured. She opened her mouth, ready to change the subject, and then changed her mind. Perhaps she would feel better if she confided in her friends.

'Last night Jack told me that he had feelings for me, that he'd never come between a husband and wife, but that he wanted me to know,' she said, admitting half the story to test the waters.

'Cheeky bloody devil!' Dot remarked.

Flo sighed. 'I think that's sweet.'

Alice caught the look of concern on Mary's face. 'What do you think?' she asked.

'It all depends on what you said to Jack.'

275

'I told him that Luke and I had problems,' Alice said hesitantly, unable to read Mary's expression. 'But I said we were committed to one another and that we had made vows.'

'Good for you,' Dot chimed in.

'As long as you really feel like that,' Jean chirped shyly. 'I mean, when you fall in love, you fall in love.'

Alice looked at the younger girl in surprise. What did she know about Alice's feelings? She felt a hot fury rise. 'I am not in love with Jack. I am a married woman; Jack was just my friend. He got confused, that's all.'

'Was? Flo asked bluntly. 'Aren't you going to see him again?'

'No,' Alice replied hotly, unable to meet Jean's gaze. 'It's for the best if we have nothing do with each other from now on.'

There was a silence then as the girls reflected on Alice's words.

'That's a shame,' Mary said eventually. 'But probably for the best if you want things to improve with Luke.'

'Mary's right,' Dot said softly. 'Jack was a nice fella, I'm surprised at him really, but he does wear his heart on his sleeve.'

'A lot of the Yanks do that,' Flo said wisely. 'I've seen them at the pub all gabbing about the women they've loved and lost back home.'

Dot rolled her eyes. 'Lot of fuss about nothing. Easy come, easy go for them from what I've heard.'

'Not Jack,' Alice protested. 'He adored his wife. Was devastated when she died.'

'I know.' Flo smiled sagely. 'But no matter how nice he is you're better off without him. Plus he's got a kid as well – you don't want a complicated friendship when there are children concerned.'

'Which is why I don't blame Mary for being cautious about David's suggestion,' Alice said, successfully steering the conversation back to her friend. 'It's a lot to think about.'

Mary nodded gratefully. 'It is. Then of course there's the fact David still doesn't want me getting called up. He worries, he says.'

'Have you been called up yet?' Alice asked.

'No.' Mary shook her head. 'I mean I'm busy enough with the Red Cross, so I'm not looking for anything extra.'

'Have you seen much of Rose up there?' Dot asked suddenly. 'I feel like she's disappeared. I asked her along tonight to help out but she said she was too busy.'

'She's so different these days – she seems withdrawn,' Flo said sadly.

Jean's eyes widened. 'She shouted at me the other day.'

'Rose?' Alice exclaimed. 'Never in this world. She doesn't have it in her.'

'She did that day,' Jean replied. 'I just told her I thought she was ever so brave for coming back to work like she did after her accident. She snapped that there was more to her than her white stick and one day people would see that.'

There was an intake of breath amongst the girls at Jean's revelation. 'I would say that sounds unlike her too,' Mary sighed, 'but she's been so off with me and Malcolm lately – when she's in of course.'

'Where is she then?' Alice asked. 'As if I couldn't guess.'

'With Joy,' all the girls, bar Jean, chorused.

'Why is she spending so much time with your sister?' Flo queried, bewilderment filling her face.

'I don't know. But what I do know is if Joy is involved it's not likely to be good news.'

Dot frowned. 'I thought you and her had made up now.'

'We have, sort of. But a leopard don't change its spots and Joy's a filthy great big leopard. Ever since Joy came to her rescue that day at Mayfair House, Rose has been besotted.'

'It's true,' Mary agreed, 'and I don't think it helps that she's missing Tommy more than she lets on. She *still* won't agree to him asking for compassionate leave.'

'Well, perhaps it's time we made her see sense,' Dot said firmly. 'She's changing beyond all recognition, girls, and we need to do something about it.'

As the girls nodded Alice felt a flash of relief. Together they might be able to get Rose back on the straight and narrow, even if the same couldn't be said for her sister.

Chapter Forty

The sound of crying woke Alice from a deep, dreamless sleep. Sitting upright she came to straightaway and snapped on the bedside light, only to find Arthur's cheeks were flaming red as he bawled his eyes out.

The sight of him scrunched up like an old paper bag, as he beat his fists against his sides tugged at her heartstrings. He had been sleeping through the night for weeks now. Was this because of her? Was he crying like this because she had been working too long and hadn't been around for him as much as she should? Or was he in pain?

'Come on, sweetheart,' she said in a soothing tone, trying to calm him.

If anything Arthur's cries became louder and more persistent and so she hurriedly checked him to see if he needed changing. Realising that he didn't, she decided to try feeding him instead. Taking a quick look at Luke, she saw the bedspread draped over his head was moving and she felt a flash of alarm. The last thing she wanted to do was upset Luke; he was always dreadful if he didn't get a full night's sleep and the last thing she wanted was an argument in the middle of the night.

Hurrying towards the door, she made to open it before Luke was properly disturbed. Only as she laid her hand on the doorknob she realised it was too late.

'Alice love, what's going on?' he asked in a loud whisper.

Turning around, Alice couldn't resist smiling. He looked like a little boy with his hair mussed up and eyes half open.

'Ssh, go back to sleep,' she replied in hushed tones. 'It's just Arthur.'

'Is he all right?' Luke asked, rubbing his eyes.

'Fine. I'll just feed him and he'll go out like a light.'

'All right.' Luke looked relieved. 'Would you like any help?'

'At feeding him?' Alice asked in horror.

Despite the earliness of the hour, Luke couldn't help smiling at his wife's stricken face. 'Well, I could give him a bottle, but no, I just meant I could perhaps make you a cup of tea for when you'd finished.'

'That's very sweet of you, but please, just get back to sleep.'

Much to Alice's surprise, Luke got to his feet. 'Alice, let me help you,' he begged. 'You're at work all day and with the baby at night. I want to do something for you.'

Looking at the concern etched across her husband's face Alice felt love flood through her. Leaning across to kiss his cheek, she gazed at him tenderly. 'What you've just done is more than enough.'

With that she took their crying son down the stairs and prepared to feed him, feeling bowled over with surprise. Settling herself down in the chair, she decided to savour the moment with her child. As she rocked him contentedly in her arms, his breathing became calmer and he fell into a deep sleep. She allowed the weight of his head against her chest to soothe her. Was it possible she, Luke and Arthur could be the happy family she always dreamed they would be?

Despite the interruption in the small hours, Alice arrived at work feeling lighter, brighter and far more like herself than she had for some time. It seemed that she wasn't the only one, as walking on to the shop floor she saw Flo standing by the gleaming glass cash register, humming to herself while she flicked through the sales books.

'Blimey, you're chirpy,' Alice marvelled.

'I am more than chirpy, I am over the moon.' Flo beamed, peering over the counter. 'Last night was a roaring success. Look at all these sales books; we filled them with orders.'

Alice took a look at the paperwork and saw Flo was right. The books were teeming with orders from customers who were keen to order the utility prints and make their own utility garments.

'We haven't been this busy for a long time!' Alice exclaimed.

'It's had a knock-on effect on leather goods too. And hats. The girls were telling me all about it last night. Before the stitching event got started lots of customers were buying accessories to go with their new outfits.'

'Before they had even made them,' Alice remarked drily.

Flo giggled. 'You know what our customers are like. They adore the chance to buy anything they can that's Liberty's – war or no war. Our fashion parade gives them the perfect excuse to do just that.'

About to pass the books back to Flo, Alice caught sight of Mary and waved her over. 'Look at these!'

'I'll take those, thank you,' Mrs Claremont thundered from behind them.

Whirling around, Alice saw the woman's face was contorted with anger as she snatched the books from Mary's hand. 'You shouldn't be looking at these, you work in carpets,' she hissed, before turning to Flo. 'And you certainly shouldn't be looking at them either. They are none of your concern. I am head of this department. As such it will be me that looks at them and decides if the new customers are our kind of customer.'

Alice looked at Mrs Claremont in astonishment, her good mood evaporating in an instant. As she took in the look of disgruntlement on her boss's face Alice felt a wave of anger. 'You're really going to go through these books and decide who is a good customer and who is a bad customer?' she exclaimed, hands on hips. 'After we all worked our fingers to the bone at the stitching evening last night, an idea you insist was yours and yet you didn't even come to the event!'

Mrs Claremont's jaw dropped open. 'I beg your pardon – how dare you talk to me like this? I am your supervisor; you will treat me with respect.'

Warming to her theme, Alice leaned forward so her face was just inches from her boss. 'I know you've had me hauled over the coals for insubordination before now, and you'll probably do it again, but you're ruining Liberty's, do you hear me, ruining it! Your lies, your demand for respect are killing what's special about the place.'

As Alice stopped there was a silence as Mrs Claremont looked at her in pure fury. Her grey eyes were alive with anger yet she looked almost satisfied at what Alice had just done.

'You stupid girl,' she said, a hint of a smirk playing on her lips. 'I'll have you moved from your precious fabrics if it's the last thing I do.'

With that the woman turned her back and marched straight up the stairs. Alice looked at the other girls in shock. 'What have I done?' she whispered.

'You were brave and you said what needed to be said,' Mary said supportively.

Flo nodded in agreement. 'You did that, but blimey, Alice! She's going to string you up for this, you daft mare.'

For the rest of the day Alice found she was barely capable of working at all as she thought about her outburst. She was always so calm, so respectful of her superiors, but Mrs Claremont had got under her skin and for the life of her Alice couldn't understand why. She supposed it had something to do with the pressure she was under thanks to Luke and Jack. Yet she knew that it was really about Mrs Claremont and the way she ran the fabric department. It had all changed after that day in the café, she mused. The moment she had said that the Liberty girls were her family, Mrs Claremont had withdrawn completely, and since then had gone out of her way to be awkward and unfriendly. It made no sense, Alice thought desperately, but then neither did what she had just done. She had worked at Liberty's for a decade and never once been in trouble; instead she had been proud to have worked her way through the ranks. Yet all that looked as if it would count for nothing as Mr Button and the board would surely throw her out on her ear. Alice hung her head in shame. How could she have been so stupid as to throw her job away like this? What would Luke say? They needed the money. What had she been thinking of?

Towards the end of the day Mr Button had called her to his office for a quiet word before she went home.

Standing before him, she felt as if she were back at school with the headmaster reading her the riot act for coming in late. Now as Mr Button sat behind his desk to tell her how disappointed he was in her, Alice found she couldn't disagree.

'I'm sorry,' she said and meant it. 'I went too far.'

Mr Button's eyebrows shot up so far his forehead they disappeared into his hairline. 'Yes, Mrs Milwood, I would categorically agree that you went too far.'

At the use of the term Mrs rather than Alice, she couldn't help wincing. Mr Button was one of the fairest but kindest men she knew. If he was talking to her this way then she had to deserve it.

'Would you like me to gather my things?' she asked quietly.

'Of course I wouldn't like you to gather your things,' he snapped. 'What I would like is for you to respect Mrs Claremont.'

'But—'

Mr Button held his hand up to stop Alice talking. 'But nothing,' he said firmly, cutting her off mid-flow. 'I have never seen such blatant disregard for an acting head of department. Mrs Claremont is conscientious and she deserves your respect.'

At that Alice bowed her head in sorrow. Mr Button meant the world to her, he was the father she had never had; she hated the fact she had let him down so badly. 'I'm sorry. I wish there was more I could say.'

'I beg of you to say nothing,' he fumed. 'Your tongue has got you in enough trouble today.'

'Yes, sir.'

There was a silence then as Mr Button took off his glasses and glanced out across the windows. Alice followed his gaze over the bombed-out city – such devastation, she thought, not just out there but in this store too.

'If only you girls understood just half the pressure I am under to make this shop work during wartime,' he said, putting his glasses back on and turning to face her. 'I have the family and the board, as wonderful and understanding as they are, begging me to make sure this store doesn't go the way of others with no stock, no reputation and no staff. I don't just have to think of the next day and the next week but the next year and what may happen if this dreadful war does or doesn't end. This endless bickering between staff members is of no help whatsoever.'

Alice closed her eyes in despair. She felt horribly selfish. If only she had thought for just one moment, stopped herself from opening her big mouth, then perhaps the one man who had always treated her with kindness and respect wouldn't be looking at her as if he wished she had never darkened his door.

'Truly, Mr Button, I know I keep saying it but I am sorry. I shouldn't have reacted as I did. I know I have let you down.'

Mr Button nodded. 'You *have* let me down, Alice. That's the incredibly sad thing about all of this. You were a staff member I relied upon – but no more. Now go home, report to me next week while I think about what happens next.'

Chapter Forty-One

When Alice got home all she wanted to do was curl up in a ball and weep. She had made such a colossal mess of things; she had no idea how she was ever going to make it better. It was half past four and by rights she should still have been at work, but now with her job in limbo she had nowhere else to be aside from the Bell Street terrace.

Sliding her key into the lock she hoped she would have the house to herself. Sadly, as she stepped into the hallway she realised that was unlikely because she could hear Dot and Luke having a heated exchange.

Pausing just for a second in the hallway, she toyed with the idea of slipping out of the front door and running away. She felt too tired to deal with any more arguments today. But then, as she peeled off her coat, Alice realised with shocking clarity that the reason she was in this mess was because she hadn't behaved as well as she should have. Now was the time to put that right.

'What's going on with you pair?' she asked wearily, stepping into the kitchen.

Luke and Dot both turned to look at Alice, thunder in their eyes. Standing opposite one another, either side of the kitchen table, they looked for all the world as if they were about to go into battle.

'I'll ask again, what's happened?' Alice said evenly.

Dot was the first to speak. 'This young man of yours thinks it's perfectly acceptable to bring his mates around to my house, sit in my kitchen and drink beer in the afternoon while I'm looking after his child.'

'And I've told you until I'm blue in the face that three servicemen, injured like me, discussing how we're going to get back to doing what we're good at over one bottle of beer each is not something to be ashamed of,' Luke roared.

'You've been in this house, under everyone's feet, feeling sorry for yourself for too long now,' Dot continued as if Luke hadn't spoken. 'And although I appreciate it's difficult for you, lad, it's high time you sorted yourself out and made a fist of being back here.'

'Dot,' Alice cried, stepping forward in Luke's defence. 'Don't be so hard on him. He's trying.'

'Whether I'm trying or not should be of no concern,' Luke said, his voice taking on a steely edge. 'What should matter to you is that I am the man of this house and I know best.'

At that Dot let out a knowing laugh just as the sound of Arthur wailing from upstairs echoed through the room. 'Is that right?' she said over his cries. 'Alice, talk to your husband while I go and sort out the little 'un. I hope that when I come down he's come to his senses and got a bit more respect about him for who's actually paying the bills around here.'

As Dot pushed past him to walk up the stairs, Alice glanced at Luke and saw his hands were balled into fists. A red flush of anger crept up his neck, and she knew that it was a blessing Dot had walked away.

She pinched the bridge of her nose. Despite everything that Chris had told her she did feel sorry for her husband. He had always been a proud man and returning from whatever had happened in France, with his leg injured and his job – his reason to get up in the morning – all taken away from him while his wife and landlady provided would no doubt take its toll. Alice eyed her husband carefully. The last thing she wanted to do was anger him further. She had known him long enough to know sympathy was the very last way of getting through to him.

'Luke, sit down,' she began crisply as Arthur's cries continued to echo overhead.

'I'm fine where I am,' he said through gritted teeth.

Nodding as if expecting that answer, Alice pulled out the chair next to him and sank into it. Rubbing her hands over her face she thought of what to say next. 'Luke, you're a good, and proud man,' she began, lifting her chin to look at him. 'And I know how hard you've worked to continue to provide for this family, even when you weren't here.'

Luke's face softened at the compliment. 'I have always worked hard,' he growled. 'I have always faced my responsibilities, and that woman' – he jabbed his forefinger on the table as if to emphasise the point – 'that woman upstairs has no right to judge me.'

'I know that,' Alice said, doing her best to remain calm. 'You know Dot – she was just lashing out. Perhaps she's had a bad day with Arthur. You know how he kept us up last night. She didn't mean anything by it, I'm sure.'

Luke sighed and shook his head. 'I was just letting off some steam with some old RAF friends. I don't see what's wrong with that?'

'There's nothing wrong with that,' Alice said carefully. 'I understand that you feel you need to get together with your RAF pals. I'm the same with Liberty's – those girls see me day in, day out, they know the ups and downs. No doubt these blokes will appreciate what you went through in France far more than I ever will. I'm not stupid, Luke. All I ask is that we try and remember this isn't our house as much as we might want it to be. We've both got to be respectful to Dot. She does enough for us both as it is.'

'And I suppose that's my fault, is it?' Luke snapped. 'I'm that much of a failure I can't even provide a roof over my head for my own wife and child now?'

'That's not what I mean,' Alice said wearily. 'What I'm saying is that this war has put us all, rich and poor, in shocking situations, situations some of us could never have imagined. People who were bombed out like we were are living all over the place and we're lucky to have a roof over our heads at all when so many don't. It's got bugger all to do with providing for your family, Luke, and everything to do with getting through these dark days. We're here, we're together, that should be enough.'

As Alice trailed off she could still hear Arthur crying. More than anything she wanted to go to him; she had a feeling she knew how to reach her baby son far better than she knew how to reach her husband at that moment. She tried to read his expression, to see if any of her words had hit home. But his face was blank and Alice had no idea what else to say. Deciding to do what she knew she was good at, she got up to tend to Arthur, only for Luke to reach for her arm. At his touch she turned round and saw such despair in his eyes, she felt a flash of sorrow.

'Help me,' he begged. 'I'm drowning without the RAF. Truly, it's as though I don't know who I am any more. I want to serve my country, but I don't know how.'

'If you really want to serve your country then why not find something else do?' she suggested hesitantly. 'The RAF may not need you at the moment but there are plenty of others that would.'

'Who?' Luke scoffed.

'The Home Guard for one. A young man like you would have a lot to offer.'

There was a pause then as Luke's expression changed. For a moment Alice thought she had finally got through to him, but he turned back to the table and swept his hand right across it, sending half-full cups of tea and the pot crashing to the floor.

Alice leapt to her feet. 'What are you doing?' she shrieked, standing well back from the shards of china that flew into the air.

'The Home Guard?' he said, his voice dangerously low. 'You honestly believe that I, a flying officer in the RAF, should join the Home Guard? I'm used to life on the front line. It's where I belong, not in the bloody Home Guard with a bunch of old codgers. Christ, Alice. You've got no idea.'

There was silence then as Alice looked at the debris that surrounded them and then back at her husband. Her whole life was chaos, she realised. Her job, her marriage, her ability to be a good mum. As for the man standing before her, she had felt for some time Luke was little more than a stranger but right now he was unrecognisable. The old Luke would never have lost his temper like that.

In that moment Alice felt another stab of frustration. She felt as if she was failing on all fronts. Right now she wanted to hit her husband where it hurt. 'And I suppose Hélène did understand, did she?' she spat, unable to hold back any longer. 'I suppose Hélène would never have suggested you do something useful for your country like join the Home Guard.'

Luke's jaw dropped with shock. 'What did you say?'

'You heard,' Alice growled. 'I know all about your affair with your French tart. If you want to go and lay down the law I suggest you go and do it with her.'

Luke just stared at her and for a moment Alice couldn't tell if he was going to hit her or apologise. In the end he did neither, instead he pushed back his chair and went to walk out of the door – only to bump into Dot.

'Far be it from me to pry, but is what I heard right?' Dot gasped. 'You were carrying on with some woman in France rather than returning to your wife and child?'

Shaking his head in fury, Luke tried to push his way past the landlady but Dot was having none of it. Squaring her shoulders she stood, hands on hips in the doorway, making it impossible for him to pass.

'What have you got to say for yourself, eh?' she snarled. 'You've a lovely wife and kiddie and you've treated them appallingly.'

Luke bent down and pushed his face into Dot's. 'Everyone around here acts like you're the oracle, like you know better than everyone else, but I know different. You're a dried-up bitter old widow with no family of her own to interfere with so you meddle in everyone else's affairs. I feel sorry for you.'

By now Alice had heard enough. This stranger, this imposter, this man was not her husband and she could barely bring herself to look at him.

'Get out,' she snapped. 'Get your things and get out of this house. I can't bear to have you near me.'

Luke's head whipped round. Eyes contorted with anger, hair stuck out at angles, he was lost for words. 'What?' he eventually spluttered. 'You can't throw me out. I'm your husband.'

Alice took a step towards the man she had thought was the love of her life. 'In name, perhaps. I'm tired of your lies, your deception and your attitude since you got back. I don't know who you are any more, Luke Milwood, and I want you gone.'

'And where am I supposed to go?' he growled. 'Not a lot of call for injured ex-servicemen like me.'

'I'm sure you'll find somewhere,' Alice spat. 'I'm sure Hélène will have you.'

At that Luke went white with shock. He took a step towards Alice and made to grab her arm, before catching himself. Taking a step back, he pushed past Dot, opened the front door and slammed it shut, all without ever once looking back.

Chapter Forty-Two

After Luke's shock departure, unsurprisingly, Alice and Arthur had barely got a wink of sleep. So when someone started banging on the door before dawn broke, Alice found she was wide awake. Padding down the stairs, doing her best not to wake Dot – an unlikely feat, she knew – she threw open the door and found Joy standing on the doorstep.

'What are you doing here?' she gasped.

Smartly dressed in her Mayfair House uniform of black dress and matching shoes, Joy looked both defiant and sympathetic. 'I won't stay long,' she said in hushed tones. 'I just wanted to let you know that Luke turned up at the hotel last night.'

Alice glanced furtively to her left and right, looking for flapping ears. The houses were tightly packed on Bell Street and while she knew it was unlikely that she could keep her business to herself forever, she wanted to keep the fact she'd thrown her husband out quiet for a few hours at least.

'Come in,' she said quietly. As Joy stepped inside, Alice hugged Arthur close to her, as though her son could protect her from whatever news Joy had to impart.

'I just thought I'd let you know that Luke arrived at the hotel last night begging board and lodging.'

Alice blinked at Joy in surprise. 'I thought the hotel would have been the last place he would have gone.'

'Apparently the bed and breakfast Chris stayed in was full and he didn't know where else to go,' Joy said matter-of-factly.

'I'm amazed you said yes.'

'He is your husband, Alice.' Joy sighed. 'I may not like him, but that doesn't mean I won't help him – he's family, remember. Dad taught us that: you always help out family and no matter what he's done he is still Arthur's father.'

Alice felt a pang of love for her sister. There were times when Joy surprised her with the compassion that she was capable of showing. 'What was he like?'

'Angry,' Joy mused. 'In fact, he was shaking he was so furious. Kept going on about how you had humiliated him, how he was a man, how it wasn't right that he had been thrown out by his wife.'

'Shouldn't have been messing about with another woman in France then, should he?' Alice fired.

Joy blanched. 'He told me that there had been a misunderstanding, he didn't say he had been cheating on you with other women.'

'Just one woman to be precise.' Alice recounted the painful details of Luke's time in France. By the time she had finished, Joy's eyebrows were hoisted so high Alice wondered if she would be in a state of disbelief forever.

'I'll get rid of him,' she fumed. 'He asked me to vouch for him with the manager, which I did. Thanks to me he's got free bed and board in exchange for a bit of hotel maintenance. Had I known what he had really done I'd have kicked him out on his ear as well.'

Alice shook her head before reaching forward to hug her sister. 'I know that, and I'm grateful. But if you don't mind I think it's better he stays with you. Like you say, he's Arthur's father.'

'Are you sure?'

Nodding, Alice gave Joy a watery smile. 'I am, darlin', but I can't tell you how much I appreciate you coming round to let me know, thank you.'

'You're welcome,' Joy replied quietly.

There was a pause then as the sisters looked at each other; the love that ebbed and flowed between them was not lost on either of them.

'I think you're being very brave, Alleycat,' Joy said softly.

The nickname had Alice choking back tears as she spoke. 'Not brave, just practical.'

Joy shrugged. 'I'd have torn him limb from limb for betraying you like that.'

'The thought did cross my mind, but it's not the right thing to do.'

'But he didn't just lie to you, Alice,' Joy seethed. 'He tried to make a fool out of you. You can't stand for that! You have to teach him a lesson and get revenge.'

As Joy stopped speaking, Arthur started to cry. Doing her best to quieten her son, Alice shook her head at her sister. Joy had absorbed so much from their father, including the mantra that one of the greatest crimes of all was humiliation, something you never could or should forgive.

'Joy, I don't see it that way and neither should you,' Alice said as quietly as she could over Arthur's cries. 'Dad had some warped, twisted ideas – getting revenge on someone for humiliating you was one of them.'

'It's not warped,' Joy said firmly. 'It's about honour. Luke has treated you and Arthur appallingly!'

'He has,' Alice agreed. 'But the best form of revenge is to move on.'

Despite Mr Button's insistence that Alice see him at the beginning of the working week, due to meetings, schedules and other commitments that seemed to get in the store manager's way, Alice didn't actually see him until the following Wednesday morning. By then she was still feeling more than a little shell-shocked. She had no idea what her store manager would have planned for her, but for the first time in her working life she found that she didn't care. Saturday evening's episode seemed so long ago now that she struggled to even remember precisely what had happened or why. As Mr Button encouraged her to take a seat, Alice found she was moving but it was as if she were in someone else's body; she couldn't quite focus but as the store manager started to speak Alice did her best to concentrate.

'I have given this a great deal of thought,' Mr Button said gravely, leaning forward in his chair as he addressed her. 'As I said, you are a highly valued member of the staff here at Liberty's but I have to set an example and show that insubordination will not be tolerated. That's why I think the best thing to do is send you back where you started.'

'Sir?' Alice frowned, unsure as to what he meant.

'I mean that I think the best way of setting an example is to send you back to the bottom of the ladder – a bit like snakes and ladders, if you'll permit the analogy.'

Alice shook her head. She couldn't think straight.

'I mean I'm sending you back to the stores. You'll work with Mr Wilmington again.'

At the mention of the word 'stores' Alice felt very much awake. While she was happy to take on any role Liberty's deemed fit, a return to deliveries and loading, where she had started her working life at Liberty's, wasn't just a demotion but, it seemed, a humiliation too.

'Sir? The stores?' Alice tried. 'I'm a sales assistant. At the very least allow me to work on the shop floor.'

But Mr Button merely shook his head as he handed her a slip of paper. 'I'm sorry Alice, but the decision has been made. Mr Wilmington is expecting you. That chit of paper I've just given you is for your overalls. I'm sure they'll have one in your size.'

Chapter Forty-Three

The warm summer days and lazy summer nights continued as July progressed. It had been almost a fortnight since
Alice had told Luke to leave the house and she was finally
beginning to relax both at home and work. Her new job in
the stores wasn't anywhere near as bad as she had feared
and Mr Wilmington had welcomed her with open arms,
handing her some overalls and encouraging her to drink
as much tea as she wanted.

It made a welcome change, Alice had to confess, and
instead of fretting about the future she did her best to
simply embrace and appreciate each day at work and
with her son. It was Arthur who was really helping her
get through. Watching him change and grow, seemingly
every hour, gave her a renewed purpose. She couldn't
help feeling it didn't much matter what happened to her
– everything she did, everything she would do was for
her son.

But of course it was her very own Liberty girls who
ensured she didn't slip away. She didn't have the strength
to tell them everything, only that Luke had left. Thankfully
none of the girls had pressed her and Joy hadn't uttered
a word about what had happened. Alice wanted to repay
the favour, which was why tonight, as she helped Mary,
Flo, Jean and Rose get ready for the next community stitch
night, she had insisted Joy come along.

'Over here,' she called, waving to her sister, who was
still dressed in her Mayfair House uniform.

'How are you, Alice love?'

'Fine. Did you bring your hat like I asked?'

"Course. Not sure how much difference it'll make to this dress though. I've never got on with navy.'

'It'll make the world of difference.' Flo smiled. 'I want to show the women tonight that dressing cleverly is all about accessories.'

'And that's what will win them the fashion parade title?' Joy nodded in understanding.

'Precisely,' Alice replied as she tucked a stray lock of hair behind her ears, only for Joy to peer closely at her neck.

'What's that black mark?'

'What black mark?' Alice asked, doing her best to wipe it off.

'The one that you're frantically rubbing at,' Joy said sarcastically. 'What's going on?'

Alice exchanged a guilty look with Flo, who gave her an encouraging nudge. 'Go on, tell her.'

'Tell me what?' Joy hissed impatiently.

Alice sighed. 'I don't work on the shop floor no more.'

Confusion crossed Joy's face. 'What do you mean? Have you got a promotion into the offices then?' she asked, turning back to look at Rose, who was busy answering some of the women's questions about sewing. 'Only you never said anything when I saw you last week and Rose hasn't said nothing neither.'

Alice looked at the floor. 'No, well, I'm embarrassed, you see. Thing is …'

'Will you spit it out?' Joy snapped.

'The thing is she works in the stores now,' Flo said helpfully. 'Mr Button said that as she had a mouth like a delivery driver combined with no respect for her superiors, she could work in the loading bay until she learned some manners.'

Joy's hands flew to her chest in shock. 'Oh my days! Alice! You're never humping and lugging boxes about like the fellas, are you?'

Miserably Alice nodded. 'It's my own fault. I shouldn't have spoken to Mrs Claremont the way I did.'

'She had it coming,' Flo said loyally over a pile of material. 'It's just a shame she's succeeded in getting you moved because frankly, Alice, fabrics isn't the same without you. Now, with Mary still in carpets, I'm the only one there that knows anything about the stock, or even pattern-cutting.'

Alice frowned. 'But Jean's coming on leaps and bounds.'

'She is,' Flo agreed. 'But Mrs Claremont doesn't want me training her up. Says I make mistakes that cost the company money so she doesn't trust me to do it. Only problem is Mrs Claremont is doing it herself and as she knows next to nothing about fabrics Jean's making a mess. This whole situation's a bugger's muddle.'

'So what do we do?' Alice wailed.

Joy shrugged. 'Talk to Mr Button. He's not unreasonable. I'm sure, Flo, you could tell him the problems the department is having and say that it would be better for you, Alice and Mary to work together again for the good of the store.'

Alice smiled at her sister affectionately. 'When did you get so wise?'

Joy flushed at the compliment. 'It had to happen sometime,' she replied just as Mary clapped her hands together.

'All right, everyone, I think we're ready to start,' she called over the din of chatter. 'Today we're going to do something a bit different. Each of us is going to come around and examine your work tonight. We'll make suggestions on your stitching technique along with things you can include like accessories to help make your outfit a success for our fashion parade.'

'And the winner of the show still gets a leather bag,' Mrs Hillingdon, one of Alice's customers, piped up. 'That is the prize, isn't it? That's what is says on all the posters.'

Mary grinned. 'Yes, that's still the prize. The fashion parade is in just a fortnight now, right here in our lovely store, so, ladies, we need to get our fingers stitching.'

The women needed no more encouragement than that, and immediately got to work. Together with Flo, Mary and Jean, Alice walked amongst them, chatting and offering advice. She paused beside one young woman dressed in a bus conductor's uniform whom she recognised as a regular.

'I'm Alice, one of the staff here. I just wanted to say that's a beautiful print. I've always had a soft spot for this ivory with the tiny flowers.'

'Hilda.' The woman smiled back, her cat-like green eyes bursting with friendliness. 'Me too – it was my old wedding dress.'

Confusion passed across Alice's face. 'Don't you want to keep hold of it?'

Hilda shook her head. 'After leading me a dog's life for years he finally left last month, and good riddance, I say.'

'But you must be devastated!' Alice exclaimed. 'Do you have children?'

'Two sons,' Hilda replied, a warm smile flashing across her face. 'John who's eight and Barry who will be seven next month. They were evacuated down to Devon when war broke out but I went and got them back. It was selfish perhaps but being without them was too much of a cross to bear, I missed them that much.'

Alice nodded her head, understanding only too well. 'I'd have probably done the same. My lad's only a few months old but even the thought of having him evacuated sends shivers down my spine.'

'It was the same for me,' Hilda replied. 'John and Barry are the light of my life in a way my husband never was and never will be.'

'But aren't you worried about your sons growing up without a father?'

Hilda snorted with laughter. 'You must be joking. My boys are better off with no father than a father like that.'

'I'm sorry,' Alice said hesitantly, unsure what to say in the face of such bluntness. She was all for calling a spade a spade but she wasn't one to air her dirty laundry in public either.

Hilda shrugged, her bright red hair falling past her shoulders. 'Don't be. He took up with a fancy piece three doors down. Thought it'd humiliate me, but in fact I couldn't be more delighted. He's someone else's problem now and it means all the money I earn can go on me and my boys, and anything left over can go on transforming pretty fabric like this.'

Alice smiled at Hilda's confidence. She did seem genuinely happy with the way things had worked out. 'Do you miss him?' she asked suddenly. 'I mean do you wish things were different?'

Hilda put down her sewing then and looked wistful for a second before she replied. 'No I don't. I mean when we got married it was wonderful, and when my boys came along I thought we would be the perfect family. But then he changed. Got a job as a rag-and-bone man and slowly he started to become someone I didn't recognise. He was carrying on with Ida May for years behind my back so it was a flipping great big relief when he finally left me for her.'

'And you really don't feel humiliated?' Alice asked bluntly.

Hilda threw her head back and roared with laughter, revealing a row of pearly white teeth. 'If anyone's humiliated it's Ida May. She's got to deal with him forever more now.'

Alice smiled. 'It's good you feel that way.'

'It is. And my boys do too. You see, it's always been their happiness I've put first. It's why I never threw him out beforehand: I thought the boys needed him in their lives. I mean every child needs a father, don't they?'

'Unless it's a bad one,' Alice replied in understanding.

'Exactly,' Hilda said knowingly, and returned to her sewing.

As Alice continued to walk amongst the women she began to think about her own situation with Luke. The truth was that since he had gone she hadn't missed him at all; if anything she felt somewhat relieved she no longer had to deal with his erratic behaviour. But of course she knew that he couldn't go on living in a hotel forever and eventually they would have to talk about the future and how they would repair their marriage. Unless he chose to leave her for Hélène of course, and at this particular moment in time Alice couldn't decide whether that would be a blessing or a burden.

Glancing up at the clock she saw it had gone eight, and time to end their stitching evening. The women had done well, she thought as she surveyed them all, heads bent over their work. Some of them had never held a needle before in their lives, much less cut a pattern, yet all of them had taken to the challenge with enthusiasm. This war, Alice realised, in many ways had been a blessing. It had given some women a freedom that they had never experienced before. Yes of course they still had the responsibilities of running a home, caring for children and looking after a husband, but with men on the front line jobs previously only ever done by men had opened up for them, show-ing them a new way of life. Maybe, Alice thought with a start, the problem wasn't all Luke, perhaps it was her too? Perhaps she had become different since war had broken out? She had always been good at fending for herself – she'd had to be when her father left – but she had always been grateful for Luke's protection and care. Perhaps since Luke had joined the war effort she had become too good at taking care of herself.

Now as the women gathered their belongings together, Alice saw Mrs Claremont walk briskly across the floor towards her.

'Mrs Milwood,' she began crisply, and summoned the remaining Liberty girls. 'I'm afraid I have some bad news.'

'Oh?' Flo asked.

'Yes. I'm afraid it won't be possible to hold the fashion parade at Liberty's after all. The board feels that it will be too dangerous to have that many people in store after hours.'

'How ridiculous!' Mary exclaimed.

Rose gasped. 'So what do we do?'

'We can't let these women down,' Alice said determinedly. 'Some have made real progress, not just with their stitching but with their confidence at learning a new skill.'

'I agree,' Mrs Claremont said, surprising everyone. 'I'm appalled, to be honest with you ladies. The evenings have done a lot to restore the store's coffers, and of course having Betty Fawcett as judge has brought us a lot of publicity, not to mention the fact that donations to charity will be lost. In my opinion the board has been very short-sighted, but I'm afraid we *will* have to cancel.'

The girls looked at one another helplessly. After all their hard work, it had come to this?

'There must be something we can do?' Alice wailed.

'What's happening?' Joy asked, suddenly appearing from behind with her hands full of needles, threads and buttons.

'Liberty's say we can't hold the fashion parade here after all,' Rose groaned. 'We're going to have to cancel it.'

'Can't you hold it somewhere else?' Joy asked, dropping a spool of thread to the floor in the process.

'At such short notice?' Alice grimaced. 'The parade is due to be held in two weeks' time. Nowhere can accommodate us that soon.'

'Plus we don't have the money,' Flo said curtly. 'I may not work in the offices any more but I knew the budgets inside and out, and there won't be any money set aside to hire anywhere.'

'What about Mayfair House?' Joy said suddenly. 'You could hold the event there.'

The girls looked at Joy in surprise.

'They'd never let us go in their fancy hotel, would they? Surely they wouldn't have room?' Jean asked cautiously.

'There are two ballrooms.' Joy shrugged. 'They're never both in use at the same time, especially now with the war. My boss Mr Henderson is very understanding. I'm sure if I explained it was for charity he would let you have it for free.'

Alice looked at her sister as if she could kiss her. 'You would really do that for us?'

'Obviously.' Joy smiled. 'We're family.'

As everyone hugged and patted Joy, Alice stared at her sister in open-mouthed wonder. She had never seen her sister behave so selflessly before and it was a side she was enjoying seeing. Who would have thought it – her sister to the rescue yet again.

Chapter Forty-Four

There was no doubt about it, Alice thought as she stared up at the red brickwork, the evening sun beginning to dip behind the clouds, Mayfair House really was the perfect setting for Liberty's fashion parade. It had been almost a fortnight since Joy had suggested that the hotel hosted the show and in that time her sister had worked wonders, organising, liaising and generally providing support when Mr Button fretted about holding a Liberty event off Liberty's premises.

In short she had been wonderful, and Alice wondered what she would have done without her. Stepping inside the hotel reception, which no longer seemed as grand and imposing as it had the first day she had arrived for tea all that time ago, she marched on into the ballroom. The scene took her breath away. Joy had taken the task seriously enough to try and recreate the feel of the shop floor. Aside from the rows of stiff-backed wooden chairs, which lined a makeshift stage area, Joy had somehow managed to get hold of a roll of red carpet which she had laid down the middle. At the front a small table with three chairs was set up – clearly the judging table – behind which stood rolls and rolls of fabric from the stockroom, the likes of which Alice couldn't remember selling since before the war.

'Blimey!' she whistled, taking stock of the bright, delicate silks. 'How many do you think we're expecting?'

Joy smiled as she hauled another chair to the front of the room. 'We've only got a couple of days to make sure everything's perfect, Alice. Besides, if you prepare for success you can expect success.'

Alice looked at her in surprise. 'Wherever did you hear that?'

Joy laughed. 'Cook told me the other day when she was trying a new recipe with powdered egg.' Standing up straight she held her hands aloft as if to show off what she had been doing. 'So what do you really think? The hotel's as excited as Liberty's about the parade.'

Alice looked around her, taking it all in. 'It's incredible,' she whispered. 'It all looks so stunning and I can't believe you've done all this for me.'

Joy smiled stiffly. 'I wanted to help you. You've helped me out often enough.'

'I'm your sister,' Alice replied uncomfortably, 'of course I would help you out. Throwing you out was helping you out, though I know you won't see it that way.'

'I don't,' Joy said evenly. 'But I do know that you weren't being malicious. It's not your fault everything in life has always fallen into your lap.'

Alice blinked at her sister in surprise. 'You keep saying that, is that really what you think?'

'Yes and no. I mean you found the love of your life in a cinema queue; it was an old mate of Dot's that got you the job in Liberty's. I'm just saying you don't know what it's like to really struggle.'

'I can't believe I'm hearing this,' Alice snapped impatiently. 'You seriously think I don't know what it's like to struggle? Don't you remember me working my fingers to the bone to keep you out of the care homes when Dad buggered off? Don't you remember me encouraging you to concentrate on school and to leave the likes of Shirley Allbright alone? It was as though she was pulling you one way and me the other when Dad left.'

'I know you mean well, but you don't understand.' Joy shrugged as if Alice were speaking a different language. 'You've got to respect the old ways. Shirley is as much a part of South London's past as Dad was. You may not like it but you have got to respect it.'

Letting out a deep sigh, Alice sank into one of the stiff-backed chairs beautifully decorated with a ribbon made from a utility fabric remnant. There were times it felt as though it was three steps forward and two steps back with her sister.

'I only ever wanted the best for you, Joy,' she said eventually. 'I didn't want you having the childhood I endured.'

'There's only four years between us!' Joy scoffed.

'And it felt like a lifetime.' Alice smiled sadly up at her sister. 'It was me that was bailing Dad out the nick, me that was dealing with his corrupt mates wanting their share of the spoils, and me that had to deal with the scores of women that worked for Dad, who he cheated out of their profits.'

'I am sorry you had all that to cope with, truly I am. But you and Dad were worlds apart. He did a lot of good as well, you know.'

'Like when?'

'Like the time he gave all that money to the children's home, and the time he took Christmas dinner up Bedlam hospital.'

'All with money and food he'd nicked one way or another!' Alice protested hotly.

'He only ever took money from the rich, those that could afford it,' Joy fired back. 'Shirley told me all about it. Alice, I know you don't understand, but the one thing Dad did drum into me was loyalty. Shirley, well, she's an old friend of Dad's; out of respect for him I should help her.'

Alice opened her mouth to protest but Joy held a hand up to silence her. 'While she may not be getting her life together in a way you approve of, she is trying and I'm not going to let her down.'

'But you would let *me* down,' Alice said coldly.

'That's different! You know it's not like that. Honestly, you drive me mad sometimes.'

'Then perhaps we should agree that it's best not to talk about Shirley!' Alice forced herself to speak brightly, looking away from Joy and around the room itself. 'Blimey! You've made it look just like Liberty's in here.'

Joy smiled. 'That was the plan.'

'And you did it all by yourself. I can't believe it,' Alice marvelled.

'Well, not quite all by herself,' a male voice boomed.

Jumping up and whirling around she glimpsed Luke standing nervously in the doorway. Turning back to Joy, she stared at her thunderstruck. 'What does he mean?'

Joy toed the floor nervously. 'When Luke found out what was happening he wanted to help.'

'Why?' Alice asked bluntly.

'Because you needed help, Alice,' he said, coming into the ballroom.

She looked at him then and gasped in disbelief. The progress he had been making since he had been at home seemed to have disappeared. His face was lined and grey, and he had lost the weight that he had begun to put on.

'I'm your husband, Alice,' he said simply. 'I know I haven't made a very good job of it but I want you to be happy. I want to be the one that makes you happy.'

Alice turned to Joy once more. 'Is this down to you as well?

'Well, I think you should talk. You are married and that counts for something. Whatever you decide to do next, Alice, I think you should hear Luke out. He does love you, in spite of everything.'

Alice stared at her sister in disbelief. 'Since when did you two become such good friends?'

'We're not,' Luke said quietly. 'But since Joy was kind enough to help me get lodgings at the hotel, we realised that although we may not like each other all that much, we do have one thing in common: you.'

'Exactly,' Joy chimed in. 'Which is why I'm going to go now and leave you both to it.'

With that she disappeared out of the room, leaving Alice unsure if she wanted to cuddle her or strangle her. Instead she sat down again and looked up at her husband expectantly. 'Well?'

Luke rushed to sit in the seat beside her. 'I want to say I'm sorry. I'm sorry for all of it. Time apart has shown me how important you are to me. I should never have lost my temper like that. I can see why that would have upset you. I know your father didn't have the greatest control over his emotions and no doubt when you saw me lash out like that you thought I was like him. But I'm not your father, Alice.'

'No, you're a cheater 'n' all,' she said drily, folding her arms.

Luke hung his head in shame. 'There's nothing I can say to that other than I'm sorry. I could tell you that I was afraid, I was lonely, I wasn't sure if I would ever see you again.'

Alice roared with laughter. 'And you thought the best way of coping with missing me would be to jump straight into the arms of another woman. I'm sorry, Luke, but it's all just too much to bear.'

'Please, Alice,' Luke tried again. 'I know I have behaved so, so badly, but you're my wife, Arthur is our child, we should be together.'

'Should we?' Alice asked in disbelief. 'Because since you've got back you've done nothing to show me that you want to be a family and everything to show me that you want to be back with Hélène. Did she see your temper as well?'

As Luke opened his mouth to speak, Alice held up her hand to stop him. 'I don't want the details, thank you. It's just a shame you couldn't have told me any of this yourself and I had to hear it from your brother.'

'I know,' Luke whispered. 'I knew I should have told you, but the whole thing was tearing me apart. I had to confide in someone. Chris was devastated at what I had done, sickened in fact. I'm not surprised he told you. He called me cowardly for not doing it myself.'

There was a silence then. Sitting there, Alice felt as if she had been put through an emotional mangle. She was sick of worrying about her husband's behaviour and whether he loved her and her son. She was sick of treading on eggshells whenever the subject of his health or his war work came up. But most of all she was sick of her marriage being a problem.

'What do you want to do?' she asked wearily.

'I want to come home,' he said earnestly. 'I want to show you that I am the husband you married, that I can be again.'

'But what if it's too late? We've both changed. War has seen to that,' she said, her voice cracking with emotion.

'I'll never stop trying to show you,' he said hurriedly. 'Alice, please.'

Alice rested her head in her hands; she didn't know what to do. Sometimes honesty was the best policy, she thought. 'I need more time to think.'

A flicker of anger crossed Luke's face. 'How much?'

Alice lifted her head and shrugged. 'I don't know. This is about Arthur too. He has to come first. I'm not saying I don't want our marriage to work – we made vows – but I need time to come to terms with everything that's happened, the way you betrayed me.'

'But I've said I'm sorry,' Luke replied incredulously. 'Why can't you forgive me?'

Alice fixed her gaze on her husband. She could see how much pain he was in and wanted to make it better, but she also knew that she couldn't rush into something she wasn't ready for. 'More than anything I want to say yes and forget what happened. I just need time to get over it, to learn to trust you again if we're going to make this marriage strong.'

Alice saw that Luke was broken by her words. 'You're saying that you've given up, aren't you? Just tell me honestly.'

'No.' Alice shook her head vehemently. 'That isn't it at all.'

'Do you still love me?' he asked in a small voice.

'I . . ' she began, thoughts of Jack flitting into her mind as she did her best to bat them away. 'I want to love you, Luke.'

'But you don't love me now?'

She shook her head again, feeling tears prick her eyes. 'I don't want to lie to you. Can you understand?'

Nodding, Luke got to his feet. 'I understand. I understand that you don't love me any more.'

With that he turned and walked out of the door, leaving Alice feeling as if her heart would break.

Chapter Forty-Five

The pub was packed to the rafters with people soaking up the long summer night. Everywhere Alice looked she could see people enjoying a glass of something with a loved one or sisters gossiping over the day's events. It was the sunshine she decided; it put everyone in a good mood no matter what.

After Luke left her in the ballroom Alice had felt bereft until Joy found her sitting in silence on the chair. Without a word she had pulled Alice to her feet and, with their earlier misunderstanding forgotten, together they had caught the bus back into town. Getting off at Oxford Street, the girls had walked down Argyll Street, along Carnaby Street before pausing at the French Pub. Once inside Joy got Alice a port and lemon and then promised she would be back in just a few minutes. Sure enough, Joy returned only this time she wasn't alone: she brought reinforcements in the form of Flo, Mary, Jean and Rose.

'Look who I found.' Joy beamed, before going to the bar for a round of drinks.

Alice smiled gratefully up at her friends. 'You didn't have to come here.'

'Where else would we go?' Mary said softly. 'Joy said you'd had an argument with Luke.'

'Not so much an argument, more a disagreement.' Alice sighed. 'He wants to come back and I'm not ready to let him.'

'Has he apologised for losing his temper like that?' Flo asked, taking the drink gratefully from Joy's hands.

'He has, but I said I wanted a bit more time to think,' Alice replied slowly. 'I know he means well but I don't want things to go back to how they were.'

'Not that simple with a kiddie though, is it,' Jean muttered darkly. 'Sometimes you've got to just make the best of it.'

Alice frowned. Jean didn't know the half of her situation, and she didn't really know why the young girl was here. She was about to say as much when she caught sight of some bruising above the girl's left temple. Their eyes met and Alice could tell Jean knew she had spotted the tell-tale mark. Silently she could feel the girl begging her not to say anything and Alice was more than happy to oblige. In fact she was more than happy to leave maudlin subjects such as the state of her marriage well alone and just enjoy a drink with her friends. She hadn't told them half of what had gone on with Luke and as far as she knew Dot hadn't revealed the truth either. Although she knew she was no victim, Alice didn't particularly want to air her dirty drawers in public just yet .

'So tomorrow it's our final community stitch night before the big parade,' she said brightly, changing the subject.

Jean nodded. 'Mr Button says he's thrilled. Thinks the board will be sorry we couldn't hold it at Liberty's.'

'Well, at least this way Mayfair House gets a bit of publicity, for helping us out,' Rose said sagely. 'But of course it's all down to Joy, she's saved the day.'

'Couldn't agree more.' Alice held her glass aloft. 'I think we should raise a glass to my sister – to Joy.'

As everyone clinked their glasses together, Alice was surprised to see her sister flush with embarrassment. 'Thanks, everyone, but I was just happy to assist.'

'And you've been wonderful,' Rose said loyally. 'I think we can all agree that we'd have been lost without you.' She grimaced in the direction of Alice.

At the glance, Alice felt stung. She wasn't sure what she had done to fall into Rose's bad books today but she clearly had a bee in her bonnet about something.

'So how is life in fabrics?' she asked, looking away from Rose.

'Don't ask me,' Mary groaned. 'I'm still in carpets steering customers down the wrong path. Honestly, girls, why Mr B. agreed I would be a good fit for carpets I really don't know.'

'Perhaps it's because you spent time in Ceylon,' Rose said innocently. 'Maybe he thought you would have a bit of extra knowledge.'

'Rose!' Flo snapped. 'What did you bring Ceylon up for? You know Mary doesn't like talking about her time there.'

Mary laid a hand on Flo's forearm. 'It's fine,' she said softly before addressing Rose. 'Perhaps you're right,' she went on crisply. 'But as I spent most of my time there on my sister's tea plantation I didn't get to find out a lot about carpets.'

There was silence then as Rose looked away, embarrassed. Joy patted her arm reassuringly. 'Why don't we pop to the bar, get some more drinks?'

'But you just got a round?'

'Well, you can never have too many.' Joy chuckled. 'Come on, Rose.'

With that the two girls went to the bar, leaving Mary, Flo, Jean and Alice looking at one another bemused.

'What on earth was all that about?' Flo asked, aghast.

Alice shook her head. 'I don't know what's got into Rose. Sometimes I feel as if I don't know her at all. She would never have spoken to us like that six months ago.'

Mary nodded. 'She's the same at home. I know Malcolm's worried about her. I'll try and talk to her – in fact I could probably do it while I'm at work and nobody would notice. At least it would give me something to do.'

Alice smiled sympathetically. 'I'd like to say that it's the same in the stores, but I'm rushed off my feet. I'm getting muscles on my muscles too.' With that Alice flexed her bicep, leaving the girls in stitches.

'We miss you in fabrics,' Jean said shyly.

'We certainly do,' Flo agreed. 'You and Mary are wasted in other departments. When we were all together we had such a wonderful time.'

'And that reflected on to the customers,' Mary agreed. 'I'm sure sales were up when we were there.'

'They were.' Flo sighed. 'But with the fashion parade, sales have shot up anyway, even though customers aren't happy. Mrs Claremont doesn't let them loiter like we always used to.'

A sad silence fell as the girls finished their drinks.

'How's the singing been going?' Mary asked eventually, turning to Flo.

'Good thanks. But I'm thinking about giving it up. It's making Neil so unhappy. Every letter I've had from him these past two weeks is full of how he doesn't think it's right for me.'

There was a chorus of disappointment from the girls but Flo waved their concerns away. 'I haven't made my mind up yet. I know I'm angry with Neil for telling me what to do, and I know I love singing and honouring Aggie and all she meant to me by doing it. Yet I also know for the sake of my marriage I can't keep doing something that's making Neil so unhappy. He's suggested I turn Aggie's house into a guest house instead.'

Alice raised an eyebrow in surprise. 'A guest house along with a full-time job! Blimey, would you cope?'

Flo shrugged. 'It'll be company for me which is what I really need, along with more money, which we'll need when we have children.'

'You're not expecting already, are you?' Mary exclaimed gesturing to Flo's flat stomach.

Flo laughed. 'No, not yet. But I won't want to waste any time when Neil next comes back from shore leave.'

Alice whistled. 'You're not letting the grass grow.'

'What's the point? Who knows what or where we'll be in five years' time? Might as well enjoy ourselves while we're here. That said' – Flo looked at her watch – 'I need to go. I'm singing tonight and they're usually good tippers on a Thursday.'

'I'll come with you,' Mary said. 'I need to get back and check on Malcolm.'

'And I need to get back too.' Jean sighed. 'My sister will be cross if I'm too late.'

'I'll wait for Joy,' Alice said, gesturing to the bar where her sister and Rose were deep in conversation.

'All right.' Flo smiled. 'See you tomorrow.'

As the girls waved goodbye and walked out of the pub, Alice stood up to chivvy her sister along. Crossing the floor towards the bar area, she saw Joy whisper something to Rose, then quickly flee from the pub.

Frowning, Alice was about to chase after her, when something out of the corner of her eye caught her attention.

Whirling back to look at Rose, she watched in disbelief as her friend leant against the wooden bar, then casually slipped her hand into the coat pocket of the man beside her.

Immediately Alice recognised the sleight-of-hand movement as her sister's signature scam and her blood boiled. Quickly she glanced around to see if anyone else had seen what she had, but she knew already that nobody had. Joy was a master when it came to pickpocketing and it looked as though she had trained Rose well.

Alice had to hand it to her. Joy had always been skilled at training the young and defenceless and she knew that what many saw as Rose's disability Joy would recognise as an advantage. With breathtaking clarity Alice realised precisely why her sister had befriended Rose all this time and it wasn't because she liked Rose or wanted to help her, it was because she knew nobody would expect a partially blind girl to be a thief.

Alice watched in disbelief as Rose slipped the wallet into her own pocket before turning and walking directly out of the pub, white stick firmly in hand. Anger flooded through her as she realised that the reason Joy had suggested they come to this pub for a drink wasn't so Alice could see her friends but so Rose could easily pickpocket in a pub she knew.

As the wooden door of the pub swung back and forth Alice was rooted to the spot, unable to believe what she had just seen. But then she galvanised herself and rushed out. She knew now she would never be able to save her sister, but there was perhaps a chance she could help Rose.

Chapter Forty-Six

It didn't take long for Alice to find her friend and sister. Joy would have trained Rose to walk directly around the corner and, sure enough, as Alice hurried along the pavement and turned right, she saw Rose and Joy huddled together down a dark, narrow alleyway. Getting closer Alice could see another woman had joined them, tall with thick black hair and a raucous laugh that echoed down the passage; Alice felt her blood boil at the sight of her dad's old mate: Shirley Allbright.

'Oi!' she shouted, no longer able to help herself. 'What the hell do you think you lot are doing?'

At the sound of her voice, the girls jumped and Alice didn't miss the flicker of fear that passed across Rose's face. Joy, naturally more brazen, merely rolled her eyes as Alice approached, exchanging a knowing glance with Shirley.

'Well, come on, what are the excuses this time, Joy?' Alice said with a sneer. 'You got Rose to nick stuff for you as a one-off?'

'That's right,' Joy said evenly. 'I told you: I just wanted to help Shirley out. She needed a friend but that's it now.'

'Yes, she was just helping me out,' Shirley echoed, lighting a cigarette, the amber glow giving her heavily made-up face an almost clown-like quality. 'Now run along, Alice, before I make you.'

Alice laughed at the threat. 'Oh Shirley, sweetheart,' she said with a shake of her head. 'I've been seeing women like you off since I was in nappies. My old man might have been a right sod but he taught me a thing or two and don't you forget it. So do me a favour and don't make idle threats at me. They won't wash.'

To Alice's surprise, Shirley backed down. 'I was only saying,' she muttered sulkily.

Alice turned to Joy; the expression on her sister's face was so indignant it was almost comical. 'When are you going to stop lying?'

'I don't know what you're on about,' Joy said hurriedly, nudging Rose out of silence.

'That's right, it was a one-off, a bit of a dare,' Rose said quickly.'

'Don't give me that. I saw that sleight-of-hand movement – it was no one-off. That was a move you've got Rose to perfect. Tell me, Rose, how many times have you really done it?'

At the accusation Rose coloured. 'A few,' she admitted.

'"A few",' Alice echoed in disbelief. 'And you think that's really friendship, do you? Someone who gets you to steal for them?'

'It's not like that,' Joy said quickly. 'Rose and I really are friends.'

'That's right.' Rose's voice was firm and she took a step towards Alice, who, to her surprise, found herself shrinking back. Rose was wearing an expression Alice had never seen before; she looked like a furious cat, ready to pounce on her prey. 'You all think I'm so pathetic, don't you?' she began, her voice so low, Alice struggled to hear her.

'Of course we don't. What makes you say that?'

Rose let out a bitter laugh. 'Yes you do. You all do. Ever since I went blind you've all thought I'm this poor little terrified mite that needed looking after. Not one of you has ever seen me as Rose, a person capable of so much more. Joy saw that; she was the only one that did.'

Alice had heard enough. 'No, she didn't, she used you.'

'No. She gave me a chance to do something different with life, to have some fun.'

'But stealing? You've never stolen anything in your life. Don't you feel even slightly guilty?'

A flicker of remorse passed across Rose's face and Alice felt a flash of hope, only for it to turn to frustration as Rose's features set in mutinous lines. 'Let me tell you something, Alice. All you've done is moan about Luke. Some of us have real problems – I lost my sight, and it's never coming back—'

'You don't know that,' Alice said, cutting across her friend. 'There's still every chance—'

'Oh come off it!' Rose roared. 'You don't believe that any more than I do. And you know what, I don't mind any more. I used to – until I met Joy, I felt like killing myself, I hated my life that much.'

Alice's expression softened. She had no idea her friend felt that way. Slowly she reached out a hand to comfort her but Rose pushed her away. 'Rose love, I didn't know. Why didn't you talk to us? We could have helped.'

'Helped?' Rose scoffed. 'How would you have helped exactly? None of you apart from Mary knew anything about first aid for a start. If you had, my sight might not be as bad as it is now. Mary did what she could but the rest of you stood there like lemons.'

'Rose, no, it wasn't like that,' Alice exclaimed, only for Rose to cut her off.

'It was exactly like that,' she snarled. 'I lost my sight, not my hearing. You were all standing there wondering what the hell to do; if it hadn't been for Mary I might not have got even the very barest of sight back. You know what, Alice, I shouldn't say this but I hate you all for not suffering like I did. What had I done to deserve this?'

Alice felt a knot of fear begin to grow. How had she not known Rose felt like this? What could she do? After the accident, Rose had always talked about forgiveness, even when she confronted one of the men who was behind the hooch ring that had sent her blind in the first place. Now she was blaming her friends? This all felt like it had come from nowhere and Alice was about to say as much when Rose spoke again. 'For months, Alice, while I sat in that little office in Liberty's doing half the job I used to, learning braille, I saw no point to anything and I used to fantasise about the Jerries dropping another bomb on us. When you got caught that day in Bath, I felt jealous! Can you believe that? If only it had been me, I thought, if only I'd been killed in that blast. But Joy helped me realise I was still me, that I still had something to offer.'

Alice clutched the sides of her head; she felt as if she were spinning. She glanced at Joy, who was standing there, her expression unreadable.

'What was it she made you realise you could do?' Alice said evenly as she lowered her hands to her sides. 'That you could have a career thieving? What do you think Malcolm or Tommy would say?'

At that mention of her father and husband Rose hesitated, but only for a moment. 'I don't care. Because no doubt they would see me as the rest of you do, as some poor little girl to be pitied. Joy has shown me how to have fun and I like it.'

'And how long do you think you can keep that up for?' Alice quizzed, ignoring Rose's self-pitying tone.

'When will you realise I couldn't care less?' she spat. 'From now on I'm doing what I should have done a long time ago and that's look out for myself.'

With that Rose stepped back looking satisfied. Alice decided to try another tack.

'You know how many times Joy here's been cautioned by the police? It's a wonder she wasn't doing time with Shirley.' Alice cast a glance at the older woman, who remained silent, still smoking her cigarette. 'You want the same for yourself, Rose? You think that you hated your life before Joy came along, imagine what it would be like behind bars? Or better yet go and see Mrs Matravers, the woman – unlike me and the friends that care about you – who actually *did* send you blind.'

As Rose went to speak, Shirley stubbed out her cigarette and let out a tiny, sneering laugh. 'Oh, you're so self-righteous, Alice. Your father hated that about you, did you know? In fact he hated you full-stop; ashamed of you, he was, and he had every right to be. Little goody two shoes – you made him sick.'

'I'm glad,' Alice fired, Shirley's words having no impact at all. 'I'd have been worried if I'd done something to make him proud. You always were too worried about what Jimmy Harris thought of you – I s'pose that's why you never amounted to much in his organisation. You were too busy saying yes to whatever was asked to think for yourself. Still, you've always been as dense as the National Loaf, Shirley, so it's probably just as well.'

As Alice finished, Shirley rushed towards her, ready to strike. Sensing what was coming, Alice stepped neatly out of the way and couldn't help laughing as Shirley ran straight into the wall behind her, the collision causing her to fall in a heap on the ground.

'You stupid cow,' Joy snarled, rushing to Shirley's side. 'How could you do that? Where's your respect? Shirley should have crowned you – it's no more than you deserve. Not to mention the fact you've made a fool out of me. How could you?'

'Joy,' Alice began wearily, 'I've begged you, I've pleaded with you, I've even threatened to cut you out of my life, but none of it has any effect because you still can't see the damage you're causing. So from this moment I'm choosing not to care what you do. You can nick off whoever you like, just don't involve me in any of it, because you know what? You're dead to me now.'

'You don't mean that,' Joy scoffed, still crouching beside a woozy Shirley. 'You'll be back to bail me out. You always are.'

'Will I?' Alice said with an air of finality in her voice. 'I'm done. I can't take any more and roping my friend into your tawdry games is a step too far. So from now on, I never want to see you again, do you understand?'

'Until you change your mind!' Joy tried again.

'Rest assured: I won't change my mind.' Alice shook her head in disbelief at the scene before her. There was Rose standing loyally beside Joy who was trying to haul Shirley to her feet. 'I've been kidding myself all this time that you would eventually grow up and become the woman I know you're capable of becoming, but I know you won't. And I can't have you in my life any more. I need to protect myself and my son, so this is it, Joy.'

As Alice fell silent, Joy locked eyes with her, but she said nothing. In that moment, Alice was filled with sadness as she realised there was nothing else left to say. In one night she had lost a husband, a sister and a friend. She had never felt so empty or alone in her life.

Chapter Forty-Seven

The rain thundered down as Alice arrived at work the next morning. Once again, following the drama of last night, she had barely slept, with thoughts of Rose and Joy swirling around her head all night.

Arthur had picked up on her misery and grumbled all night long, and so by the time she donned her brown overalls ready to start work she was already exhausted.

Thankfully, Percy Wilmington, the elderly storesman who ran deliveries like clockwork, was a gentleman. Though he had no problem with women working for him while his men were off fighting, he did think that young women raising babies deserved to be cut a bit of slack, especially when they arrived with bags as black as coal under their eyes. So he arranged for Alice to sit in the office and go through a backlog of paperwork while he furnished her with several cups of tea, much to her surprise and delight.

'If I haven't said this before,' she said, smiling as Percy pressed her third cup of tea into her hands, 'you'd make someone a lovely wife.'

Percy threw his head back and roared with laughter. 'That your way of asking me, Alice Milwood?'

Alice chuckled. 'I don't think the present Mrs Percy Wilmington would thank me for that.'

'Maybe not. Mind you, she does have her moments when I shine my boots and leave polish all over her clean floor.'

'I can see why she might be tempted to trade you in,' she agreed, taking a sip of her tea and allowing the warm liquid to soothe her soul. 'Thanks for letting me sit in the office today.'

Percy smiled. 'No problem, love. You look done in – if you don't mind me saying.'

'I don't mind you saying,' Alice replied. 'Let's just say I've a bit on my mind.'

'I can see that.' He patted her hand. 'But you're doing me a favour sorting through this lot. I hate paperwork, always have; it's not something I've ever been any good at. More of a hands-on fella, if you know what I mean?'

Alice nodded as she set her tea down on the only spot on the desk that wasn't covered with paper. 'Only too well. How many months you been sitting on all this?'

A flush of guilt passed over Percy's lined face. 'About three,' he mumbled.

Raising an eyebrow, Alice said nothing. She knew how important it was to Liberty's that they kept good records; if the board got wind of Percy's poor admin skills he'd be strung up.

'What did you do before you got me to do it?' she asked, reaching for another box, which to her delight was marked fabrics.

He sighed wistfully. 'Before war broke out my right-hand man Reg Lake did 'em. Now, Mrs Claremont helps out on occasion when she can see we're in a muddle. Otherwise my missus has a go when we're really stuck. '

Alice laughed. Although she could see Percy was struggling she knew he meant well. 'Leave all this to me. Paperwork's my speciality, especially when it's marked fabrics. I'll have it shipshape for you in no time.'

Percy smiled gratefully at Alice. 'You're a lifesaver, love.'

As Percy returned to the loading bay, Alice dutifully returned to the box of papers. She knew that deliveries kept copies of all the orders, packing notes and delivery slips and each had to marry up with a copy of the sales order that would have been filled out by the relevant sales assistant. In theory it sounded easy but there were so many loose bits of paper in no particular order Alice had a feeling she would have her work cut out.

Still, she thought with a sigh as she got started, it was something to take her mind off her troubles. She had always believed in the power of hard work, and this task was no different. When she had got up that morning, Dot had tried asking her what was wrong but Alice hadn't felt like talking and had instead suggested that she bring Arthur to the final stitch night that evening and she would talk about it then. She realised she was banking on Rose not turning up; after all she seemed to have lost interest in Liberty's and in fact anything that didn't revolve around Joy.

If she hadn't caught Rose pickpocketing the night before, Alice would have felt sorry for her. Alice also knew that this version of Rose, this disgruntled, fed-up and angry version of the Liberty girl she had known for years, didn't marry up with the girl she knew of old. Alice was sure that if she and the rest of the Liberty girls could find a way to help Rose then she would return to her old self and together they could help her rebuild her life into one that made her happy.

However, that all seemed like a pipe dream after the way Joy had manipulated Rose. Just the thought of her sister made Alice's blood boil. Joy had gone too far this time, and Alice wasn't sure if they would ever find a way back to one another. All she could do was hope that in time Joy might genuinely learn a lesson and they could perhaps be reunited. That day, however, seemed a long way off and for now sifting through these papers seemed less complicated.

So far it wasn't as bad as she expected. Despite the cavalier fashion in which everything had been thrown into the box, things were tallying together, yet she was stuck on this one particular piece of paperwork for an order for Beath's. It was for the two-hundred rolls of utility fabric that had seemingly been placed by Flo and had caused all the trouble. Alice could see straightaway that Flo had in fact ordered the two-hundred rolls despite her intention to only order twenty. But what was strange was that on the receipt and invoice, only twenty had been paid for. Perplexed, Alice rooted through the box trying to find the carbon copies of the sales-book order that would have been kept by the Counting House, along with any other notes that might explain the discrepancy, but she could find nothing.

'Percy,' Alice called, heading out to the bay. 'Can you come in and help me with something?'

Peering over from some boxes he was busy packing into a crate, he issued an instruction to one of the girls and came straight over. He laughed, seeing Alice's bemused face. 'That paperwork getting you down?'

'It's this,' she said, pulling out the Beath's slip. 'I can see that Flo took down an order for two hundred rolls of fabric for Beath's but it seems they only ever paid for twenty. Where is the invoice and refund for the remaining one-hundred and eighty they sent back? I'm struggling to get everything to match up and I can't file the paperwork properly without everything in order. Would you have any idea where they might have gone? Would there be another box of fabric paperwork, do you think?'

Taking the slip from Alice's hand, Percy scratched his chin thoughtfully before his face broke out into a broad smile. 'Ah, that's that hush-hush rush job Mrs Claremont wanted sorting. She might know something about the paperwork on this if you can't find it.'

Alice frowned. 'What job?'

'Beath's,' he said emphatically. 'Mrs C. said there had been a mistake over at the Counting House. Flo had taken an order for two-hundred rolls and, regardless of the money that had been taken, we had to send them and settle the rest later. She said we weren't to bother Flo, what with her having a hard time with her aunt.'

'So will the refund slip for the one-hundred-and-eighty they returned be over at the Counting House then?'

Percy shook his head. 'No, all the paperwork from them is here ready to marry up. Stores is the last piece of the jigsaw if you like – that's why we get everyone else's paperwork. Put it to one side if you can't find it now. In my experience this sort of thing always turns up.'

'All right,' Alice sighed, grateful not to have to tear her hair out looking for something that could be anywhere.

'It was a funny old do, though, this order,' Percy said as he handed her back the paperwork. 'Mrs Claremont came down all of a dither and said that Beath's was an important customer and we had to get these two hundred rolls all sent down the same day.'

'The same day?' Alice exclaimed. 'How on earth did she think you were going to do that?'

Percy laughed. 'Well, I dunno how we did, but we did. I did say I was worried about doing it without seeing the paperwork for such a large order, never mind the receipt showing payment, which our drivers – as you know – always carry so the order can be checked when it's delivered. But Mrs Claremont insisted that this was a very special order. So we got 'em down there, only for Beath's to say that wasn't what they'd ordered and they'd actually ordered the twenty that they had paid for.'

'What did Mrs Claremont say?' Alice asked quietly, her heart beginning to pound.

'She said there had been a terrible mix-up; she would talk to Mr Button and to Beath's. She begged us not to say anything about it. She reckoned that poor old Flo hadn't filled the forms in properly but that she would sort it all out and we weren't to worry. She said what was important was the Liberty's and Beath's relationship as it was fragile and it would be no good if we started shouting the odds saying they had got it wrong and they had ordered the two hundred rolls.'

Alice thought for a moment. She remembered how Flo had come to her in a state, unable to understand how she had got an order so wrong.

'So what did you do?' she asked.

'We arranged to take back a hundred and eighty and leave 'em with the twenty they'd paid for.' Percy sighed. 'This sort of thing happens very rarely though. Usually we would have a carbon copy of the order form, receipt and invoice for every order, which then go next to our delivery slips and get filed in our red book. But this time, we've only the delivery slips.'

With that Percy pulled out a huge red file that showed the deliveries and cancellations that had been made, along with copies of any monies repaid.

'That is strange,' Alice said. 'So there are no sales dockets at all for this order?'

'Only the top copy for the two hundred that Flo wrote down at the time which of course the Counting House kept,' Percy admitted. 'However, I suppose poor old Flo was having a hard time after her auntie died. It was lucky Mrs Claremont was there to sort it all out for her.'

Alice bit her lip. 'Yes it was rather lucky.'

'She's a good sort,' Percy said as he turned to go. 'Don't worry too much about those missing papers. Perhaps have a word with Mrs Claremont if you get stuck? She'll be only too happy to help you, I'm sure. She was so worried about letting Beath's down that day.'

As she watched Percy return to the loading bay Alice felt a knot of annoyance form in her stomach. She wasn't quite sure what had happened, but she had a sneaking suspicion that Flo had been framed.

Chapter Forty-Eight

Arriving at the last stitching night before the parade to the sight of Arthur in Dot's arms, with his gummy smile and chubby cheeks, lifted Alice's spirits tenfold.

Greeting Dot, she scooped her son into her own arms, and as she held him close, burying her head in his soft, fine hair, she inhaled the unique sweet smell that was pure Arthur and felt the knot in her shoulders loosen. For a brief moment she felt a pang of guilt that his father wasn't able to enjoy these simplest of moments. After all, that had been all she had wanted when Luke was missing: for them to be one happy family. Who was she to put a stop to that? For her boy's sake, shouldn't she try to make things right one last time?

'I thought you were going to be here for the whole evening, not the last ten minutes,' Dot grumbled, interrupting her thoughts. 'His lordship here has been getting right upset his mother isn't about.'

'Sorry,' Alice said with regret. 'There was something I had to do.'

'Don't tell me Percy had you sorting through even more paperwork!' Mary smiled as she came across to greet Alice. 'I popped in at lunchtime and he said you were too busy to take a break. What was so important?'

Alice gave a knowing smile. 'I'll explain it all in a minute, but first is Rose here?'

Mary shook her head. 'She hasn't been in all day. She was feeling very unwell when I left for work this morning and asked me to let the superintendent's office know she was poorly.'

'Why did you want her?' Flo asked.

'I didn't,' Alice replied bluntly. 'I want to talk about her and for that I want to make sure she's not here.'

There was a pause as the last of the stitchers bade them all goodbye and made their way out of the door. The girls waved and said, 'See you tomorrow night,' then looked expectantly at Alice.

'There's no easy way to say this, but I caught Rose pickpocketing last night.' As the girls gasped in disbelief, Alice continued grimly: 'But that's not what I'm worried about. When I spoke to her afterwards she told me she hated her life and that up until she had met Joy, she wanted to do away with herself.'

'Why didn't she tell us how she felt?' Mary protested. 'I know she hasn't said a word to Malcolm; he would be devastated.'

'I thought she was being so strong,' Flo replied thoughtfully. 'She seemed to have been remarkably accepting.'

'I think she was *too* accepting,' Alice mused. 'She was screaming in the street last night that she felt Joy was the best thing that had ever happened to her. And if that wasn't bad enough she told me she thought we were to blame for her blindness. She said she hated us for the fact we hadn't lost our sight when she had.'

'That's terrible,' Flo said sadly. 'And that's why she's pickpocketing?'

'I suppose she wants to feel something other than sorry for herself,' Mary murmured. 'Crime will do that, I suppose.'

'But what's she blaming us for?' Dot cried indignantly. 'I mean, what the hell have we done? It's not like we poured the flaming whisky down her throat, is it?'

'I don't know, girls,' Alice answered. 'But I do know that something has to be done. We can't let Rose fall through the cracks like this.'

'What would her poor father say if he knew what she was up to? Or Tommy?' Flo exclaimed.

Alice shrugged. 'She doesn't care. Says she's not remotely bothered what they think. Joy's the only one she's interested in, says she makes her feel as if she's alive.'

'And go hang the rest of us, I suppose.' Dot sighed. 'Well, I think you're right, Alice, something has to be done but I don't know what. I imagine that the more we tell her not to hang about with Joy, the more attractive she'll become.'

'Precisely,' Alice agreed. 'I don't think we have to rush into this. Whatever we do now we need to think carefully about.'

'I suppose having a word with Joy is out of the question?' Mary offered, only to be met with a roar of laughter from Alice.

'She was there when I tore strips off Rose. Looked at me all smug as Shirley Allbright told me not everyone is cut out to be a goody two shoes like me.'

'Cheeky cows,' Dot growled.

'That's what I said,' Alice sighed. 'Still, I thought we could try and put our heads together and help her. I mean, Rose isn't Joy, she doesn't have to end up going the same way.'

'Perhaps a simple chat with her will do the trick?' Flo suggested.

Alice grimaced. 'Based on last night's performance I very much doubt it, but perhaps once the dust has settled?'

'In the meantime that doesn't explain why you couldn't get to the stitching night, lady,' Dot said. 'So come on, what were you up to?'

'And come to think of it, where's Jean?' Flo frowned. 'She said she would be on hand to help tonight.'

'These young kids,' Dot snapped. 'No sense of responsibility.'

'Actually, Jean was helping me,' Alice said in a hushed whisper. 'I've asked her to get Mr Button for us; she should be along in a minute.'

Flo frowned. 'What on earth are you up to? And why do we need Mr Button?'

Alice clapped her hands together excitedly. 'Every cloud has a silver lining. Today poor old Percy felt so sorry for me in deliveries he asked me to sort through the department's paperwork.'

'That's a silver lining?' Dot scoffed. 'I should hate to be around if Percy's handing out treats.'

'Wait!' Alice insisted. 'While I was going through the paperwork I found a discrepancy with the order that got Flo demoted.'

'How do you mean?' Flo asked quietly. 'I know I made the mistake – I was distracted, finding the job too much for me.'

Alice shook her head. 'That wasn't it at all. You didn't make the mistake, Flo, but someone made it look as though you had.'

Confusion crossed Flo's face. 'I don't understand.'

With that, Jean suddenly arrived clutching a piece of paper. Her face was flushed and she looked as if she had run a marathon.

'Where's Mr Button?' Alice asked.

'In with Mrs Claremont.'

Alice gasped in despair. 'So he's not coming?'

Jean shook her head. 'He's coming and he's bringing Mrs Claremont too.'

'Alice, what the hell is all this about?' Dot cried.

'I'll explain when Mr Button gets here,' Alice replied, turning her attention back to Jean. 'What's Mrs Claremont doing here?'

'Ensuring preparations for the fashion parade are in order, Mrs Milwood,' Mrs Claremont said crisply, approaching swiftly with Mr Button following closely behind. 'We were in rather an important meeting when Miss Rushmore interrupted us saying we had to get to the crypt immediately.'

'It's all actually worked out rather perfectly, Mrs Claremont,' Mr Button said smoothly. 'You see, girls, I have some rather exciting news which I will make official next week; however, I don't think Mrs Claremont will mind if I share it now?' he asked, turning to the older woman.

As she smiled and nodded her head, Mr Button's face broke into a broad smile. 'I have great pleasure in announcing that the board, the Liberty family and I have all agreed that Mrs Claremont will become deputy store manager. She has proven herself to be an excellent leader and I'm thrilled.'

As Mr Button finished, Alice and the girls looked anxiously at one another before realising that they were now supposed to congratulate Mrs Claremont.

'That's wonderful news, Mrs Claremont,' Dot said, realising someone had to say something. 'You must be very proud.'

'I am,' Mrs Claremont said evenly. 'I've plenty of plans for this place. My replacement in fabrics will be announced in due course but in the meantime Miss Rushmore here will do a wonderful job of running the department.'

Alice saw Jean had gone pale and she felt a flash of anger. Jean was a nice girl but too young and inexperienced to run a department. The responsibility was far too great, and Alice knew that Mrs Claremont had only suggested it so she could keep a firm grip on fabrics while she continued her bid to run the store. This had to stop.

Drawing herself up to her full height, Alice felt a pang of worry. This wasn't the way this was supposed to turn out at all. She'd been hoping for a private word with Mr Button with the rest of the Liberty girls around her for support.

Nervously she cleared her throat and glanced at Jean, who nodded and pressed a heavily creased piece of paper into her hands.

'I just wanted to talk to you about the incorrect order Beath's received recently, sir,' Alice said.

'Oh?' Mr Button frowned. 'I thought we had dealt with this, Mrs Milwood. I'm not sure, for Mrs Canning's sake, there's a lot of sense in dragging it up.'

'Actually there is, sir,' Alice tried again. 'You see, new evidence has come to light.'

Mrs Claremont snorted. 'New evidence! What do you think this is? A courtroom drama in the Old Bailey?'

'What is this new evidence?' Mr Button asked quietly, ignoring Mrs Claremont.

'Today, whilst I was working in the stores, I was asked to sort through the deliveries paperwork. To cut a long story short, I was unable to find any carbon sales orders for either the two hundred or twenty rolls Beath's ordered.'

'You must have done,' Flo insisted. 'I wrote the order out for two hundred, which was entirely my fault as I knew Beath's only wanted twenty. I remember speaking to them about it and being pleased it was such a big order. I must have been distracted, there was so much happening, and then of course Mrs Claremont was good enough to resolve it for me while I was away on compassionate leave, and I didn't know anything about all this until they rang me. It was all my fault Alice. I knew they wanted twenty rolls but I wrote down two hundred. I made a terrible mess of it all.'

'The thing was you didn't make a terrible mess of it, Flo.' Alice spoke evenly.

'We've dealt with all this,' Mrs Claremont said with a wave of her hand. 'Mrs Milwood, I don't understand why you're pushing Mrs Canning like this. Forget it.'

'I won't forget it because I found the carbon copies that went missing. And they clearly show that Flo did write down an order for twenty rolls.'

There was a collective gasp as Alice produced the carbon copies.

'Let me see those,' Flo demanded, taking the papers from Alice's outstretched hand.

'I've also got the original,' Alice continued. 'It was stashed with the carbon copies. It seems the Counting House never had the original order and were entirely reliant on a conversation with Mrs Claremont about the mistake. However, if you look at the original top copy in Flo's order book you can see quite clearly that it states she took an order for two hundred; the only trouble is that where twenty has been crossed through and two hundred has been written in full in its place – as we must always do with orders for more than a hundred – you can quite easily see that firstly this isn't Flo's writing, and secondly this handwritten two hundred isn't visible on the carbon copies as it should be.'

'What on earth does that prove?' Mrs Claremont scoffed. 'Mrs Milwood, you're wasted in deliveries. With these crackpot theories you ought to be Miss Marple.'

Flo snapped her head up as she handed the papers to Mr Button for examination. 'It proves that I didn't make a mistake, but someone made it look as though I did.'

'I must admit, Mrs Canning, this is all rather strange,' Mr Button said hesitantly as he pored over the carbon copies and the original form. 'But who on earth would do something like this?'

'Can I see those?' Mrs Claremont said, examining the papers in Mr Button's hand. 'I must say that this is all very strange. I shall make it a priority to look into it when I take up my new post properly next week.'

As Mrs Claremont went to stuff the papers in her bag, Alice stretched out a hand to stop her. 'I think we can clear up the mystery quite easily here and now,' she said, turning to Jean. 'Miss Rushmore, would you mind telling everyone how I knew where to find these papers?'

'Because I knew they were hidden at the back of the cash register,' Jean said in a small voice.

'Are you admitting to this?' Mrs Claremont gasped in surprise. 'Why would you do this to poor Mrs Canning?'

Alice glanced at Jean then, and saw her face flush with annoyance. 'I never did nothing to Mrs Canning,' she shouted suddenly. 'I shoved them papers there because you told me to throw 'em away. Only trouble was, I didn't think what you were doing was right. Unlike you, Mrs Canning and Mrs Milwood were trying to help me learn about fabrics; you just wanted me to be your lackey. So I hid 'em, because one day I knew the truth would come out that you were the one who made it look like Mrs Canning had made a mistake.'

At that Mrs Claremont let out a short burst of laughter. 'Don't be so silly, Jean. I shall discuss this with you further next week. Don't worry, Mr Button, I'll get to the bottom of this.'

Only Mr Button looked grave. Alice could see his eyes were filled with fury and his nostrils were slightly flared. She didn't think she had ever seen him look quite as angry as he looked now. 'This has been sorted out quite satisfactorily now, Mrs Claremont,' he said slowly. 'The words "two hundred" have been written in your hand.'

Mrs Claremont's hands flew to her throat. 'Now, Mr Button, I can assure you that I had nothing to do with this and I'm shocked you think I would stoop so low.'

'I don't think it, I can see it with my own eyes,' Mr Button snapped as he took the papers from Alice's hands and jabbed at the offending numbers. 'Mrs Claremont, I cannot believe what I'm hearing. You have been responsible for causing trouble for one of my most loyal and capable staff members when she was facing a particularly gruelling time.'

'Please, Mr Button, it wasn't like that. You must believe me,' Mrs Claremont begged. But Mr Button shook his head at her in disgust. 'It gives me no pleasure at all to say this, Mrs Claremont, but I'm afraid you have left me with no choice. As of this moment your employment is terminated. Don't come back tomorrow.'

Chapter Forty-Nine

Alice knew she ought to be delighted that not only had Mr Button thrown Mrs Claremont out on her ear but that she and Mary had been reinstated to fabrics. Yet somehow she felt surprisingly flat as she began her walk home, Arthur fast asleep in his pram, as she went over the events of the evening.

As well as reinstating Mary and Alice, Mr Button had offered Flo the chance to have her old job as deputy store manager back but she had refused. Instead she had simply asked if things could go back to the way they had been with her in charge of fabrics and Alice as her deputy.

Astonished, Mr Button had agreed, before commending Jean for her bravery in speaking out against her boss for wrongdoing. All in all it had been a success and with the fashion parade now only a day away Alice knew she ought to feel overjoyed with life when instead she felt listless: so much so that she had refused the other girls' invitation to go for a celebration drink, and instead insisted she needed to take Arthur home. The truth was she felt so deflated that even if she hadn't had a baby to care for, she would have refused – she just wanted to be alone. There had been so much to think about lately, so much that had gone wrong, it felt as if her life was being continually upended and she needed a few minutes to take stock.

Rounding the corner and heading in the direction of the Tube station, the sight of a young couple walking in front of her caught her eye. Dressed in his army uniform, he looked as if he was home on leave for a couple of days, while his wife, who looked just as smart, dressed in a navy tea dress, seemed torn between doting on the baby in the pram she was pushing and the husband with his arm wrapped around her shoulders. As she watched him drop a kiss lightly on the top of the woman's head, she felt a stir of jealousy. That ought to have been her. She was supposed to have had that life, she thought bitterly. When Luke came home she'd thought she would be able to give Arthur the family she always wanted for him, but it seemed Luke had other ideas. A cheating father was not what she wanted for her child, but then again, she thought, looking into the pram where her son was sleeping contentedly, did she want a future for him where both parents were at war or, worse, living apart?

Glancing again at the couple ahead of her, Alice felt a sudden resolve. She wanted to try and give that happy family to Arthur and she wasn't ready to give up without a fight. She didn't know what the future held for her and Luke, but she owed it to Arthur and to herself to find out.

Before she could change her mind Alice made an abrupt turn in the street, almost waking Arthur in the process. Then, with a quick tug at the sleeve of her cardigan, she walked determinedly west in the direction of Mayfair House.

Just half an hour later after catching a bus in Regent Street, Alice had arrived outside the red-bricked building, heart pounding as she tried to summon up the courage to step inside.

She still hadn't decided quite what she would say to Luke. Should she tell him that they ought to sort out their differences for the sake of their son, or should she admit to the kiss with Jack and reveal she was still hurt about Hélène but that she was prepared to try to forgive and forget?

Neither seemed a better option than the other, and frankly the more Alice thought about it, the less she knew what she wanted to say. Now as she stood in front of the hotel, the uniformed doorman looking at her as if she were slightly unhinged, Alice gritted her teeth and walked straight into the foyer.

Heels clacking across the marble floor, she smiled at the receptionist who she knew was a friend of Joy's. 'Is Luke here? I just thought I'd pop up and see him.'

The receptionist grinned at Arthur and ran her finger down the handwritten ledger on her desk. 'He hasn't signed out so yes, he should be in. Leave the pram in the corner if you like, save you the trouble of taking it all the way up there.'

'Thank you!' Alice scooped out her still-sleeping boy.

She knew Luke was staying in the staff quarters at the top of the hotel. She walked down to the lift at the far end of reception and pressed the call button.

As she waited for the lift to appear Alice tapped her foot nervously on the marble floor. Would he be pleased to see her, or would he simply tell her to get out? After all, the last time they had seen one another she hadn't exactly given him an awful lot to feel hopeful about. Still, she thought as the lift pinged open in front of her, that was then and this was now. All she could do was hope that together they could find a new way forwards.

As the lift raced upwards, the scream of the lift shaft became so loud that Alice was terrified Arthur would wake up and start screaming himself in protest. But amazingly, as if sensing the magnitude of what his mother was about to do, Arthur slept through it all, stirring only briefly when the lift ground to a halt on Luke's floor.

Stepping out into the corridor, Alice managed a smile. These maids' quarters were in stark contrast to the marble floors and vaulted ceilings in reception. Here the corridors had concrete floors and bare brick walls, and as Alice crept past door after door, she had a feeling that the rooms themselves would hold only a single bed and not much else.

Eventually she found Luke's room. Rapping on the panelled wooden door she hoped Luke would let her in without fuss, as Arthur was heavy and her arms were beginning to ache.

Impatiently she waited but there was no reply so she rapped again and pressed her ear to the door to listen for sounds of movement. 'Luke,' she called. 'It's me. I thought we could talk.'

Listening again, she thought she could hear the sound of voices and frowned: he must have the radio on. She rapped again, but there was still no reply, just the echo of laughter.

Glancing down at Arthur, who now felt like a baby elephant in her arms, Alice tried the handle. Amazingly the door wasn't locked and she was able to walk straight inside. Only as she pushed the door open and took a step into the room she found herself wishing she could turn back time, for the sight in front of her left Alice thunderstruck.

A wave of sickness crashed over her as she made sense of the scene before her. Clothes had been flung across the room, a tangle of tops and bottoms immersed in their very own rumba, while a half-drunk bottle of port with two glasses rested on the bedside table.

Alice's gaze swept past the debris of what had obviously been up until now a very good evening and took in the sight of two figures lying naked in a single bed. Rooted to the spot, she fixed her eyes on her husband who was lying in a jumble of sheets, his head propped up on the pillow, looking for all the world as if he were about to face court martial.

She watched the colour drain from his face.

'Alice,' he began hurriedly, 'I can explain.'

Alice held up her one free hand to stop him. She wasn't interested in what Luke had to say. The scene before her told her everything she needed to know and she realised with a disgusted thud that the time for talking was over, that there was nothing that Luke could say that would make anything about this situation better. As her eyes left those of her husband's she turned her gaze to the other figure, because lying next to him, sheets clamped around her chest as she stared at Alice, her green eyes flashing defiance, was her sister.

Chapter Fifty

Even though it was entirely inappropriate under the circumstances, Alice wanted to laugh. She had spent years trying to help Joy and set her on the right path. Now, here was Joy truly demonstrating what she thought of her sister and Alice knew that Luke would have been only too willing an accomplice. This was a man who had set up home with another woman, leaving his wife to think he might be dead. Sleeping with her sister was surely just the next step in the road. It was sad really that they couldn't have been a bit more imaginative.

'And what exactly can *you* explain, Joy?' Alice asked, her voice steady and even despite the fact her heartbeat was roaring in her ears. 'Can you tell me why you and my husband are curled up together in this single bed? Is it because you're freezing cold in the middle of summer perhaps? Is it because you're working on some new rationing project where clothes are not required, or is it because you two are a pair of dirty, cheating little sods who want ripping limb from limb?'

Joy sat up and smiled smugly at her sister. She looked like the cat that got the cream. 'There's no need to be like that,' she replied in a mocking tone. 'Think about Arthur. Think about your family.'

Alice looked at her sister, ready to open her mouth and tear strips off her for her behaviour as she usually did, despite the fact she was carrying Arthur. But she knew this was exactly what Joy wanted. It was so pathetic that Alice almost felt sorry for her.

She turned her gaze back to her good-for-nothing husband. To think she had been considering falling to her knees and telling him about her kiss with Jack. It was clear to her now just how much the war had changed things, putting distance between Alice and Luke both physically and emotionally, so that when he met Hélène he had allowed himself to be swept away. By the time Luke had returned, Alice had changed too. Not only had her son become the apple of her eye, but she had become more confident and capable too. She didn't need Luke the way she used to. Alice glanced down at Arthur, who was now beginning to stir. She had spent so long trying to create a perfect family life, and to give him opportunities that she'd never had, that she'd forgotten to worry about whether or not the man who was his father was worthy of such a title.

'Alice,' Luke tried again, cutting into her thoughts as he tried to pat down his mussed-up hair. 'Please can you forgive me? I made a mistake. I was feeling low after our exchange yesterday. It's been so hard for me since I got back from France; I don't know who I am any more. This meant nothing. I'm sorry, I got carried away, Joy was there, we had some port, we got lost in the moment – you know how these things go.'

Alice had heard enough, and all she wanted to do was get out of that tiny room that reeked of whatever the pair of them had been doing and return to the safety of the Elephant and Castle.

Squaring her shoulders, she lifted her chin in defiance and held on tightly to her son. 'Then let me make it a little easier for you,' she said with a hint of steel to her voice. 'I don't want you in my life any more, or Arthur's. In fact, I don't ever want to see you again. So go back to Hélène in

France, go to your brother's in Wales, or set up house with Joy here for all I care. As long as you don't darken my door again, Luke Milwood, I really don't care what you do.'

A flash of anger crossed Luke's face. 'I think you do care and you will care. You are my wife. You're stuck with me.'

Alice took another look at the scene before her and said nothing. Instead she turned to go, pulling open the door, only to swing round and face her husband and sister, one more punishing delivery to make. 'You two deserve each other. Luke, we may never be able to get a divorce, so yes, legally perhaps Arthur and I are *stuck with you* as you call it. You may even insist on coming home, and living in a house where nobody wants you. I can't stop you doing that. But know that in my heart' – she banged her hand against her chest for emphasis – 'you died the moment I received that letter telling me you were missing.'

Chapter Fifty-One

The following morning Alice got up to find Mary sitting at the table, her face glum, while Dot busily buttered toast with the barest scraping of spread as if her life depended on it.

'What's up with you two? And Mary, what are you doing here? You don't live here no more.'

'Malcolm and Rose have been up since the crack of dawn arguing.' Mary sighed, resting her head in her hands. 'I thought I'd escape and come here for a cup of tea before work. It was hell to listen to.'

'What were they rowing about?' Alice asked, placing Arthur on the floor as she took a sip of tea.

'Malcolm found out about Rose's pickpocketing. He discovered the wallet she took from the man's coat – although all the cash was gone, his Identity Card was in there and of course it all came out.'

'We've *got* to get through to Rose somehow,' Alice said urgently.

'I know.' Mary nodded, her eyes filled with concern. 'That's what me and Dot have just been discussing.'

'Is that why you're upset then?' Alice asked, turning to Dot.

'Partly,' Dot replied curtly, 'and partly because George's sister's coming today.'

'Your husband George?' Mary quizzed.

Dot nodded.

'Vera?' Alice exclaimed. 'But why? She's not seen you for ages.'

'Exactly.' Dot sighed as she took a bite of her breakfast, sending crumbs across the work surface. 'She wants something. Wrote to me last week saying she was coming over from Bromley to see me today.'

'When was the last time you saw her?' Mary asked.

'Must be two Christmases ago.' Dot sighed again. 'She always manages to find something wrong. I haven't dared tell her I'm courting. I can only imagine what I'm meant to have done this time.'

Mary frowned. 'Why would she be upset? George has been dead twenty-five years.'

'Because in her head I should still be wearing black and in mourning,' Dot said, rolling her eyes. 'George always thought she was a daft mare as well, so he never had much to do with her when he was alive.'

'So will you tell her today then?' Mary asked. 'About Mr Button? I mean if he's mentioned marriage.'

'Yes, you've kept that very quiet làtely.' Alice chimed in. 'Has that all gone off the boil? I thought you were considering it.'

Dot shrugged. 'He hasn't even asked me, so there's nothing to consider.'

'But if he does?' Mary persisted.

'Then I have to say I don't know, girls.' Dot pushed her plate of toast away from her. 'I love Edwin, but I'm not sure I could get married again, not now.'

'You're never too old to get married again,' Mary offered. 'Life's short, Dot.'

'I know that! It's not the shortness of time that bothers me, girl, it's the length of marriage! They ought to dish out medals for length of service – Alice will tell you.'

Alice held her hands up. 'Don't talk to me about marriage! I'm hardly the world's greatest advertisement for it. Anyway,' she said, swiftly bringing the subject back to

Dot, 'it's not exactly like Vera will be here for long, is it? Quick cup of tea and she'll be off, surely?'

'Let's hope so. I shouldn't be so mean about her. She's my last link to George, but the trouble is she's still so possessive over him and she's been worse since her Reg died five years ago.'

'Was Reg her husband?' Mary asked.

'That's right. They wed the same time as me and my George, had two children together. Sam and Violet, who must be about your age now – I haven't seen them for a long time either.'

'She could just want to say hello,' Alice mused.

'Never in this world.' Dot sniffed, pulling her plate of toast back and taking a large bite. 'What's up with you anyway?' she asked, regarding Alice thoughtfully. 'You've a face like a busted clock.'

Alice sighed. She had half thought about lying but decided there was no point. The truth would come out sooner or later – it always did. 'Last night I went to find Luke to talk to him about repairing our marriage.'

'Good idea, love,' Dot said sagely, jerking her head towards Arthur. 'That kiddie needs a dad.'

'That's what I thought, and still do think,' Alice replied. 'Only trouble is that I don't think Luke is fit to be Arthur's father. When I arrived at Mayfair House and went up to his room I found him in bed with another woman – Joy.'

Mary's jaw dropped open with shock. 'Oh my goodness.'

'That two-timing little sod,' Dot seethed, putting her toast down in disgust. 'And as for her, if I lay eyes on that little madam again I'll crown her! Who the hell does she think she is?'

Taking a deep breath, Alice lifted her chin and looked at her friend and then her landlady. 'I will never forgive Joy for this. I mean, sleeping with her own brother-in-law is low, even for her.'

'You know she only did it out of revenge, don't you, love?' Dot said, echoing Alice's own thoughts on the matter. 'Much as I want to string the little cow up for this, you know this was never about her wanting Luke.'

'I know. This was all about those daft codes of honour my old man used to bang on about.'

'Oh yes.' Dot raised a knowing eyebrow. 'Your old mum used to tell me about 'em. "Always get revenge on someone if they make you look a fool" was one of his favourites.'

Mary stared at them in disbelief. 'You think that's why Joy slept with Luke? Because of something your father said?'

'Joy was and I suppose still is a real daddy's girl, Mary.' Alice sighed. 'I think if she could have she would have followed him to the States.'

'You did your best for her, love,' Dot insisted.

Alice shrugged, feeling helpless. 'That may be so, but I didn't realise quite how angry Joy was with me. You should have seen her face when I caught them both. It was as though all her Christmases had come at once. She looked so pleased with herself. I think she imagined telling me all the details afterwards, but for me to catch them at it, well, that was the icing on the cake.'

'I'm shocked,' Mary exclaimed. 'I mean I thought I knew better than anyone how low sisters could go, but what Joy has done, no matter what her motivation, is despicable. As for Luke, I knew you were having problems but how on earth did he think that sleeping with your sister would fix them?'

Alice let out a bitter laugh. 'I don't think he thought about me for a moment. I think he thought about himself, and that's what he's been doing for months.'

'How do you mean?' Mary asked.

Alice looked down at what was left of her cup of tea. When Chris had first told her of Luke's betrayal she'd thought she would fall to pieces, but now, in her home, surrounded by women who truly loved her, she felt oddly calm.

'I mean that Luke could have come back from France a lot earlier,' she admitted, her voice shaky. 'Chris told me when he came to visit that the reason Luke didn't come back sooner wasn't because he was waiting for the right time to make his escape. It was because he'd fallen in love with a French Resistance fighter named Hélène. The only reason he returned at all apparently was because this Hélène was making noises about marriage and that wasn't something Luke could do – given he was already married.'

As Alice's words hung in the air there was a silence; Mary and Dot exchanged looks of incredulity.

'I can't believe it,' Mary said at last. 'How could he deceive you like that?'

''Cos he's got the morals of an alley cat,' Dot growled, lifting her butter knife in fury and waving it in the air. 'I tell you this, he'd better not think about coming back here or he might have another injury to worry about besides his gammy leg. I hope you're not thinking of having him back, love? He wants stringing up for what he's done.'

'Does Luke know you know?' Mary pressed.

Alice nodded. 'Yes, I told him some time ago. He apologised, said it wasn't what I thought ...' Her voice trailed off; repeating the excuses he had fobbed her off with made her feel so weak and used – she couldn't bear to repeat them.

'What will you do now?' Dot asked bluntly.

Alice raised a smile. It was typical of Dot to be so practical. 'I don't know,' she replied honestly. 'I know that I can't forgive both of these betrayals but divorce? I don't know if I can do that either. The expense, the stigma of it all …'

'And yet he's the one that's left you with this decision,' Dot snapped angrily, getting up to clear away the breakfast things.

'I just cannot think about this any more. All I know is that us girls are back together in fabrics from this morning and we've got the fashion parade at Mayfair House tonight.'

'And work is often the best place to find an answer to our problems,' Mary reasoned. 'Now shall we go up there? The last thing we want is to be sacked for tardiness.'

Mary needn't have worried. After an effortless Tube ride into the centre, the girls were ten minutes early for work and delighted to find Flo behind the cash register going through the previous few days' orders.

Mary chuckled. 'It's as though you've never been away.'

Flo beamed in return. 'It feels so wonderful to be back here. I should never have left. Fabrics is my home.'

'We're all back where we belong,' Mary chimed in, just as Jean approached the girls, looking nervous.

'Hello, Mrs Canning,' she said cautiously.

'Jean! I'm looking forward to working together,' Flo welcomed her. 'Now, I know how you did things with Mrs Claremont but when I ran fabrics we did things a bit differently.'

'All right.' Jean nodded nervously.

'There's no need to look so afraid.' Alice smiled encouragingly at the youngster. 'Trust me, you're in safe hands, but you've a lot to learn.'

Flo nodded in agreement. 'Now, I want you to know everything about this department so you can thrive, but I need you to trust me.'

'I'll do anything, Mrs Canning.'

'Good. In that case, we'll start you in the stockroom, familiarising yourself with all the fabrics. Mary will show you.'

Jean nodded. 'Very good, Mrs Canning.'

'Before you go, shall we just sort out tonight's parade?' Flo said.

Alice checked her watch; there were five minutes to go before they opened. 'I think everything is under control. Jean, did you arrange with the women that we would all meet them at the hotel?'

Jean nodded. 'That's right, Mrs Milwood. I said I would meet them at six to set everything up before the event at seven.'

Alice nodded her approval. 'Excellent. I'll bring spare buttons and threads, just in case.'

'And I'll go on ahead with Jean to sort everything out at the hotel,' Mary said kindly. 'That way you don't have to spend any more time with Joy than you have to.'

Confusion passed across Flo's face. 'What have I missed?'

'I'll tell you about it properly later,' Alice replied. 'Let's just say Joy has been up to her old tricks and plenty more besides.'

'Oh my days, Alice,' Flo said sympathetically. 'You do whatever you need to do then.'

Alice smiled gratefully at her friend. 'Thank you.'

'Now, is there anything else we need to organise? I take it Betty knows where she's going tonight?'

'Yes, I've confirmed everything with her, Mrs Canning,' Jean explained. 'She will meet Mr Button at the hotel, but there is just one more thing I wanted to tell you.'

'What is it?'

'I've agreed to see Mrs Claremont for a cuppa next week. There are a few bits she left in the staffroom and I offered to get them to her. I know she behaved dishonourably, and I don't want you thinking I agree with what she did, but … well … this has all been a bit out of character for her.'

Alice nodded in understanding. 'That's very good of you, Jean.'

'Is she all right?' Flo asked quietly. 'Mrs Claremont, I mean?'

'She's all right. A bit shell-shocked, I think. It was well known in gifts how she hard she worked, and she expected the same from everyone else. A lot of the girls hated her for it, but I always felt sorry for her. I suppose that's why she took me under her wing a bit, because I never took any of the things she said to heart.'

'Why did you feel sorry for her though?' Alice quizzed in hushed tones as the shop's door was thrown open to the public.

'Rumour was that she'd been shunned by her family and friends many years ago. Even her own kids didn't want anything to do with her. Liberty's was her life; she gave it everything she had,' Jean said with a sigh. 'I knew what it was like to want to create something of your own, so I suppose I cut her a lot of slack where some of the other girls couldn't.'

'That was kind of you,' Flo said gently.

'I don't know about kind.' Jean's voice was sad. 'I just felt that she was someone that would blossom if you gave her a bit of kindness. I knew she had the good of the store at heart. But when I moved across to fabrics I couldn't believe what I was seeing – such cruelty. She was never so mean in gifts. The lies, the deception, the ambition in taking your job, Mrs Canning, and the way she always tried to do you down, Mrs Milwood. I had never seen her that way – it was like she was possessed. It was why I had to speak up, Mrs Milwood, you know, about the sales dockets she told me to get rid of. I knew it was wrong, but I didn't know what else to do.'

'You did just the right thing,' Flo said soothingly. 'Don't worry about it any more.'

As Flo snapped her notebook shut and stuffed it into her pocket, the first thrum of shoppers shuffled through the store.

'Just one final thing,' Flo called as Jean turned away.

'Yes?' Jean replied cautiously.

'There's no Miss or Mrs in this department. We're all on first names here.'

'All right, Flo,' Jean replied hesitantly.

'Good. We'll make a proper fabric girl out of you yet, Jean!'

As Jean smiled, Alice felt a flush of pride. Her personal life might be in disarray, but now she was back in fabrics where she belonged with a new girl to nurture and train, she felt as if things were finally slotting back into place.

Chapter Fifty-Two

As Alice got off the bus and walked along the road towards Mayfair House, she felt a sudden chill, despite the warmth of the evening and the flowers and shrubs out in full bloom. It wasn't lost on her how she had walked up this road twenty-four hours ago, unaware her world was about to be obliterated.

Now, with every step, the roar of her heartbeat became louder in her ears as she fretted over what she might find tonight if she saw Luke or Joy. Taking a deep breath, she told herself to calm down. After all, she had no idea if either of them would be there, although she imagined it was certainly possible given Luke was helping with odd jobs around the hotel and Joy was a waitress in the restaurant.

Still, she thought, she had nothing to be ashamed of and she refused to be pushed into a corner because of the actions of others. As her heels clacked across the pavement, she found her thoughts straying to Jack. Since their kiss, Alice had done her best not to think about him, telling herself that no good would come from picturing his face or allowing herself to wonder what he might be doing with his days. He had no place in her life, she had told herself sternly. Her loyalties and her priorities had to lie with her husband. Yet despite what she had told herself, Alice had ached for him. She missed the way he understood everything she said without question, and the way he talked with such love about his life at home and of course his son. He was honest, Alice realised, honest and straightforward, and that had never seemed more attractive. In that moment she couldn't resist bringing Jack to mind. With a sharp clarity, she realised that just the image of him gave her the strength to face whatever lay ahead.

Alice was just allowing herself to wallow for the first time in weeks in memories of Jack when she became aware of a sharp, acrid smell filling her nostrils. Nearing the hotel, she looked upwards and was astonished to see plumes of thick grey smoke filling the air. She narrowed her eyes to try and make sense of it. For all the world it looked as though there had been a raid, but she hadn't heard the tell-tale wail of Moaning Minnie, and strangely there were people everywhere. In fact, she suddenly noticed there seemed to be more people on the street than usual as they ran away from the smoke.

Whirling around to try and ask someone what was going on, she suddenly saw Hilda from the sewing nights and hurried towards her. 'Hilda!' she shouted. 'Are you all right? What's going on?'

'Oh Alice,' Hilda replied breathlessly. 'It's terrible. The hotel's on fire.'

'What?' Alice gasped. 'When? Are you hurt? What's happened?'

'I don't know any more than that,' Hilda said shakily. 'Mr Button told everyone to meet in the café on the corner of this road. He said we could do a head count there and try to work out what's what.'

'Is it bad?'

Hilda nodded. 'I ain't seen nothing like it in any of the raids I've been in.'

With that Hilda ran off, leaving Alice with the taste of fear in her mouth. What about Arthur? Dot had him. What if he was hurt? Quickly she pushed through the throngs of people coming towards her and turned into the road that led to the hotel. Reaching the end she gasped in horror, unable to believe what she was seeing. The once beautiful building was now a towering inferno with flames soaring from every window. Thick black smoke was everywhere, covering the hotel like a shroud, while all around her the sounds of screaming reverberated as people desperately tried to scramble for safety.

Alice felt panic rise. Arthur would have been at the hotel with Dot. Frantically she looked around for anyone she recognised, her pulse racing. She couldn't bear the thought of a world without her son in it. Just at the moment Alice thought she was about to collapse in shock, she felt a tap on her shoulder. Whirling round, she came face-to-face with a calm-looking Dot clutching a tear-streaked Arthur.

'Oh my baby,' she wept with relief as Dot pressed him into her arms. 'I thought you were dead. Oh Arthur.'

With that she squeezed her son so tight he started to cry again, which made Alice hug him ever tighter. 'I thought I'd lost him,' she sobbed.

She felt Dot place an arm around them both. 'The place was already on fire when me, Edwin and the girls arrived,' Dot explained as she guided Alice back to safety on the other side of the road.

'So everyone is safe?

Dot nodded. 'Look,' she said, gesturing to Flo, Mary, Jean, Mr Button and Betty Fawcett, who were talking to the civil defence teams to try and work out how they could help.

Another wave of relief swept across Alice as she realised how much worse this could have been, but then a nasty thought jolted her from within – not everyone was accounted for.

'Where's Luke? And what about Joy and Rose?' she demanded.

Dot clamped her arm firmly around Alice's shoulders. 'Rose is with Malcolm over by the first-aiders,' she said, gesturing to the twosome in the corner. 'But as for Luke and Joy, I have to admit I haven't seen them.'

Helplessness exploded inside Alice. She had to do something. 'Can you hold Arthur?' she begged.

'Why?' Dot asked, perplexed, as Alice bundled her son back into Dot's arms.

'Because I need to find Luke and Joy.'

'Alice, don't be so daft!' Dot called after her, but Alice drowned out the sound of her landlady's pleas. She had to find out where her sister and husband were. No matter what had gone on between them, they were a part of her life, her family and her history – she had to know.

Once again she pushed through the crowds fleeing the hotel. As she neared the entrance, the heat from the flames soaked her face with sweat. She saw a team of volunteers frantically working to put out the blaze with stirrup pumps, yet the water they were throwing over the flames seemed to be having little effect.

'Scuse me, miss,' a voice boomed in her ear. 'Where do you think you're going?'

'I need to find my family!'

'You're going nowhere, love,' the fireman said firmly. 'Now I need you to get back to the other side of the street please.'

'No – just wait a minute,' Alice wailed, but the fireman wasn't interested; he was shoving her back across the road.

Just then she felt a tug on her sleeve. Turning round she came face-to-face with Luke, smeared with soot and with a torn jacket. She flung her arms around him. 'Thank God. You're all right. Have you seen Joy?'

'No,' Luke replied stiffly as he pulled away.

The feelings of relief Alice had been enjoying just seconds earlier evaporated as quickly as the puffs of smoke emanating from the hotel. 'What, not today? Not at all? When, Luke?'

Luke shrugged, looking uncomfortable. 'I don't know Alice. Not since last night.'

'Well, haven't you tried to look for her?' Alice spluttered in disbelief. 'She's your sister-in-law and someone you're quite fond of if last night's anything to go by!'

A flicker of what looked like guilt passed across his face. Looking down at his feet she saw his kit bag, which appeared to be stuffed full.

'What's going on?' she asked crisply.

'Nothing,' Luke said, hoisting his bag on to his shoulder. 'Look, Alice, I'm sorry but I've got to go.'

'Without helping?' Alice cried. 'There's a fire ripping through the hotel! You're a serviceman, Luke. It's your duty to go in there and help.'

'I'm not going back in there,' Luke scoffed, 'I've only just got out.'

'But what about Joy?' Alice begged again. 'Luke, you've got to help me find her.'

But to her amazement Luke shook his head, his caramel eyes failing to meet her blue ones. 'I can't, Alice. I can't climb the stairs to help – my leg … I'm useless.'

With that he turned on his heel and pushed his way through the crowds. Alice stared at his retreating back in disbelief. If ever she needed more confirmation that the man she had married was long since gone it was there in every step he took away from her.

As he disappeared she felt a wash of sadness pass over her. The man she had married would have fought his way through the flames, regardless of the state of his health. The man walking away from her now was nothing more than a stranger.

Regardless of what had happened between her and Joy, she had a duty to find her; Joy was her sister, her family, and that meant something. Glancing up at the building, she shuddered with horror. The blaze was continuing to rip out the heart and lungs from the hotel and she knew it was a fool's errand to go in there now. Every inch was covered in flames, and debris was flying through the air with all the speed of a fighter aircraft. The best thing to do would be to properly check the crowds. Joy was like a cat with nine lives; there was every chance she was out here somewhere or even in the pub.

Weaving her way through the throng Alice searched for any sign of her sister. Desperately she checked with other members of staff but nobody knew where she was. Alice refused to give up, but when she turned back to face the hotel Alice felt the knot of fear in her stomach grow ever larger. Survivors were still pouring out of the building as fire officers and volunteers braved the flames to bring people out alive.

Suddenly she spotted a shock of blonde hair that looked familiar and she rushed towards the woman. 'Joy!' she screamed. 'Joy! It's me.'

But as the woman whirled around it was clear that it wasn't her sister. 'Sorry,' she muttered, 'I thought you were someone else.'

As she continued her search Alice couldn't ignore the panic that was now rising within her. Where was Joy?

Just then Alice saw a woman stumble out of what was left of the hotel entrance, covered in black soot, clothes torn and ir singed at the ends. The woman looked exhausted as she careered all over the road carrying a lifeless body blindly in her arms. Unable to tear her eyes away from the scene playing out in front of her, Alice's heart was in her mouth as she recognised the flame-red hair and glasses, one of the lenses cracked and broken.

'Rose,' she screamed, 'Rose! What are you doing?'

But Rose paid her no heed as two firemen took pity on the blind girl and took the body from her arms. As the figure was set down on the pavement, Alice ran towards her friend, then gasped in shock as she realised that the person Rose had rescued from the blaze was none other than Joy.

Chapter Fifty-Three

Alice flew towards the motionless body lying on the crowded pavement. Pushing her way through the throngs of people she eventually reached Rose and Joy's side and crouched down by them.

She could tell Joy needed help fast. Her clothes and skin were badly burnt and her once blonde hair was now the colour of a chimney sweep.

'Joy,' she said, pressing her face close to her sister and listening for the sounds of breathing, only to find there was none. 'Joy!' she tried again, but still her sister remained still.

Cold fear gripped her heart as she stole a glance at Rose. She could see Rose, bruised, with cuts on her face and a dress that was badly ripped, needed medical help.

'Rose, are you all right?' she asked quietly, but Rose didn't answer. Instead she took the broken glasses from her nose, wiped the soot from her mouth and shouldered Alice out of the way. Bending over Joy, Rose began the resuscitation procedure they had all been taught at the first-aid nights.

In that moment Alice adored her friend for all she had done for her sister, recognising that it had been pure love that had powered Rose through the flames to try and save Joy. Yet Alice could also see that her heroic attempts had left Rose with barely any strength, she needed medical attention herself and it was time for someone else to help Joy.

'Let me,' she said, laying a hand gently on her forearm.

Alice expected Rose to resist but she didn't; instead she let Alice perform the vital mouth to mouth. As Alice's breath flowed from her mouth into her sister's she prayed that no matter what had gone on between them she could give Joy the life force she so badly needed. Despite their differences they were connected through blood and history, and Alice wasn't ready to say goodbye – not yet.

Yet no matter how hard Alice breathed or how hard she pumped Rose's chest, she could see that her efforts were useless.

'Come on, Joy,' she urged as she pounded her sister's chest again. 'Come on!'

'Alice, I think it's too late,' Rose said quietly. 'She wasn't breathing when I found her.'

But Alice refused to give up. 'No!' she screamed. 'No! My sister will not die here in this fire.'

Pressing her lips to her sister's face again, this time Alice didn't just blow all the oxygen she could into her sister's mouth. Now she made sure the heady concoction was filled with love. Letting out a deep exhalation, the life they had shared together flashed before her eyes. The way their mother had died as Joy arrived. Then later the way they had played Knock Down Ginger together and the way their father left, leaving Alice to fill the gap of both parents, the way she had done her best to pour the love they couldn't straight into her sister's soul.

As Alice let the last of the breath out she leaned back, tears spilling down her cheeks, and looked at Joy's face, willing her to wake up. But she continued to lie still and Alice knew she had failed her sister yet again.

Turning to Rose for help, she was astonished to see that her friend had gone and in her place stood a Red Cross volunteer. 'Let me look at her please, love,' the woman said in a sympathetic yet firm tone that brooked no argument.

Wordlessly, Alice stood up and let the woman begin her work. It felt like forever that Alice watched the capable redhead perform the resuscitation routine on her sister and with each round Alice found herself bargaining with God. She vowed to be a better mother, a better employee, a more loyal sister, and most of all she vowed she would no longer fail Joy as she had done so recently by turning her back when it was clear her sister needed her more than ever. Joy had done some terrible things and hurt Alice to her very core, but Alice knew that Joy was also just a child, incapable of growing up – exactly like their father.

As she continued to watch the volunteer work on Joy she felt as if she were about to fall when suddenly she felt two steadying hands on her shoulder. Turning around she saw Mary on one side of her and Flo on the other. In the background stood Dot, holding Arthur in her arms.

With the girls she loved surrounding her, Alice felt strength bloom in her heart. When the Red Cross volunteer stood up with a grave look on her face, Alice knew she would need that strength more than ever. 'I'm sorry, love, she's gone,' the woman said gently. 'Was she a relative?'

Alice nodded, the lump in her throat making it difficult to reply. 'My sister.'

'We'll take care of her from here,' the redhead said kindly. 'Have you anyone who can take care of you?'

With tears pooling in her eyes, Alice nodded again as she gestured towards Mary, Dot and Flo. 'I've got my other sisters with me now.'

With that the Red Cross volunteer smiled and arranged for Joy's lifeless body to be transferred to the morgue.

Once she was gone, Alice reached her hands out for her son, and silently Dot handed Arthur to her, only too aware of the comfort the baby would now bring.

'I am so sorry,' Mary said. 'I can't believe this.'

'Neither can I,' Flo said gravely. 'Joy was so young; she had her whole life ahead of her. No matter the mistakes she made, she didn't deserve this.'

Alice lifted her head from Arthur's and gazed tearfully at her friends. 'She deserved a lot more than this, she deserved more than me. This is my fault. If only I'd been more patient, shown her the right path, been more forgiving, then maybe she wouldn't have died tonight. Maybe she would be living in a farmhouse somewhere as a Land Girl, or married with children while her husband fought overseas. Either way, perhaps she would have been happy.'

There was a loud snort as Dot stared at Alice with disgust in her eyes. 'Alice Milwood, you stop that right now,' she said firmly. 'I know you're upset and you've every right to be, you just lost your sister, but don't you dare go rewriting history in your grief. You were mother, father, sister and friend to that girl. You got her out of trouble more times than most would have done and it's not your fault Joy chose to go down her own path. You did all you could for her, Alice, you should be proud not ashamed.'

'Dot's right. If anyone should be sorry it's me,' said Rose timidly.

Glancing up, Alice saw that their friend had now managed to rejoin them and her heart went out to her. The girl had clearly been patched up by the Red Cross. She leaned heavily on her white stick with her one good arm, while her other arm hung in a sling. As for the cuts and bruises on her face, Alice could see they had been cleaned and disinfected.

Rose gestured at Mary, who soon got the hint and guided Rose to sit on a small patch of wall by the roadside.

'Rose love, what have you got to be sorry for?' Dot asked, peeling off her coat and placing it around Rose's shoulders.

Tears brimmed at Rose's eyes but Alice could tell she was doing her best to remain strong.

'For everything. For the way I treated you all, for the way I've behaved, for not reaching Joy fast enough. I've let you all down; I know I have.'

With that Rose broke down, the tears that she been holding at bay cascading down her face as fast as waterfalls, great sobs convulsing her body.

'Darlin',' Alice said gently, putting her own grief on pause for a moment, 'this is not your fault. You were brave when nobody else was. You're a heroine – surely you see that?'

'No, no, no,' Rose wailed, rocking backwards and forwards in horror on the wall. 'I've let Joy down. She's dead because I didn't get there faster. I didn't know where I was going, but I knew Joy would be inside somewhere and her cries helped me find her. Then when I found her, she was silent. If only I wasn't blind, I would have found her quicker, reached her sooner, maybe she wouldn't have inhaled so much smoke. I'm so sorry.'

'Listen to me, Rose,' Flo growled so suddenly her voice sent shockwaves of surprise down Alice's spine. 'I don't want to hear one more word out of you about how you've let people down because of your sight. You marched into that building with no thought for your own safety and you tried to save your friend. Don't you think that takes guts?'

'That's right,' Alice agreed. 'My own husband ran away and he'd slept with Joy the night before so what does that say?'

At that Rose looked at Alice in astonishment. 'Joy slept with Luke?'

Alice nodded. 'Yes. I found them together. It's ironic that was the last time I saw her. I'll never get the chance to make things right with her now.'

Now Rose was on her feet; she reached out an arm and placed it comfortingly on Alice's shoulder. 'I didn't know she would do that. I knew she was upset with you after the other night, and I knew she wanted revenge. I'm ashamed to say I encouraged her.' Rose's voice faltered. 'I was just so furious with you all, especially you.'

Alice stared at her friend, aghast. 'Me? Why?'

'Because that night you took something from me I thought I would never feel again – happiness. I knew stealing was wrong, but it made me feel so good. As though life could be exciting again. I felt invincible; then you came and spoiled it all. That's why I encouraged Joy when she started going on about getting back at you for showing her up in front of Shirley, but I was so wrong, and I've realised that, I've been so wrong about so much.'

As Rose broke off she wept some more and this time the girls didn't try to stop her. Instead they stayed with her and supported her until finally she had cried herself out.

'You know, I didn't mean what I said, Alice.' Rose hiccuped as she wiped her face with the back of her free hand. 'I don't resent you or hate you girls. I don't know why I said that. I wanted to lash out I suppose. I was jealous; I resented the fact none of you lost your sight when I did.'

'Perfectly understandable, darlin',' Dot sympathised. 'There isn't a saint among us who wouldn't feel the same.'

'I don't know how you were so forgiving at all,' Flo marvelled. 'I mean, I would have wanted Mrs Matravers to pay immediately.'

'But she has paid, hasn't she?' Rose said sadly. 'And yet that still wasn't enough for me. I still had to take it out on you girls, my wonderful friends who have always been there for me.'

'And we always will be,' Mary said softly, 'you don't get rid of us that easily.'

A ghost of a smile played on Rose's lips before she spoke. 'I think I just wanted to feel something different. When I met Joy, she made me realise I could be anything I wanted to be. I stopped hating my life and myself so much; she showed me another way. Joy said that life had already treated me badly, so what was the point in being well behaved?'

'Was that when she got you to pickpocket?' Alice asked.

Rose nodded. 'Joy needed the money for Shirley Allbright, and I wanted to feel a release, I wanted to experience something other than the pure misery I had been feeling for months. I felt so worthless, so useless, as if my entire life had been for nothing. Nobody would want me.'

'Is that why you've kept Tommy away all this time?' Mary asked, the truth suddenly dawning on her.

'Yes,' Rose replied in a small voice. 'He won't want me if he sees me like this. I don't want to be a burden to him, not when he's already coping with so much so far from home.'

'You've got to put yourself first for once,' Alice said firmly. 'Tommy loves you. He's not going to leave you because you're partially sighted.'

'That's what Joy said. And she said that even if he did I should have some fun first. So she took me drinking and gambling. We went and courted GI soldiers – well, Joy did, I just accepted their drinks. We went dancing and I realised I was so much more than a blind girl, I was Rose Harper again.'

'And how do you feel now?' Alice asked cautiously. 'Do you still want to harm yourself?'

'No. If anything tonight has made me realise how wrong I got it all. You girls have always been here, and I realised that if one of you had lost your life in that fire I would be lost without you. I am so sorry for all I have done wrong. Please will you forgive me?'

Alice kissed Rose on the cheek, and wrapped an arm around her. 'Darlin', you're our friend and you always will be. There is nothing to forgive.'

Chapter Fifty-Four

Dressed in their finest black, the Liberty girls gathered at the church in Kensal Green to say goodbye to Joy just ten days later. Following the devastating blaze, Alice had gone from acceptance to denial as she struggled to come to terms with what had happened to her sister. She had woken frequently in the middle of the night, heart pounding, brow dripping with sweat as images of her sister dying on the pavement became too much for her tortured mind.

In fact, Joy, along with two other young girls from the Mayfair House staff, had died from smoke inhalation. The hotel had been devastated at the tragic loss of such young lives. It turned out that the fire had started in the kitchen but had been impossible to contain and had spread quickly. The hotel manager had contacted Alice and said that once the hotel was rebuilt they wanted to name a suite after Joy as a tribute.

Alice had of course agreed, thanking them for their kindness, not mentioning how ironic it was that they wanted to name a suite after Joy when she had never been sweet in her entire life.

The grief Alice felt enveloped her every single day, the anguish of it taking hold of her in a vice-like grip without warning. She could be busy serving a customer, or at home caring for Arthur, and suddenly she would feel the sadness sweep through her, threatening to throw her entirely off course. The strength of these feelings terrified her, but thankfully she had her precious Liberty girls, who had been a tower of strength since Joy's death. Together they had rallied around, ensuring Alice didn't have anything too taxing to deal with on the shop floor, and were always with her during her lunch or tea breaks so she didn't have to be alone. They also gently helped remind her of the things that continued to make life worthwhile: her wonderful son, of course, and her job.

Alice wasn't sure she would have got through the last few dark days without them, and now she was hoping to count on them again as she prepared to say goodbye to her sister for the final time.

The one thing she hadn't counted on was receiving a letter from her father that morning. She had sent him a telegram informing him of Joy's death, but hadn't expected a reply, so it had come as something of a surprise to find an envelope written in a hand that was familiar but which she momentarily couldn't place – until she checked the postmark and saw it had been mailed from overseas.

Her hand had trembled as she ripped open the envelope and taken in the few lines her father had written.

4th August 1942

Hello Alice,

I'd ask how you are but following your telegram I can only imagine. Alice, sweetheart, your note knocked me for six. I can't believe it – my precious little girl. I was so proud of her, she's a loss to the entire world. I have no doubt she'll be sorely missed, especially by you, my girl. You two always belonged together, it's why I left you and her together, because you loved the bones of each other and I knew it was the right thing to do.

Still, knowing that Joy did everything she could to uphold the Harris name – that gives me strength. Shirley wrote to

me the other day and told me how well Joy was doing with
helping her out and getting the old business up and running.
Said she had a little blind apprentice who was coming along
nicely too.

I know you always thought you were too good for what I
did, but you ate the food that my spoils put on the table and
you never complained neither when my business endeavours
put clothes on your back.

Think about it, love – you could do worse than go into
business with Shirley. She'd get you started, and in time
your boy could take over the business and the Harrises could
rule the streets of South London again.

I miss you, sweetheart, don't be a stranger,

Your loving father

As she read through the note two or three times, Alice's
blood began to boil – so Joy *had* used Rose. It was sick.
Alice shook her head in sadness – she knew she would
never tell Rose. She might have flung the accusation at her
during that fateful night but Rose would have thought she
was just lashing out. The truth would break her heart.

She turned back to the note. What a fool Jimmy was,
she thought angrily. He had rewritten history, having
no idea what his 'business endeavours' had cost his
girls. That bit about leaving them together because they
adored each other was nothing but fantasy. Jimmy Harris
had done what suited himself without a thought for anyone else, just as he always did. As for starting the family
business up again, with Arthur one day at the helm – the
idea made Alice sick to her stomach. This man had never
been a father to her, let alone a loving one; she and Joy,
though it was sad she never realised it, had been better
off without him.

Now, as she stood in the packed church, Mary and Dot either side of her for support, Alice did her best to forget her father and instead focus on the vicar standing at the altar delivering his eulogy. He had asked her a lot about Joy in the days leading up to the service, and Alice found that despite recounting the criminal, selfish and down-right reckless behaviour Joy had often demonstrated throughout her life, there had been many instances to tell him about when Joy had also been a kind and thoughtful sister and friend.

Alice found that she revelled in the chance to relive happy childhood memories, such as the time when she and Joy had delivered food parcels to their elderly neighbour, Joy even saving some of the food on her own dinner plate so the old lady wouldn't go without. That gesture had moved Alice, and proved to her without doubt that her sister wasn't wholly bad, she had simply been misguided.

Looking around the church as the opening bars to 'Jerusalem' sounded Alice tried to find Shirley Allbright in the crowd, but was glad she could see no sign of the woman Joy had mistakenly thought was her friend. She had never belonged in Joy's life; she didn't belong in her death now either.

Turning back to the front she concentrated on the hymn instead. This had been one of her sister's favourites and Alice intended to sing her heart and lungs out, wanting her sister to know she would forever be in her heart.

As the service drew to a close and the vicar led every-one outside, she said a little prayer for Joy. 'I'll never forget you, sweet sister,' she whispered.

Alice stepped out into the bright August sunshine, the cheeriness of the day in stark contrast to the pain she felt in her heart as she took in the sight of her sister's final resting place. Her legs felt heavy and the knot in her stomach grew ever larger as she realised this was the moment her sister would be committed to the earth and she really would never see her again.

For a moment Alice stood there, looking up at the sky and wondering where she would find the strength to do such a thing. She had lost her mother, her father, her husband and now her sister, who at just twenty-two had barely had a chance to make anything of herself. As the breeze fluttered through the trees, Alice turned away and found her gaze came to rest upon her friends standing by the burial plot, encouraging smiles on their faces. She knew that it would be her girls who would help her find the courage for one of the most difficult moments of her life.

'You all right, darlin'?' Flo whispered as Joy's body was lowered into the ground.

'I will be.' She nodded as the vicar gestured for her to throw a clod of earth on to the coffin.

'It was a beautiful service,' Rose murmured as she took her own turn at throwing a handful of soil. 'I never knew all that stuff about Joy. She was a good girl at heart, Alice.'

'Rose is right,' Mary said in hushed tones as she joined the girls. 'I think Joy would have been very grateful for all you have done for her today.'

Alice smiled weakly as she balanced Arthur on her hip; he had been incredibly quiet throughout the service. 'I hope so. I don't feel as though I was very kind to her at the end.'

'And some people don't deserve to have kindness at the end,' Dot said firmly. 'Just because they're dead don't mean you have to start telling lies about 'em. Joy was a liability and she did you plenty of wrong turns. I'm not saying she was all bad, but don't go round making out she was a saint when you think back on her either.'

As all the girls turned to stare at Dot in disbelief at what they perceived to be sheer heartlessness, Alice simply roared with laughter. 'You're a tonic, Dorothy Hanson, you really are.'

Walking towards the exit, Alice braced herself for her final duty: thanking everyone for coming and saying good-bye, when Dot's cry cut across her thoughts.

'What the hell's he doing here?'

Alice turned to follow Dot's gaze and realised she was looking at Jack Capewell. As her eyes roamed across his figure she felt her stomach flip. How handsome he looked in his uniform.

'I'll just go and see what he wants,' she murmured. 'See you girls at the gate.'

Without waiting for a response Alice walked across the graveyard towards Jack. The closer she got the more agitated she felt; yet the moment his face lit up when he saw her, all those nerves melted away. It pained her to admit it, but Alice felt a pang of longing as she took in the scent of his musky aftershave. The scent tugged at her heart, and she realised she had missed him more than she would have imagined possible.

'Alice.' He smiled warmly. 'I'm sorry, I know you don't want to see me, but I wanted to come when I heard what happened to your poor sister. I wanted to pay my respects.'

'That was very kind of you.' Alice meant it. 'It's really nice to see you again.'

'And it's really good to see you too,' he said gently.

'How are you? Are you still stationed in London?' Alice ventured, moving on to safer territory.

Jack nodded, the sunshine highlighting his eyes. 'For the moment at least, yes.'

'And how's Jack Junior?'

'Getting bigger by the second, according to my sister.' He laughed, reaching into his pocket. 'She sent me a picture of him – you wanna see?'

'Of course!'

At the sight of the little boy, she felt a bubble of happiness rise up inside. It was clear that Jack's sister had taken the boy to a professional photography studio for the snap, but like all little boys at his age, his hair was mussed up and his clothes ever so slightly dishevelled. But the way he grinned right into the camera, his eyes sparkling, meant that his excitement at having his image captured on film was right there for everyone to see.

'That's one gorgeous little boy!' She beamed as Arthur grinned in delight at the picture too.

'As is this little guy. He's grown!'

Alice rolled her eyes. 'He's heavy too. You want to hold him?'

'You bet I do!' Jack scooped Arthur into his arms, and then pretended to drop him because he was too heavy. 'Boy, you're a handful. Just like your mom.'

'Oi!' Alice teased.

Watching them for a moment she felt a jolt of surprise at how right they looked together. For a brief moment she wondered what it would be like if she, Jack and Arthur became a family. Would it be as perfect as this picture in front of her?

Then just as quickly Alice banished the thought from her mind. It was wrong to think that way. No matter what was going on between her and Luke they were still married and, besides, it wasn't fair to lead Jack on like that.

'I'd better go and start saying goodbye to people,' she said, taking Arthur from his arms. 'We're having a wake at the pub after work for Joy. You'd be welcome to come.'

'I can't. I'm on duty tonight. Maybe see you another time?'

'That would be nice,' Alice said firmly. With that she turned to go, until an idea sprang to mind. 'Actually, we're having a bit of a party at the store on Saturday night.'

'Saturday night?' Jack looked at her quizzically.

'Yes, it's the fashion parade,' Alice explained. 'We were supposed to hold it at Mayfair House the night it got burnt down so Mr Button suggested we hold it in the store after all. Everyone's welcome; we're going to toast Joy and the other girls that died in Mayfair House. It would mean a lot if you would come.'

Jack looked at her and then scratched his chin. 'All right. I'd like that very much.'

'So would I,' Alice replied gently.

Chapter Fifty-Five

It wasn't until Alice found herself sandwiched between Dot and Flo in the pub around the corner from Liberty's that she felt the knot of tension she had been carrying in her shoulders all afternoon start to disappear.

Arthur was being cared for by Doris from next door again, and now, in the bosom of her friends, with adult company, and a port and lemon inside her, she finally felt she could relax.

'To Joy,' she said suddenly, raising her glass.

'To Joy,' everyone echoed, clinking their glasses against hers.

'She will be missed,' Rose said quietly.

'She will.' Alice agreed. 'Which is why I only want us to remember the good times with her.'

'That won't take long,' Dot muttered under her breath, earning herself a reproving glare from Alice.

'I know we say it all the time,' Flo began, changing the subject, 'but what with Aggie's death and now Joy's it really does make you realise how short life is.'

Mary nodded. 'I was thinking exactly the same thing myself. Joy's death has put things into perspective for me.'

'How do you mean?' Flo quizzed.

Mary paused for a second. 'I mean I've done some thinking and I've decided to write and tell David that I want us to get married as soon as possible and apply to adopt Mrs Matravers' baby. After all, once we're married I will be the child's aunt.'

'Mary, that's wonderful,' Flo gasped in delight.

'I think you'll make a lovely mum!' Alice beamed. 'Well done, Mary, I know you won't regret it.'

'Thanks, girls.' Mary flushed. 'I mean we obviously want to go on to have our own children, but we want to give David's niece a real home.'

'So have you heard back from David yet then?' Alice asked.

Mary shook her head. 'I only decided last night so I posted the letter before the funeral. I keep picturing his face when he reads it.'

'He's going to be so thrilled,' Flo exclaimed, the evening light dancing on her chestnut mane.

'He is.' Rose nodded. 'But I suppose that means you'll be leaving Dad and me now?'

Mary looked confused. 'Why?'

'Well, you'll be getting married, you'll want your own place,' Rose reasoned.

Mary patted Rose's hand. 'Not for a bit yet, I don't imagine. We don't know when David's coming back or even if they'll let us have Emma. I mean although Mrs Matravers is in prison for the foreseeable, she might object.'

'If she does, she'll want her head testing on top of everything else,' Dot said darkly.

'Well, I think it's great news.' Flo grinned. 'We should use Joy's death as an example to us all to try and carve out a bit of happiness for ourselves while we can.'

'I certainly have been,' Rose said quietly. 'I've been thinking too and I've realised that the first-aid nights made me happy. I've spoken to Mr Button and he says I can start them up again if I want to.'

Alice felt a flush of joyfulness. 'That's wonderful news, Rose.'

'It certainly is,' Flo agreed. 'We'll help you any way we can.'

'Just say the word,' Mary added.

'And can I just say it's about time you came to your senses, Rose, love,' Dot said sagely. 'All that law-breaking never suited you. Stick to what you're good at.'

At the older woman's searing honesty the girls broke into raucous laughter before raising their glasses again in a toast.

'To happiness,' they cheered in unison, and Alice found herself nodding fervently in understanding as she took a sip of her drink. She had been thinking about her own idea of happiness for some time now. She had wasted so much time trying to create the perfect family life and it had all been for nothing; perhaps she too needed to consider taking a different path.

'And I've got some other news too!' Rose's excited voice pulled Alice from her thoughts.

'Oh yes?' Alice grinned expectantly.

As Rose took a sip of her drink before she spoke, Alice took a moment to observe her friend. The cuts and bruises on her face were healing nicely, and the sprain in her wrist was almost better as well. Best of all she had some colour in her cheeks, as though she was no longer weighed down by the burden of living a life filled with unhappiness and resentment.

'Come on then, out with it,' Flo urged. 'You look like the cat that got the cream.'

Rose blushed shyly. 'I heard from Tommy this morning. He wrote to say he's coming home next month. He's got the compassionate leave I kept saying I didn't want him to take.'

At that the girls broke out into a loud and happy cheer for their friend.

'How long is he home for?' Flo asked above the noise.

'Just seventy-two hours, but I couldn't be happier. I've missed him so much all these months, I should have said yes before, but I didn't want to be a burden to anyone.'

'You weren't a burden at all,' Flo put in loyally.

'Except when you were playing silly beggars with Joy,' Dot said, earning herself a shake of the head from everyone at the table. She shrugged. 'Don't look at me like that, you know I'm telling the truth.'

There was a series of good-natured groans then as Mr Button approached the table. 'What did I miss?' Mr Button called over the racket. 'And would any of you fine ladies like a drink?'

'Ah, Mr B., I'm glad you're here. Perhaps you can keep Dot in line.' Alice chuckled, before spotting Jean standing behind him. Immediately she shuffled along the bench so there was room for the young girl to sit down.

A smile played on the store manager's face. 'I think the man that can keep Dorothy Hanson in line is a braver man than I am. Now, drinks, girls?'

As the girls shouted their orders Alice turned to Jean and was astonished to see how unhappy she looked. 'Are you all right?' she asked sharply.

The younger girl nodded.

'Then why do you look as if you lost a pound and found a tanner?'

'No reason,' Jean replied, her gaze fixed firmly on the table.

'Now you know you're amongst friends here, Jean,' Mr Button said firmly as he returned with the drinks and set them on the table. 'I'm afraid I found her outside crying,' he said to the rest of the group.

'I'm going to be homeless,' Jean muttered.

'Why?' Flo gasped.

'The landlord's kicked my sister and me out. He's putting the rent up and we can't afford it. We've got a week to find somewhere.'

'Oh Jean, what will you do?' Mary asked in concern.

'I don't know. I'll sort something out.'

'Will you go somewhere else together?' Alice tried again.

'I want us to,' Jean said in a small voice.

'Then why don't you move in with me?' Flo suggested out of the blue. 'I've got plenty of space since Aggie's gone and I could do with the company.'

'So does that mean you've decided to give up the singing and open up a guest house like Neil wants?' Alice asked.

Flo sighed. 'I don't know. All I know is I've got space, I'm taking it one step at a time and it'll be a pleasure to have Jean move in.'

Jean's face had lit up in surprise. 'Are you sure, Flo? I don't want to be no bother.'

'Why would you be a bother? Like I said, you're doing me a favour. Why don't you and Bess move in on Sunday?'

'We'd like that.' Jean grinned happily. 'Thank you.'

'Seems we're all setting up homes for waifs and strays.' Dot grinned. 'I said I'd take in Violet from next week.'

'Vera's girl?' Alice said, looking puzzled. 'Why?'

'She's got a job up Marks and Sparks, ain't she,' Dot explained, slurping her stout. 'I said she could stay with us. That's what Vera wanted to butter me up about. Even brought me half a pound cake 'n'all. Dry as a bone, mind, but cake's cake.'

Mary frowned. 'But where will you put her?'

'In the little box room, I suppose, on the put-up bed,' Dot replied. 'It was good enough for Joy for a few weeks.'

Alice made a pshawing noise. 'You can't do that. She's your family. She should have a proper bed.'

'She'll be all right, she's young yet. She could sleep on the floor and still have a good night.'

'Unlike the rest of us.' Mr Button chuckled authoritatively. 'But Alice does make a good point, Dot. You can't let the girl live indefinitely in the box room.'

Dot bristled. 'It's a perfectly good room.'

'And I was perfectly happy in there,' Mary added, not unreasonably.

'That's as may be but it's not a good solution long-term, is it?' Mr Button pointed out. 'Perhaps you should think about moving somewhere a little larger, Dorothy.'

Dot raised an eyebrow as Mr Button met her gaze. 'Like your little house up Galleywall Road you mean?'

Mr Button shrugged. 'It's bigger than yours. I'm only making a suggestion.'

Alice hid a smile and decided to have some fun. 'But surely you're not suggesting Dot move in with you now, Mr Button? I mean the two of you aren't married. What would people say?'

Dot shot her a warning stare. 'That's enough out of you, lady.'

'What have we missed?' Flo asked innocently as she sensed mischief and wanted to join in.

Mr Button leaned back in his chair and observed the table. 'Absolutely nothing, Flo. I have been merely looking for ways to convince Dorothy here to allow me to make an honest woman out of her.'

'And I told you we would have this conversation another time,' Dot replied firmly. 'We've hardly been back together five minutes and you want me down the aisle already.'

Mr Button reached across the table for Dot's hand. 'Only because I don't want us to lose any more precious time,' he said softly. 'All I'm asking you to do is think about it.'

Dot pulled her hand away and smiled before giving Mr Button a shake of the head. 'I *will* think about it.'

Alice said nothing as she grinned at the couple sitting across from her. They were made for each other; anyone could see that. Why Dot was so reluctant to marry again, she wasn't sure. It could be the chance at a wonderful fresh start. Alice drummed her fingers on the table and thought for a moment. All around her things were changing. Perhaps it was time for her to start making some changes too.

She cleared her throat. 'Actually I've got some news of my own.'

As the girls and Mr Button looked at her expectantly she felt suddenly hollow. The news she had been expecting and dreading in equal measure had arrived squarely on her doorstep that morning, and she had spent most of the day pondering the contents.

'I had a letter from Chris this morning,' she announced. 'He wanted to say how sorry he was about Joy.'

'That was kind of him,' said Dot.

Alice nodded. 'It was. He also wanted to tell me, because he thought I deserved to know, that Luke has gone back to France.'

'What!' Flo gasped. 'Why? How?'

'To be with Hélène,' Alice said with a courage she wasn't quite sure she felt. 'He said that Luke had told him he was sorry but that the war had shown him he didn't want to live a life of misery with me and his son when he could be living a life full of happiness with the woman he loves. I imagine that even though France is occupied, as he got out, and has his friends over there now, Hélène would be able to arrange his re-entry just as easily.'

'But won't the RAF be upset? Isn't that desertion?' Mary tried again.

Alice shrugged her shoulders feeling helpless. 'I don't know if he's told them what he's done or if it doesn't matter because he's on sick leave. I suppose I'll find out if the RAF turn up on my door asking where the hell he is in a few months' time. For now, all I can do is try to deal with everything that's happened.'

'Alice, sweetheart, I'm so sorry,' Mary said soothingly. 'I can't even begin to imagine how you feel.'

'You're better off without him,' Dot said sagely. 'He was a changed fella the moment he came back from France. Alice, darlin', I know the path you're on now won't be easy, but trust me, this is better in the long run.'

'But what am I going to do?' Alice cried, all her bravado from moments earlier gone in a heartbeat. 'I don't know if I'm supposed to divorce him, let him go or what? The shame of it all!'

'It could be more shameful to live with a man who treats you badly,' Rose said wisely. 'You deserve better than Luke, Alice, and I think you know that.'

Alice nodded. 'The thing is, in my heart of hearts I've known for some time that I don't love Luke. I did love him but he hurt me too badly.' She paused, taking another sip of drink for courage. 'The truth is I've fallen in love with someone else but I know I can't do anything about it.'

'Why?' Dot frowned. 'After all Luke's done to you, you're still worried about betraying him? I think that ship's sailed, darlin'.'

'It's … it's not Luke,' Alice said haltingly, 'it's Arthur.'

'Arthur?' Mary quizzed.

'Because of the shame all this would bring him,' Alice admitted with a heavy sigh. 'Not only does he come from a family full of criminals but his father's an adulterer. All I ever wanted was to give my boy the family I never had – well, I'm making a right bad job of it. Falling in love with another man would be the cherry on the cake. What would people say?'

'Bugger other people,' Dot snapped, banging her fist firmly down on the table. 'They don't count for tuppence when it comes to your happiness – you and Arthur are the only ones that matter. And I tell you something else, my girl: you keep saying how you wanted to give your boy what you never had? Well, you already are. You're giving him love.'

'Dot's right,' Flo agreed. 'I've never seen a mother more in love with her child.'

'You dote on that boy,' Mary said firmly.

'Better to have one wonderful parent than two bad ones,' Mr Button added, looking a little awkward amongst all this emotional talk. 'I think you're being far too hard on yourself, Alice.'

'I know you are,' Dot insisted. 'I take it this fella you've fallen for is Jack?'

'Yes. I think I fell for him the moment I met him, but all this time I've pushed him away. He might not even want me now.'

Mary snorted. 'Then he's as big a fool as Luke.'

'If there's one thing I've learned throughout the past year, Alice,' Rose said quietly, 'it's that life is short and happiness is hard to find. As well as agreeing to Tommy coming home, I've decided to make the most of every drop of happiness that comes my way from now on and I suggest you do the same. The thing about happiness is you never know when it's going to come around again.'

Chapter Fifty-Six

The Saturday after the funeral was the day of the fashion parade. Alice opened the blackout blinds, feeling full of hope for the day ahead.

Admitting the truth about Luke and her feelings for Jack to her friends had helped clear her head. She felt as if she could look forward to a future, albeit an uncertain one; at least she would no longer be looking back.

From now on her focus was her son, it really was as simple as that. With Luke no longer around, and likely never coming back, she was free to think about herself and Arthur. And the first thing she needed to consider was moving out. Alice didn't want to be a burden when Violet arrived and deep down she thought it might be time to find her and Arthur a family home of their own, even if it was only a room together in someone else's dwelling. She ought to stand on her own two feet; after all, it was the two of them against the world now.

But first there was something else she had to do. Since Joy's death she had felt as if she and her father had unfinished business. She had sent him a telegram letting him know that Joy had died, and his reply had infuriated her. Yet her sister's sudden passing had given Alice time to reflect. Joy had been the last connection to her father, a man she had never wanted anything to do with when he was living under the same roof, never mind when he was thousands of miles across an ocean. Without Joy in her life any longer, Alice had no reason to have anything to do with Jimmy Harris, but she wanted to say goodbye in the way she had said goodbye to Joy.

Pulling out her writing pad from her bedside cabinet, Alice began to scribble.

15th August 1942

Dear Jimmy,

Thanks for your letter the other day. I'm sure you'll be glad to hear that Joy's funeral went off all right. The church was standing room only as everyone came out to pay their respects. You're probably thinking that so many people turned up because they wanted to say goodbye to the daughter of one of the great criminal masterminds. In fact nobody from your old gang days turned up – not even your precious Shirley.

This is one of the hardest letters I have ever had to write, and in fact I didn't even know who to address it to. It doesn't feel right calling you Jimmy, but it feels even less right calling you Dad. Since Joy's death I've realised that there are so many things I want to get off my chest, but I also know that there's no point. You'll believe what you want and no amount of persuasion from me will have you seeing otherwise.

I've spent years hating you, resenting your decision to leave us penniless while you set up shop in America, taking your money with you. It's taken me a long time to see it, but actually I know now that your leaving was the best thing that ever happened to Joy and me. The truth is that I don't feel anything towards you at all now. You're just some old crook who stitched everyone up – your own family included – in pursuit of your own happiness. I spent too long blaming you for the way my life turned out. I'd always thought I needed rescuing, but I know now that I'm stronger than

391

*I thought, and more confident and capable too. I'll stand
on my own two feet, though I would never be the woman I
am today without you. We may be related but I've learned
over the years that family isn't always made up of the people
you're connected to by blood. You aren't my family, Jimmy,
never have been and never will be – so please don't contact
me again.*

Alice

Once she was finished, she sealed the envelope and felt as
though a great weight had been lifted from her shoulders.
She hadn't known she felt like that but now she'd got it all
down she felt like a new woman.

Quickly, she got Arthur washed and ready for the day
ahead, and then she concentrated on herself. Pulling
open her own cupboard she ran her eyes across the array
of clothes that hung inside. There wasn't much in there
that hadn't been patched to within an inch of its life, she
thought wryly. Eventually selecting a plain cream dress
with short sleeves and a high neck, her gaze came to rest
on the wedding dress that hung next to it. Without thinking she allowed her fingers to roam across the soft silk, and
she closed her eyes as she remembered the day she wore it.
She had felt like a film star as she pulled on the exquisite
gown, her mind full of thoughts of her future and all the
promise it held. The silk had swished gently around her
legs all day as she stayed close to her husband's side, and
Alice remembered how perfect she had thought life would
be. But that was all in the past, she mused sadly, shoving
the dress back.

'Dot, are you coming to this meeting as well?' Alice
called as she walked into the kitchen and found her landlady making tea.

Dot nodded as she poured the liquid into two cups. 'Edwin says it's important we're all there.'

'Yes, he said that to me. He even said I could bring Arthur into work if I was stuck for someone to look after him. That's how important it is.'

Dot lifted an eyebrow. 'Is that right? Tell you to stick Arthur on the till 'n' all, did he? Think the customers might have summat to say about that.'

'Not our customers,' Alice said loyally. 'Very kind, they are.'

'True,' Dot admitted with a smile.

'Anyway' – Alice glanced at the clock on the mantel – 'whatever it is, we'd better get a move on. If we're late he'll have our guts for garters.'

'Including Arthur's,' Dot finished dramatically.

An hour later and all three were on the shop floor of Liberty's waiting for Mr Button to appear. As Arthur gurgled contentedly in Alice's arms, earning herself looks of envy from some of the other shop girls, she couldn't help feeling proud of her son. 'Your very first day at Liberty's,' she whispered into his ear.

Just then Mr Button appeared at the top of the staircase flanked by another man Alice hadn't seen before. 'Who's that?' she mouthed to Mary, who was standing next to her.

Mary shook her head. 'Attractive though, isn't he?' she murmured.

'If you like the angry, brooding look,' Flo hissed from behind. 'Whoever he is, he looks like he got out of bed the wrong side this morning.'

'And judging by that walking stick he's carrying, I'm guessing there's only one side of bed he *can* get out of,' Dot said knowingly.

As the two men muttered between themselves Alice took time to assess the stranger. He was shorter and younger than Mr Button; Alice guessed he was in his late thirties. With a stocky build and an intense brooding look that came from his deep-set brown eyes, the man, whoever he was, gave off an air of slight menace. Alice shivered; he reminded her of the film star John Wayne.

Once Mr Button turned back to face the staff and smiled, the stranger caught her staring and locked eyes with her. She felt a pang of concern, until she realised that within that brooding look, there was something else too – a hint of gentleness perhaps.

'Now then, everyone,' Mr Button said loudly. 'Many thanks to you all for coming in early this morning for this extra special meeting. As you know, since Mrs Matravers left us, we have been in a state of flux regarding the post of deputy store manager. First Mrs Canning took over the role, but she believes she is more suited to her previous role as fabric manager, and of course Mrs Claremont was going to step into the breach for a short time, but as you all know she is no longer with us, creating a vacancy. However, this morning I am delighted to let you know all that has changed. Ladies and gentleman, and of course young man' – he smiled, gesturing towards Arthur – 'I would like you to welcome our newest addition to the Liberty family, Henry Masters, who will be joining us as our new deputy store manager from today. He used to be sales manager at Bourne and Hollingsworth many years ago so he knows an awful lot about our store and what we're trying to do here.'

Mr Button finished and there was a polite round of applause from the staff as Henry Masters took a step forward to address the staff. 'I am delighted to be here,' he said in a rich Yorkshire accent. 'Mr Button and I served together in the army many years ago and I am delighted to join him here in this wonderful store and serve with him again. Over the coming weeks I shall be making a point of getting to know you all, spending time in your various departments and understanding how you all work. I appreciate that Liberty's is a very different kind of shop. We have a rich history, a greater variety of stock and the most beautiful and unique store in the world. I am honoured to serve here and serve amongst you.' He paused for a moment to clear his throat. 'However, I have a few rules. I'm fair and I can promise you I will always listen, but treat me like a fool and you'll be sorry. That said, I look forward to a good and decent working relationship with you all.'

At that Henry Masters took a step back and allowed Mr Button to take centre stage once more. 'Well, everyone,' he beamed, 'I want you all to do everything you can over the coming weeks to make Mr Masters feel welcome. And of course he will be joining us this evening for Liberty's very first fashion parade!'

At that there was a thunderous round of applause before everyone returned to their departments.

'Did you know anything about this?' Flo asked Dot as they made their way to fabrics.

'Not a thing,' Dot grumbled. 'And he usually tells me everything.'

'I thought he had dreamy eyes,' Jean said in a faraway voice.

'I thought he seemed quite brusque,' Mary said as she took her place behind the cash register. 'Did Mr Button really never mention anything to you about him when they were in the army?'

Dot rolled her eyes. 'What is all this? I don't know everything.'

Just then the girls heard the sound of heels clacking across the floor in a hurried fashion. Spinning around, Alice was surprised to see Hilda, one of the women she had got to know at the stitching evenings, walking determinedly towards them, her face a picture of panic.

'Girls, I wanted to let you know I'm pulling out of the parade tonight,' she babbled.

'Why?' Alice gasped in shock. Hilda had made a lovely frock from her old wedding dress and was using an old hat she had smartened up with new buttons to set it off.

'My dress is ruined,' she wailed. 'Barry started cutting it up to play with. I'm going to kill the little sod. Acting right up he was,' she added angrily.

'Surely you can repair it?' Dot said, aghast.

Hilda shook her head, tears pooling in her eyes. 'It's ruined. I can probably make a skirt out of it now, but it'll need measuring, cutting out again and all sorts.'

Alice's heart went out to her. This parade had meant so much to Hilda; it was such a shame it had all come crashing down around her in this way.

Then like a bolt from the blue, a thought struck Alice. She and Hilda were about the same size. Perhaps there was a way she could help the woman after all. 'Do you have to be anywhere now?' she asked quickly.

Hilda shook her head. 'Mum's got the kids and I ain't due at the WVS until later. Why?'

'I think I might have something we can customise quickly for you. If you don't mind popping over to my house a bit later on, I think we can make you a gown that's fit for a queen.'

Chapter Fifty-Seven

It was just past lunchtime when Alice left Liberty's, her mind filled with ideas of the beautiful yet simple dress she would create for Hilda to wear later that day. She had a feeling, too, that Hilda would understand the importance of what she had in store, and couldn't wait to share her ideas with her.

With a few moments to spare before Alice met Dot to collect Arthur, she decided to stroll along Carnaby Street and take in some of the window displays. Between her son and her job, Alice rarely had any time to unwind, and she thought it would be nice to take a leisurely stroll along the lively street with nobody to please but herself.

She had only walked a few steps, the blistering summer sunshine already searing through her summer dress, when she suddenly saw the café where she and Mrs Claremont had shared a cup of tea when she returned to work. Looking at the large sign that hung outside advertising tea whatever the weather, Alice felt a pang of sorrow at the thought of her former manager. Yes, she had behaved badly, but if there was one thing Joy's death had taught her, it was how important it was to forgive and move on – after all, with the country in the grip of war, you never knew when you might get the chance again.

Checking her watch she saw she had just enough time for a cup of tea, and decided to throw caution to the wind and treat herself. Pushing open the door, the jangling of the bell overhead alerting every café-goer inside to her presence, she found an empty table. She was just about to take a seat at the one nearest the window when the sight of the woman opposite made her stop dead in her tracks. There, drinking tea and eating a scone, was Mrs Claremont herself.

For a moment Alice stood rooted to the spot, unsure what to do. Should she pretend she hadn't seen her or should she go and say hello? It felt like hours that Alice agonised over the decision, but in the end it was made for her when Mrs Claremont lifted her head and caught her eye.

Alice made her way over to Mrs Claremont and smiled gingerly. 'A pleasure to see you here. Do you mind if I sit?'

Mrs Claremont rewarded her with a grunt. 'It's a free country.'

Taking that as a yes, Alice perched opposite and ordered herself a pot of tea from a passing waitress.

'I didn't expect to find you here,' Alice remarked, desperately searching for something to say. 'How have you been?'

'How do you think I've been, Mrs Milwood? I've lost my job and without references I am struggling to find another.'

Alice blinked in surprise. 'Mr Button won't give you a reference?'

'No,' Mrs Claremont said curtly. 'He feels that my ten years of loyal service count for nothing.'

'I'm sorry,' Alice said, meaning it too. Surely a reference wasn't too much to ask?

Mrs Claremont sighed and pushed away the paper she had been leafing through, giving Alice a chance to take in her appearance. Her former manager looked gaunt. Her already lined face seemed hollow, while the blue jacket she wore was threadbare on the elbows and hung from her frame. She wasn't eating, Alice realised, and with a start she understood that it might not be through worry over what had happened, but because she simply couldn't afford to.

'Why don't you let me talk to Mr Button about a reference?' Alice offered. 'I'm sure I can persuade him.'

Now it was Mrs Claremont's turn to look surprised. 'You would do that for me? Why?'

Alice shrugged. 'Even if you don't work at Liberty's any more you're still one of us and we always look after our own. You may have made a mistake but I don't think there's anything to be gained from making you suffer more. You and me – well – we're not so different, Mrs Claremont. We both raised our children single-handed, and this is one lone mother reaching out to another, offering a hand.'

As Alice brought her speech to a close, Mrs Claremont let out a hollow laugh. 'Oh, Mrs Milwood, you really are too kind. You didn't deserve the way I treated you and for that I'm sorry.'

'That's all right,' Alice said softly.

But Mrs Claremont shook her head. 'No, it's not all right. You see, I treated you all badly in fabrics, not because I thought you were terrible at your jobs, or because I thought I was so much better, but because I was jealous of you all.'

'Jealous?' Alice echoed in disbelief. 'What on earth did you have to be jealous of?'

'Your bond, your friendship, the way you treated one another like family. You see, I had nobody to help me in the way you do, Alice. I tried not to let it get me down but I'd find myself going home alone and thinking back to the days when I was looking after my children by myself. I envied the help you have and the more I thought about it the more I hated you for it. I kept wondering how my life would have been if I'd had my own Liberty family to help. Would I have struggled as much? And so I wanted to make you understand what it was like to suffer. It's why I moved Miss Holmes-Fotherington to carpets and you to the stores.'

'But it makes no sense. We'd done nothing to you,' Alice exclaimed.

Mrs Claremont nodded sadly. 'I see now that it was wrong of me. When we shared a cup of tea in this café all those weeks ago I thought we did share a bond. I thought we were two peas in a pod, rearing our children alone without anyone to lean on. I wanted to help you, give you a leg-up, but then I discovered that alone was actually the very last thing you were.'

Alice shook her head in disbelief. 'I can't believe you had nobody, Mrs Claremont. Surely there was one person you could turn to?'

'When my husband was killed, I was like you,' Mrs Claremont said, a faraway look in her eyes as she remembered the past. 'I had lots of family and friends who wanted to help. What I didn't have was any money. My Alan worked at Alexandra Park Racecourse. He was a weak man and got into debt with a notorious gang called the Newcastle Mob. When he died, his debt passed to me, and with two children to raise and no money coming in I had to do whatever it took to pay the debt off and put food on the table.'

'I'm sure you did what any mother would have done,' Alice breathed.

'Perhaps,' Mrs Claremont sighed, turning her gaze to meet Alice's. 'I did some things I'm ashamed of, Mrs Milwood, but I did what I had to.'

'You must have been relieved once your debts were settled?'

Mrs Claremont let out a small sob. 'My freedom came with a price. The Mob let slip the lengths I had gone to in order to pay back what was owed, and once everyone found out what I had done they turned their backs in shame.'

'Is that why your children left?' Alice gasped. 'Because they found out what you had done?'

Mrs Claremont nodded. 'They wanted nothing more to do with me. I begged them to stay but they felt what I had done was disgraceful.'

'What about your family? Your friends? Surely they could see why you did it?' Alice cried. 'You had no choice.'

'Not one,' Mrs Claremont replied matter-of-factly. 'They all thought the children would be better off without me and said that the honourable thing to have done would have been to have gone to the police.'

'But if you had done that, then the Mob could have come for you another way,' Alice said, understanding. 'And then your children would have been orphans.'

'Precisely,' Mrs Claremont said with a grim smile. 'I did what I had to for my children, for our survival. But my family and friends thought my behaviour unforgivable and turned their backs. For the past few years I had nobody. When I met you, Mrs Milwood, I thought that we were kindred spirits, but when I saw the support you had I let jealousy get the better of me. Out of all the things I've ever done, Mrs Milwood, that's the one I regret the most. I'm sorry.'

Alice reached across the table and clamped her own hand over her former manager's. As her eyes roamed the face of the older woman, she could see in an instant the toll that years of pain and worry had taken. She realised she recognised Mrs Claremont. Not because she knew her, but because she had seen women just like her, defenceless, powerless, broken women that her father had taken advantage of, all for his own ends. He had destroyed hundreds of women like Mrs Claremont – but not any more. In that moment Alice realised she had the perfect opportunity to atone for some of the crimes her father and her sister had committed.

'Could you pop into Liberty's later, Mrs Claremont?' Alice asked suddenly, getting to her feet. 'We're holding the fashion parade tonight. Could you come in before it starts?'

A flash of concern crossed Mrs Claremont's face. 'Yes, but why? Nobody will want to see me there.'

'Trust me when I say that they will. Now don't be late.'

With that Alice left the café without saying another word. There had been enough suffering, enough talking, now was the time to make a change.

Chapter Fifty-Eight

The scene before her took Alice's breath away. The large floor space beneath the crystal chandelier had been transformed from its usual grand walkway linking the departments and now looked as if it belonged in a Parisian couturier. Rows of velvet-covered chairs stood underneath the chandelier with a centre staging area in the middle for everyone to walk down and display their outfits.

On either side of the chairs, mannequins dressed in rolls of utility fabric had been neatly stacked to create a colourful display and as for the grand sweeping staircase itself, Alice could see each step had been polished until it shone.

Clutching Arthur tightly, wisps of his baby hair tickling her chin, she could see already that the space was a thrum of activity with guests waiting for the parade to start. As Alice got closer she saw that there were three chairs laid out in one corner, and that Flo was sitting excitedly at one end, complete with a notebook in one hand and pen in the other.

'What are you doing in a judge's chair?' Alice asked, bewildered.

Flo turned to her, excitement etched across her face. 'Mr Button has asked me to be one of the judges! Isn't that brilliant?'

'But why?'

'Mrs Claremont was supposed to be doing it, don't you remember?' Flo hissed. 'So Mr B. has asked me to join him and Betty Fawcett on the panel instead. Now go, Alice, we're about to start.'

Rudely sticking her tongue out at Flo, Alice briefly smiled at Betty, then found a seat next to Mary, Rose and Dot.

'I was beginning to think you weren't coming,' Dot grumbled.

'I was just helping Hilda,' she replied, settling Arthur on her lap.

'Yes, what was that all about?' Mary asked.

Alice chuckled and tapped the side of her nose. 'You'll see shortly.'

Turning over her right shoulder to assess the crowd, she saw that the place was packed, with some even standing at the back. There were quite a few faces that she recognised, she thought, smiling at a couple of regulars, but plenty she didn't. Scanning the crowd, Alice saw to her delight that Millie and Doreen from Jolly's had turned up. She waved to them, excited they could be here for this wonderful event celebrating the very best of Liberty's. With a flash she remembered the drapery manager from Jolly's, Mrs Downing. Her friend would have loved to be here for this, Alice thought sadly. She had made Jolly's her world after her husband had died and this would have been like Christmas for her. There was one face that still hadn't arrived though, she realised: Mrs Claremont. Alice had got to the store early this evening and managed to talk to Mr Button before the event. He had been extremely understanding, all things considered, but Alice had a feeling that the generosity he had been feeling might disappear if Mrs Claremont didn't put in an appearance soon.

Alice shook her head free of her worries and dropped a kiss on her son's head. Tonight was supposed to be happy, she thought, pushing all sadness aside as Mr Button took to the stage.

'Ladies and gentleman, it gives me great pleasure to welcome you all to this, the very first Liberty fashion parade. Please put your hands together and welcome our judges, the wonderful actress Betty Fawcett, who has honoured us with her presence here tonight, and our head of fabrics, Mrs Florence Canning.'

There was a deafening round of applause as Betty stood up and blew kisses at the crowd. Alice couldn't help chuckle; Betty had always known how to work a crowd. As for Flo, she just smiled, looking utterly starstruck.

'Now, many of you know we were supposed to hold this parade a couple of weeks ago at the Mayfair House Hotel, which very sadly burnt down the night of our event,' Mr Button continued. 'Our thoughts and prayers are with everyone who was affected by the blaze.'

There was a pause then as Mr Button cleared his throat once more, and Alice suddenly felt a set of eyes burning into her. Turning to her left she saw Jack sitting just a few chairs along. The love and kindness in his gaze was not lost on her and she felt a yearning for him like no other.

Lost in her emotions, Alice almost didn't notice the thunderous applause that came as the first of the night's entrants took to the stage. Shaking herself back into the present, Alice concentrated on what was happening in front of her and pushed Jack to the back of her mind.

The women taking part in the parade had worked so hard over the last few weeks and Alice felt a flash of pride at their creations. Some of these women – like Mrs Hillingdon, she thought with a smile as she watched her show off a skirt she had made – had never held a sewing needle before in their lives. What they had achieved was incredible and they should all be thrilled. But as Hilda took her turn on the makeshift podium Alice felt real gratification – she had truly endured more than most to come out on top.

Looking at Hilda now as she walked confidently in front of the throngs of people who had gathered for the show, Alice clapped loudly, cheering her on.

'Why do I recognise that dress, Alice?' Dot asked as Hilda passed them. 'I'm sure I've seen it before.'

Alice nodded. 'It's my wedding dress. Hilda and I tore it apart. We kept the dropped waist, but shortened the sleeves.'

Dot's jaw dropped in shock. 'Not your wedding dress! Why?'

'It's time to look forward not back, and hanging on to that dress when my husband and I are no longer together is living in the past. It's the future I'm interested in now.'

As Hilda came off the stage there was yet more enthusiastic clapping. Alice glanced over at the women and saw Jean was sitting at the end of the row ably making sure the contestants had everything they needed. Alice watched her and grinned. She had a feeling that with the right training Jean would become a very capable member of the fabric department.

Now, Mr Button took to the stage, accompanied by the perennially glamorous Betty Fawcett. Dressed in a utility gown made from the latest Liberty striped print she looked breathtaking, Alice thought.

'Thank you, everyone.' Mr Button called over the applause. 'I think you will agree that all our contestants did a wonderful job tonight of showcasing not only how magnificent our Liberty utility fabric is but how delightful it looks in these new styles – wouldn't you agree, Miss Fawcett?'

'I certainly would!' Betty beamed, waving to the crowd. 'I have long been a fan of Liberty's, as you know, and I can promise you that all my friends will be stocking up on their utility fabric here when rations allow. I think what these women have proved tonight is what can be done with very little, and the imagination shown with new and old fabric is absolutely amazing.'

'Have you and the judges agreed on a winner?' Mr Button asked.

'We have. It was a very difficult decision but we felt that the last lady, Hilda, wore such a beautiful outfit, and we all agreed it was a fantastic way of showing what you can do with what you already have.'

At the announcement everyone was on their feet cheering and Alice couldn't have been more elated. She and Hilda had worked hard that afternoon to make the simple dress Alice knew would fit Hilda like a glove. And now, knowing that her old wedding dress had made way for a bright new future for Hilda gave Alice a great feeling of hope.

'Well, that's it, ladies and gentleman,' Mr Button said as Betty presented Hilda with her prize. 'Our Liberty fashion parade is at an end but I do have some rather good news. The parade has been such an unexpected success that we will be making community stitching sessions a permanent event. So, if you or your friends would like to come along to the store on Friday evenings and learn how to make one of these fabulous creations with our very own fabric girls, then come along.'

The girls looked at one another in surprise and Alice barked with laughter as she turned to Dot. 'I won't even ask if you knew anything about this.'

'When will you learn that man tells me nothing?' Dot giggled, but then her smile vanished. 'What the hell is that old cow doing here?'

Alice turned to follow her landlady's gaze and saw she had spotted Mrs Claremont making her way in. 'Dot, leave it. I asked her to come.'

'You did?' Rose gasped. 'Why?'

'Because Mrs Claremont was stupid and made some poor decisions, but that doesn't mean she deserves to spend the rest of her life being punished. I've recently discovered she's been dealt more than her fair share of bad hands – just like the rest of us. She deserves a second chance.'

'You must be joking,' Dot snorted.

Alice looked at her earnestly. 'I'm not and I really would like your support.'

'I don't know, Alice,' Mary said warily.

'Neither do I,' Dot added, 'but you know that if you want our support you've got it.'

Alice smiled gratefully at her landlady and friend just as Mr Button and Mrs Claremont appeared. 'So what did you all think?' Mr Button said, acting for all the world as though he didn't have a sacked member of staff by his side.

Dot nodded. 'Wonderful, Edwin, a worthy winner.'

'Yes, Hilda was a triumph,' Rose offered.

'She was, wasn't she!' Flo was beaming as she came up to join the little group. Spotting Mrs Claremont her face dropped like a stone. 'Oh, hello there, wasn't expecting to see you.'

'None of us were,' Dot said bluntly. 'So why are you here, if you don't mind me asking, Mrs Claremont?'

The former fabric manager gazed at the floor looking uncomfortable while Mr Button addressed the group. 'Mrs Claremont and I have spoken at length and we have agreed that she will return to Liberty's. Not in a managerial capacity, you understand; instead she will return to gifts as a sales assistant.'

At the news there was a sharp collective intake of breath as the group tried to make sense of what they had just been told. The silence was broken by Mrs Claremont clapping her hands together.

'If I may,' she said in a gentle tone that Alice had never heard before, 'I would like to say something and that is I'm sorry. I truly am sorry for the way I treated you all. I know I don't deserve your forgiveness, but please believe me when I say that I have come to realise how very wrong I was. If I could undo what I did, especially to you, Mrs Canning' – Mrs Claremont turned to Flo and shook her head in sorrow – 'then truly I would. But I can't. The only thing I can do is apologise over and over and promise you that when I return to this glorious store I shall endeavour to spend every moment I can making up for what I did.'

At that the rest of the girls looked at each other and smiled before Flo spoke. 'There's nothing to forgive. You're one of the Liberty family, Mrs Claremont, and we always forgive and we always forget.'

'It's the Liberty way,' Rose said softly.

Chapter Fifty-Nine

Once the prize-giving had finished and Hilda had uttered a thousand thank yous to Alice and the rest of the Liberty girls for all their help, Alice stifled a yawn.

'Well, I suppose I'd better be getting back.' She stood up with a sleepy Arthur in her arms.

Dot looked pointedly at Jack who had been waiting patiently for a moment with Alice but was now slipping on his coat. 'Isn't there someone you need to speak to before you go anywhere? That poor man's been hanging about for you long enough.'

Alice toed the floor uncertainly. She felt a flash of nerves even though she had invited Jack along.

'Go to him,' Rose urged. 'Tell him how you feel; it's time.'

'She's right,' Mary said sagely. 'I know you're nervous, but you don't need to be. He's a good man.'

'Indeed he is,' Dot added quietly. 'You don't have to make no promises to each other tonight, Alice. But you deserve to be happy. Now why don't you give me Arthur and I'll take him back with me.'

Seeing Jack was coming towards her, Alice steeled herself. She knew what she had to do, what she wanted to do, and she wasn't going to shy away from this chance at happiness any more. Handing Arthur to Dot with a kiss, she walked straight over to Jack, meeting him under the chandelier.

'I'm so glad you came,' she whispered.

Jack smiled, the wide easy grin that she recognised as if it were her own, lighting up his face. 'Me too.'

Alice felt suddenly shy. 'Do you perhaps want to go for a walk outside?'

'All right,' he replied, guiding her gently towards the door.

Outside, Alice took a deep breath and she realised Jack was doing the same. 'I don't know why I'm so nervous!'

Jack smiled as he lifted his chin with her forefinger. 'I know why I am. I don't usually fall for married women, much less do anything about it. But you, Alice, I can't think about anyone else but you. I've loved you from the day you crashed into me in Bath.'

'And I you,' Alice cried, the truth of her feelings rising to the surface and with it all the emotions she had tried to bury. 'I tried for so long to deny it, to tell myself you didn't mean anything at all to me, but you mean *the world* to me; I don't ever want to lose you.'

Jack clasped each of her hands and rested his forehead against Alice's, his breath warming her cheek. 'But you're married, honey. We can't do a thing while you're married.'

'But I'm not,' Alice spluttered tearfully, 'I mean, I suppose officially I am, and that will take some working out. But Luke and I aren't together any more.'

A look of confusion and then hope crossed Jack's face. 'How can that be?'

Tearfully Alice told him the entire story. Of how he had slept with Joy and then deserted her, their son and finally his country to set up a new life with Hélène.

'I've no idea what this means. I don't know if you and I can have any kind of future together.' Alice sniffed. 'And even if we were to try there would be the stigma of it all. I'm a married woman; I don't know what it's like in the States but here people love nothing more than to gossip.'

Jack laughed. 'They like to gossip back home too. But you know what, Alice? I don't care about gossip there and I don't care about it here either. My darling, you are the woman I want to be with for the rest of my life. I would walk to the end of the earth for you, and even if we don't know what our future together looks like or how we can work it out, just knowing that we both want the same thing, the chance of happiness together, is more than enough for me.'

Tears of relief splashed down Alice's cheeks as she let out a long breath. She hadn't realised how worried she'd been about what Jack would say to her unique situation with Luke.

At that Jack gathered her in his arms; then he bent down and pressed his lips against hers, filling Alice with a desire she didn't know it was possible to feel. As she gave into the sheer deliciousness of his kiss once more, she savoured the delight that came from knowing this would be the first of so many kisses together. As they finally broke apart and she looked up into his eyes that were filled with nothing but love, Alice knew that she had finally found the man who would help her create the family she had always dreamed of, but she also knew she had found a man she deserved. Jack wasn't someone who wanted to rescue her and he wasn't someone she needed; instead he was someone she wanted. The death of her sister had taught Alice that happiness was short-lived, that it needed to be grabbed with both hands, no matter how difficult that was. Although she didn't know what the future had in store for her and Jack, Alice was smart enough to realise that it wouldn't be a fairy-tale. She had long given up on the idea of a perfect upbringing for Arthur, but what she hadn't given up on was ensuring his childhood was filled with love. If she and Jack forged a life together Alice knew that it would be messy, complicated and sometimes painful. There was an awful lot they needed to resolve, but for now, in this moment, Alice revelled in the delight of her own happy ending.

Welcome to

Penny Street

where your favourite authors and stories live.

Meet casts of characters you'll never forget,
create memories you'll treasure forever,
and discover places that will stay with
you long after the last page.

Turn the page to step into the home of

Fiona Ford

and discover more about

The Liberty Girls...

Character Profiles

Alice Milwood

Blonde-haired, blue-eyed Alice is twenty-six years old and was born in Elephant and Castle. Her mother died giving birth to her little sister Joy when Alice was four leaving her father, Jimmy Harris – notorious criminal and leader of The Elephant Boys – to care for them. Eventually Jimmy's criminal past caught up with him and he fled to America, leaving the girls to fend for themselves. At sixteen things started to look up for Alice when she secured a Saturday job at Liberty's and became bosom pals with Flo. At twenty-one she found happiness by marrying RAF Flying Officer Luke Milwood, and in December 1941 made Liberty's history by giving birth to her baby son Arthur on the shop floor. She now lives with Dot Hanson, in her South London terraced home.

Flo Canning

Flo is twenty-seven and with her twinkling green eyes, chestnut hair and peaches-and-cream complexion she is easily the most glamorous of the girls. Like Alice she grew up with only one parent after her mother disappeared when she was small without explanation. Her father, Bill Wilson, was a petty thief and so Flo was brought up in Islington by her aunt Agatha. She too started life at Liberty's as a Saturday girl, swiftly working her way up the ranks to become manager of the eponymous fabric department. On Boxing Day 1941 she married the love of her life, Neil Canning, who is currently serving in the Navy.

Mary Holmes-Fotherington

With her raven hair and green eyes, twenty-five-year-old Mary has a striking appearance and a background far removed from the rest of the Liberty Girls. Born and raised in Cheshire, Mary had a privileged start in life and was expected to attend finishing school before war broke out. Yet she disobeyed her father and joined the ATS keen to serve her country. Through no fault of her own Mary was dishonourably discharged from the Women's Army in 1941 and found herself in London, estranged from her family and rocked by scandal. Fate smiled down on Mary and she moved in with Dot and Alice and found work in the fabric department of Liberty's. Her past eventually catches up with her but not before she finds love in the form of handsome doctor, David Partridge.

Rose Harper

The youngest of the Liberty Girls, Rose is twenty-one and married to her childhood sweetheart, Tommy, who is away serving in the Army. A talented seamstress with glasses, long auburn hair and blue eyes, Rose works in the office of Liberty's. Her kind-hearted nature and generosity of spirit mean she is thought of fondly by the Liberty family. When she is poisoned after drinking illegal hooch and goes blind, the Liberty family show how much they value her by helping her return to work. With her mother and husband away serving their countries, Rose lives with her father, Malcolm, in Elephant and Castle just streets away from Dot.

Dorothy Hanson

Dot's quick wit and habit of saying just what she means ensures she doesn't suffer fools. She has greying chestnut hair, grey eyes and at forty-eight she is the matriarch of the group. She lives in Elephant and Castle in the terraced home her husband George left her after he was killed in the last war and frequently takes in waifs and strays. Dot recently joined Liberty's on a part-time basis, helping out in the fabric department, and has rekindled her romance with Edwin Button, Liberty's store manager, after more than thirty years apart.

Dear Reader,

Firstly, let me thank you from the bottom of my heart for picking up a copy of *The Liberty Girls*. It means the world to me that you have chosen to spend time with Alice, Dot, Mary, Flo, Rose and their special Liberty's community.

People often ask me where the inspiration to write a series set in this wonderful store came from. It all started one dreary February day. I used to work near Liberty's and one lunchtime I found myself inside. With time to spare, I saw things I hadn't taken much notice of before: intricate wood carvings, sweeping staircases, a glass-panelled roof, pretty little rooms that made you feel instantly at home and of course the goods themselves – exotic and unusual treasures sourced from around the globe. Liberty's was as breathtaking inside as it was outside.

But it was when I walked up the main staircase and caught sight of a plaque dedicated to staff killed during the Second World War that I got goosebumps. I wondered what life would have been like for the workers all those years ago. Liberty's employees would have spent their days surrounded by beauty – but outside the chaos, devastation and sheer ugliness of the Second World War would have dominated their lives.

Liberty's was never bombed during the blitz, and I wondered if the store became something more than a shop during that period. The plaque suggests that it was a place of community, a refuge for both workers and shoppers away from the horrors of war. Suddenly an idea was born and the first book in the Liberty Girls series was published last Christmas.

These days I am never happier than when I am in this Liberty's world – where the girls have come to feel like old friends, and the difficulties they face feel as real as the dilemmas in my own life. I am thrilled to be making a start now on book three in the series. I hope you will join me for the next instalment, which follows the adventures of Flo and the Liberty girls as they cope with the challenges of 1942, relying on each other and the spirit of Liberty's to survive.

Like all authors, I always love to hear from readers. If you would like to share a Liberty's memory, let me know what you see in store for the girls, or simply say hello, feel free to drop me a line by visiting my Facebook author page: facebook.com/fionafordauthor.

Lots of love,

Fiona x

The Human Cost of the Bath Blitz

The scene where Alice stands on Pulteney Bridge, with a German pilot just yards away ready to gun her down, sounds like the stuff of fiction but in fact it's completely true. During my research for this book, I uncovered several accounts of Bath Blitz survivors who claim German pilots flew so close to them during that fateful weekend that they were able to see the whites of their eyes.

Incorporating the story of the Bath Blitz into *The Liberty Girls* was particularly poignant for me as Bath is my home town. Growing up I was well aware of the tragedy that had struck the city, but it wasn't until I started researching this book that I realised how detrimental the damage had been.

To put it into perspective, up until the 25th April 1942 the Georgian city of Bath had been relatively protected from the onslaught of the Second World War, aside from a couple of stray bombs that had fallen in 1941, tragically killing a handful of people.

The historic spa town was largely safe from the Germans. Unlike its more industrial neighbor Bristol, which was frequently bombed thanks to its ports, Bath was so peaceful it was almost possible to believe war didn't exist there. Certainly this was a view the government took and Bath was not seen as a high priority to defend. Yet what many don't realise is that Bath was in fact a key contributor to the war effort. Not only had the Admiralty been evacuated to Bath in the thirties from London, but the engineering works, Stothert and Pitt, were building Navy torpedoes and gun mountings for the Army. Bath, it could be argued, was a legitimate target for German attack.

The history books say that after the two German port cities of Rostock and Lubeck were bombed earlier in 1942, Hitler wanted revenge. Apparently he wanted to attack British cities filled with heritage and culture, to try and ebb away at the British spirit, which seemed to be unyielding, no matter how many bombs were dropped. Goebbels, minister of propaganda, suggested the beautiful cities of Exeter, Bath, Norwich, York and Canterbury would make good targets after studying the Baedeker Guide to Britain. However, it's worth noting that this has been refuted by historians who argue the Baedeker story is nothing more than a piece of propaganda.

Whatever the reasons, on a clear moonlit evening, as Bathonians enjoyed their Saturday night in the city, eighty German planes took off from occupied France with only one mission – to decimate the city. The first explosive fell half a mile east of the city and many residents who saw the flares thought Bristol was in for another night of torment. However, as the flares became louder and brighter, panic grew as people realised Bath was the Germans' intended target. This was the start of a two-day campaign which saw the Germans damage much of the city, including Kingsmead – the residential area of Bath – Stothert and Pitt's engineering works, Lansdown, Julian Road, the gasworks, and much of the railway line. The world-famous Assembly Rooms, which had only recently been restored, were also blitzed along with the city's grand Regina Hotel, while fires tore through the Circus and Royal Crescent.

The death toll stood at 417, the largest for any of the towns hit during the Baedeker raids, but it was the human stories that came out of this appalling raid that captured my imagination. Take for example the GP, Mary Middlemas, who was killed instantly while taking a break from caring for her patients to get something to eat. Harry Hemming, who at twelve pretended to be eighteen so he could work as a messenger boy across the city. It was Harry who saw firemen fighting fires on Pulteney Bridge as the Luftwaffe flew close to the volunteers, and Harry who saw them gunned down to cause maximum mayhem. It was also Harry who got so close to the Germans he had to dive into the doorway of a sports shop for shelter – just as Alice does in this book.

Then there were the three boys who were remanded at Bath Juvenile Court, charged with damaging a loo and shelter, who didn't appear at court the following week. There was also the fourteen-year-old girl who was trapped under the rubble for three days before she was rescued. And we mustn't forget thirteen-year-old Doreen Williams, whose father had been a volunteer fireman since the outbreak of war. Although he wasn't technically on duty during the second night of the raid he wasted no time in volunteering to serve his city once more. Putting on his jacket, he said goodbye to his family – and that goodbye is the last word Doreen heard her father say, tragically, just like so many others who never came home.

These are just a handful of the stories to have come out of that terrible weekend, but I hope that by reading this novel you will get a sense of how much of an impact the raids had on the wonderful city of Bath. We are fortunate in some respects that the Germans' plan to destroy the city failed. Although they caused a great deal of damage, for some reason they left the north of the city untouched, leaving the Pump Rooms, Roman Baths, Circus and Crescent relatively unscathed.

Today, a war memorial dedicated to those men and women who lost their lives during that weekend stands at the entrance to the city's Royal Victoria Park. These inspirational men and women, like Doreen Williams' father, and Harry Hemming, who chose to look fear squarely in the eye, should continue to be remembered and celebrated. I am sure you will agree these first-hand accounts of social history are important to preserve in whatever way we can.

Hear more from

Fiona Ford